Praise for *Bluebird*

'*Bluebird* is engrossing: a sharp-witted a[...] contemporary world and our contemporary families. Yet the satire is never smug and the characters never lose their complexity or their individuality. Malcolm Knox's writing now has such confidence and clarity that he is exhilarating to read. He's a maestro, and I didn't want *Bluebird* to end.'   Christos Tsiolkas, author of *Damascus* and *The Slap*

'Malcolm Knox is in scathing top form with this brutal takedown of white male nostalgia, real-estate greed, wasted privilege and bronzed-Aussie delusion.

'Gordon's an unlikely hero, trapped in the collapsing halfway house of his marriage, his elderly father's crumbling tyranny, loyalty to his abysmal friends—and the toppling Lodge, the symbol of everything he can't bear to lose. The novel perfectly skewers the hypocrisy, racism, class warfare and misogyny at work in the power-plays of ageing surfside gladiators, clinging to their personal and communal mythologies of an Australia that no longer exists, if it ever did. It's a mark of Knox's supreme skill that he can render his protagonist's failures with such ruthless clarity, yet somehow elicit such genuine sympathy that I found myself desperate for Gordon, urging him on to step up, and save himself.

'Filled with biting observations about our culture and our families so starkly insightful they make you gasp and read them out loud, *Bluebird* showcases Knox's dexterity as a satirist more savagely astute than ever.'   Charlotte Wood, author of *The Weekend*

Praise for *The Wonder Lover*

'A strange and beautiful creation. It reveals Knox to be an author of a controlled virtuosity with few peers in this country. Indeed, along with 2011's *The Life*, it marks a considerable leap in Knox's formal ambition: an evolution thrilling to watch unfold.' *The Saturday Paper*

'Malcolm Knox has established himself as one of the most ambitious and exciting fiction writers at work in Australia. It is a testament to Knox's talent and creativity that we remain, throughout, excited by the ambition and potential of this novel. We marvel at this writer who stretches himself, and for that reason we read much of *The Wonder Lover* in awe of its creator's inventiveness.' *Australian Book Review*

'This is one of the big books of the year. You know that phrase that critics use about a writer at the peak of his powers? Well, this is the time to apply that to Knox, who has been one of our most significant writers mining aspects of contemporary masculinity for a while in novels like *Summerland* and *The Life*.' Caroline Baum, *Booktopia*

'Malcolm Knox has . . . made a speciality of interpreting the lives and emotions of men . . . Genuinely original and intriguing.' Katharine England, *Adelaide Advertiser*

'Few authors have such a sharp eye—or stylish pen—for the secret lives of men.' Jennifer Byrne, *Australian Women's Weekly*

'Malcolm Knox's *The Wonder Lover* is a book in love with language and the possibilities of storytelling. I loved it.' Christos Tsiolkas, *The Saturday Age/Spectrum*

'I loved it. Wonderful and sad. Sad and wonderful. He is a brilliant writer.' Don Watson, ABC Book Club

'Gradually unfolding the three marriages, with the tone growing more dark and complex, it becomes an exquisitely wrought dissection of one man's downfall and a reminder that of all the records and extremities Wonder encounters, the most revelatory is the damage human beings inflict on one another.' *Sunday Age*

Praise for *The Life*

'A vivid and essential piece of work.' *Australian Book Review*

'It confirms what ought to have been more widely recognised, that he [Knox] is one of the most considerable of our novelists in what is at least a silver, if not a golden, age of Australian fiction.' Peter Pierce, *Sydney Morning Herald*

'Malcolm Knox explores the inner life of men with both surgical insight and heartfelt compassion . . . *The Life* digs in deep.' Michael McGirr, *The Age*

'Plot is one thing, mere reviewer's necessity, but voice is another. Here is where the novel seduces and converts . . . it is clear Knox is on to something here. He has written a vivid and essential piece of work.' Adam Rivett, *Australian Bookseller & Publisher*

'*The Life* is also just a bloody good read.' Stephen Romei, *The Australian*

'You don't have to be a surfer or be familiar with the story of Peterson to appreciate Knox's superb storytelling and his rhythmic, evocative prose in homage to one of Australia's most intriguing sporting characters.' Greg Stolz, *Sunday Times*

'Knox has never written better than in *The Life*. Page after page is radiant with the energy.' Geordie Williamson, *Weekend Australian*

'The book is worded in the crackling stream of detritus that flows from Keith's broken mind—a sort of *Catcher in the Rye* for Antipodean surfers.' *Inside Sport*

'I envy the confidence and the naturalness of that book—it moves and shrugs, completely itself, like a wave.' Charlotte Wood, *Bookseller & Publisher*

'If Winton is an aria, Knox is early Rolling Stones.' *The Guardian*

Malcolm Knox was born in 1966. His award-winning novels and non-fiction titles have been published in Australia and internationally. A journalist with the *Sydney Morning Herald* since 1994, he has won three Walkley Awards for investigative journalism, magazine feature writing and sports journalism, as well as a Human Rights Commission Award. He lives in Sydney with his family.

Bluebird

MALCOLM KNOX

ALLEN & UNWIN

SYDNEY · MELBOURNE · AUCKLAND · LONDON

First published in 2020

Allen & Unwin
83 Alexander Street
Crows Nest NSW 2065
Australia
Phone: (61 2) 8425 0100
Email: info@allenandunwin.com
Web: www.allenandunwin.com

A catalogue record for this book is available from the National Library of Australia

ISBN 978 1 76087 742 2

Set in 13/18 pt Granjon by Bookhouse, Sydney
Printed and bound in Australia by The SOS Print + Media Group

10 9 8 7 6

MIX
Paper from
responsible sources
FSC® C011217
www.fsc.org

The paper in this book is FSC® certified. FSC® promotes environmentally responsible, socially beneficial and economically viable management of the world's forests.

For my family

For my family

FIRST
PART

FIRST
PART

Bird's eye

When I close my eyes and think of Bluebird, I picture it from above. I glide on the sea breeze, hold my position, and turn my salted beak upon them. Avian and condescending—they have called me worse. An outsider, I arrived with an innocent gaze to which they imputed evil character. I was a vulture waiting for my host to die before feeding on his flesh, which tribal magic turned into their own. I was predator, scavenger and judge, an unhappy triple threat.

They were wrong! I am but a gull drawing circles on this cloudless sky. Until I act, I watch. There below, a white van knifes into the last space in the top car park. Clothes are shrugged off, a wetsuit zipper fumbled in excitement. A square of wax grates over a surfboard, doors are locked and keys stashed in wheel well, footprints skip over the dune and down the sand. They float on the water as I float, without a wingbeat, upon my lighter element.

Over here, more. Latecomers who thought they were early risers discover what those in the know already knew. It's going to be one of those days. You wouldn't want to be caught napping. Earliness is the stamp of belonging.

A rustic signboard stands at the top of the dune path. When I arrived here, the VISITORS WELCOME *sign had been burnt mute by persons unknown. Its charred cinders, trodden into the sand to form a foot-blackening compound to tattoo departing soles, represented honesty.*

More recently, a newly-appointed deputy general manager of the local council declared that a new sign had to be erected. What, he asked in a printed leaflet, is a place without a sign? A public plebiscite (participation rate <20 percent), given three alternatives, settled on a new slogan: Bluebird. Like No Other. *The popular favourite—* Car Park Full—*was not among the options.*

Within hours of the sign's erection, guerrilla graffitists vandalised, or corrected, it to Bluebird. LikeS No OtherS. *And so it remains, like its burnt predecessor, eloquent in its defacement.*

Bluebird whispers a history of self-concealment. If I cast my eyes to the smoggy horizon (no, I don't go there either), I flinch from the high-rise nightmare of Ocean City, that beach camp of four million. In the old days, Bluebird was OC's last secret, the land that public transport forgot. Old Bluebirders chose weatherboard obscurity, the pride in self-sacrifice, the decency of being overlooked by each property boom. Bluebird was OC's blind spot, under-value its badge of honour. Any suggestions of a train link from OC to Bluebird were greeted by pitchforks.

Alas, out of sight has lost the battle to out of mind. Preservation from access couldn't ensure preservation from progress. Bluebird's quest to be Nowhere has been surrendered. Nouveaux Bluebirders—expat English bankers, locals made good, adventurers from the far side of the harbour, blue-chipsters and craft beer barons, rock royalty, fashion designers, self-styled purveyors of digital-age culture—and they call me a parvenu?—have scorched this earth. From its ashes arise mirrored shrines for maximally magnified self-reflection.

And here come the daytrippers. Ugh. Sunlight bounces off windscreens in the bottom car park on the flat between the surf club and the electrical substation. Families insert into overflow parking in the grass lot beside the firehouse. Nippers parents are bickering about how much space between cars is really necessary. Having deposited their children in the care of the surf club—Sunday morning babysitting service—they queue for early-opening caffeine at the Beach Cafe. I own that. Hate me if you will, Bluebird, but I own you too.

Out on the water, surfers jostle for the main break. The day's first threats echo with the first birdsquawk. Hello, friends! Less combative surfers filter out to the sub-premium take-offs. Council lifeguards, erect Desert Foxes in their beach buggies, plant red-and-yellow patrol flags and chequerboard buffer zone lollipops, and megaphone border-force instructions to surfcraft riders: 'Attention in the water!'

When was paradise lost: an hour, a decade, two centuries ago? Even I miss Old Bluebird, and I wasn't there. I have contracted the local infection: crippling nostalgia.

I tilt my wings away from this scene to the sea, from human faces to cliff faces. Try as it may, all that restless meat cannot spoil Bluebird's native glory. A claw of sandstone clasps its jewels: surf club, ocean bath, open-air public shower, refoliated dunes, alpha to omega told by one smile of golden sand and a drenching of scents: salt, wrack, sandstone, Norfolk Island pine resin. Not just a beach, but the idea of a beach. Everything in its right place.

At some point, each new arrival will ask the Bluebird question. Surfers and swimmers gazing from the warm water, walkers and waders, bakers and bathers, even tough old birds like me ponder the houses and unit blocks cascading at illegal angles down the cliff faces, the six-storey apartment tower teetering on pillars shrouded in scaffolding for concrete cancer surgeons to cut out the corruption of bygone bad habits.

How did they get away with that?

We ask it of the rough-as-guts males barnacled to the rocks, the melanoma farmers practising their military surf club march-past on the sand, the hard men out on their big boards, working-class relics in a high-end landscape.

How do they keep getting away with it?

A question, like a fire, needs a provocation, and Bluebird's raised middle finger to the monuments to greed and folly and rapacious optimism is one structure that clings to the sandstone cliff in the southern corner, defying gravity, connected to the world by a pair of wooden staircases, one leading up via four zigzags and a narrow pass between two duplexes to the street, the other thirty-three steps down to a jump rock onto the sand; staircases like rope ladders on which the building is paralysed, unable to climb or descend. A gob of bleached driftwood and cement render thrown against the cliff face, surely it must slip into the sea. This house is not an answer but a question: absolute beachfront yet virtually inaccessible, sitting on premium real estate that is somehow not real estate at all, a historic abuse protected by custom.

How the fuck did they get away with that?

That is The Lodge, and if you have to ask what The Lodge is, you're not a Bluebirder.

Gordon and Kelly Grimes are living there now. They used to rent an ex-housing commission cottage near the high school, but separated after Kelly fucked Gordon's best mate. As separations go, theirs was unorthodox: Kelly and their sixteen-year-old son Ben moved out of *the broken family home and into The Lodge, followed by Gordon himself, thanks to the manipulations of Kelly's widowed wicked stepmother, who, for good measure, claimed the queen room. Kelly has the double, separated by half an inch of asbestos sheeting from the bunk room, which is occupied by Gordon, his twenty-two-year-old goddaughter Lou, and Ben.*

Lodge and family: held together by the gravity of their fractures.

What have they got away with? As the godless say, pull up a pew. Long story.

Gordon

ON THE DECK OF THE LODGE, GORDON GRIMES SCREENED HIS eyes. The sun was playing peek-a-boo over a bank of clouds that would soon burn off, summer continuing its insurgency against the season formerly known as spring.

Hearing a whistle from his left, Gordon turned to see his bearded young neighbour waving cheerfully. David Archer's humble grin spoke of disbelief at their shared good fortune. Gordon, on edge due to both an ongoing dispute with Archer and the underlying fact that Archer's fortune was built on a more solid economic base than his, raised his hand tentatively, torn between the suspicion that Archer was taking the piss and the greater anxiety that his friendliness was genuine. Archer cupped his hands worshipfully to the sky. In their single mediation session before the dispute was given a court date, Archer had referred to this headland as Bluebird's 'dress circle', which Gordon took to mean that the people down below must be actors.

Gordon, bracing against his balcony rail, might have held a premium ticket, but he felt far from premium. He had got away with nothing except the view.

He swept his eyes over the beach. Six ancient clubbies were practising their march-past, pausing around the reel to debate who would pick up which corner. Six into four never did go. Mathematics, like their opinions, stood immutably against progress. Gordon squinted down at the top car park, where his crew had been rolling up since the pre-dawn. He could pick them out of the Sunday crowd just as animals, in a mass of humans, see only the fellows of their species. Morning surfs complete, they milled about, a cluster of non-working working folk falsely remembering empty waves, bandying hot air and urban myth.

Snake, tradie in tradies' heaven, first in the car park as usual in his customised van fitted out with shadow boards for metalwork tools and a seven-stick surfboard quiver, was flying on a vertical run of surf talk with Red Cap, a fifty-one-year-old who no longer surfed because of reconstructed shoulders dangling from synthetic tendons, yet still the most regular of the regulars. On days like this, Snake and Red Cap claimed the sunrise like respondents to a call to prayer; if they were not first here, the Bluebird sky might fall in.

Firie Sam clambered up the dune path to join their conversation around the green-painted park chair that Kelly had christened The Bench of Broken Dreams. Mid-fifties, handlebar moustache and fruity voice box, mobile loans officer by day, safety officer with the volunteer rural fire service by days off, an anomalous Old Bluebirder in gainful employ, Firie Sam was unzipping his sleeveless vest, its shine like sealskin. Nobody knew how Sam maintained a supply of that discontinued line of zipper vests; there were rumours of a long-ago stock theft.

Old Bluebirders didn't arrive so much as occur. Tonsure Man, whose stringy beard and luxuriant mullet appeared on loan from the yarmulke of exposed wrinkled-apple skin atop his head, was exchanging information with the tattooed nude-nut Cnut, whose name was likely Canute or Knut, going by his Nordic facial planes, but who spells in the surf? Cnut by nature, therefore Cnut by name. Up popped the obligatory Macca and Chook, one per beach from here to the border, and an interchangeable posse of Maccalikes and Chookalikes. There now was the sole woman in the pack, the eight-time state champ, her ebullient hoarse monologues piercing the morning. Friendly with everyone and remembering no-one's name, the eight-time champ formed a surf-buddy couple with Japan Ned, a Bluebird resident since the Japanese eighties. Japan Ned had not mastered a comprehensible English beyond 'Good out' and 'Shit out', all he needed for car park conferences. You lost yourself in contemplation of his carved white grin and his bewitching, almost edible skin tone. It was said that Japan Ned's nickname originated with a local cabinet-maker and surfer who likened Ned's complexion—so darkened by daily exposure to a sun that had turned him into a mid-Pacific race all his own—to the colour of japanned wood, but it was also said that none of the local tradies could be quite that eloquent.

This bunch, every morning of the year. Permanent holiday. How *did* they get away with it?

But yeah, Gordon knew:

Snake, divorced, had moved back to Bluebird to live with his widowed mother.

Red Cap, divorced, also lived with his widowed mother.

Tonsure Man, never married, lived in Bluebird in a bachelor flat beneath his widowed mother's house.

Cnut, never married, lived in his car.

Firie Sam, divorced, had moved with his widowed father into the disused firehouse.

Japan Ned, who could only be divorced, lived nearby, no-one had worked out where or with whom.

The eight-time state champ had made nothing from the sport but lived on the clifftop, prime possie, doctor's wife.

And now the turd dropped into the bowl.

Rocking up to work the car park like a party host was Doug 'Dog' Gilsenan, a Bluebird lifer who had marked his fiftieth year by switching from surfing to stand-up paddleboarding so he could continue to bully the south-end peak in a world of seven billion potential blow-ins. On big days, small days, in-between days, good days and shit days, Dog, his face a voodoo mask of factor-50 war paint, statuesque on his paddleboard, picked off the best waves, sounding his warning with a shrill whistle as he careered down the line in his budgie smugglers. Dog would fancy himself a marble Caesar, though the parabolic folds of his flesh toga were the legacy of no greater conquest than the recovering sugar user's weight loss.

Gordon saw the group ripple away from Dog's merry greetings. The eight-time state champ cut herself into silence. Snake shuffled back to his van with Red Cap. Firie Sam went to the shower to wring out his zipper vest. Tonsure Man and Cnut scratched the ground with their toes.

'What you reckon?' Dog would be saying to Japan Ned, the only one on whom he could rely for a response.

'Shit out,' Japan Ned would say with a smile that was not for Dog.

As if he had only graced them with his presence while on his way to more pressing business, Dog feigned not to notice their snubs and made for The Lodge, the rest following him with their eyes as he crossed the grass down to the corner of the beach. He stepped from the jump rock onto the staircase. He cock-sparrowed up the wooden stairs, straining his ribcage to flatten his man boobs, marshalling energy against age. He paused on the middle landing so he wouldn't sound puffed-out on arrival, while pretending to appraise the house clinging to the rock face. As a property lawyer, Dog perceived The Lodge as a list of litigation risks. *Something* had to be done.

Did it? From the inside looking out, possession was nine-tenths of the law and eleven-tenths of fuck-you. For Gordon, The Lodge was a monument to the glorious and improbable reign of *nothing*: a manifestation of the human will to resist change, a temple dedicated to miracles within miracles. Weather-beaten couches, tables and other furniture of the 'found' variety, including two queen beds and a double bunk, had been human-chained down the staircase from Cliff Street into The Lodge, not a soul could remember when. For Gordon, The Lodge was a mighty ruin, a castle redoubt worth the last drop of its defenders' blood.

But Dog was a can-do guy. A semi-retired practitioner who ran his own race and much else, Dog lived with his wife Sally in the penthouse of the newest unit block behind the surf club, their kids having moved to interstate universities. As an empty-nester needs a hobby, Dog's hobby was Gordon's wife. When that had begun to go off like yesterday's milk, Dog had refocused his attention on Gordon, his stated project to fix up his best mate's life and stop it from going so badly wrong again.

Gordon went inside and knocked an agreed double-rap code on Kelly's door. Moments later she was a blur up the steps to Cliff Street, clothes bunched under her arm. Gordon preferred not to reflect on his actions, protecting *her* from having to see *him*. Funny old world.

Dog entered the basement below Gordon's feet, where his two paddleboards, Malibu, foamie, mini Mal and surf ski were stashed on the damp sandy slab. An honour system, Gordon thought with a grimace. Now Dog's sun-creamed face appeared at the top of the internal stairs, his smile powered by the renewable energy of discovering that his boards had not been broken into small pieces.

'Master of the house! Coffee up?'

Dog pulled himself up on the last banister post, but before Gordon could warn him the wooden newel came off in his hands. Dog shrugged, made to screw it back into place, but then tossed it to Gordon, who stared at it for a moment before dropping it in his board shorts pocket, another job for the list.

'Don't know how long you can keep squatting in this death trap,' Dog said, bending towards the kitchen as if climbing a mountain, exaggerating the subtle uphill slope of the living room floor just as he had affected not to feel the three flights from the beach.

Gordon filled the electric jug.

'Macchiato, champ.' Dog nodded at the gleaming La Marzocco espresso machine against the kitchen's back wall.

Gordon switched on the jug and placed a tin of instant beside it.

'Lou gone out?' Dog said with sad eyes.

'Early start for everyone.'

Among other initiatives, Gordon's goddaughter had bought the commercial Italian machine on Afterpay and begun popping out cafe-quality coffees to the amazement of all comers. But Lou was the only one who knew how to use the La Marzocco, so its hours of operation were limited.

Gordon and Dog tested the theory about a watched jug.

'So,' Dog said, 'all on ya tod.'

'All on me tod.'

Gordon moved to the painted open shelf, still stocked with the mismatched crockery that had been there when he moved in six months earlier, alongside an indecently expensive handcrafted ceramic tea-and-coffee set imported from Kyoto. Gordon stared dumbly at the Japanese cups, and felt Dog staring too. They knew exactly what was what, the pair of them. Gordon reached for a cracked Big W mug and set it in front of Dog's sun-spotted hands, alongside the tin of instant.

'Not joining me?' Dog said, a sigh passing through his words as the Kyoto moment drifted astern. Gordon wondered if he and Dog would ever have the big talk. They had not mentioned the event, and Gordon was fairly sure that Dog was tortured by the uncertainty of not knowing how much Gordon knew. Which was the problem with, and the beauty of, never talking about it. Gordon felt like they were in a silent six-month game of blind poker in which neither player would dare look at his own cards, for fear of confirming bad news. Sometimes Gordon wondered if he and Dog were waiting for time to bury what had happened, as was local custom. Why say anything, if time would step in and do the work for you? But then again, it would also be just like Dog, unable to stand the guilt anymore, to spill out his confession when there was nothing left to say. While feeling a little sorry for whatever inner torments roiled beneath Dog's factor-50, Gordon did not feel sorry enough to open the subject. It was never too late in life for a man to discover suffering. And once Dog had discovered it, his pain wouldn't mean anything unless he was allowed to experience its full richness.

Gordon shook his head. 'Lou's spoilt me.'

'Fuck she's good. It's a crime not to charge for it.'

Dog reached into his pocket and slid something across the melamine breakfast bar. He withdrew his hand, leaving a five-dollar note. The Queen glared past Gordon, it seemed, too exasperated with him to meet his eye. He turned the note over to spare his embarrassment and pushed it back towards Dog, who threw up his hands as if it was infested with germs.

'I don't want your money. Especially not for instant,' Gordon said, feeling the headache of a ritual conversation coming on. 'You know council would have my guts for garters if I was running a business here.'

'It's only five bucks.'

'We're zoned strictly residential.'

'I insist.'

Dog was always leaving cash, one stone that, as he saw it, killed a flock of birds. Help a mate out. Just the right thing to do. And, in place of any meaningful spoken, written, texted, emailed or emojied words, a gesture of apology.

But only a gesture. If there was a chance that Gordon did not know about him and Kelly, the stupidest thing Dog could give him was a concession of guilt.

Dog turned the note back over. As QEII was his witness, he said, 'I'm begging you.'

Gordon eyeballed the Queen, whose resemblance to his own mother was so strong, he was surprised at not having noted it before. The similarity in mid-century marcelled curls and worldview set off a chain reaction of Norma Grimes-voiced reproaches in his head. You are the world's worst actor, Gordon. I can see through you a mile away. Everyone around here takes you for a man of peace, too good for this world; you and I know better, my son.

He sometimes wondered how long he could keep it up. Why not take Dog's cheeks in his hands, lock eyes, draw him close as if for a kiss, and then drive his forehead, with such force that it lifted his feet off the ground, into the juicy sun-creamed bridge of Dog's nose? Was it better to be thought of as too good to be that bad?

Behind Gordon's back, the water boiled. Dog smacked his lips and uttered empty murmurs of anticipation.

On the other hand, Gordon thought, maybe he should be grateful. He wouldn't be here in The Lodge if not for Dog. Funny, funny old world. Any funnier he might stop crying.

He pocketed the five-dollar note.

'I'm going downstairs to clean up.' He nodded to the sugar on the shelf. 'You know where everything is.'

Kelly

GORDON DIDN'T GO DOWNSTAIRS TO CLEAN UP. HE CONTINUED through the basement, descended the wooden stairs, crossed the beach and walked behind the surf life saving club to the Beach Cafe, which was, like most of Bluebird's profitable enterprises, beneficially owned by his absentee stepmother-in-law.

The conversation with Dog had given him a neuralgia that could only be remedied by espresso. Gordon scored his drug of choice from Paolo, one of a pair of lecherous Italians who sublet the hole in the surf club wall from Leonie.

'Cash!' Paolo exclaimed at the sight of Dog's five-dollar note. 'Old school!'

Fuck off, Gordon said, or thought he said. The next person to say 'old school' when he produced cash would get a fist in the gob. Or they would if Gordon did that kind of thing instead of what he actually did with his fist, which was drive it into his pocket.

With the bar stools taken, Gordon sat at one end of the communal trestle table and watched Paolo and his business partner,

Lucio, playing to national stereotype by flirting with the bored local women lining up for their fix. Chatty Paolo and gruff Lucio were faithful to the twenty-two-year-old Milanese models they lived with, so it was all a bit of fun, middle-aged lycra queuing up each morning to pay to be mocked by lingering brown eyes and accented sweet talk. At least the relationship between the Italians and the local men was garlanded by a merkin of honesty. Amid the tidal pheromone backwash, the male natives had no time for Paolo or Lucio, and the feeling was mutual. Some of the less happily married locals thought these boys were an actual rather than a theatrical threat to the morals of the Bluebird community, and Paolo and Lucio were too macho to deny it. This mutual misunderstanding had the Beach Cafe doing a thriving trade while teetering on the brink of a punch-up.

'I didn't think you could afford a coffee out.'

Too late, Gordon realised that one of the local women being moistened by Italian hospitality was his soon-to-be ex-wife. Kelly landed beside him with a weary sigh. She hitched a maroon singlet strap over her shoulder from where it had slipped down her arm. He'd last seen that singlet bunched in her hand. Where had she changed, he thought. In the alley beside David Archer's house?

'Don't mind me,' he said.

'Let me guess.' One of Kelly's gifts was to ride over the top of Gordon's occasional pettishness. 'Dog gave you cash for something, and the only way you can deal with it is by getting rid of it as fast as you can.'

Gordon had long given up trying to tell her she was right.

'So you come down here and put it into Leonie's pocket. My stepmother wins again.' Kelly allowed herself a smile, which, when Lucio came over with her cappuccino, she transferred effortlessly to the taciturn Italian, who growled *Signorina* as if he would devour her if only he could be bothered.

'*Signora*,' Gordon corrected Lucio's departing back.

Gordon and Kelly sipped their drinks and shared a companionable moment, he imagined, going Dutch on victimhood. Kelly's feud with her stepmother had a long history in which the punishment for her infidelity was the latest outrage. Its roots lay in jealousy, originating when Leonie married Kelly's father: logistically convoluted but psychologically simple. By contrast, Gordon's relationship with Leonie, as well as being hard to explain in a family-tree botanical sense—she was the foreign-born second wife of his deceased father-in-law—eluded pat explication. Leonie had gifted him one of the three issued shares of the company that owned The Lodge, a port in the storm of his marriage breakdown, and with it responsibility for its insurmountable bills, knowing full well that Gordon was the type of man who, having been given this extraordinary bounty, would be reluctant to ask her or anyone else to fund the maintenance costs which she, Leonie, so airily overlooked. In one act, giving Gordon a share in The Lodge had made him a rich(ish) man on theoretical and unredeemable paper, while stripping his cash reserves to the bone. He could get why Leonie wanted to fuck with Kelly. But whether she wanted to help or punish *him*, give him the chalice or the poison in it, he had not the faintest idea. She had saved him out of sympathy; it was not beyond her to be ruining him out of carelessness.

'Can I make a radical suggestion?' Kelly said. 'Get a job. I did. It can't kill you to try.'

The constitution of the company that owned The Lodge was, like the Russian Duma or various People's Committees, a democratic autocracy. Of its three shares, only Leonie's had voting rights. Kelly had inherited her share of The Lodge twenty years earlier from her father Noel Chidgey, but, under the terms of his will, was prevented from monetising it without Leonie's approval. Six months ago, after cheating on Gordon, when she would have loved to sell her share and start up somewhere else, Kelly had asked Leonie for that approval, but Leonie had refused. So Kelly moved into The Lodge with Ben. Her restricted financial condition might force her to wear, as she called, a 'fixed chagrin', but Kelly, who hated the house she had grown up in nearly as much as she hated her stepmother, had no intention of staying in The Lodge long-term. The Lodge was merely a stepping stone on her path to escape. She would find a way around Leonie. She had rejoined the workforce, managing an aromatic candle emporium in the tourist hub of Capri ('Seven miles from the city, a million miles from care', but, if you asked Bluebirders, too fucking close, thanks very much), to make ends meet while waiting for that happy day when some change in circumstance, such as Ben finishing school, or Leonie falling from a cruise ship or suffering a fatal pedicure mishap, freed her from the hideous tumbling-down house and this miserable beach.

'I have,' Gordon said. 'But I'm not like you.'

'Employable.'

He lowered his head.

'You're not that useless, Gordon. There must be something out there that isn't customer-facing.'

But customer-facing was all that was left, and Kelly, attractive, fit and trim, able to play any convivial role in exchange for her needs being met, was speaking from the higher status of one whose very appearance did not trigger customer complaints. Gordon was a shambling ruin, his scant resources of social conformity exhausted by the putting on of clothes each morning. What could he do? His chosen trade—he had been a journalist and long-serving editor of the now-defunct *Bluebird News* until he followed his staff into redundancy at the age of forty-seven—had gone the way of lamplighting, wet nursing and elevator operating. Some local-paper journalists were still, like radioactive waste, rolling over into new half-lives, but Gordon hadn't been able to summon sufficient energy for the 'citizen journalism' that had taken up residence on the internet but seemed a fancy name for what used to be known as the letters page. He was good for little else, in too deep for career reinvention. As far as he was concerned, it could all go to bloggery. In his first year of redundancy, when his family had still been intact and he needed to keep putting on a show as protector and provider, he had sent out begging letters hawking himself as a freelance copywriter and subeditor. One company replied that they had no position available but would keep him on their 'flies'. He thought about sending a correction as evidence of how much they needed him, but heeded Kelly's warning that it wouldn't get the reaction he hoped for.

After that, he had done some thinking. If the family cut their costs right back, they could exist on his trickle of income from the journalistic afterlife—irregular press releases for local businesses, a short-lived foray into 'mentoring' (too customer-facing, it turned out), the patchy investment earnings from his redundancy payout—until his superannuation came through. This strategy of exhausted desperation, or desperate exhaustion, far from making him an outlier, embodied the Old Bluebird state of mind in the new Bluebird demography. Nobody he knew worked. 'You gotta work to live, not live to work!' claimed Tonsure Man, who had never held a job for more than six months. 'What's the point of living in God's Country if you're the working dead?' asked Red Cap, who had last worked in the pre-internet age. Old Bluebird was a workers' aristocracy, except for the work part. Work was beneath them, even if living in their elderly mothers' spare rooms was not. So, after his fruitless efforts at finding post-redundancy employment, Gordon had decided to finally acknowledge member-ship of his own type—and fuck it, he thought, why not; he was as Bluebird as anyone else. When Kelly had raised the occasional murmur about just how frugally they had to live to stretch out his redundancy, Gordon had replied, 'Something will turn up.'

Then something had turned up: Kelly left him. And then something else turned up: he followed her.

'Leonie only wants to bring our family together,' Gordon had said to Kelly when he arrived at The Lodge with his bags.

'She'll bring something together,' Kelly replied, but let him in.

Gordon, unlike Kelly, loved The Lodge with all his heart. He had always loved it, and now that he found himself living in it, he didn't ever want to leave. He was its custodian. His personal attachment to The Lodge was a true marriage. As a boy, he had helped paint the basement for old man Chidgey, and he had stashed his surfboards and taken his showers and learnt to drink beer and lost his virginity in this living museum to the milestones of his adolescence. Old Bluebirders generally looked at each other with a fundamental aesthetic forgiveness; having known each other all their lives, they still saw the youthful beauty, the prime of life, buried under the wrinkles and sun damage and double chins. (That Dog and Kelly could still see each other as hot young spunks, memory enhanced by cocaine goggles, was a big contributor to Gordon's problems.) The Lodge embalmed Gordon at the zenith of his promise, and he still saw The Lodge's best face beneath the decay and mould and water damage and structural unsoundness. He saw the architectural intent behind the 'feature wall' of diagonal pine veneer placed randomly beneath the breakfast bar. He saw the craftiness in the brown macramé curtain over the kitchen window, enabling him to spy on incoming visitors without being seen. He relived the 1970s in the design of naked women in the black-and-white downstairs shower curtain. Where most houses tended to be refurbished in one fell swoop, dated like layers of geological catastrophe in sedimentary rock, The Lodge was a permanent work in process, bits improved at whim, and with its haphazard ageing Gordon felt a true kinship. They were made for each other, Gordon and this building that had fallen so miraculously into his hands. The one thing he had loved his whole life, without any reservation, free of the capacity to disappoint, was The Lodge. The community, like the newspaper and the old Bluebird Literary Institute (now an organic food store), like Bluebird High School and the post office and the police station, had been submerged beneath the Ponzi scheme of real estate tumbling down the headlands. The Lodge was the last remnant of what Gordon considered civilisation. He would save it. As each house was knocked down and the world 'discovered' Bluebird, Gordon's love for The Lodge had hardened into something akin to a mission. Chance had made him the protector of Bluebird, the steward of history.

And yet, maintaining The Lodge required such daunting upkeep. Gordon was exhausted from being so daunted. At four o'clock each morning, he was dragged out of his thin watery sleep by the list of what he needed to do to save The Lodge that very day: more maintenance, more begging. As with a prisoner who wakes from the freedom of his dreams to find himself in his cell, Gordon's early hours were an agony of quiet recognition. He liked to envision himself standing against the future, but he suspected Kelly was right and he was just hiding from it, hoping the future would continue its good grace of washing past The Lodge, forgetting to sweep it, and him, away. His habits of inaction were his illness and his cure. His passivity, his admirable goodness, was driving everyone crazy, not least himself. But he had his reasons. Private reasons. There was more than one evil to stand his ground against.

Kelly was wiping froth off her upper lip. 'We ought to free up this space,' she said, glancing at a large group, some sort of office brunch party, eyeing the communal table. 'Oh, Gordon, you've got to do something. We can't both be down here hiding from Dog.'

'At least we're not drinking International Roast.'

'I'm serious. You have to tell him you know.'

'Can't I enjoy keeping him guessing?'

'I'd say yes if that's what you were doing.'

'Instead of what we are doing, which is ignoring it until it goes away.'

'You're not the one who should be feeling ashamed,' she said with a disarming absence of emotion.

What Gordon couldn't admit to Kelly, if she wanted to raise the subject of shame, was that a few weeks ago he had come to this very cafe to ask for a job. Fatigued with insomnia and desperation, he had mentioned his need for cash to Leonie, as a hint that she might take some responsibility for The Lodge's outgoings or, as Gordon thought of them, outpourings. Blithely, Leonie had said, 'Go to the Beach Cafe. I'll call them. All you have to do is mention my name.'

So Gordon had sidled up to Lucio at the counter, leant close, and said significantly: 'Leonie.'

'What?' Lucio had replied, showing his teeth.

Gordon repeated what he thought were the magic words. 'We. Together. A job. You. Me. *Leonie*.' For some reason, his English had deserted him and he felt the need to speak pidgin with an Italian accent.

'The fuck is wrong with you, mate?' Lucio said with a menacing steadiness.

Paolo had stepped out from behind the espresso machine.

'Yeah! What the fuck is wrong with you?'

Gordon wouldn't have been bothered by a threat from Lucio, but the ever-ingratiating Paolo losing it with him came as a shock. There was a disturbing intimacy to Paolo's question. Clearly the Italians thought Gordon was making some accusation or, worse, suggestion in relation to them and Leonie. But their hostility hinted at something personal about him that had been disgusting them for a long time. Did they even know him well enough to be disgusted by him?

He could tell neither Kelly nor Leonie about this debacle, and prayed that word would not get back.

'Ah, we've got a big group?' a voice was saying now, male, twenties, passive-aggressively metrosexual, its tone pettish, as if continuing a conversation already started. Gordon raised his eyes as far as the speaker's ankles—bare, sockless between cuffs of dark-blue twill and expensive leatherwork—and made no sign of leaving.

'Come on, Gordon.'

Kelly was on her feet. Gordon remained. A commotion ensued as metro-fuck-knuckle and his group distributed themselves around smaller tables they dragged together. Gordon ignored their huffs until a dumpy woman in her fifties, incongruous among the party, some kind of office administrator he guessed, said, 'Excuse me, sorry to disturb you. Do you mind if we use your table when you're done?'

Kelly was rolling her eyes. 'I'm going to work.'

Gordon gave the dumpy woman a warm nod and cleared his table. As the party moved in, Gordon said to fuck-knuckle, 'Hope you learnt something from your elders.'

The man blinked at Gordon as if affronted by a violation of vagrancy laws.

'Show a little courtesy,' Gordon said with a nod towards the quiet and now unfortunately embarrassed older woman, 'and you'll get what you want.'

As he walked off, he heard one of the party murmur, 'What is wrong with that guy?'

'Everything,' he heard Lucio sigh.

'Gordon, you are *so* your own worst enemy,' Kelly said once they were out of earshot. It struck him that his point had been lost, because the real audience for his actions, the office party, would forget him instantly whereas someone who was not its audience—Kelly—would figure that Gordon, after all these years, was finally cracking up.

'I think I could contribute a lot to a customer-facing business,' he said. 'It just has to be done the right way.'

Kelly studied him for a long moment, as if conducting an assessment. 'Sometimes I wonder if there really is something wrong with you.'

Well, Gordon thought as he watched her hips swing off towards the bus stop, it is a widespread problem, the underemployment of the middle-aged. It wasn't his fault, it wasn't laziness and defiance, it wasn't a tired fuck-you, it wasn't a reversion to adolescent surliness. It had to be something important, a social phenomenon. He had had so many reasons to think that the problem—the cause of all his problems—was someone else, a long list of suspects, or better still, some*thing* else. But what if it really was just him? *What is wrong with me?* The considering way Kelly asked made him think she had been discussing him with others. What if she was right? Or what if his worst enemy was inside himself, a dark shadow blocking the doorway through to the brightness other people seemed to think lay on the other side of the mornings they woke into? As he set off from the cafe, he mouthed the words. *What the fuck is really, really wrong with you, Gordon?* The question—never mind whatever answer it might be harbouring— carried the sickening stench of truth.

Ben

GORDON SPENT THE DAY AS A REFUGEE FROM HIS HOME. UNLIKE
Kelly, he didn't have a job to go to, only a series of barely necessary activities in Capri which he tried to dignify by listing on a lined pad under the heading *Tasks*, their sole useful purpose to spare him the scene which, in his current mood, he preferred not to face.

For many years The Lodge had been the daily clubhouse for Gordon's cronies, but only in the six months since moving in had he realised that they camped in there literally every day. Red Cap and his mother Josie would be doing jigsaw puzzles; Tonsure Man would be going through the bookshelves and second-hand clothing bins; Cnut would be napping on Gordon's bed; Snake would be on the phone lying to his clients about how flat-out he was; various shifts of Chookalikes would be rotating in and out, not a single item of footwear between them; and lording over them all would be Dog, sticking his nose where it ill belonged.

By mid-afternoon, Gordon judged that Ben must be home from school and Lou from TAFE. The breeze had swung onshore,

28

clearing Bluebird's prized main break of all but a couple of surfers. As he climbed the wooden stairs, he heard loud voices from above. A red cap moved behind the picture window. Josie's voice pierced the air like a crow's caw. Something in her irritated tone told him that Dog was in the conversation.

He banged the downstairs door with an intentionally heavy 'Alert! Dad approaching!' slam. Whenever the crew were upstairs, Ben retreated to do his homework in the damp concrete basement alongside everyone's dumped shit and unused surfboards. Lou, who was trying to set up a pay-per-use 'lending library' of surf-craft, had renamed it the Boardroom. It smelt of salt water and sand and surf wax and fibreglass and wee. Two of its walls were painted in black gloss, as if someone had started on a dungeon but lost the will. Gordon was sad to think that this was where Ben felt most comfortable, but he could see why nobody would want to spend longer than necessary upstairs with that noisy mob or in the bunk room where Ben slept, with Gordon and Lou, like convicts forced to share quarters on an uncomfortable voyage. It dismayed Gordon to sleep in the same room as his son and goddaughter; he shuddered to think how icky it must be for them.

Ben sat with his back to the Boardroom door at the fake-wood school desk Gordon had rescued from the tip and lugged down from Cliff Street to The Lodge at the expense of a slipped disc, an early gesture of post-separation atonement. He had installed it at the Boardroom's tiny aluminium-framed window, so if Ben craned his neck he could see Bluebird Beach. It was an archi-tectural characteristic of The Lodge's era to prioritise protection from wind over the view: of the upstairs bedrooms, the two on the beach side of the house, with potentially superb vistas, were each limited to a single, high, narrow pane of frosted glass. Only from the balcony could you know where on earth you were. Downstairs, Ben spent more time on his feet squinting at the waves than on his backside studying. Kelly said it was the worst place to put a desk for a kid with Ben's condition. But when Gordon had shifted the desk away from the window, Ben moved it back.

To Ben's right was a handmade American pewter object in the shape of Atlas holding up the world. Atlas's spread arms, a recent $280 purchase from Eastons, held Ben's fifty-cent biro. Gordon felt a flush of love for his son, the last person in Bluebird who would think of asking Gordon what was wrong with him. Ben had inherited his mother's best features—her olive-skinned good looks, her honesty, her fundamental sense of fairness—which offset the selective blindness, proneness to skin infections, indecisiveness, allergy to common sense and other too-florid-to-name legacies with which his Grimes side had lumbered him. 'Breed with someone better than you!' Gordon's father Ronald, a eugenicist tyrant in the twentieth-century tradition, used to bark at him. 'All the strongest characteristics come down the distaff side!' Gordon had certainly found someone better than him to breed with, out of his league even, but this beautiful boy was more than enough recompense.

'How was cricket practice?' Gordon asked, his eyes on the penholder. You couldn't talk to Ben and look into his eyes. 'They're like dogs,' the paediatric psychiatrist had said of Ben's type of attention disorder. 'They'll only look at you while you're not looking at them.' When he heard this, Gordon felt sorry for the doctor. The man clearly didn't know dogs.

'Wait, what?' Ben gave his all-purpose response. With Ben, if you were banned from repeating anything you said, or if he was banned from repeating everything he said, the sum total of your communication would be zero.

'How was cricket?'

'Good.'

Another all-purpose response. A maths test he flunked, a school musical in front of a thousand people, an all-time surf, a shit surf, a date . . . Ben would assess each, supremely non-judgemental, as 'good'.

'Get a bat?'

'Wait, what?'

'Did you get a bat?'

Ben mumbled something.

'What?' Gordon said.

'They ran out of time.'

'Get a bowl?'

'What?'

'Did you get a bowl?'

Ben mumbled something.

'What?' Gordon said.

'Some, at the end.'

'How's your catching?'

Ben, everyone knew, couldn't catch tinea in a public shower.

'What? Um, good.'

'It's a long season ahead, I'm sure you'll get more of a go.'

'What? Oh. Yeah, hundred percent.'

Ben adored his cricket, which Gordon thought, just quietly, was a more clear-cut symptom for his diagnosis than was revealed by any of the psychometric testing they had put him through. This cricket season showed no sign of varying from his other five years in the one team St Pat's could muster. Ben was listed in the team sheet as 'bowler', which meant that he wasn't permitted to bat. If he ever bowled, it was in junk time when games were either well won or lost. Which meant Ben was a specialist fielder, except that fielding, more than batting or bowling, was his Achilles heel. He didn't like dirt or foreign matter on his hands and had a particular sensitivity to pain in his palms or fingers, so he had no hope of stopping a hard cricket ball. He had a strangely uncoordinated throwing motion that propelled the ball forty-five degrees off course. If his team had twelve players available, despite an official rotation policy, Ben was frequently twelfth man. Gordon's secret definition of a successful day of cricket was that Ben finish without becoming aware that the other boys were giving him shit. Yet Ben wouldn't miss a practice or a match, which, aside from infuriating Kelly when it was her turn to drive him across Ocean City on a Saturday morning and sit for six hours until the pointless exercise was over, was, in Gordon's view, an open-and-shut clincher for his type of Asperger-ish, ADHD-ish, non-specific, nameless disorder-ish Thing.

'You doing homework? Need any help?'

'Wait, what?'

'How's your schoolwork going?'

'What? Good.'

The boys' Catholic school Ben attended was across the road from Bluebird (aka Bloodbath) High School, where Gordon and Kelly had gone in the 1970s and 1980s. Bloodbath was no longer an option, having been converted into a high-performance selective unit for super-talented daily migrants bussed in from other parts of OC. Bloodbath High, suddenly and shockingly one of the top academic schools, lost its connection with the suburb surrounding it. Nobody knew those kids; you never saw them at the beach.

For Ben, who was never a chance of sitting even the entrance exam for Bluebird High, there were few options between the new

Bloodbath, Cobcroft Boys' High, and those temples to wannabeism, the co-ed private schools St Claire's and Chalk Farm. Neither Gordon nor Kelly was Catholic, but Kelly had had Ben strategically baptised to qualify him for the convenient and relatively cheap St Pat's. In happier days, Gordon and Kelly had agreed on St Pat's as a best of all worlds for Ben—and the Catholics were not like they used to be, everyone assured them. Since Jude Oxenford, who had been a schoolmate of Gordon and Kelly at Bloodbath back in the day, had taken over as principal, St Pat's had become off limits for priests and therefore, supposedly, safer for children.

'Sure you don't need help?' Gordon said, cutting his eyes at the laptop open on Ben's desk. He pretended not to have noticed Ben hurriedly changing screens.

'What? I'm good.'

Ben was such a late developer that he was sixteen before he started to hide things from Gordon and Kelly. This had coincided with the separation, so it was hard to tell the difference between Ben punishing them or just growing up.

'So you reckon I should move Up North?' Gordon said.

'Wait, what?'

'Your mum told me, after we got back. You reckon I should leave The Lodge, head up there?'

In the recent school holidays, Gordon had taken Ben to Beckham Bay, an eight-hour drive north of Ocean City, where they had stayed with Gordon's cousin Rachel, her husband Jason and their three girls. Up North was Bluebird unspoilt, the other side of history's sliding doors. On a stretch of lagoon sand, a temporary community re-formed during each school vacation: families ate together and gossiped and socialised in ways they never could in their regular city lives. In that pop-up enchanted hamlet, you enjoyed more community with your one-week-a-year neighbours than the pests you put up with for the other fifty-one. When Gordon went Up North he didn't know if he was in his element or in a cage. This time, his first holiday without Kelly, he wondered if his natural element *was* a cage.

'Me. Up North. Without you,' Gordon said.

'What? I dunno. Maybe.'

'Is it for my sake, or to give you an excuse to see that boy?'

Ben had been so happy Up North, just the two of them, that he even told Gordon he had met a boy. Ben had come out a year ago, but in Bluebird it had been a theoretical matter; he'd seemed as far from meeting a boy as he had seemed, when they thought he was straight, from meeting a girl. But Up North, for four days there had been shared volunteer bushland regeneration work, campfires and moonlit walks. It brought Gordon to tears when Ben made his confession. Boys his age didn't tell their fathers things like that. For all the swings of Ben's condition, the round-about was the delayed onset of adolescent disillusionment with his father. A significant roundabout it was, in the circumstances.

'I could never leave you and everyone,' Gordon said, trying not to feel hurt by the suggestion. He leant forward and tried to hug Ben, who turned sideways, making an authentic hug impossible. Pre and post diagnosis, Gordon had persisted with his attempts to exchange bodily warmth. Ben's aversion didn't matter to Gordon; it was the trying that counted. Gordon had applied the same philosophy with Kelly, who didn't like his hugs either. Maybe she had some brand of ADHD too, and all that was needed to save their marriage was an amphetamine prescription. Whatever. Failing with Kelly didn't mean he had to stop hugging Ben.

'You all need me too much,' he said into the bristling crown of Ben's head.

Ben mumbled something.

'What's that, mate?'

'When's Mum home?'

Gordon gave a shrug as non sequitur-ish as the question. Ben was asking when his mother got home as if this were a normal event for a normal family. But when Kelly arrived 'home', if that was what The Lodge was, Gordon would, by agreement, make himself scarce. By the unspoken terms of their new disposition, they could spend time together as pairs but not as a trio. To pretend to be a family would confuse Ben. All those other people blowing in and out of the house papered over and accentuated the awkwardness, among those people the lingering bad smell who was the prime cause of their troubles.

'Want to join us upstairs?' Gordon asked, knowing that the best way to get Ben to focus on his homework was to offer a poorer alternative.

'Wait, what?'

'Want to join—'

'Are all the people hanging around?' Ben cut in.

'Just the dregs.'

'I've got so much work.'

'No worries, I'll call you when dinner's ready.'

Gordon started for the internal stairs. Up North, he had come to the cliff's edge of the big explanation session, which was what their holiday was meant to be about, but he had failed to take the leap. How to explain to any sixteen-year-old, let alone one with Ben's peculiarities, the logic of the separation? Ben seemed tougher on Kelly than on Gordon (if you asked Kelly), but possibly he was tougher on Gordon than on Kelly (if you asked Lou). Whenever Ben tried to blame his mother for what happened, Gordon deflected responsibility to himself, saying he had given Kelly plenty of reasons to lose patience. Ben didn't seem to take this in, but you never knew how much Ben was taking in. As Jude Oxenford put it at parent-teacher night, 'It's not that Ben isn't highly intelligent—he is—it's just that the input and output jacks are not where we usually find them.' And whose, Gordon had silently replied, were?

Lou

GORDON TROMPED UPSTAIRS TO RECLAIM HIS HOUSE FROM THEIR clubhouse. At the top of the stairs, he took the banister newel from his pocket and screwed it back into its place, but could tell, from the lack of resistance, that he had lost the thread. Unable to bring himself to consider another handyman job, he left it there to wobble in wait for its next victim.

Dog held court over Red Cap and Josie, who were at the card table working on a jigsaw puzzle of Van Gogh's *Starry Night*.

'And after he drops in the second time, he goes, "I'm a local, I've lived here five years!" And I go, "Try fifty years, champion." That shut him up. Nothing gets up my nose,' Dog concluded, 'more than blow-ins who act like they own the place.'

'Cos it's *your* job to act like you own the place,' Josie said, without looking up from the jigsaw.

Josie had popped in earlier that day to ask Red Cap for a lift to the shops but her plans had been derailed by free food and the irresistible pull of the two-thousand-piece Van Gogh.

Josie and Red Cap formed a mother-son tableau that would have been touching if not for their constant bickering over jigsaw puzzle technique. Red Cap was a systematiser, piling the edges and corners and separating them by colour, laying the ground-work before joining pieces, whereas Josie operated on instinct, trying connections if they 'felt right'. Red Cap had just gone to the trouble of separating two pieces that had come joined, due to a factory error, by their paper backing. 'Why do you have to make things harder for yourself?' Josie said. Her fifty-one-year-old son, unemployable and a convicted criminal, replied, 'It would be unethical.'

'Get out of it, you, that's my son's pile!' Josie slapped away Dog's hand. Dog did not see jigsaws as a cooperative enterprise. Instead, he would steal pieces that Red Cap had patiently sifted, jam them into spots where they didn't fit, and pretend they did, showily tap-tapping them in and seeking acclaim.

'Ten bucks says I find the next piece,' Dog said. 'Gordo, you gunna back me in? I'm a genius at post-impressionism.'

'Save it for the jury,' Josie said.

Gordon, wondering if the installation of a closing-time bell in The Lodge would cause any effect other than high dudgeon among these people, went into the kitchen, which was separated from the living room by an inexplicable Wild West louvred saloon door, chest-high at the top and knee-high at the bottom, swinging open at the centre. He cleaned out the microwave, a morass of hot chocolate after an accident involving possibly Tonsure Man or Red Cap but most likely Dog, whose attitude to cleaning was that it was all part of the service.

'Eh, Gordo, what's this one like?'

Tonsure Man had come to the saloon door from the sunroom, now known as the library, waving a paperback thriller, a question mark on his face.

'Cleanser,' Gordon said, not a compliment but a code. A 'cleanser' was the term they had used since boyhood for taking a crap. When applied to a book it meant it passes the time, but it's shit.

'Like his others?' Tonsure Man flashed the author's embossed name and fanned the pages.

'Customer guarantee: no different from his others.'

'When you gunna get some decent reads? I'm starting to wonder if I'm becoming an intellectual snob.'

'When Lou has cash to go down to Lifeline and buy more selectively,' Gordon said. 'Till then, we're relying on what people offload when their old folks die.'

'I heard that,' said Josie, who had only a Gideon's Bible, six Margaret Fultons and a shelf of completed crossword puzzle books to bequeath.

Tonsure Man went back to searching the shelves. Since the demise of the Bluebird Literary Institute, the nearest public library was too far away for Bluebird locals, many of whom, like Red Cap and Tonsure Man, fancied themselves big readers but couldn't afford new books. As well as introducing the library concept to The Lodge, Lou also served focaccias and Vietnamese rolls and, in her spare time, ran surfboat crew training in the twilight and dawn hours for girls who weren't welcome at the Bluebird Surf Life Saving Club.

'She's a beauty, that bird,' Josie declared.

'I don't know how she does it,' said Tonsure Man, marvelling at anyone who could fit more than a surf session and three coffee dates into a single day.

Tonsure Man took another thriller off the shelf and waved it questioningly at Gordon, who had read everything. 'You'll like that,' Gordon replied. He moved to the shelf and tightened the books against the obscene $300 bookend, inlaid with New Zealand jade, he had bought from Eastons with the same stolen card he had used for the Kyoto tea set and the Atlas penholder. Gordon gave the bookend a caress, seeking virtue.

Perusing the flyleaf, Tonsure Man said sceptically, 'I don't read Australian books.' Few did. 'Australian books' reminded them of school.

'Trust me, it'll be worth your while,' Gordon said, with a keen appreciation of the worth of Tonsure Man's while.

'So what you gunna do?'

Tonsure Man had this way of changing the subject without warning onto a larger subject that hovered in his head but required some guesswork to ascertain. It was as if Tonsure Man had been conducting a silent conversation with an imaginary Gordon that he was now setting free without remembering that the real Gordon had not been part of it.

'About . . . ?'

'Everything,' Tonsure Man said, waving the thick paperback to sum up the vastness of the problem. 'Red Cap's old lady, all the old ladies around here, they'd be totally stoked if you could set this up as a proper community centre. You got the machine, Lou's itching to run the place as a coffee shop, you could do it all, make some cash too.'

'A community centre.'

'Fucken access mate,' Red Cap called from the card table. 'How are they gunna get up and down the stairs? Even I'm struggling,' he said, rubbing his destroyed shoulder as if that might soon prevent him from loafing about doing nothing. 'Josie's doing it tough, aren't you, Mum? Nearly fucken kills you to get in and out. Gordo, why don't you get Mrs C to build one of them travelator things?'

Red Cap called Leonie Chidgey 'Mrs C', evoking the image of a plump and jolly grandmother rather than the gym-fit, duck-pouty, Botoxed-and-liposuctioned-to-within-an-inch-of-her-life despot who called the shots here.

'Don't think they're called travelators, but I know what you mean,' Gordon said.

'Yeah, them chairs you can hop on and press a button,' Tonsure Man said. 'Whee! Solve all your access problems, eh.'

Gordon did not see the tortuous access as a problem so much as the best thing The Lodge had going for it.

'Lou's a go-ahead chick—you could really make something of it,' Red Cap said. 'You just gotta get Mrs C on board. Suck up to the old bird, fucken sort out the ownership.'

'It is sorted,' Gordon reminded him.

'Ar, that fucken bullshit.' Tonsure Man flicked an angry hand, and to be honest, Gordon couldn't have phrased it better. 'It can't be spread among the three of youse. If you're not careful you won't have any choice: we'll be forced out and the whole place'll be gone. Fucken shitten *fuck*!'

Tonsure Man's eyes filled at the emotion of, first, losing The Lodge, which like other locals he regarded as his birthright, and second, of losing it to the real enemy, the money that landed in Bluebird freshly laundered and itching to renovate. As usual with TM, the finer points of the argument were jumbled but the thrust was well-intentioned.

41

'It's not right,' Red Cap continued, subsiding into the ratty cane sofa beside Tonsure Man, who was using the Australian novel as a fan. And it's also not right, Gordon thought, what they say about small communities trapping people in their past. Red Cap, a maths teacher at Bluebird High before Bloodbath turned selective, had slept with a final-year girl student, which made him technically a child sex offender and earned him the sack from the education department and a two-year good behaviour bond from the District Court. That was twenty years ago, and Red Cap had never held down a steady job since. Unemployment had turned him into a full-time surfer, but he had over-surfed and ruined his shoulders beyond even medical science's capacity for repair, so, like his unfortunate former student, he was fucked every which way. Yet he'd not done what someone in his position with any sense of shame did, which was move away and start up a life where nobody knew him, a new identity, maybe even a different-coloured cap. Instead, Red Cap had stayed put. If your small circle is inside a huge city, the past doesn't necessarily stick to you: people churn through and those who stay are so dizzied by the ambient change that they cling tight and forget each other's blemishes. The disgraced are your neighbours, but time closes around their disgrace. Everyone remembered that there was *something* about Red Cap, but anything else was mere details. New people came in, like Japan Ned and Cnut and Snake, who wouldn't give a fuck about Red Cap's past. The important thing to them was not some silly shit he did in the 1990s, but the fact that he was in the top car park every morning at The Bench of Broken Dreams, talking surf, chained with them to this beach and this great tree, The Lodge, that they would not allow to be cut down.

And Gordon, too. Memory was everywhere and nowhere, a suffocating blanket one minute, a puff of cloud the next. He too carried an aura of 'bloke who's done stupid shit way back', but who remembered exactly what?

'Might as well be you that gets control of all this,' Red Cap went on, casting an eye around the falling-apart furniture, the saloon door, the diagonal pine feature wall below the kitchen bar and the yellowing books. He rested his hand on the opening of the laundry chute, beside the bookshelf, which might once have led to a laundry but now led to the Boardroom, allowing a clear line of hearing from upstairs to down. 'Anyone else'd fuck it right up.'

Gordon sensed that the slope in the living room floor was increasing. He took a glass marble out of the sparsely stocked cutlery drawer and placed it on the floorboards. It set off towards the balcony, taking a direct route past Red Cap, Josie and Tonsure Man, and warping past Lou, home from TAFE, coming out of the bunk room adjusting the strap of her swimsuit over her shoulder, her training uniform fitting her like the skin of an apple. Twenty-two years old, tanned and fit from ironwoman training, curveless as a thumb, Gordon's goddaughter fascinated the hell out of Tonsure Man, Red Cap and Josie, who looked up from the jigsaw puzzle to gawk shamelessly at her musculature.

The marble rolled past Dog, who was silently beseeching Lou to make him a coffee. Ignoring him, Lou pulled on a baggy Champion sloppy joe and Adidas tracksuit pants over her swimsuit. She was either the cutting edge of youth fashion or a donation bin picker. Add it to the list of things Gordon couldn't decipher anymore. No—never could. Who was he kidding. But no doubt about it, his goddaughter was a tonic. Whenever he saw her capability—the best word to describe Lou's approach to actions as simple as dragging a surf ski off the beach or making a coffee—he received a shot of optimism. It seemed self-evident that life would be harder for each new generation, but Lou gave hope that the human race was on the improve. Hope: why did you have to look so hard to find it?

'Can't you get her to notice me?' Dog asked Gordon.

'I think she already has,' Gordon said, eyes on his watch. He followed the marble and picked it up when it fell into the slot for the balcony sliding door, a loose aluminium strip raised and irreparably kinked from people tripping over it. Kelly had christened the annoying metal strip the Shitfuckerpoobum. Replacing that aluminium strip was one of his *Tasks*. He'd gone to the hardware store today, but Shitfuckerpoobums were more expensive than he'd thought, so he'd crossed it off his list. His *Tasks* all ended up with a line drawn through them at the end of the day, a ladder of horizontal rungs that gave him equal satisfaction whether they had been completed or avoided.

'How many seconds?' Dog said.

'Eleven,' Gordon said, crossing the room, uphill, to return the marble to its drawer.

'It was, what, fifteen when you moved in?'

'Thirteen,' Gordon replied defensively.

'Still a change,' Dog said. 'It gets below ten, you're gunna have to tie the furniture down.'

Tonsure Man, who was sorting through the donated clothing bins Lou had set up beside the lending library, emerged with a onesie in each hand—in the left a spotted cow, in the right a dinosaur—and commenced speaking as if he had been waiting for Lou for a pitiably long time.

'What kind of stain would rule out a onesie?' Tonsure Man asked. 'The cow's got something small but real crusty, and the dinosaur's got one that's big and dark but maybe not a biohazard.'

'To humans or dinosaurs?' Lou said, inspecting both onesies. 'Dinosaur can survive, but the cow's for the abattoir.' She handed the onesies back to Tonsure Man, who put the cow back in the clothing bin.

'It's a real service you're doing, love,' said Josie. 'I can't get over their attitude at the church. I'm never going back.'

After finding that the churches turned up their noses at clothes without tags attached, Lou had asked, 'But who would donate new things?' Second-hand clothes were being dumped in landfill, so she decided The Lodge could distribute them—there had to be people in Bluebird desperate enough to take used clothes but too proud to go to a church. It was Lou's unwritten rule that if you took something from The Lodge, you left something else: books for the library, a board game, a cake, a bag of coffee beans, even a few dollars if you felt so inclined. Up to now, the only takers for donated clothes were Tonsure Man, Red Cap, Cnut and Snake, who took what they fancied and left bugger-all in exchange. And the only one who left cash was the one whose money was not welcome.

'You don't go anyway, you're an atheist,' Red Cap told his mother, who was beetling to the kitchen.

'Agonistic!' Josie retorted over her shoulder, before putting on a wet smile and saying to Lou, 'We were hoping you might crank up the coffee machine one last time, dear?'

Lou rolled her eyes at Gordon. 'I've got my squad coming.'

'You're doing wonders with those kids,' Josie said ingratiatingly. 'If you don't mind me saying so, you're a loss to motherhood.'

'And a gain to everyone else,' Red Cap added.

'The parents should be paying you,' Tonsure Man said. 'If it was the fucken BSLSC, they'd be up for four hundred a season.'

'You know she's not allowed to charge,' Gordon said. 'She can't even crowdfund,' he added, to show he was aware of her latest tricks to help him.

'You're a miracle worker!' said Josie, who was inclined to dewy-eyed sentiment when it came to Lou. Ever since there had been surf clubs, there were talented kids walking out on them. A motivated few would move to another club, but most quit. Lou spotted a chance to run an informal, stress-free girls' board training and racing group out of The Lodge. Gordon had raised the peril of council permits, but Lou pointed out that there was no law against a group of crusty male surfers using The Lodge as a clubhouse, so what was to stop young girls doing the same?

'Okay, I get it, you want coffee,' Lou said. Gordon followed her to the La Marzocco. 'You don't want to give it a crack?' she asked.

Gordon shrugged. 'I wouldn't want to do anything to the machine.'

'It doesn't take a uni degree, only ten minutes of your undivided attention.'

Lou had been nagging Gordon to let her teach him the skills of the Italian masters. He, overcome by the certain knowledge that even on a La Marzocco his coffee would taste like burnt rubber, had managed to wriggle free.

'I specialise in instant,' Gordon said.

'Or that's what Kel says!' Dog yelped from the living room.

Lou widened her eyes at Gordon. 'Did he actually say that?'

Gordon looked at the floor. The kitchen was developing a similar slope to the living room.

'I'm not making him coffee,' Lou said. 'It's a waste of my spit.'

'Squad's not here yet. I'll watch and learn.'

Gordon's transparent ulterior motive for avoiding learning the machine was to make Lou indispensable. She had told him how sad it was that she was the best new arrival into his life; sad because of the circumstances of her coming, sad because she would leave before he was ready. 'How do you know when I'll be ready?' Gordon had asked. She let him work that one out for himself.

The coffee machine's signals lit up and Lou went to work, darting about the controls like the pinball wizard she used to be until the night Snake, Cnut and Macca drank enough vodka Red Bulls to hatch the great idea of pitching The Lodge's KISS-themed pinball machine off the balcony, an act for which they made amends by helping Lou cart the brand-new La Marzocco down from Cliff Street. Gordon poured himself a glass of water and sat at the melamine breakfast bar.

'How was Up North?' Lou asked. 'We haven't really had time to talk about it.'

'Ben didn't tell you?'

'Ben told me how it was for him. I'm asking how it was for you.'

'Good,' Gordon said.

Without raising her eyes from the coffee machine, Lou wound up her middle finger.

She carried lattes in Duralex tumblers to the living room for Josie and Tonsure Man. To Red Cap's abject look, she said, 'Okay, okay,' and came back to the machine.

'You didn't answer.'

'Didn't answer what?' Gordon said.

'Do you ever listen?'

For thirty years his wife had been asking this, as if their marriage were a royal commission into the question of whether Gordon Grimes ever listened. In his defence, Gordon thought it was more complicated than not listening—more a matter of his declining ability, with age, to do two things at once: listen, for example, while thinking. But explaining that to Kelly, or now to Lou, was to confirm that he was not only a man who didn't listen but one who believed it was somehow correct and justifiable and *interesting* that he didn't listen.

'Well, the big town at Beckham is still the perfect site when they test a neutron bomb. Take out the humans, it'd be paradise. Ben didn't like it either. Too many white witches.' Ben had been scared by the kids his own age with the weary eyes of under-aged burnouts. 'But he loves where we go, to the camp on the lagoon.'

'He said you looked ten years younger the moment you cracked your first home-brew. He told me you'd be happier if you moved there. He said you could buy that newspaper your cousins have been trying to sell.'

'Ben's my life coach now.'

Lou shot him a savage look, warning him not to belittle his son, least of all when he had better ideas than Gordon's. She took a fresh latte to the living room for Red Cap.

'There's a reason they can't find a buyer,' Gordon called after her.

After setting up a vet practice a few years earlier, Rachel and Jason had indulged themselves and bought the *Northern Daily*, a two-town five-sheet rag, at one minute to print media's midnight. Gordon had made the mistake of confiding in Ben his casual dream of taking over the *Daily* from his cousins, overseeing its conversion to digital, and entering semi-retirement as an Up North micro-magnate. His big mouth. Ben must have told Lou, who wasn't the first woman to seize one of Gordon's rare moments of candour and bang him over the head with it.

'You only need to admit to yourself that you hate it here.' This was Lou, back in the kitchen. 'You don't surf anymore. Too many people, too claustrophobic. All you lot talk about is how much better Bluebird was in the old days. Okay, so stop mourning the past, pack up and go Up North, do yourself a favour!'

'I can't go while my parents are still . . .' Gordon almost said 'alive', but he didn't quite mean it like that. Or he didn't want to sound like he meant it like that.

'You can still come down and see your parents; they don't actually need you. You spend your whole time putting up these fake obstacles.'

'Ben's not a fake obstacle. I can't move him up there before he's done with school.'

'He didn't say anything about *him*!' Lou waved her hands in exasperation. 'Ben wants you to do what's good for *you*, for once in your life!'

Gordon tried not to feel hurt that Ben and Lou wanted him to move away. It made a kind of sense, if he could talk his mother-in-law into letting him sell his share of The Lodge—and if he could ensure The Lodge was left in safe hands—but unfortunately making sense was like physical exercise. Some was good, but too much sent you into meltdown. And in his shape, you couldn't do it two days in a row.

To change the subject, he said, 'How much do I owe you for food?'

Gordon had for some time been trying to reimburse Lou for the coffee beans, focaccia bread, Vietnamese groceries and other expenses she incurred feeding the hungry masses. She rebuffed him always, but this time she grinned mischievously. Gordon thought she was going to accept, but she opened a kitchen drawer and produced a stuffed envelope which she pushed across the breakfast bar.

'For you.'

Gordon lifted the flap, saw green and yellow notes, and slid the envelope back at Lou with his knuckles as if scared of leaving a fingerprint.

'Where did you get that?'

'I did a fundraiser. Two, in fact. While you were away. We had music, food, dancing—I got seventy people in.'

'Tell me you're kidding.'

She pushed the envelope back, like a puck on a shuffleboard table. 'You need money. I want to contribute.'

'We'll get slammed by council. Running a business out of here?'

'So what? All they can do is send you a cease-and-desist letter.'

'You don't realise. Fixing it up for the inspections alone will cost more than we could ever raise, let alone the improvements they'll force on us. It's what they require you to spend, that's how they get you.'

'What they don't know can't hurt them,' Lou said. 'You really have to let me help.'

Gordon was about to raise more objections, but Dog was in the doorway with a face calibrated between pathetic and abysmal, an empty Big W mug dangling from his finger.

To Gordon, Lou said, 'I think I can hear my squad arriving.'

Dog nodded genially, as if Lou ignoring him was a shared joke.

Children's voices drifted up from the lawn.

'Right on schedule,' Gordon said.

'They don't play by my rules, they don't get to train,' Lou said, fixing a seawater plug into her ear.

'How else will they learn discipline?' said Dog, the soul of indiscipline.

'Have fun,' Gordon said to Lou's broad back as she pushed out through the saloon door. At the top of the staircase, she removed the wobbly newel and placed it by the laundry chute where Gordon could not forget it.

Dog nodded at the envelope. 'What's that, champ?'

'Nothing,' Gordon said, slipping the money into his pocket before going into the bunk room to add Lou's clothes to the load of washing he intended to put on, the last *Task* waiting to be crossed off. He carried the clothes to the top-loader on a platform outside the back door of the kitchen, filled the tub and switched it on. The second-hand washing machine had no fixed running time, making up its own mind whether to take one hour or three. You knew it was nearly finished when it entered its spin cycle and wobbled violently enough to shake the walls.

Handling Lou's clothes, Gordon swallowed back a fur ball of emotion he didn't want to cough up in front of the others. He'd had little to do with Lou through her childhood. Twenty-two years ago, after naming him godfather to their only daughter, a role Gordon intended to take as seriously as he took his stewardship of all anachronisms, his friends Dave and Sue had moved interstate. Each birthday, Gordon sent Lou a gift and a card with a thought-through message about 'life'. 'It's the one birthday you never forget,' Kelly pointed out caustically after he forgot one of hers. 'A girl you never see, your omigod-daughter when you're not even a Christian, and yet you have her birthday in your diary and not your wife's. Not to mention your mother's, which is coming up very soon and I bet you haven't bought anything, and no, I'm not doing your shopping for you. But Lou? You've never met her, but you never forget her. Shows your priorities.'

Gordon had taken that to heart, where diverse colonies of guilt were accumulating like plaque. He did care for his goddaughter; he was just waiting for a chance to prove it. And then, five months ago, when his own life was lying in pieces around him, Gordon received devastating news. Dave, at forty-nine, had died of a stroke. Weeks later, a man who had been attempting to 'console' Sue was seen driving her into a national park. That afternoon the man was found in his car, alone with an empty card of Endone. Sue was listed as a missing person, but police treated the case as a murder-suicide. Gordon had flown in and, discovering that he was the nearest Lou had to a parent, blurted out an invitation that she had, astonishingly, accepted, despite not knowing Gordon as more than a name on an annual birthday card.

Even Kelly had admitted that the omigod-daughter's arrival was a breath of fresh air. At her home, Lou had had to drive three hours to her nearest surf club every weekend to swim in Antarctic waters. Here in Bluebird, with the beach at her doorstep, landing a part-time job at a local day care centre, enrolling in a childcare course at TAFE, and setting about transforming The Lodge, she had landed in a version of heaven. She deserved to, having fallen direct from hell.

In the kitchen, Dog was still waiting with his mug.

'Looks like you're getting instant again,' Gordon said, and went off with his *Tasks* list in search of a pencil.

All filler no killer

GORDON WAS COOKING SAUSAGES WHEN HE RECEIVED A TEXT
message from Kelly asking about his dinner plans. It was not, as
it might once have been, an obliquely angled proposition. Recent
events had re-encrypted the inquiry: Kelly was wondering if it
was safe to come home.

Gordon contemplated lying.

Sausages, he typed.

As he clipped and skinned beans, covered them in a bowl
with a pat of butter and put them into the microwave, his phone
hummed again.

just you and B?

Gordon was almost knocked down by a wave of sorrow. A fifty-
year-old woman shouldn't have to go through this. This was for
twenty-year-olds sharing a flat with people they hated.

Numbers still fluid.

He looked to the balcony, where Dog, Josie, TM and Red Cap
were gathering, he imagined optimistically, to mount a group

53

assault on the car park. His hopes were raised when Josie poked her head past the sliding door and said, 'We should give you some family time,' as if it was her idea to leave.

Tonsure Man ducked back to the clothing bin to grab his Australian book, the dinosaur onesie, a T-shirt and a set of winter pyjamas he had set aside.

'Later, Gordo,' TM said, jingling a set of car keys in farewell, before disappearing through the front door. He, Red Cap and Josie had a system to avoid her having to climb stairs: she entered The Lodge from above on Cliff Street but left via the beach below, disproving the common belief that what comes down must also go up. While Josie and Red Cap left by the back door down the beach stairs, Tonsure Man would fetch Josie's car from Cliff Street and drive it down to the beach car park, where she and Red Cap would be waiting. It was a perfect little circle, just as long as Tonsure Man didn't forget to pick them up. There had been times when he had driven straight home and gone to bed, only to wake up the next morning wondering why Josie's car was in his driveway.

Gordon was midway through texting Kelly to say dinner would just be himself, Ben and Lou, who was back from training and taking a shower, when Dog poked his laughing-clown head over the saloon door.

'Sausages, champ!'

'Ben's favourite,' Gordon said, heavying up the hint for Dog to leave. But Dog didn't do hints. His will was stronger than Gordon's, and his observance of the forms of Bluebird mateship unbeatably cunning.

'Music to my ears. I've got the munchies. Or I will in ten minutes!' He waved a wiry-looking joint and trotted out to the balcony.

'Shit,' Gordon muttered. He was changing his text to say Dog was staying to eat, when an incoming message from Kelly saved him the trouble.

ok ill eat out

When Gordon took the food out to the card table, the wind had dropped and the lights from the toilet block at the north end of Bluebird shimmered on the bay. Like man's best friend resting after a long walk, the beach inhaled and exhaled, small waves sighing on the sand.

Gordon laid the four plates on the $220 French jacquard tablecloth Lou had placed delicately over the jigsaw puzzle-in-progress. She nodded at the fourth plate.

'You've got to ban him from The Lodge. Nobody would argue.'

'You're quick to judge a person you barely know.'

'Saves time.' Lou sighed. 'Gordon, you're so understanding. What the hell is wrong with you?'

'That seems to be the question of the day.'

Ben was drawing shapes with his finger on the tablecloth: one of the tells for his retreats into his safe interior. Here was their refugee crisis, a child taking shelter from warring adults.

But Gordon couldn't bring himself to ban Dog. If he let himself go in that direction, he could not say where he would stop. Gordon, who believed it was his responsibility to his fellow Bluebirders, whatever he really thought of them, to be the Bigger Man, said, 'Dog's been annoying forever. Where's the justice in banning him now?'

A moan escaped Lou.

'You think you're old school, you do things the Bluebird way, but actually you're just gutless.' She flicked a napkin at his face, accidentally hitting him in the eye. 'We can dump him at sea, shark food, nobody would ever know,' she said with disturbing matter-of-factness. Far from recoiling from conversations about murdering people and dumping their bodies, Lou relished them. This was the problem with the long-lost part of reconnecting with your long-lost goddaughter. The long-lost was the histories that wised you up on who it was you were talking to. He was pretty sure she was joking. 'I keep telling you,' she said. 'I'm trying to help you catch up with your own life, only you won't let me. Is your eye okay?'

Gordon was rubbing his eyelid, which was stinging quite badly, like he'd been shot point-blank with a spud gun. 'Yeah, all good.'

'Ah! Isn't this nice!' Dog said from the sliding door, bald head gleaming. As he stepped inside, he tripped on the aluminium track and fell forward, staying on his feet by reaching forward to the broken staircase, where the exposed screw from the broken newel dug into his palm. 'Shit!' He wrung his hand in pain.

Lou and Ben exchanged a satisfied look.

'Shitfuckerpoobum,' Ben corrected him.

⌒

Ben dug a hole in his mashed potato and filled it with sauce. Lou cut and ate her beans one at a time. Not even the ridiculous tablecloth could make Gordon happy. Pushing against the awkward silence, Dog kept smacking his lips as if savouring a gourmet banquet.

'These are butcher's special, right?'

Gordon's plate was clean.

'Cheapest ones I could find,' he said. 'All filler no killer.'

'You know, it's not poor diet that causes problems for men our age,' Dog said, 'it's the speed at which we consume our poor diet. What's the rush?'

'He just wants to get it over with so you go home,' Ben said, picking up his plate and taking it to the kitchen. Lou followed him.

'Ben,' Gordon said.

'You're just as bad,' Ben called over the saloon door. 'There's a meme going round at school: *My wife and my best mate ran off. Gee, I miss him already.*'

Gordon closed his eyes and sought the energy to disappear. Dog was frowning with the dual effort of first trying to understand, and then appearing not to have understood, the joke. He emerged from this mental swamp with an innocent eye-roll—*Kids!*—and said to Gordon, as if he'd just had a good idea, 'Well! Might be time for yours truly to make myself scarce. But first'—he gave Gordon a wink and twisted his head towards the balcony—'let me do you a favour.'

Outside, Dog took three businesslike drags on a grubby-looking joint with the efficiency of an asthmatic on his Ventolin, and offered it to Gordon.

'Some favour,' Gordon said. He hadn't smoked since the twentieth century, and wasn't likely to start again on this roach glistening with Dog's slobber. 'Tempting as it is.'

'Your loss.' Dog sucked back and squinted through the twilight at the five surfers clustered on the main break. 'That Ned out there?'

'My eyes aren't good enough.'

'Can't believe he'd do this, it was a minor run-in.'

'I heard something went on. Your fault, I assume.'

'Pig's arse!'

That morning, Dog had taken a wave from the outside shoulder off Japan Ned, which led to a dispute over whether Dog, as a stand-up paddleboarder, had priority because he was on his feet, or Japan Ned had right of way because he was positioned on the inside of the wave. Two laws of the surf, incompatible with each other. You'd have needed a lawyer to sort it out, except that one of the parties to the action already was. Two middle-aged men who had peacefully shared the break for decades had emerged from the froth shouting obscenities at each other. Ned's, while in Japanese, were certainly obscene. Dog made his point about being on his feet, and the former state champ had chipped in, 'Fucken paddleboarders—fuck off and take the kook waves on your own.' Even Japan Ned motioned aggressively towards the north end, where no self-respecting local would go. This sent Dog into a tirade in which he undiplomatically mentioned the war, or words to the effect of 'Tora! Tora! Tora!', which in turn plunged Japan Ned into a menacing brood, and he soon left the beach.

'Just apologise,' Gordon said.

'For what? I was on me fucken feet first!'

'For mentioning the war.'

'Oh right.' Dog studied his dangling ember. 'I can't make head or tail of what he's saying. The risk is if I mention the war again, even if I'm apologising for the first time, he might take it the wrong way. He might even go and surf at Capri. I couldn't have that on my conscience.'

'You're on a roll,' Gordon said. 'Maybe when you've had a run-in with every last person in this place, you can consider your work done.'

'Hundred percent, there's something in the air, people are all on their fucken rag.' A maudlin flush came over Dog. 'Even Benny's giving me the stink-eye. I've got no idea what I've done.'

Gordon shook his head to put an end to the subject. He might have it all out with Dog one day, but not here, not now. Where did you start? Gordon and Kelly were 'working it out', they told people, but Kelly had worked him out a long time ago. The marriage had been like bushland drying out for lack of rain. Dog was just the convenient spark, Kelly's match. As Gordon's father used to say, when tapping a cigarette out of its packet, 'You got a match? My bum and your face.' It had been Kelly who decided incineration was what the marriage needed. She just didn't think through all the consequences. Such as everyone ending up here.

'Listen . . .' Dog said through a confidential shaft of smoke out the side of his mouth. 'There were a couple of developments while you and Benny were Up North.'

'Developments,' Gordon said, trying to quell the anxiety waking up in his gullet.

'Chinese agents sniffing round the Hilton.' Dog was referring to the Bluebird Hilton, the pub and bottle-o tucked between the surf club and the shopping strip. After buying it at the bottom of the property cycle, Gordon's late father-in-law Noel Chidgey had overseen the Hilton's transformation from the Beirut of the beaches into the money-printing factory of poker machine and liquor trade and self-abuse that it was today. The Hilton was the jewel of the Chidgey empire. It was the Hilton that made Leonie, its present owner and licensee, a rich woman.

'Chinese agents?'

'Matter of time, bud.'

'Chinese agents', spoken so significantly, did not refer to intelligence agents of the Chinese government or even agents provocateurs of Chinese appearance. In the shorthand of Bluebird Beach, 'Chinese agents' meant local real estate agents with previous connections to clients who might or might not have been Chinese. They only needed to have sold a house to somebody who looked Chinese. Hence Ken Grainger, of First National Northcliffe, 'Born and Bred on the Beaches', was a 'Chinese agent'. His Brazilian-born ex-wife Cara, the co-franchisee of the rival realtor L.J. Hooker Sorrento, was also, somewhat confusingly, a 'Chinese agent'. They were, Dog liked to insinuate, everywhere.

'I heard it on the coconut wireless. They get the Hilton, you know what that means.'

'All it means is that you're shit-stirring. You're Leonie's solicitor; you know what her plans are.'

'Yeah, but I can't tell you, can I? That would be a breach of client confidentiality. But I can tell you about the Chinese agents.' Chinese agent sightings spun the Bluebird rumour mill like a hurricane on a wind farm. 'They get the Hilton, they'll get The Lodge,' Dog went on. 'She's not going to hang on to it. The Chinese buy it up, knock it down, build a palace, leave it empty fifty weeks of the year. These fucken beaches, look around us— most of these massive piles are operated by robot lighting systems, CCTV controlled by security guards in Shang fucken hai. Lights are on, nobody's home.'

'Leonie's not interested in selling,' Gordon stated, although, come to think of it, he had seen Ken Grainger sniffing around the Hilton yesterday morning. Said g'day to him while he walked up the shops for milk and a paper. Gordon didn't know if he was blocking out reality, as Dog probably thought, or if he possessed a higher wisdom. Despite the evidence, Gordon refused to concede that the arrival of wealth had to eradicate Old Bluebird. He just wouldn't. Leonie giving Gordon his one-third share had been a statement that she *cared*. She was a *good* person. Or, if not good, strategic. The Lodge could survive if Gordon could believe it strongly enough, a miracle of mind control like bending a spoon, beyond optimism, operating on the far side of hope, passing through to some dark occult faith.

'Why would Leonie be acting in your interest?' Dog said. 'What are you to her anyway?'

Some random klutz who happens to be family, Gordon thought. 'I trust one thing about her, which is how much she wants to fuck up Kelly.'

'Champ. What do you think I've spent my working life doing?'

Gordon didn't want to say. From his experience, Dog had spent his working life avoiding work and stealing waves. And wives.

'Standing in court representing fuckers after deals like yours go pear-shaped,' Dog answered his own question. 'This amount of money, this amount of aggro, someone's going to end up in front of a judge, I'm telling you.'

'I'm more likely to be in court for murder.'

'Murdering who?'

'Who do you reckon?' Gordon said, letting this sit for a moment before tossing his head towards David Archer's house and adding, 'You know I've got a court date this week.'

'Course I know,' Dog said, and possibly he did. But he was shifting from foot to foot and looking around suspiciously, as if he felt the ground rumbling, the karma train approaching. 'You're naive, buddy. Always have been. You reckon Mrs C hates Kel that much, she'll guarantee you can go on living here till the day you die?'

'She has a track record.'

'Not when there's no commercial interest in it for her.'

'There's no commercial interest in her giving me my share of this place.'

'Have you even seen the contract?' Dog's eyes narrowed.

'I signed it.'

'Yeah but did you read it? I was fucking there! You don't have a clue what's going on.'

'It seemed rude to go through it,' Gordon said. 'In the circumstances.'

'*It seemed rude,*' Dog echoed, shaking his head in disgust. 'Has it struck you that Leonie picked you out for this deal precisely because you're the type of clueless cunt who would be so grateful that you would see it as unforgivably rude to read the fucking contract?'

'Well,' Gordon said. The possibility had struck him down to the last insult, but it was among such a multitude of possibilities striking him at that emotionally fraught time, he was too busy trying to fend them all off to pay special attention to just one.

'Champion.' Dog settled a world-weary look on his oldest friend in the world. 'The party's over, and you won't see the empty fridge coming till after it's hit you. That's your problem, Gordo. You just let life sweep you along like flotsam, yeah, all good, fate will provide. But you'll end up like every incurable optimist: fate's gunna fuck you up the arse.'

Once he had disentangled Dog's mixed metaphors, Gordon's jaw firmed to deny the charge of optimism. A chorus of voices screamed in his ear, Kelly, Ben and Lou, *Now. Let him know. Now.* But suddenly it was Dog who looked nervous, his eyes swivelling.

'Can you feel it?' Dog asked. 'I can feel it.'

'I feel like I should've had a lawyer when I got that contract.'

'Bit late now. How rude to hire a lawyer when Leonie's being so good to you? Lawyers are lying cunts. Anyway, I've got a bad feeling; I gotta get out of here. Coming for a wave tomorrow?'

Every day Dog challenged Gordon's vows to stop smoking dope and stop surfing Bluebird, with a persistence that suggested loving friendship and fraternal care but felt more like a tick burrowing into Gordon's armpit.

'You surf, and make it up with Ned,' Gordon said.

'What the fuck *is* that?'

For a moment, Gordon saw a flash of panic on Dog's face. The ground was indeed shaking. There were not many objects on the open shelves in the living room—no photographs, knick-knacks or anything suggesting shared memories, most of their things remaining in storage—but the crockery rattled. Dog's eyes were flashing as if that karma fridge was coming, and it wasn't aimed at Gordon.

'You really would murder me?' Dog said quietly. For a second, Gordon saw himself reflected in the wetness of Dog's brown eyes, a terrifying moment of shared recognition: that if Gordon dropped his nice-guy mask for one instant, out would jump the frothing homicidal maniac.

'Calm down.' Gordon put Dog out of his misery. 'The washing machine's on spin.'

'Jeez, I was shitting meself there!'

With an uneasy laugh, Dog made a phone call and let himself out the front door to climb the stairs to Cliff Street, where his wife Sally would be waiting in her car like he was eight years old and she was his mum picking him up from a play date.

Gordon and Lou followed Ben to bed early, none wanting to wait up for Kelly. Gordon lay in his child-sized bunk, imagining himself rolling downhill like the marble with the slope across the living room, jumping the Shitfuckerpoobum and tumbling off the balcony all the way down to the beach.

Hours later, when the sliding door opened and closed and he heard Kelly trip on that same Shitfuckerpoobum and swear quietly and go to the bathroom they all shared and then her bedroom, he was still awake, fizzing with worry, cataloguing the number of ways in which he was well and truly fucked. He felt the presence of that shadowy man, that faceless nightclub bouncer, standing in the doorway between himself and sleep. Gordon still hadn't worked out a way past him. It was a waiting game, and at this stage of life waiting was the only skill he had left. He set himself for an all-night face-off.

Kelly's bed wheezed as she flopped onto it. He heard her cough and sniff, or maybe sob. He looked across the bunk room at Ben, who hadn't moved: a sure sign that he was still awake. Above him Lou sighed, conscious, impatient with her thoughts. It was after midnight and that made four of them, each unhappy in their own way, lying on their backs, listening to each other's breath.

NEXT
PART

NEXT PART

Bird's eye

How do they get away with it? Truth be told—and this should be apparent after spending one day in his worn-out thongs—Gordon is getting away with nothing. Day by day, dollar by dollar, degree by degree of slope in that living room floor, Gordon is failing at the Bluebird way of life. He is failing to get away with it.

Though I would like to think of myself as a benign seagull, or even, in my moments of flushed self-regard, a guardian angel hovering over Gordon, from down there I am seen as a wicked witch, long-nosed with a wart on my chin, malevolent on my flying broomstick.

Yet I am as much a passenger of history as they, powerless to change The Lodge's character. History is an elephant, plodding to its destination, and we are fleas riding on its skin. Ancient as I am, could I have done anything about the Great Depression, when The Lodge was abandoned by its first owners and fell into disrepute as a tramps' camp? In the late 1940s it was turned over to the Returned Servicemen's League for diggers to dry out and, like the driftwood cladding, die in the sun. It was then that the building gained its name; at arbitrary hours of the month the diggers' home became the meeting house of a breakaway chapter of the local Freemasonry. By the 1960s, the official Masonic Lodge, a neoclassical showpiece of the ambitious seaside metropolis Capri, aggressively requisitioned the house and sold it to the Chidgey family of automotive lubricants and brake fluids fame. Was that my fault too?

Enter the love of my life. Could I have pulled strings on that force of nature? Patriarch, businessman, Mason and sometime mayor Noel Chidgey was said to sit up in The Lodge like the Prime Minister in Canberra. Noel was, if nothing else (and many said he was exactly that: nothing else), lucky, selling his automotive business at the top of the lubricants and brake fluids cycle before his annexure of a controlling stake in the Bluebird Hilton. Soon after, alcohol and gaming laws were favourably reformed and Ch-, as they said, ching! Noel and his first wife of sainted memory, Gladys (nee Mishra), raised their children Kelly and Carl in The Lodge until Gladys died from a burst aortic aneurysm at forty-five. Cue violins. Carl and Kelly were reaching adult age and, without Gladys's unifying love, the Chidgey family spun centrifugally: Kelly from a planned into an unplanned marriage; Carl to the mysterious exile of a university arts degree on the far side of Ocean City, none of the family quite sure if he had gone boho or hobo; Noel to increasingly frequent grieving widower's holidays in exotic locations, which may or may not have started before he became said grieving widower.

During one of these trips, or possibly an earlier visit, Noel met a twice-divorced accountant named Leonie. I enter the story—finally! A respectable period having passed since Gladys's death, I demanded Noel take our private arrangement public. Having hooked Noel and moved to Ocean City, I went full stepdragon, treating Kelly as more step than daughter, a contempt that was mutual, for Kelly dismissed me as a living insult to the holy memory of the unimpeachable Gladys. I viewed Kelly as a spoilt heiress and carrier of that peculiar strain of bigotry, the dark-skinned racist, the minority minority-hater, the recent arrival whose loathing was aimed at the more recent. Finding Kelly's assumptions of Australian racist prerogatives wonderfully comical, I could never resist the temptation to bait her. You will have to forgive me my leisure activities.

The Lodge, which we owned mortgage-free, became unoccupied after Noel's death in 2000 during the Ocean City Olympic Games Torch Relay, for which he partially completed the Northern Beaches leg. Noel's death, televised on the nightly news as he got the staggers up Bluebird's shopping strip to hand the torch to the president of the BSLSC Tony Eastaugh (who received it from the teetering brake fluids king and, in true Olympian spirit, sallied forth without a backwards glance), emancipated my gift for sharp business practice. It was I who engineered the nifty tax-efficient restructure of assets into family trusts that sugar-highed the Chidgey fortune. Upon Noel's death, two of the trust shares in The Lodge went to me and one to Kelly. The vanished Carl was summarily disinherited, but for Kelly there was a catch: I held the trust's sole voting share, which meant that she could not sell, add to or borrow against hers without my express permission, which, I made clear, would come in my own sweet time.

Whatever I did with The Lodge, I was too smart to tinker with the engine of Chidgey wealth and soul of the community: the Bluebird Hilton. I had the Hilton to make the money, The Lodge to have fun with. After Noel's death, I lost the taste for the sewer of prejudice and resentment that was Bluebird and fled to more congenial climes—my son from my first marriage, Tino, required my loving attention in Thailand—leaving my properties to be managed by my conveyancer and probate solicitor, Douglas Oscar Gilsenan. Empty, The Lodge fell *into disrepair and became a de facto clubroom for the conveyancer and his cronies, the locals Noel had still perceived through memory-tinted eyes as his children's playmates, but who had ripened into the underemployed, sun-damaged, life-raddled dead-enders who could not let go of Bluebird, the last hold-outs grimly defending the beach's last unrenovated property. The ghosts of those rehabbing diggers returned to The Lodge to possess its denizens, who bear the war wounds without the war.*

I'm not so bad, am I? I might not have held much belief in this family, but I believe strongly in Family. After Kelly's act of sabotage against her marriage, my responsibility was to keep Family together. Gifting a share in The Lodge to Gordon was the very least I could do.

But alas, although my extraordinary munificence has enabled Gordon to move into The Lodge and remain with his family, he struggles to feel as grateful as he thinks he ought. Most nights, as he lies awake fretting over cost and complication and compromise, he fears he has been lured into a trap by his love for this house. Conserving history and saving his family feels like an unbearable burden. He is too ashamed to ask me for help.

I suspect that there are shames wrapped inside Gordon's shame, guilts within his guilt. So desperate is he to avoid confronting his shame and guilt, he has turned for his financial salvation to the one person whose need for secrecy is as vital as his own. And in finance, secrecy merely makes the introductions for illegality.

Silly, silly, silly boy. Like everyone who knows him, I wonder why he makes life so hard for himself. What, dear Gordon, is the matter with you?

The firehouse

NOTHING COULD MAKE GORDON GRIMES'S HEART CHIRRUP QUITE as tunefully as a morning like this: clouds throbbing with rain, sea the colour of dreadnoughts, squalls on a sou'-easter devil wind whisking the water into foam quiffs. Ben was off to school early, Kelly had disappeared to work and Lou, bound inside a scarf, had headed out to meet a friend on her way to TAFE.

Bluebird Beach was scoured of humanity. Even Red Cap was cowering indoors, Snake had a job on, Cnut had not been sighted, and Dog, when he saw the forecast, had hurriedly arranged a client conference in Mirage Chambers, his virtual legal office which comprised a receptionist and a conference room. Mirage was the pop-up solution for legal practitioners who would not or could not afford, or would not be accepted into, a legitimate Ocean City firm. Dog would lurk in the toilets until his clients arrived, and then appear in the conference room laden with important documents, bubbling with confidence about their case, backed by the authority of his Potemkin Village chambers. It was the deception, as much as the peppercorn rent, that appealed to him.

Behind the top car park, the cafes had pulled down their wind-snapped awnings and given their shivering staff the day off.

For Gordon, then: a surf day.

He hadn't given up surfing; he'd just given up surfing with people. Pristine days with sweetly groomed swell, bringing masses of board riders to Bluebird, kept Gordon indoors. Only on filthy days did he take his board from its cover, wax up, pour himself into his wetsuit and trot happily down to the rain-whipped sand.

Firie Sam Eastaugh, in board shorts and zipper vest, was already out at what passed for a south peak in the confused mess. Gordon bobbed next to him. They didn't say hello: a waste of body heat. Gordon watched Sam stroke into a limp moment of chop that somehow stood up into a rideable wave.

'How's it been?' Gordon asked when Sam paddled back.

'Puke, but puke on me own. Here—go.'

Sam nodded Gordon into an unpromising knob of water which, to Gordon's surprise, turned into a half-decent ride.

'Careful we don't make it look too good,' Sam said. 'The Zillas will be out.'

Gordon squinted back to the beach, half visible in the rain, but no fix-chasing Brazilians were in sight, just Japan Ned suiting up in the car park.

'Saw your old lady up the shops yesterday,' Sam said. 'I was thinking about how back in the day she tried to keep you out of the water. She was terrified you'd get a taste.'

'I have to go see her and Dad,' Gordon said. 'I've been avoiding them since Ben and I got back.'

'Yeah, she knows. You're a bad son.'

Sam took a wave that only he could have spotted. Sam was a big man of big parts: big nose, big brown eyes, big tussock of greying black hair plastered over his big forehead, big handlebar moustache foresting his big mouth, and a jaw so stupendous it made the rest of his features seem small. To outside eyes he and Gordon would have looked like indistinguishable middle-aged blurs. In fact, Sam was fifty-four to Gordon's fifty, a seniority that defined their relationship as cleanly as if they belonged to a traditional, age-respecting culture. Old Bluebirders could still see their young selves in each other, and Sam would always be the big boy to Gordon, charismatic and scarred, the one who told him what to do.

'I did have the fear, but that was what hooked me,' Gordon said. 'Remember those big days?' They didn't make days so big, so clean, so perfect, so free, anymore. He wondered if he was staying in Bluebird like a second-coming zealot, hopped up on the return of paradise.

'What you never saw was what it did to your mum. Probably lucky for you.'

Sam took another wave. Gordon waited, thinking about Norma. He really had to go see her. Sam paddled back and sat on his board.

'Funny thing is, I don't fear the ocean anymore,' Gordon said. An accidental drowning, while probably an unhappy business to go through, sometimes presented itself as the solution to his problems.

'Me neither,' Sam said.

'But you've still got the stoke.'

'You can't come out on a day like today and say you've lost your stoke, brother.'

'These are the only days I come out. You're out every day.'

'I'm a sick puppy. Anyway, if you don't like the crowds you could go the Dog route,' Sam suggested. 'Stay competitive, just give yourself a bit of help with your choice of craft.'

'Dog still wants to win,' Gordon said.

Sam let that pass, out of respect for the awkwardness of Gordon's situation or because he saw a wave. This time, he paddled hard but the slab of chop petered out. Gordon heard him swear.

'Here comes Ned,' Gordon said. Two unknowns and the seven-time state champ were following Japan Ned into the water from the car park. Soon the clouds would lift and Bluebird would fill with people who used not to exist at this time of year: mothers' groups, able-bodied sunbathers, Zillas, clusters of what Gordon's mother, too burdened by her own preoccupations to care for the eggshells she was walking on, called 'people of the dark-haired persuasion'. People of every persuasion, Gordon thought, and more of them. Fucken people. Whoever they were and whatever your prejudices, they didn't used to pack out the sands of Bluebird on a workday. Maybe it was the workday, not the people, that had changed.

'One beach, one clan, one club,' Sam said. 'Bluebird's great singularity.'

'I thought I was the one who spent all day pining for a non-existent past,' Gordon said. 'It was never just one club here.' He gave a nod towards The Lodge, its cement-rendered lower level giving the butter-yellow impression of a surf clubhouse. The relationship between the Bluebird Surf Live Saving Club and The Lodge had, since Noel Chidgey's time, alternated between simmering hostility and outright war, and Noel chose that yellow as a direct provocation to the club. He had recruited Gordon and

Sam from the local rats to paint the basement in exchange for a case of Tarino orange soft drink. Gordon, Sam and the ghost boy who made them a gang of three.

'Yeah nah, I'm not pining for it,' Sam said. He shot a piercing look at Gordon through the rain. 'You ever think of him?'

'Dog? He makes sure I see him every day, so there's not much chance to forget.'

'Not him.' Sam was looking wretched, as if he had been delegated to convey bad news for which he didn't have the words.

Japan Ned was beside them.

'G'day, Ned,' Sam said.

'G'day, Ned,' Gordon said.

'Shit out,' Ned said.

'Yeah, flogging a dead horse,' Gordon said. 'Hey, Ned, you cleared the air with Dog? He'll probably come down when the weather clears up.'

'Shit out!' Ned said again, white teeth glowing.

A comatose drawl came from the beach loudspeaker. 'Attention in the water. Those fibreglass surfboard riders, please paddle to the north of the flagged area. Fines of up to two hundred dollars apply.'

Gordon didn't believe what he was hearing, and then seeing. A clubbie was ploughing out on his knees, his rescue board slapping against the chop.

The public loved clubbies: they were volunteers, they saved lives, they sat deep in the Australian marrow. The truth was that nine in ten were officious fuckwits. Gordon recognised Ryan Stoyle, Ben's PE teacher and cricket coach, prize knob, all-round small-town hero.

'Nice day for it!' Gordon shouted.

Stoyle showed no recognition: or, to be precise, he showed that he was not prepared to recognise Gordon.

'I'm going to have to tell you to paddle south of the flags,' Stoyle said with the automaton emotions and bristling self-importance of a highway policeman. 'I have the authority to confiscate your board and fine you two hundred dollars.'

'Mind if I ask why?' Gordon said.

'It's illegal for a fibreglass surfboard rider to be within the flagged area.'

'Why?'

'Beach regulations.'

'I mean why are you out here? There's not a single person on the beach. They'd have to be mad, day like this.'

'You were asked to paddle out of the flagged area.'

'I'm not in the flagged area.' Gordon nodded towards the beach.

'You're in the buffer zone.'

'Buffer zone from what?'

'Flagged area.'

'Where there are no swimmers. You can't fine me for being in the buffer zone.'

'If you're in the buffer zone, I can move you on.'

'So I have to move out of the buffer zone to stay clear of where there are no swimmers.'

Stoyle paddled closer. For a moment Gordon thought he was going to square up. Anyone with any experience knew that you could not effectively attack another surfer while on water. The fighting got done later, in the car park.

Gordon back-paddled to keep out of arm's reach. Stoyle spun his board and sat up.

'You've drifted between the flags,' Stoyle said.

76

'You've drifted out of your mind.'

Suddenly, Stoyle clutched his stomach as if he had been gut shot.

'Fuck!'

'Should have worn a wettie,' Gordon said, paddling away to the south, where Sam and Ned had drifted on the rip. He could hear Stoyle cursing as he tried to unwrap the bluebottle strands from his torso.

'I'm off,' Sam said. 'You getting changed at your place, Gordo, or coming straight up to mine?'

'Be right with you,' Gordon said. He paddled for a wave that stood up on the inside and gave him a surprising trim into the beach. He undid his leg rope and was tying it around his board, watching Japan Ned try to get going on a limp grey peak, while Sam bellied in.

They went up the rain-firmed beach with the confident tread of people who walk on top of sand. 'Sand people' was one of those quirky micro-insights of Ben's into a truth which habit had ironed from Gordon's perception. As he walked, a little swell of love for his boy hiccupped Gordon's breath. They passed the Bluebird Surf Life Saving Club, painted the same yellow as The Lodge's basement, its national pennant riding its flagpole like an erect middle finger, returning the gesture. Two blue-shirted council lifeguards peered down from the watchtower, shared a word, laughed. Gordon and Sam climbed over the crest of the sand path and descended the decking slats on the landward side of the dune.

Another squall hit them as they crossed the middle car park, passed the electrical substation and rounded the firehouse. They put their boards on their heads against the rattling hail. Behind the exit for the fire engines was a multi-level surfboard rack. Sam was not the only volunteer firie with an addiction. He and Gordon slung up their boards before rinsing off in the open-air showers.

Sam tossed Gordon a towel and they climbed the back stairs. Gordon was surprised to see a furtive shape, a tattooed bald male in board shorts and a black windcheater, hunched at the screen door, sliding something out from under the mat. It didn't take a moment to work out who it was, because Cnut had, at some time in his murky past, decided to have a face tattooed on the back of his head, the snarling features of that face being, approximately, Cnut's own. Cnut never answered questions about his unique tatt, but it was understood that he had many enemies, in the surf and out, and his markings were like those of an animal designed to deceive its predators.

On seeing Cnut slip a mauve manila folder under his arm, Gordon glanced at Sam, who was unfazed.

'Got it all, mate?' Sam said.

Cnut shoved the folder behind his hip as if preparing to deny possession. He forged down the steps past Gordon and Sam, grunting, 'Yeah, all good—you saved me life.'

'Get it signed and notarised and you're sorted,' Sam called after Cnut.

To Gordon's questioning look, Sam shrugged. 'Drug dealers need home loans too.'

'Cnut's buying in the area?'

'Laundering, you might call it. He's put together a stake he needs to stash somewhere. No place better than property. He's putting down forty percent on a one-bedder in Capri, we're loaning him the rest.'

Gordon shook his head in amazement. It was years since anyone in his acquaintance had been a buyer, not a seller, of real estate.

'Cnut'll end up richer than us all,' Sam said as he took his house key out of a waterproof neoprene pouch he stored in a potted geranium and inserted it in the screen door lock. 'He's in a recession-proof industry.'

'Real estate?'

'Marching powder.'

'Backed in by the Bluebird Building Society,' Gordon said. 'Operating out of a condemned firehouse.'

Sam grimaced as he fiddled with the key, which stuck in the lock. 'Don't diss your mobile loans officer. The parent company likes to keep a local presence and the shareholders don't have to know that we only exist as telephone support working from home.'

He had worked all his life for the Bluebird Building Society, of which his father Tony had been the local branch manager. Acquired by one of the Big Four mega-banks during the financial shakeout of the 2000s, the building society's shopfront in Bluebird was shut down, sold off and converted into apartments, but the name was kept alive as a 'virtual branch', staffed by no-overheads loans officers like Sam, peddling the mega-bank's products under the Bluebird Building Society letterhead. Sam did take a few liberties, lending to his friends, cutting corners, or, as he put it, Keeping Local Alive. As Sam saw it, the mega-bank couldn't have it both ways: it couldn't keep marketing the BBS as the 'locals only' branch and not allow some tolerance for the clients who made the society what it was. And besides, half his BBS workmates were making profits for the bank by selling life insurance to dead people.

Sam wrestled the screen door open and ushered Gordon inside. The firehouse comprised two empty offices, now makeshift bedrooms, and a large meeting room with a window overlooking the back of the dunes and the BSLSC. Gordon dragged a desk chair out of one of the offices; the Bluebird fire station had become redundant since the consolidation of the beaches' services into a 'superstation' two suburbs north, where the fire engines, equipment and professional firemen were based. With professionalisation and corporatisation, the volunteer rural fire service to which Sam had belonged had been disbanded. In the country Gordon grew up in, firemen, like soldiers, were grumpy mavericks with chips on their shoulders; now they were male models in tight overalls, superheroes in superstations.

He followed Sam into the kitchenette, a bench against the club-room's western wall equipped with a single sink, oven, one-burner stove and mini-fridge. Sam had enhanced it with a small espresso maker. Soon he conjured two unexpectedly authentic flat whites.

'Get this inna ya.'

'Everyone's a fricken barista,' Gordon said.

Gordon and Sam sat and sipped and looked at the back wall of the surf club.

'Shit of a day,' Gordon said, smiling at the pebbly rain drumming the window.

'Just how we love it.'

'Remember how we used to think those old pricks were mad, running down in their budgies to swim the bay on days like this?'

'Yeah and we're those old pricks now.' Sam raised his cup. 'Toasting each other with coffee. What the fuck's the world come to?'

'What's the plan for this place?' Gordon asked. The volunteer firehouse's future always seemed to be hanging by a whim of the state government property department or a connection with the local mayor. Miraculously, the place hadn't been turned over to developers. For a time it was protected by the influence of

Sam's father over the local press, back when there was a local press and Sam's father had influence. Before the bureaucrats decided there couldn't be fires so close to the beach. All that water—what could go wrong? Now the firehouse's survival seemed a marvel of benign neglect.

'It can't go on,' Sam said. 'The land value's too high to keep a firehouse in this location. It's like we're under a rock that nobody has turned over. They will.'

'And convert it into another fuck-off house,' Gordon said.

'Fuck-off units,' Sam corrected him. 'More yield in it. For retired pricks who managed to hang on to their dough. So they can flip the bird at the likes of us.'

'It'll kill the old folks. Kill history.'

'I wouldn't sentimentalise it, brother,' Sam said with a twinkle. 'We did our best to kill this place ourselves, if you'll remember.'

'We thought there was no tomorrow. There were quite a lot, it turned out.'

'All pretty much the same as the todays.'

As boys, Gordon and Sam, together with Gordon's elder brother Owen, had been members of the BSLSC where Sam's father Tony was president. Having imbibed the obscurely origined but deeply felt tribal hatred of clubbies for firies, the three boys figured that they could become legends of the surf club if they burnt down the firehouse. As the youngest, Gordon would do anything Owen and Sam suggested. Their compound of petrol and sticks and dune grass was blackening the exterior wall and climbing towards the flammable wooden eaves when Gordon panicked and ran off, terrified of what they had unleashed, to raise the alarm.

Sam had subsequently grown fascinated with the firehouse and the men and engines that emerged from it. Girls led changes in history, and Bluebird girls loved the men who rode the sides of the engines. Sam would leave the BSLSC and become a fire service volunteer at eighteen, devoting his weekends to back-burning drills. Gordon had pondered becoming a firie until Sam's place as the most influential presence in his life was taken over by Kelly, who convinced Gordon that he was better than that. Kelly would change her mind about him, but too late. Gordon went off to the *News*, and the weekend demands of journalism had put paid to volunteer fire work. It was one of those sliding doors that had slammed shut on him, spiritually jamming his fingers.

'If I knew then what I know now about how to set fires, we would've been more successful.' Sam took a sip of his coffee. 'Fuck that's a good brew, even if I say so myself.'

It was one of the many-textured ironies of a life on Bluebird Beach that Gordon and Sam were now the old crusties drinking coffee in the building they had tried to incinerate. Up to then, Gordon's mother had forbidden him from coming near the fire-house because of a widely held suspicion about the Bluebird firemen. As it turned out, Norma was right about the suspicion, but thirty metres out on the location.

'Your old man about?' Gordon asked.

Sam nodded towards the back of the building. On cue, a convulsive cough came from the toilet. 'How's yours?'

Gordon shrugged. 'No change.'

'Still giving your mum hell?'

'He's a student of history,' Gordon said. 'He believes in triumph through attrition.'

Gordon's father Ronald lived in a nursing home, technically suffering end-stage kidney failure but living the infuriated dream of perfect health. Gordon's mother Norma visited Ron every day so he could shout at her for locking him up among half-dead geriatrics. By night, Ronald plotted break-outs in order to fulfil his deepest wish: to get behind the wheel of his car and drive into the countryside to relive holiday trips to the dams, mines, power stations and other engineering wonders he had inflicted on Norma, Gordon and Owen in the 1970s.

'I wish mine wanted to escape,' Sam said.

A volley of indescribable toilet noises answered.

'Listen.' Sam lowered his voice and leant forward. Gordon noticed a rime of coffee froth on his friend's moustache and wanted to wipe it for him. 'I've got my computer, we can do your visit, but I can't let the old man know. He'll blab it all over town. How much are you down to?'

'About two weeks,' Gordon said. 'So yeah.'

Sam finished his coffee, his eyes darting towards the bathroom where Marianas trenches of mucus were being hawked up. 'You know, you can't keep eating the house forever.'

Gordon gave a nod to what was a pro forma piece of advice, cover for the moment Sam ever got pulled up in front of an investigation where he would have to state honestly that he had warned the customer about the inadvisability, or illegality, of his borrowing practice.

'I can try,' Gordon said.

'That's not what you're meant to say at this point,' Sam said seriously.

'Okay. Thank you, Samuel. I know it is bad financial practice to keep drawing down on my equity and living off the cash flow and repaying it out of fraudulent revaluations. And it's hypocritical for me, having been a conscientious objector to the property ladder all my life, to live on the proceeds of that same Ponzi scheme which is killing Bluebird. That what I'm meant to say?'

'You, ah'—Sam looked from side to side as if what he was about to say was more questionable than what he was offering to do—'you had any more ideas about raising the cash elsewhere?'

'Lou's been trying to push cash my way from her fundraisers. A month of her events would cover my bills for, ooh, a week? She tried to give me eight hundred bucks the other day. It's not worth the guilt. I went and deposited it straight back into her account.'

Sam nodded. 'You thought about getting a hand from Norma?'.

It wasn't the first time Sam had suggested the ultimate self-sacrifice. Gordon would literally choose a painful death in preference to borrowing money from, or moving in with, his mother. He would not dignify Sam's question with a response. Instead he said, 'I've got a court date coming up with my neighbour. I'm still blocking his excavator from getting in to do his reno.'

'Oh, that.'

'I'm thinking he might offer me a settlement. It's a two-million-dollar project. What's ten or twenty grand between friends? You'd think he'd throw me that much to make me go away.'

'Yeah, but you don't have a legal leg to stand on.'

'I've got a strategy.'

'A strategy,' Sam repeated.

Rather than invent what this strategy might be, Gordon skidded onto a new subject. 'Dog says Leonie's up to something with the Chinese.'

'Selling The Lodge?'

'And the Hilton.'

'Well that'd save your arse.'

'I can't believe she'd do it to me. You know, Red Cap told me the other night that saving The Lodge was my mission in life.'

'Easy for Red Cap to say.'

'But he's right. With all the shit that's gone on, it's the one thing that gets me out of bed in the morning. How to save the fucking place. Hence why I'm back here again, doing dodgy deals with you.'

Sam's eyelids drooped with his moustache. Gordon wondered if he had said the wrong thing, but no; the toilet door had banged open and Tony Eastaugh was bearing down on them, surprisingly nimble considering his plastic left foot.

Tony came to a wobbly stop behind Gordon's shoulder, forcing Gordon to rearrange himself so as not to rick his neck. Tony's lack of consideration for the comfort of others, Gordon reminded himself, was not, or not only, a sign of age. The guy was a lifelong prick, and it was somehow consoling to see the inner prick untouched by the decay that was eating up the rest of him.

'You've been on holidays,' Tony announced, peering at Gordon over the top of his smeared reading glasses. Tony wore these glasses permanently, but he never looked through their lenses, only over or under the rims, depending on whether he judged the situation demanded a significant peer over the top or a sneer down the nose. With Gordon, he toggled between both. 'Must've been strange not having your wife.'

Sam was mouthing: *Ignore him*. In eighty years, Tony Eastaugh had never taken the slightest interest in anybody's domestic life unless it gave him an opportunity to twist some blade.

'How's your foot, Mr Eastaugh?' Gordon asked.

Tony glared under his glasses and bared his teeth as if Gordon had replied to his precise jab with an energetic if misdirected roundhouse.

'We're going to the races this weekend,' Sam said, 'and Dad won't even let me take him to an air-conditioned box. He wants to be down in the ring, sniffing the horseflesh. He reckons you can pick a winner by the smell. Makes it pretty hectic, though, getting a man with one leg down to the bookies and then up to the stands. Coffee, Dad?'

'It's meant to be a laxative,' Gordon said. 'I read it in a magazine at the doctor's surgery.'

'Bullshit,' Tony said, still glaring implacably over and under his reading glasses at Gordon, as if deciding which angle would best answer his questions about this young nitwit. 'Been drinking it all my life and it binds me up.'

Sam took the empty cups and rinsed them at the sink. 'From the sound of what was going on in there, I'm not sure he needs a laxative.'

'I can tell you, from what was going on in there,' Tony said, 'I need a doctor.' He farted exuberantly. 'That's good, no follow-through.' He peered insistently over his glasses at Gordon. 'You didn't answer about your holiday.'

'It was good, Mr Eastaugh,' Gordon said. Fifty years old and he still felt a child before the club president, the big man of Bluebird. Tony's hair, the colour of pissed-on snow, lifted and fell with a puff of breeze. He was wearing a frayed yellow BSLSC polo shirt and board shorts, no shame or long pants to cover the join between his veiny left shin and his prosthesis. Feeling sympathy for Tony's infirmity and guilt for his uncharitable thoughts, Gordon shook off his revenant teenage surliness. 'Ben had a fantastic time and even did some volunteering work.' He hoped that this would earn some approval from Tony, who had devoted his life to volunteerism, outside the part of his life he had devoted to intimidating the crap out of young boys and conning investors out of their savings as the founding manager of the Bluebird Building Society Investment Advisory Service. There were so many unexploded mines in a conversation with Tony, Gordon suddenly caught an image of himself in some Cambodian battlefield, missing a limb or two of his own from previous missteps.

'The culture of volunteering is dead,' Tony pronounced. 'These kids only do it for points in their Duke of Ed. How can they call it volunteering if they get something out of it?'

'Ben asked me the same question,' Gordon said. Another scoring punch for Tony. Ben had been a regular community volunteer as a younger kid, but what adolescence had started, his parents' separation had finished off: he'd lost all interest, unless helping Lou counted, which it didn't. Gordon was thrilled when, on the holiday, Ben allowed himself to be taken to the Beckham lagoon bush regeneration project for a couple of six-hour days. On their way home, Gordon asked Ben if he would do some more volunteering on their return, but Ben said, 'No, Up North people do it because they care for each other. In the city it's crims doing community service and kids who want to be school prefects beefing up their CVs. Everyone's out for himself.' Gordon had refrained from replying that Ben's interest in the bush regeneration project had coincided with the presence of the boy he was interested in, so perhaps it wasn't purely altruistic. He also refrained from mentioning this now to Tony Eastaugh.

'Who are those weirdos who moved up there?' Tony asked, accepting a cup of black instant from his son. Tony preferred instant, seemingly part of a broader statement of resistance against the forces of political correctness.

'Rachel and Jason?' Gordon said.

'They're not weirdos,' Sam said. 'They're his cousins.'

'Runs in the family,' Tony said with satisfaction.

If anything ran in families, Gordon thought, it was the looks in certain male lines. As if time had a sardonic sense of humour, Tony was a diminished version of his son. The bones of his shoulders were still broad but the flesh holding them together was concave and withered. The handlebar moustache was moth-eaten. The forehead was higher, to reveal a galaxy of scabs, crusts, keratoses, basal cell carcinomas and, with any luck, melanomas.

Giving himself a mental slap, Gordon said, 'Rachel and Jason are the straightest people in the Northern Rivers. They drive Beemers. Solid citizens. Never smoke dope. Three daughters at private schools.'

'That's why they're weirdos,' Tony agreed with himself. 'If you're not some hippie dipstick, who but a weirdo would move up there?'

'They were surprised about me and Kel,' Gordon said to Sam, hoping to rescue the chat they might have had before Tony's intervention.

'I wasn't,' Tony interrupted.

Sam and Gordon looked expectantly at Tony. Misinterpreting their looks as an invitation, he blurted, 'How Noel Chidgey's daughter put up with this hopeless case is anybody's guess. She saw the light before she's too old to find someone else. Mind you, she pretty much is.'

Gordon frowned at Tony, not because of the offensiveness of what he had said, which was par for the course, but because this was, more or less, what all of Bluebird said: that Kelly had been unhappy for a long time, everyone could see that she and Gordon had gone past their use-by date, and the only surprise was that she had left her move so late.

'We used to place bets on you,' Tony said. 'Pollyanna here'—he indicated Sam—'thought the Chidgey lass would stick it out, but I knew what was coming.'

'Bets?' Gordon said to Sam, who was wiping up the coffee cups.

'He means figuratively.'

'I would have put real money on it if he'd let me,' Tony went on. 'Everyone knew you two were a mismatch, but a lot of people stick together so long, despite the evidence, that people figure you must have some secret special thing that nobody else can see.'

'Usually in the sack,' Sam added unhelpfully.

'But no, there's never a secret,' Tony said. 'Noel's daughter just took longer to see what we all knew.'

Blunt and hurtful, but sadly true. Gordon's break-up with Kelly had shown him how differently others perceived him from how he saw himself. Was this what life was about? Stumbling over the bleeding obvious: that you were not who you thought you were, and that everyone else was right about you? Was the big reveal that fuckwits like Tony Eastaugh, who'd known you since you were a kid, who showed no wholesome interest in you, knew you better than you knew yourself? What an anticlimax, not to mention a poorly constructed narrative. It was the shapelessness of life, more than its sheer capacity to disappoint, that stopped Gordon from ever believing in, say, God.

'You should probably apologise,' Sam said to his father.

'Who to?' Tony said, and he had a point, Gordon thought.

Tony bumbled to his feet and drained his coffee. His fart, on rising, sounded squelchier than the earlier one. 'That's my cue,' he announced, turning for the bathroom and pushing his glasses onto the bridge of his nose as if he was going to need reading-strength eyesight for what he would find in there. Over his shoulder he said, 'You'll have to go to Chemist Warehouse for me, son.'

As Gordon watched Tony disappear into the bathroom, he wondered, not for the first time, if Tony's enmity towards him originated from something Gordon had done. No; from a specific thing Gordon had done back when Tony was Lord and Master of Bluebird Beach, captain and then president of the BSLSC, head of Rotary, vice-president of the Returned Servicemen's League, and general all-round cock of the walk, when the young boys had beheld him as a beachside deity with his barrel chest, when he bestrode Bluebird like the triplet brother of Dennis Lillee and the Marlboro Man. Every big knob from the mayor to the local member was in Tony's grip. His rule was unquestioned— except, of course, by Sam, who had once confided to Gordon that 'being my dad's son, everyone says it's like being the son of God, but it's more like being the son of a priest'. Gordon had only deciphered this allusion after a night when, aged eight, he had been showering after board training. The surf club showers were a confusing place for him from the start, where males of every age, seven to seventy, mixed in all their glory. Though he had grown uneasily accustomed to the diversity of old men's shapes and sizes, Gordon had never seen Sam's father in the showers. The skanky changing room seemed beneath Mr Eastaugh's dignity. Gordon had not seen him that night either. The older boys had had their showers, and then Gordon had taken his turn before needing to use the toilet cubicle. Sam and Owen routinely pissed in the shower, teasing young Gordon for being the only person in the club who was too squeamish to use it as a second urinal. In the cubicle, he became aware that through one of the bored-through holes in the particle-board partitions an eye was staring at him. A watery unblinking blue eye. Nobody had come in or out since the older boys had showered. The eye had been there all along.

Gordon looked down and saw, beneath the partition, a pair of horned bare feet the colour of tobacco-stained teeth. He raised his heel and stomped on one of the feet as hard as he could. His heel crunched against a joint that felt like an ankle, which buckled sideways. There was a muffled grunt and Gordon heard the slap of naked buttock on wet concrete floor. Gordon ran all the way home in the dark, bunching his clothes across his middle, too scared to even get dressed. He never told his parents. He told Owen, who laughed and told Gordon something he didn't quite understand about showering alone in the surf club. Gordon never had the chance to ask his big brother what he meant.

The next week, Gordon was on his way home from school when, outside the Bluebird Building Society, he passed Mr Eastaugh. Sam's father's ankle was in a plaster cast.

The thing about villages inside rapidly changing cities was you didn't need to move if you wanted to escape your past. You could stand right where you were, and history would change around you. In the eyes of New Bluebird, Tony Eastaugh was a generic cranky old man, anonymous, one of a dying breed. To Old Bluebird, to Gordon and Sam and Gordon's parents and Dog and Tonsure Man and their widowed mothers and all the rest of them, it was all so fucking long ago. Memory was erased by the salt- and sand-bearing wind that rubbed away the names of the dead on the Anzac memorial statue in front of the surf club.

It was like Red Cap and his sacking from the education department. The past meant everything, and yet it wasn't worth a pinch of shit. Everyone forgot. Tony was just some old guy with a plastic foot taking a bog on the other side of a too-thin door.

It was gangrene, in the end, that did for Tony's left foot. But it had never been quite right after that episode in the surf club showers. The bones never healed.

'Earth to Gordo, come in?'

Sam was sitting across the table with his laptop open at the Bluebird Building Society page. He was typing himself into some hidden sanctum, the magic pudding of mortgage refinancing, in the confines of which, concealed by who knew what disguise, Sam would transform Gordon's equity in The Lodge into a deposit in his savings account. When they'd begun, Sam had promised that this little trick could be done 'until the cows come home'. Gordon watched Sam's spotted fingers tapping the keyboard. Sam wasn't saying that anymore.

'Right, I'm in.' Sam scrolled through a complexly arranged page of columns and numbers and let out a concerned whistle. 'You're drawn right down to your limit, my friend. No more piggy bank for you at that valuation.'

'Shit.' Gordon scratched his groin and tried to decipher what he was seeing on the screen. 'I didn't realise.'

'Not a problem, let me just . . .' Sam whirred through a series of boxes in what Gordon took to be a flow chart of questions and formulae, but Sam's fingers and the screen were moving too rapidly for Gordon to understand anything except the number he saw pop up at the end.

'Hang on, did you just make my—did the value of my share in The Lodge just go up by . . . by *that* much? How do you do that?'

'I do it because I am a Fucking. Top. Bloke,' Sam said absently, focused on the screen. Now he looked up at Gordon. His eyes were an old man's. Across the room, the toilet flushed. 'Quick and lively, brother. How much do you need?'

Ronald

GORDON WAS SITTING OUTSIDE HIS MOTHER'S APARTMENT BLOCK in his Car With No Name. The vehicle, a fifteen-year-old Japanese station wagon, did have a make, model and colour, but it had been known as the Car With No Name ever since the night Gordon was organising to pick up Firie Sam from Central Station and Sam had asked, 'What car are you driving?'

Gordon, who had only recently bought the car, replied famously, 'Dunno.'

'What do you mean you don't know what car you're driving?'

'I dunno, it's a car.'

'But what type is it?'

'I told you,' Gordon said. 'It's a car.'

'Okay,' Sam said. 'Can you tell me what colour it is?'

'Nope.'

It was agreed that Sam would tell this story at Gordon's funeral. What was more Gordon Grimes than not knowing the make or colour of his own car?

When visiting his mother, Gordon sometimes had to park the Car With No Name (for the record, a gunmetal grey 2004 Nissan Pulsar wagon, currently worth less than its insurance premium) and sit for a few minutes to summon up a pleasant state of mind. Because of the heavy stone of duty sitting in his oesophagus, because he had been avoiding his parents so he could maintain the glow from his holiday Up North, he had to remind himself that he was a good person. He was guilty about not seeing them, just as Norma was guilty over her relief at having got Ronald into the nursing home, a guilt she paid for by receiving a twice-daily scourging she observed as faithfully as a bride of Christ.

And then Norma still felt bad about coming home to sleep in her own bed.

And then Gordon felt bad about thinking all of these thoughts about her.

'I am a good person,' he said aloud.

Bluebird Public School was where he found himself parked. The main school building, in post-war brick, was surrounded by a cordon of demountables erected as stopgaps while the school population boomed in the 1970s. Temporary structures had become permanent, the demountables prettified by a mural-painting project. When Gordon was at the school it was kindy to grade six, but its five-hundred-child capacity could now barely house kindy to grade two. The other thousand students had been shipped off to the spanking-new district primary school, adjacent to the selective high school formerly known as Bloodbath High, and when the latest wing was finished, the younger kids would move over there and Bluebird Public would be no more. The land had been sold to developers for conversion into upmarket townhouses, sold off the plan, the profits pocketed before the last class was taught. Who, Gordon wondered, are all these people moving in? Where do they come from and will they ever stop? The coast was a beautiful thing, but the coast was a frontier. Land ended here. While people came to enjoy the limitlessness, what they experienced was the sense of being hemmed in. There was nowhere in Ocean City more claustrophobic than the seaside.

On his passenger seat lay a gift, an expensive glass vase of Nordic design, that he had bought for Norma, an apology for not seeing her, with a secondary purpose as a self-prodding prop. The thing had been bought; therefore, it had to be given to her; in order to give it to her, he had to visit her. Gordon's mind had developed an eccentric logic. The gift had a complicated provenance. He had ridden across the harbour to Ocean City on a premium-service Fast Ferry card to make his latest grossly expensive purchase from Eastons, the high-end homewares store from which he had bought the Kyoto china, the Atlas penholder and the French jacquard tablecloth. Six months earlier, he had come into possession of both the Eastons charge card and the Fast Ferry annual pass. He didn't need or want either, and it aggrieved him that he had not come into possession of cards that might obtain things his family needed or, what he really required, cash to pay his bills. Homewares! Fast Ferry trips! Talk about the universe playing a cruel joke. But he felt a solemn duty to use the cards, and sometimes they served their mysterious purpose.

'I bought Mum a present,' he said aloud.

As a motivational speech, it didn't quite work. He couldn't bring himself to undo his seatbelt.

He picked up his mobile and called Norma's home phone, in the hope that she was out. An unanswered call could save him the trouble of riding the lift to her top-floor apartment, where he felt neither comfortable nor, if he were entirely honest, welcome. Of course Norma wanted him to visit her, as a gesture of attention, but she did not want him overstaying whatever tight-lipped welcome she gave him. Since selling the family home, Norma had sent a none-too-subtle message to Gordon by purchasing this stylish ocean-view apartment with just one bedroom: no spare room, not so much as a study nook or sofa bed. She could have afforded a second bedroom, even a third, but her pointed down-down-down-sizing told Gordon: Don't you even think of it. Gordon felt complicatedly grateful. Knowing that the prospect of sharing a home horrified her as much as it did him brought them, in his heart, closer together.

Norma's phone rang out and sent him to voicemail. *'This is Norma's phone. She is not home at the moment, so please leave a message.'* Norma had been incapable of figuring out how to record the message, so Gordon had done it for her. Feeling too weird to speak to his own voice, he hung up. He had made half an effort. It was the lack of thought that counted.

He glanced at the gift-wrapped vase, a silent witness to his deceitfulness. *Are you with me, or against me?* Gordon asked it. A thought came to him: it was Norma's birthday in a week's time. She had invited them all—himself and Ben, also Lou and Kelly—to play happy families over lunch at the Bluebird Country Club, her personal seat of power. If he gave her the vase today, he would have to buy something else for her birthday. So, best that he not see her today. He gave the package a comradely pat. *With me.*

In a brighter mood, he started his car and set off for his father's nursing home. As he drove, whistling, through the back streets of Capri, he was pulled up by an unexpected sight: that same father, bent over his wheeled walker, waiting for the traffic signal on the corner of Whiting and Bream streets. Gordon wondered if it wasn't his father but a lookalike nursing home escapee. He wouldn't put it past Ron to seed the neighbourhood with doppelgangers to throw his imagined pursuers off his trail.

When the light turned, Ron levered himself off the kerb and began his long trek across Bream. Gordon, tooted by the car behind, was tempted to leave his father to his adventure, but Ron might just make it to Norma's place, where he would unleash havoc. The man's iron will to escape was admirable, even awesome. If character is a composition of desire, Ronald Grimes was certainly a character. His desire was pretty much all there was left of him.

As Gordon kerb-crawled along Whiting, Ron gave him a distant glance and forged ahead. It wasn't that Ron had dementia, though many of Norma's friends, no doubt intending kindness, offered it as an amateur diagnosis. Ron wasn't failing to recognise his son; he was refusing.

Gordon was reluctant to make a scene. But while he admired his father's determination, he also had to stop him getting to Norma's. It was a matter of safety. Ron's kidney disease had reached the point where, as his specialist put it, his head was 'literally full of piss' and he was incapable of rational thought. Never a patient man, Ron now burnt on a permanent one-inch fuse. Norma was scared of his rages, and though Gordon had never seen any evidence of physical violence, you never knew what went on inside a marriage. Not your parents'. Not even your own.

Until this year, when Ron had still been living with Norma, as his uraemia advanced his strength had failed. He kept passing out and cracking his head on floors private and public. There was a series of hospitalisations. With his uncontrollable outbursts, his delusional insistence on driving his car, and his wild and woolly late-night forays into the medicine cabinet—to organise his pills into a Monday-to-Sunday dispenser would have been an intolerable concession to the nanny state—Norma could no longer handle him at home. Ron disagreed. But after his last fall, he was transferred from hospital to a residential nursing home, which marked the declaration of his one-man war of independence.

Gordon pulled over on Whiting and waited for Ron to wheel himself along.

'Bit hot to be out, isn't it?'

Ron paused, gave him a bland sneer, and kept going. Gordon got out of his car and fell into slow step alongside the squealing walker.

'Maybe I can give you a lift? Where are you going?'

'Don't need you. I'm taking my exercise. Unless'—Ron eyed the Car With No Name—'you'd like me to do the driving?'

'Not in this lifetime.'

If he was unable to protect himself against his father's temperament, Gordon felt an obligation to protect the public. Ron was as capable of driving a car as he was of winning a triathlon. His 1980s-era Mercedes had become a Cy Twombly of gouges from his inability to manoeuvre it unscathed out of his garage. When Ron had turned eighty, his personal doctor had refused to issue the certificate he needed to renew his licence. Ron simply kept driving. In a last-ditch effort to keep him off the road, Gordon reported him to Roads and Maritime Services as an unsafe driver. But it had all come unstuck when Ron used his authority as a Justice of the Peace to trick an unsuspecting hospital doctor into signing his all-clear, and claimed to have a new licence. Usually, Gordon's consternation at Ron's disregard for the lives of others was alleviated by a sneaking admiration for his tenacity. But when it came to driving, no.

'Okay, Dad, you want exercise? I'll come with you.'

'God strike me pink.'

As they inched down Whiting, the walker's plaintive wheels a substitute for conversation, Gordon remembered Norma's warnings to watch Ron at every step. 'You can trust him,' she said, 'as far as you can throw him.' Which was, distressingly, an imaginable distance. But really, wasn't Gordon being paranoid? It was two kilometres from here to Norma's. Even with his indomitable will, Ron couldn't be contemplating such a trek. Surely he knew it would kill him.

'Have you seen your specialist?' Gordon asked.

Ron nodded.

'What did she say?'

'She said I need more freedom.'

This was the type of bare-faced lie, almost comically provocative, that Norma would have bitten at. Not being married to Ron, Gordon let it pass.

'What did she say about your kidney function?'

'You counting me down?'

'I'm interested.'

'Well, be interested in something else. I can't remember what she said.'

The weird thing about the past few months with his father—the lying, the raging, the escape attempts—was that Gordon had begun to like him. When Gordon was a child, Ron had been something of a stranger. Gordon's chief parent was Norma, while Ron was the provider, a functionary more than a fully-formed person. Perhaps blurred by disappointment—the easier explanation—Ron had never shown any sign of wanting Gordon to know him. He had retreated behind the cover of his role. Now that Gordon saw his father for what he was, a human battered by his history and weakened by his flaws, he finally knew and trusted him. He trusted Ron to lie every time he opened his mouth, but at least this trust was real. In all those years of childhood, Gordon had placed his trust in a fantasy, a stoic father dignified by permanent mourning, his monumental Dadness, never a person Gordon could love anywhere near as much as this old liar with his eye on a death march to Capri.

'Has Mum been today?'

Ron wiped his mouth and took a theatrical pause. 'She's locked me up and thrown away the key.'

'You don't look locked up.'

Ron sniffed derisively. 'They'll have to get up earlier to keep me from cracking their code.'

The nursing home lift had a keypad with a 'secret' four-digit security code designed to stop the residents from getting out. The staff had changed the code at least once a fortnight in the months Ron had lived there, and he kept cracking it. How? Gordon wouldn't put it past the determined old devil to camp in the lift all night, start at 0000 and tunnel his way out from there.

Gordon nodded at a bandage on Ron's temple, an elastic guard on his wrist and a scratch on his cheekbone.

'You've had another fall.'

'Pfft.'

'That's why you're living there. Mum can't look after you.'

'I can look after myself.'

Gordon was unwilling to get caught in this squirrel-wheel. Ron only wanted to be in the apartment and for Norma to leave him alone. Oh, after serving him three meals a day, doing his washing and ironing, making his bed, cleaning his toilet, purchasing his medications and calling the ambulance when he collapsed, among other less savoury duties. Aside from that, he didn't need any looking after at all! Why couldn't the blessed woman understand?

'She would let you spend every day at home if she could trust you to go back to the nursing home in the evenings.'

'I will not be trusted!' Ron exploded.

'I don't think that came out quite how you meant it,' Gordon said. 'But anyway. You keep on plotting and scheming and lying, nobody will visit you.'

'Why would I want anyone to visit me?' Ron said, his face empurpling.

'I don't know, Dad. I don't know.' It was a fair point. Who needed friends at this late date? What would visitors of Ron's vintage be doing other than reassuring themselves of their own heartbeat?

'Nobody visits,' Ron said, as if winning his point, and looked into the middle distance, presenting an impeccable self-pity. He recommenced his walk and asked, 'Have you written to the JPA?' Ron had been at Gordon to write to the Justices of the Peace Association. Having been a long-serving Justice of the Peace during his career as a civil (or, as everyone called him, uncivil) engineer, Ron said in encouragement, 'You don't even need any training. You just apply, they do a criminal record check, and you're in! You're a JP!' He paused. 'You don't have a criminal record, do you?'

Justices of the Peace performed voluntary services such as witnessing signatures for drivers' licences and other important documents. Gordon had never figured out what else. The crucial perk was that they got to write their name as, for example,

Ronald E. Grimes, JP, a suffix which Ron believed gave them equal community standing to a holder of the Victoria Cross, an Order of Australia or a medical degree.

Gordon shook his head. 'I haven't had time.'

'Too busy surfing,' Ron said with a snort a decade out of date. 'You don't realise how many of your problems would be solved if you stopped surfing and became a JP.'

Gordon had long suspected that his father was trying to let him in on some kind of quasi-Masonic lurk. There are benefits, Ron seemed to hint, but I can't tell you what they are until you sign up. Wink-wink. Whatever the benefits, Gordon didn't want to be a JP. His memory was of frightening individuals rocking up at the house late at night to ask his father to witness a signature. It was always an inconvenience, never a pleasure, and probably not a contribution to society's good.

To change the subject and divert his father from his next question, which would be what he was doing for money, Gordon said, 'I've got that court date with my neighbour coming up. I'm hoping for a nice settlement.'

Ron shook his head emphatically, as if he'd known all along that the weakness of the case wasn't a matter of law but of his son's incompetence.

'What a mess you've made of it.'

Gordon stopped. 'Sorry?'

'You should be sorry,' Ron said. 'Your marriage, your son, your home. What a mess. What are you doing for money? Ever since—'

'Do you want me to bring Ben to see you more?' Gordon, desperate, cut him off. 'Would you like that?'

Old people were reputed to want to spend their last precious days with their grandchildren, and certainly Norma doted on Ben, but despite a wealth of common interests—stamps, coins, cricket, bridges, dams, trains, train tracks—Ron had never shown the slightest desire to share those passions with Ben. To Ron, the fact that there was a young boy in the family who loved what Ron also loved was mere coincidence. He had a long aversion to investing time in children. You couldn't count on them to repay you.

'The only one of you I have any time for is that girl. What's her name?'

'Lou? You barely know her.'

'That's the one,' Ron said happily. 'I always got on well with the rug-munchers. You'd be surprised at how many of them we had in the family. But it wasn't really spoken of in those days.'

'Okay, I'll ask Ben and Lou to drop in when I see them later.'

'It'll be too late for you.' Ron was waggling his index finger like an Old Testament prophet. 'What do you stand for? You've staked your existence on stopping anything from happening to that rundown dump. What's the point? How does it feel to have a goal of nothing? I can see your headstone. *Here Lies Gordon Grimes: He Made Sure Nothing Happened.*'

Gordon wanted to ask: Aren't you speaking for both of us? Isn't your version of nothing—an eventless life, an armchair and a newspaper and the ABC and Mum at your beck and call—what you always strived for? Don't tell me about *nothing*.

He took a breath. It felt good to get that off his chest. Then he realised that he'd said none of it.

'Dad, you can't hurt my feelings.'

'Oh, I wouldn't want to hurt your feelings!' Ron dismissed the accusation as a master corporate criminal might brush aside a charge of shoplifting. Hurting Gordon's feelings was beneath his pay grade. 'I could save your house for you. I'm experienced;

I know how council works. You have a valuable resource here and you won't use me, out of misplaced pride or plain stupidity—I struggle every day to guess which it is. I have never been able to decide whether you are a stubborn idiot, or just an idiot.'

'Thanks, Dad.'

'Don't thank me for the offer,' Ronald said, ever insensitive to double meanings, as wedded to the literal as if it were the staff of life. 'Accept it! I could provide professional services, your mother-in-law could pay me, you could secure your little clubhouse's future and I could secure your mother's, uh'—he paused to scratch his chin—'her security. Everybody wins—all you need to do is *listen*!'

Ron's yellowish-crimson colour didn't change, but an agitation in his fingers and neck indicated a rising tide of head piss. Gordon couldn't figure out what professional services, engineering or otherwise, his father believed he might offer. Ron had the confidence of the made-good, even if his financial success as a small cog in big wheels and his prudential planning had provided a storehouse of funds that was now—bitter irony—paying his nursing home fees. If only he ran out of money, he could escape from the home. Just as well he lacked the insight to see this.

'And you could start by contacting the JPA,' Ron concluded. 'Council and the courts would take you more seriously if you were a person of character.'

As a JP, Ronald had always placed a high value on character, an even higher one on having a certificate to prove it. A great revelation of Gordon's childhood relationship with his father was when he, Owen and Sam were punished for trying to burn down the fire station. After they turned themselves in, Tony Eastaugh went on a rampage of self-righteousness and convened an extraordinary general meeting of the surf club to expel the boys. It was a bullshit overreaction, but Mr Eastaugh was running for re-election and fancied campaigning as the president brave enough to punish his own son. The meeting was halfway through when Ron Grimes stood up and delivered an oration of Churchillian impact. He confronted Mr Eastaugh with evidence that fire-lighting had been a 'rite of passage' for generations of surf club members. Ron called in former surfboat crewmen and captains who confirmed the tradition. He produced signed affidavits from clubbies who could not attend. There were even suggestions that Mr Eastaugh himself had taken part, if not during his youth then as a 'mentor' to younger arsonists. The expulsion move backfired on Mr Eastaugh, who cut the meeting short and let the boys off with a reprimand, the first crack in the eventual shattering of the edifice that was King Tony of BSLSC.

Gordon had revered his father for outgeneralling such a huge personage. Yet, over the years, as Gordon told people about the episode, it began to seem less admirable. Ron had styled himself as the incorruptible advocate of personal responsibility, yet his shining paternal moment was to spare the boys a punishment which even Ron acknowledged they deserved. If accountability was life's keystone, the boys should have been expelled from the BSLSC. They had lit the fire. Being the one to raise the alarm didn't excuse Gordon. But Ron had stood up for them, and won. Gordon had taken his father's actions as a valuable lesson about fighting the power and not letting hypocrites win, but over the years, he understood that Ron had taught him a slightly different lesson: that those in power always have a weak spot, and suborning them was how you survived. Not character, but leverage.

Gordon nursed these warmer thoughts as he escorted his father down the road. Ron wasn't such a bad fellow, and whatever else went on between him and Norma, they still loved each other. In the right mood, they cooed like doves and bought presents and showed each other more affection and kindness than they received anywhere else. They had suffered terribly. Gordon couldn't stand as their judge, nor deny them their morsels of solace.

As Gordon had been waxing sentimentally, his father, instead of turning his walker left up Sinker Street to complete a lap of the block around the nursing home, was facing right at the traffic lights to cross Fishman Avenue into Capri. One hand on the walker, he reached out and punched the pedestrian button.

'Dad, we're going this way.'

'Going for a walk,' Ron said over his shoulder. 'Exercise.'

Ron's head hunched into the collar of his checked shirt like a turtle retracting into its shell. He leaned at a steep angle into his walker and, when the light changed, set off to cross the four-lane road. He tried to work the walker past Gordon, who blocked him with his hands raised.

'Get out of my way!'

'Dad, it's not happening.'

Ron rammed the walker into Gordon, and then tried to weave it past him. Gordon stepped into his path, edging him back off the road. Aware that cars were slowing down to rubberneck, Gordon kept his hands defensively raised, palms out.

'Dad, you can't go to Mum's.'

'Get lost!'

Later, Gordon wondered if he should have let the old man go. It was a steamy morning. Ron would have got halfway, at best, before falling in a heap. Gordon could have driven beside him like a support vehicle in an ultra-marathon. But Ron might have dropped dead. Or, worse—and more likely, knowing him—made it to Norma's. Possession was law, and Ron was possessed. If he could get into the unit, they could not legally shift him.

Gordon and his father were coupled in this mortal dance at the traffic light on Fishman and Sinker: Ron assaulting Gordon with the walker, Gordon blocking his father's path to freedom. Ron clawed Gordon's wrists, digging his nails into the soft tissue and pulling Gordon's hands towards him.

'Ball up, you weak fool!'

'Dad, what are you doing?'

'I said ball up!'

It seemed that Ron was trying to pull him closer. He began reefing each of Gordon's wrists towards his own face, one at a time. As his slack fingers kept brushing Ron's face, Gordon real-ised with a new burst of horror that his father was trying to make him punch him.

'You can't even hit me,' Ron growled.

'Of course I can't hit you! Look at the state of you!'

'You can!' Ron gripped Gordon's wrists harder and wrenched them towards his face. 'Ball up!'

'Let me go!'

'You won't hit me; you won't hit that fuckwit who stole your wife. What's it going to take, you rotten sod? Who on this earth *will* you hit?'

Gordon ripped himself clear. Ron howled in pain, wringing his hands. Gordon leant close to his ear and asked if he was all right. As the light changed again, Ron took advantage of Gordon's proximity and began throwing haymakers. Gordon bowed his head and shielded himself with his arms.

'Dad! Stop! Please!'

'Bloody idiot. Why did it have to be you? Eh? Why were you the one?'

Ron rammed him again with, Gordon felt, years of pent-up vengeance. Ron was trying to get him not just out of the way, but out of memory. This was what it had come to. After a whole life, this was what it had come to.

Astonishingly, then, Ron began to weep. His face fell into his hands.

'You've got to get me out of there,' Ron was sobbing. 'I can help at The Lodge, I can save it for you! I know all the tricks in the book. Even when your mother objected, I knew how to get past them, and now you're telling me you don't need me. Oh ho ho . . .'

'Dad.'

'You've got to talk to the doctors, your mother—they won't listen. You've got to get a man doctor to look at me. I can't bear it anymore. You've got to get me out, I can save that place for you! Don't you think you *owe* me *something*?'

'Dad . . .'

Gordon's heart was twisting. He let a hand fall on Ron's trembling shoulders.

'Hello there, you look like you need some help.'

Gordon looked around. A car had pulled up at the traffic light.

'How about a lift, Mr Grimes? It's warm out there.'

The electronic window on a carnelian red Prius had scrolled down to reveal what Gordon already knew would be beaming out at him, the one smirking face he dreaded even more than all the others he didn't want to see.

'Small world, Gordo.'

'Frontal.'

Gordon ground his teeth, regretting being caught fighting his father on this street, a list of regrets going a long way back, but most of all regretting being caught by this man.

The deputy general manager of the merged Northern Beaches supa-council stroked his beard, reddish and trimmed but kind of thinning, a match for his ginger coxcomb, ninety percent of which was not hair but the general impression of hair. Frontal, real name Michael, who had been at Bluebird Public right through Bloodbath in the same year as Gordon, Kelly, Dog, Red Cap and Tonsure Man, had gone on to greater things. He was now one rung from the top of his lifelong climb up the greasy pole of the municipal public service. What an odyssey it had been, Gordon thought but didn't say, for if he said it Frontal would be sure to take it the wrong way. Or the right way, such as it was.

'You need to take me home.' Ron collected himself and spoke to Frontal in a firm voice, like a defendant stating, 'Not guilty.'

'And where will that be today, Mr Grimes?'

Ron named the nursing home. Mugging at Gordon, Frontal got out of his car and helped Ron fold his walker in the correct manner and stow it in the hatch of the Prius. Ron chatted amicably as if nothing unusual had happened. Gordon recognised his tone: social niceties cloaking that raw angry animal. His father wasn't yielding, just switching plans.

'You need a lift too, Gordo?'

If Gordon Grimes were a toadfish, he would have been at full bloat, spines out.

'My car's just back there. Thanks.'

'We all need a Good Samaritan sometimes,' Frontal said as he clipped Ron into his seatbelt.

Gordon followed the Prius to the nursing home, to make sure his father got inside without dying or pulling another swiftie. Frontal parked in the disabled space out front. Gordon had to drive around the block to find a park. By the time he got to the visitors' register on the ground floor, he saw that Frontal had checked Ron back in.

When Gordon emerged from the elevator on Banksia floor, Jada, the efficient head nurse, greeted him with a sympathetic expression.

'Your friend has taken your father to his room. I hope you three had a nice walk.'

The nurses were not gulag guards, Gordon reminded himself. Even Ron admitted that these Nepalese were excellent at their jobs; no local would put up with the stomach-turning displays to which he subjected them.

'I don't like them.' Ron's voice was audible from the corridor. Gordon stepped into the room to find his father snug in his armchair, Frontal pouring two glasses of water before settling into the other. Why? Gordon thought. Doesn't a Good Samaritan just piss off once he's done his thing?

'They're not that bad,' Frontal was saying. 'Most of them have lived in the area all their lives.'

Gordon unspooled with relief. He had thought his father was talking about the nurses, not the residents.

'They're so *old*. They've both feet in the grave, just need someone to give them a push. Terribly depressing, the poor things,' Ron said, seeming to undergo a shift of mood. Then, remembering himself, he went on: 'They stare at me. I don't like them.'

'Aren't they people you know?'

'Why would that make me want to talk to them?' Ron asked with an unyielding look towards Gordon, prompting Frontal to glance over his shoulder and acknowledge his arrival. Like a host, Frontal nodded Gordon towards the commode in the bathroom, which doubled as Ron's spare chair. Gordon dragged it out and perched on, or in, it. 'Nobody's any good. They didn't want to know me then, and I don't want to know them now. How the mighty have fallen! Just don't tell them to come crawling to me!'

Jada came in to replace the water jug, exchanging a smile with Gordon. She asked if he wanted a chair, but he said he wouldn't be staying long. He just didn't want to leave his father alone with Frontal.

'The staff aren't bad, though.' Ron's eyes followed Jada's hips out the door. 'These Pakis, I never thought the women were much to look at, but if there's one thing about old age, it's . . . it's . . .'

'That you lose the thread of what you were saying?' Frontal suggested.

Ron refocused on Gordon. 'It's your mother's side that had it in for the darkies, I want you to know that.'

This was one thing Gordon and his father could agree on. For Norma, the most important pigeonhole for any person, in any circumstance, was their race. To Norma, Dr So-and-so or the Woman From The Health Fund was Chinese (which embraced all East Asians except sometimes Japanese), Indian or Paki (which embraced all South Asians, including Sri Lankans, Bangladeshis, Thais, Burmese and Indonesians) or darkies (miscellaneous races but also a catch-all for Chinese, Pakistanis and Indians). For Norma's taxonomic outlook on life, it was critical that everyone know that Ron was being looked after by Pakis, albeit Nepalese

Pakis. Ron's non-racism, such as it was, made a nice relief from Norma's open bigotry. But Gordon could not, to be honest, tell whether this was because Ron was not a racist, or because the non-white races were too far beneath Ron's notice for him to care about categorising. His ogling a Nepalese nurse because he was discovering a late-in-life appreciation of 'Pakis' could be a positive or a negative step, when it came to his being racist, non-racist or super-racist, if only you could tell where the starting point was.

Gordon was growing tired of thinking about his parents.

'You don't have many personal items in here,' Frontal was saying. 'When my mum was in the nursing home, you could barely move for all the family photos, albums, knick-knacks. She made it just like home.'

'And why would I want to do that?' Ron thrust his jaw.

Gordon had given up the fight to bring Ron reminders of family or home. Ron had been an inveterate stamp and coin collector, and Gordon had offered to bring his collections here for him to enjoy, but Ron had stated that he didn't want anything of value in his room 'because they'll nick it'. (So much for his non-racism.) He wouldn't even have a radio.

'I'm here under protest,' Ron said. 'I'm not going to settle in.'

'But no home comforts?' Frontal pressed. Gordon was unsure whether he was trying to trigger Ron or help him.

'Norma brings the *Herald* every morning, that's all I need.'

That said, when he stabbed his remote control like a shiv at the TV and set the ABC to maximum volume, Ron did look perfectly content, doing no differently from what he would be doing at home. He could forget for a half-hour that he had only the nursing staff and not Norma under his thumb.

'You must enjoy your loyal Gordo visiting so often,' Frontal said.

Gordon felt the insult: whereas a man like Frontal was in the prime of his career and chronically time-poor, an unemployed bum like Gordon, well, what was there to do but visit his father? He wondered if Frontal knew how little he had visited Ron lately.

'He only comes to make sure I haven't got out,' Ron said.

True, Gordon thought. Ron had never enjoyed his company. But some people change near the end. Gordon's maternal grandmother, Norma's mother Mary, had been a lifelong Catholic martyr, devoting her days to the church, Meals on Wheels, serving the poor, inviting strays for Christmas dinner, making her family's life a misery because misery meant duty to the bloody church . . . and then, right at the end, Grandma Mary decided she didn't believe in God. Normally it was the opposite; they find God as a panicked last-minute each-way bet. But Grandma Mary was adamant that she didn't want a priest, didn't want the last rites: it was all hogwash. After a lifetime of Christian devotion, she died a born-again atheist. She'd only just started thinking about it, see.

Maybe one day his father might start thinking in a new way about Gordon.

Ron blinked at the younger men in apparent surprise that they were still with him.

'Haven't you two got places to go?' He peered at Frontal. '*You* must.'

'Run off my feet,' Frontal said, without getting up.

Ron checked his watch, another old habit. If anyone tyrannised Ronald Grimes, it was Father Time. For his whole life, whenever he needed to go somewhere, he was agitated about being late. As soon as he arrived, he began to fret about getting away to the next thing. In what sliver between arrival and departure, Gordon wondered, had Ronald Grimes ever found release from the clock?

'Why do you keep checking the time?' Gordon asked.

'Drinks at four.'

'Drinks?'

'They bring a trolley. Scotch, wine, beer. You're allowed one. Well,' Ron chortled, '*I* am.'

On cue, a drinks trolley nudged Gordon out of the commode. A man whose name tag said *Nick* poured a nip of whisky into a plastic cup and bore it on a tray to Ron.

'Oh, that's good. Bugger!' Ron began the laborious process of levering himself out of his chair, which was holding on to him like a deep-sea squid. 'Highlight of my day, but I get so excited, the thought of that first sip gets me going.'

Ron shuffled towards the bathroom, taking a detour to reclaim his commode. Frontal rose to help, but Ron brushed him off with a rude familiarity that unnerved Gordon.

'You talk sense into him,' Ron said to Frontal.

'About?'

'About calling the JPA, what else? He doesn't even have to do any training—they're desperate!'

After Ron had nearly yanked himself off his feet sliding the bathroom door shut, Frontal regarded Gordon with silent satisfaction. People used to say you couldn't trust a man with a beard. Gordon had no issues with beards—how could you, these days?— but he could never trust a man who trimmed his beard with slide-rule accuracy, a precise line around the cheeks and under the jaw, the moustache equally maintained. Wasn't the whole point of a beard to dispense with shaving? Why would anyone grow a beard *and* shave every day?

Jada appeared at the door and shared some small talk with Frontal. When she left, Frontal explained: 'Overseeing nursing homes takes up a surprising amount of council time. You'd be stunned,' he added, placing a characteristically high estimation on Gordon's emotional investment in how Frontal spent his time.

The conversation was interrupted by a volley of swearing from the bathroom. Ron was either dying or having difficulties.

'You okay in there, Mr Grimes?' Frontal asked.

'Fuck off!'

Gordon felt a little happier to hear his father abuse Frontal. Ron had never held anything but contempt for that family. 'Kid's a knob, just like his knob old man,' Ron used to say. Even though the position of council manager was not a hereditary one, Frontal had inherited enough of his late father's fanaticism about rules to make it inevitable that he would one day succeed to the position Conal had held. As town clerk, Conal had ruled Bluebird and the surrounding beaches with a reinforced concrete fist for twenty-seven years. Ron Grimes, as an engineer, had butted heads with Conal in battles that the town clerk invariably won, which confirmed Ron's oft-repeated assertion: 'Money doesn't mean power. Power means power.' In Conal's time, the town clerk had not been a highly paid position, so for him there was no pleasure richer than pushing around developers who could buy and sell him. Conal was incorruptible—the ever-flowing source of his pride. Bribes, paid by developers to councillors, were the great bogey of Conal's professional life, and as a cleanskin he was able to retire with his head held high—only for a few weeks, however, before keeling over from a cerebral haemorrhage, as if the town clerkship had been safely clotting his blood for all those years.

Another frustrated growl came from the bathroom. Frontal asked through the door if Ron was okay.

'This place rations toilet paper like there's a war!'

Frontal was picking up the phone to call the nursing desk when Gordon said wearily, 'Look left, Dad. Rolls are stacked on the cleaning brush.'

Frontal was equally sanctimonious but much better paid than his father. Now that government salaries were benchmarked against the private sector to attract 'the best talent', the head counts and budgets of the new supa-councils validated bloated contracts for council managers. As deputy general manager, Frontal was earning four times a teacher's salary and double a hospital doctor's. If he became general manager, he would double this again. A council general manager earned fifty percent more than the Prime fucking Minister. If the council went through another merger, Frontal would earn as much as a banking executive. Exorbitant pay for public servants had been justified as an anti-corruption measure, inoculating them against bribes. In Gordon's view, the best insurance against corruption was to hire people who weren't corrupt. For all his other failings, Frontal was not corrupt, so paying him handsomely was a waste of ratepayers' money and a form of corruption itself, as it raised the cost of anti-corruption insurance beyond the actual risk of corruption.

Ron staggered out of the bathroom as if from a Russian winter campaign. 'Holy God, there's some cleaning up to do in there.' Spotting his Scotch on his bedside table, he proceeded at full shuffle.

'You're lucky you've still got each other,' Frontal said. 'I miss my old man every day. You realise when they're gone, you only ever have one.'

'I'm not going yet!' Ron snapped. 'Save your misty-eyed reminiscences for the funeral.'

'Mrs Grimes is suffering to see you in here,' Frontal said, all wide-eyed innocence.

'You mean Eva Braun,' Ron said.

Gordon thought: And that makes you . . . ?

'It must break her heart not to be able to look after you,' Frontal said.

'Break her bank more like it,' Ron said.

'Okay, let's go.' Gordon bounced on the balls of his feet, desperate to be somewhere else. Where else, he could decide later.

'Let me walk you out,' Frontal said. 'See you later, Mr Grimes.'

'Look for me around town,' Ron replied, raising his glass. 'I'll be the one with the ankle bracelet.'

Finding himself in the lift with Frontal, Gordon felt like he was the prisoner.

'He's a character,' Frontal said as he pressed the not-very-secret code into the keypad.

'He said you were going to end up town clerk when we were in third grade,' Gordon said.

'That's nice. I appreciate that.'

In the forecourt of the nursing home, the sun ricocheted off the concrete. The street used to be housing commission, but was now duplexes on one side and this nursing home on the other. Gordon searched his pockets for his key ring while Frontal unlocked his car by murmuring something to his phone.

'And he always said you were going to end up where you are, too,' Frontal said. 'Fathers and sons, eh? The old drama.'

Gordon located his key.

'You're going to cop a belting in court,' Frontal stated. 'The thing with your neighbour. Hard to see why you're bothering.'

'Principle.'

Frontal was nodding ruminatively. 'I get that. Sometimes I stand on the beach and look up at all those squillion-dollar places, and I see the ghosts of the old houses. This town's empty most of the year, that's the sad thing. Real estate on the beach, at today's prices, is a collectible for the super-rich. I know where you're coming from, mate.'

This town? Mate? He was such a fraud. Whenever Frontal or Conal had seen a 'town' spirit in Bluebird, they crushed it. Of all the things Gordon disliked about Frontal, foremost was his affectation of knockabout beaches banter. At school, Frontal never surfed, never belonged to the club, never played footy, never came to the ocean baths, never did much except sit at his desk in relentless pursuit of a good enough pass in geography for a traineeship in the local council to further his grand ambition to be the king pinhead in the empire of pinheads. There was nothing wrong with that—the world needed pinheads—but why not own it? Why, once you've got what you wanted, pretend to yarn with the crusty nobodies so that you can fake belonging among them while you stab them in the back and tear down their way of life? Why?

'It's you and your council that allowed it,' Gordon said.

'What you don't understand is that the forces of economics and progress are greater than local councils. We don't promote development; we're here to control its excesses and retain the essential character of the town. Bluebird has become sought-after, and that's not council's doing. That's people realising that the lifestyle that we've always enjoyed for free, they can enjoy at a price. So, inflation. Limited supply, surging demand. But Bluebird will always be Bluebird.'

Gordon wondered how Frontal could believe that Bluebird would always be Bluebird if he really did gaze upon all those empty shells that his council had approved. But maybe if you were on his salary, you could reconcile all contradictions.

'How's Kel?' Frontal asked.

'Good,' Gordon said tightly.

'Terrible what happened there, I really feel for you. She's pushing ahead with the divorce?'

Gordon considered a number of replies, but honesty—telling Frontal to fucking fuck the fuck off out of here, and fuck off while you're at it—demanded an energy he lacked right now.

'Yeah nah.'

'Expensive, divorce. I don't know how you're supporting yourself these days. It's going to be hard. Probably why you're so late with your rates.'

A liquid tide rose in Gordon's throat. The rates—the fucking rates! If Joseph Conrad lived today, his Mr Kurtz would have found a better noun than the *horror*. Gordon had forgotten to pay the *rates*. What was it up to—two thousand, three thousand he owed? He was determined not to beg Leonie. Paying council would skim off the first layer from the deposit Sam had just organised through the bank. Shit, he would have to go back to Sam for another top-up sooner rather than later.

'Local authorities look less kindly on you the longer you fail to play your part in your municipality's upkeep,' Frontal went on. 'Not right to have everyone else paying for the garbage removal, the library, the lifeguards . . .'

'The pinheads.'

'It's none of my business how you maintain your lifestyle,' Frontal said without missing a beat. 'But you realise that if there are any commercial operations going on at The Lodge, we'll catch up with you.'

'We're not making any profit.'

'It doesn't have to be a *good* commercial operation.' Frontal chuckled. 'Take a tip: don't spend up so big on the fancy imported linen and tableware. If you're raising any money, you'll need every cent for compliance and improvements. Especially hygiene, if you're selling food—that's always a kick in the guts.'

Jesus, Gordon thought, is there anything about me this prick doesn't know?

Frontal walked towards his hybrid in his tan synthetic slacks, well-shined shoes and off-white business shirt, open-necked because it must've been Freaky Friday at the council chambers. It didn't matter how inflated the bureaucrats' salaries had become, they still had a style they could call their own.

Halfway to his car, Frontal had a second thought and turned towards Gordon. People like this were never content with having had the last word. They had to have it in triplicate.

'I forgot to ask.' Frontal's disingenuousness was transparent as he arrived at his purpose. 'How's your boy going?'

'Ben?'

'I heard he's having problems again.'

It was unlike Frontal to use such outmoded terms as 'problems', a sign that he was now trying to antagonise Gordon. Frontal's dislike for Gordon was a lifelong habit. Even back at school, Frontal's resentment at the fact that his diligence and compliance received zero recognition was directed not at the alpha males, whom he hero-worshipped, but at the Gordons. Which made him pretty much the perfect personality type for a council deputy general manager. He had worked his way up the ranks, starting out as a parking inspector and giving his free time to football refereeing, a peculiar subtype of men who not only coped with opprobrium but revelled in it. Certainly, Frontal saw himself as a more evolved human than Gordon, which was confirmed by the status of his son, Daniel, the incoming St Pat's school captain, the acme of sporting hero and academic high-achiever upon whom young Frontal had gazed from an admiring distance all those years ago. Where Frontal had been a washed-out face in the crowd, Daniel was dark and delineated, commander of every photograph. Frontal had left Bluebird for one stint of his life—a university degree in public administration in England that had turned into a council job in London, for a five-year bracket of his twenties—before returning a widower (double credit points; his young Spartan wife, Soula, had died from ovarian cancer) with a miracle child, a miniature Greek god, the instrument of his revenge. The story was almost biblical, in a pinhead suburban white-bread beachside sort of way.

'Again?' Gordon said.

Frontal's frown was a bureaucratic facsimile of empathy. 'Daniel has been looking out for him, as leaders do, and he's concerned about some of the boys isolating Ben. I mean, it's never been easy to come out in a community like this.'

'Nah yeah,' Gordon said. 'Much better to keep it in the closet.'

'Our boys are at a vulnerable age.' Frontal's confidence carried a shadow of threat, the lineaments of which Gordon couldn't ascertain. 'Back in the day, we know what happened to gay sixteen-year-old boys. Fortunately, our kids are better than us. The generations mostly improve.'

Gordon could see how Frontal believed this. Daniel possessed the supreme attractions among sixteen-year-olds: a full beard shorn into robust sideburns, a precocious washboard stomach, a square jaw and sturdy eyebrows, not in his father's wispy ginger but a glossy raven-black. Definitely a generational improvement there. Unfortunately, Ben had thought Daniel was his best friend ever since kindy and, with his uniquely tuned gaydar and unstoppable fantasising, convinced himself that Daniel was potentially his special friend too. Ben had put out feelers to Daniel, who had 'responded', whatever that meant—Ben would not add details— but then Daniel had backpedalled all the way into the warmth of the dominant clique and mercilessly ostracised Ben. If Frontal knew any less of these schoolyard politics than the entire text, context and subtext, it would be surprising. You weren't meant to be too critical of a man and boy left alone by the death of the wife and mother, but fuck Frontal was one over-involved parent.

'I don't think it's a competition,' Gordon said.

'Not a competition,' Frontal repeated, perfecting his beard stroke.

'If you've got nothing else . . .' Gordon made for his car but Frontal stepped in front of him, his hands in the air, Gordon realised, in imitation of the way Gordon had blocked Ron from crossing Fishman Avenue.

'Mate,' Frontal said, his minty breath clouding Gordon's eyes, 'just think about what you're trying to save. All that shit we grew up with. Old Bluebird. Is it really worth it?'

'Some of us want to save it for our children.'

'Really? You want Ben to grow up in *our* Bluebird?'

Gordon drew a breath. 'You do it your way, I'll do it mine.'

'Sure.' Frontal clapped a hand on Gordon's shoulder. 'And listen, I hated to hear what your old man was saying to you.'

Gordon jiggled his keys.

'Just before I got out of my car, down at Fishman. What he said. *Why were you the one?* Gee, Gordo, I know we have our differences, but no son should ever have to hear that from his dad.'

Gordon stood watching, unable to move, as Frontal went to his Prius and failed to open the door. It had relocked itself in the time he had come back to deliver his truth.

Court

GORDON ARRIVED IN CAPRI'S SELF-DECLARED HISTORIC CENTRAL Business District on the morning of his court date and his mother's birthday. He knew the risks in relying on the legal system to process his case in time for lunch at the country club, but Gordon Grimes liked to live on the edge. It was a paradox of life as a bum that the less he had to do, the more he crammed what remained of his appointments, as if his body had some unconscious need for time pressure, which, if his external circumstances declined to provide, his poor decisions would create.

He circled the public car park, checking his watch, wanting to time his entry through the boom gate to maximise his chances of getting his court appearance done before his two hours' free parking ran out. Like loan sharks, the council hit you with severe penalties the instant you overstayed your generously provided gratis period. As he circled, Gordon wondered if he would always be like this, worrying himself to the grave over seven dollars for parking. If his father's behaviour was any guide, he would only get worse.

Once inside the car park, he lost a handful of what could be critical minutes after tailing a young pedestrian wearing an incipient white man's afro, Bob Marley T-shirt and what looked like chef's pants to his Skoda Yeti. Gordon planned to take his space, but Whafro got into the Yeti and sat there. Increasingly irritable, assuming Whafro was on his phone, Gordon got out and rapped on the Yeti's window.

'You're leaving, right?'

Only then did Gordon see that Whafro was not on his phone. With a street directory open on his lap and scissors in his hand, he was chopping up a mound of bush weed. Gordon thought, Bush weed? Street directories? These hipster kids.

Whafro shook his head and went on with his preparations. This was going to take longer than a phone call.

An Audi, having come up behind the Car With No Name, which was blocking the circuit, was flashing his headlights. Setting aside his nostalgic sentiments about the bush weed and the directory, Gordon puffed up to his full width and barked at Whafro: 'Out of the car park. Now.'

Fashions came and went, but smoker's paranoia was permanent. Whafro, now thinking Gordon might be a scary quasi-official adult, clapped shut his directory and fumbled his key into the ignition. Gordon went back to his car, as privately gleeful as if he had crossed a breach in time and frightened his own younger self. His momentary pleasure was broken by the Audi driver, who was shouting at Gordon from inside his soundproof bubble.

'Keep your hair on, man,' Gordon muttered.

He entered the council chambers shortly before his 11 a.m. slot, which, worryingly, turned out to be less a slot than a bracket. He sought a seat among the drunk drivers, shoplifters, fine defaulters and haunted-looking AVO-seekers bundled together at '11 a.m.'. Distributed equidistantly along a bench, none had the courtesy to make room for him. He stood, mustering peak cranky-face, above a young woman tapping her phone.

She glanced up. 'Sorry,' she said sourly, and continued tapping.

'Not the phone,' Gordon said. 'The seat.'

With a theatrical sigh, she moved six inches and, when he sat, added an extra two. He performed a furtive armpit-sniff. Okay, probably advisable to clamp his arms to his sides.

Although he had never set foot in the Capri courthouse until the last six months, Gordon was becoming a regular. He had been here for a court-ordered mediation session with Kelly. He had been here to query his rates. He had been here on Leonie's behalf to submit paperwork relating to the Hilton. And he was here every second week over some new scrap relating to cliff-side developments around The Lodge. He was here nearly as often as the spectators.

The courthouse was an example of the bygone pretensions which Capri council was progressively demolishing in favour of brand-new pretensions. The double-brick walls were topped with pediments and frills, the moulded ceiling a riot of flying putti, a trip back to when adults were allowed to take undisguised pleasure in the sight of naked cherubs. Gordon wondered how many accused paedophiles had sat here and gazed upwards, dreaming of better days. If only the ceiling could talk.

There could have been child molesters in the current bunch of uninterested parties, Gordon thought, but you couldn't tell them by sight the way you used to. When he grew up they were dirty old men in raincoats, schoolteachers, priests and peeping Tom surf club presidents. Now, they could be anyone. They could be his adversary in the current proceedings, this annoying dick from next door, David Archer, stark naked under his sharp navy-blue suit, company T-shirt and gleaming caca-brown slip-ons, grinning familiarly at Gordon.

David Archer had made his pile from stealing copyrighted images off the internet, slapping captions on them, printing them on T-shirts—all of which somehow laundered the copyright theft—and selling them online. His internet T-shirt meme empire now grossed many millions and the right, he seemed to believe, to use the path from Cliff Street to The Lodge for his workmen to transport a mini-excavator and steel girders to the puke-modernist shipping container for which he had demolished one of Bluebird's original P&O-style family homes. Gordon had refused access via the path, and David Archer had threatened him with a court order.

Gordon's initial reason for refusing was revenge for that demol-ished white house, which had been one of his take-off markers when he grew up looking at it from the surf. It belonged to the family of Neil Tasker, a school friend of Owen's, and Gordon had always loved it. Gordon lost his objection at the development approval stage—Frontal's council had yet to see a demolition it didn't like—so now Gordon was fighting a guerrilla action with the hope of a negotiated settlement. The most irritating part was that David Archer was terribly good-natured, unfailingly giving Gordon a cheery hello down the beach or up the shops or over the fence while ignoring his letters, their tone shading in time from grumpy to desperate, suggesting a cash payment 'in perhaps the high four-figure, low five-figure region'. Even now, Gordon's attempts to play the righteous nimby were falling on blind eyes. David Archer flashed his surgically whitened teeth. Entitled cunt.

An echo of Noel Chidgey's hatred of the young came into Gordon's head: *What this generation needs is a good war.*

His day took a turn for the better when the magistrate called his case early. This was unusual. When he was here with Kelly, they were inevitably last in line, the magistrate at the end of his rope. It must have been arranged as a process of escalation: auto offences first, then property disputes, drugs and alcohol, assault, murder, genocide, all the way up to marital conflict.

Today's magistrate, Tim Phelan, was a well-known Capri ex-footballer. He and Gordon had not had a conversation, other than across the courtroom, since secondary school, which permitted Tim not to recuse himself for conflict of interest. Instead of the required bow, Gordon gave Tim a chummy nod, which Tim returned. Looking good, Gordon thought.

David Archer stood up and read from a scad of correspondence about his numerous reasonable approaches to Gordon and his proposed schedule for builders to gain access down the path in a manner that would cause zero inconvenience. He omitted Gordon's shakedown letters. 'It's obviously a very difficult site for the builders to access, Your Honour,' David Archer, in flirtatiously metrosexual cadences, said to Tim. 'Your Honour' indeed, Gordon thought. Good luck with that. David Archer continued: 'And we have bent over *back*wards to put our neighbours' convenience first. The *total* time for access would be no more than *five ten-minute periods* spread over a period of *two months, all* with at *least* fourteen days' notice, and we would concede *any reasonable grounds* for rescheduling.'

As David Archer upped his rate of italicising, Tim Phelan went through the correspondence, none of which Gordon remembered reading before he'd binned it. Gordon snuck a look at his watch.

He was going to be cutting it fine with the seven-dollar charge, not to mention Norma's birthday luncheon. Why couldn't Tim have done his reading beforehand? Did they all have to stand here while he did his work? And in his comments, he kept calling David Archer 'Mr David', which riled Gordon up: it sounded like bias.

'The respondent?' Tim said, his half-closed eyes dimming on Gordon.

'Mm?'

'You're unrepresented today? I note Mr David's submissions have been prepared by legal counsel.'

'You seen the cost of solicitors?'

Tim was about to say something but checked himself.

'We've heard from Mr David at length. Have you anything to say, Mr Grimes?'

'Ah, I was thinking we might be talking about a reasonable cash settlement.'

Tim's eyelids drooped. 'How much are you proposing to offer, Mr Grimes?'

Gordon felt a blush spread over his face like a dropped tin of paint. Proposing to *offer*? It dawned on him that being late for Norma's birthday lunch might not be the absolute worst thing that could happen to him today.

'Allow me, Timbo!'

Gordon, Tim Phelan and David Archer—even some of the other cases—looked towards the voice entering the courtroom. Dog wore a suit jacket and shirt and tie, but beneath the waist-high wooden barrier, Gordon saw board shorts. He still had a smear of sun cream on his nose. He looked better outfitted for a food court than the magistrates court. He was waving a curled-up document.

'Your Honour will do,' the magistrate said. 'I take it you are representing Mr Grimes?'

'Hundred percent! And my client opposes the application. Which I guess is obvious. That's why we're here.' Dog shot Gordon a flamboyant wink.

Closing his eyes, Gordon slumped back into his seat. What the fuck was Dog doing here? He couldn't ask. At this moment it was crucial to present a united front.

'I know it's obvious, Mr Gilsenan,' the magistrate was saying. 'What I'm asking is: what are your client's grounds for objection? It seems the applicant has taken reasonable steps and conducted himself in a neighbourly way.'

'My objection is also reasonable, Teeny.'

'Mr Gilsenan,' Tim Phelan said with an audible sigh. He'd always been asthmatic. The team used to call him Teeny-Weezy Timmy on account of his size, his sighs and his thighs. 'The proper form of address, please.'

'Come on, champion, just because you're a beak you can't—'

'Your Honour will do.'

'Certainly, Teeny.' Dog coughed over the last word so that Gordon could not be sure what he had heard. What was the prick up to? 'My client reasonably holds that it's his path, his land, and if the respondent wants to knock down a house that you and I and many others have enjoyed all our lives, then he can reasonably use other access.'

'Your client is the respondent,' Tim corrected him. 'You mean the applicant. Mr David.'

'Should it please Your Honour,' Dog said, shuffling his papers.

Tim sighed again, that whistle in his nose reverberating through the court microphone. 'What other access?'

Dog leafed through the papers importantly.

'*I don't fucking know*, Your Honour.'

That woke Tim up. He turned red and spluttered at Dog to watch his language in a courthouse.

'It's the Capri local court, not the bloody Old Bailey,' Dog said.

'What other access?' Tim thundered.

'*I don't fucking know,* Your Honour.'

'This may "only" be the local court, Mr Gilsenan, but contempt can carry severe penalties. As you well know.'

Dog read from the paper in his hand. '*I don't fucking know*, Your Honour. I am reading from the correspondence between my client and Mr Archer three weeks ago. My client wrote, and I am reading from his correspondence here, *I don't fucking know, you can shove your steel beams up your arse for all I care*.' Dog turned to Gordon and stage-whispered, 'Language, champ!'

David Archer was enjoying this immensely. Gordon was not.

From there, Tim Phelan made short work of Dog's argument. 'Mr David', as the magistrate kept calling him with suspicious fondness, as if Archer were his favourite children's TV host, had taken reasonable steps, and if the respondent thought that his property rights were absolute, then he ought to reread the legislation. Gordon was losing track in the jargon of who was the applicant and who was the respondent. But he got the gist when Tim lined up his papers and tapped them on his bench and said, 'The Access to Neighbouring Land Act was legislated for precisely these circumstances: where a neighbour is unreasonably preventing development. You can't stop progress, Mr Gilsenan.'

Dog bowed. 'You can't stop progress. What's that in Latin, Your Honour? Shouldn't it be on the crest above your head?'

When he saw the effect of Dog's words on the magistrate's face, Gordon remembered Tim getting twelve weeks from the rugby judiciary for biting the university hooker's ear off.

'The application will be allowed. Mr David will submit a schedule of access, and he will not be unreasonably prevented by the respondent or anyone else.'

'One point of order,' Dog said. 'Why do you keep calling him Mr David?'

'Because, Mr Gilsenan, that is the applicant's name.'

'With respect, Teeny, his name is David Archer.'

'Consult your documents, Mr Gilsenan.'

Dog came to Gordon and brought him into a huddle over the papers, standard courtroom pose.

'Fuck,' Gordon moaned, feeling as if he'd taken a hit to the solar plexus.

'What?' Dog whispered.

'I always thought it was David Archer. Look—it's *Archer David*.'

Dog nodded ruefully. 'Fuck me. *Archer David*. Of course it'd be too much to ask for him to have a normal name.'

'Mr Grimes . . .' The magistrate was addressing Gordon now. Dog was straightening the papers in a brisk manner. Only now did Gordon suspect the true reason why Dog had sailed in to 'represent' him. Fuck.

'Your Honour?' Gordon said.

'It's a difficult site, on that cliff face. You don't suppose your home was dropped in by a helicopter?'

'The Lodge is very much pre-helicopter.'

'Whatever the manner of its getting there—and however and whenever it will be pulled down—improvement and maintenance to sites like these require cooperation. The applicant—*Mr Archer David*—has behaved as neighbours ought. You have not.'

'I . . . I suppose a settlement is out of the question?'

'I believe there has been some discussion of a settlement, though I am a little baffled as to why it was initiated by you. Should Mr David demand *compensation* for the delay caused by your intransigence, then he may take such steps.'

As Tim proceeded with an order for costs, Gordon was mulling the decision. He didn't like the sound of 'it will be pulled down'. He didn't like the sound of any of it, to be honest. He glanced to the back of the courtroom, where Frontal had materialised looking like a cat digesting its cream, and saw behind him the flash of a Chanel suit leaving the courtroom. Leonie had been watching all along.

'Thanks, Teeny,' Dog said, wrapping things up. 'See you at the Hilton.'

'Mr Gilsenan.'

'I withdraw that. You can drink on your own, as usual.'

To get to the registry desk, Gordon had to walk past the foe formerly known as David Archer, who offered his hand and said, 'No hard feelings', though his suit jacket popped open to reveal a meme that suggested otherwise.

Having failed in every department except wardrobe, and that had gone to a tiebreaker, Gordon decided to pay his fine quietly. You can't let these people win, he thought, or if they must win, they can't be allowed to enjoy it.

The registry office was a row of cubicles behind which worked three tired women, all of whom, Gordon realised, he had gone to school with. Zoe Langton, known since fifth grade as Zoo

Plankton, was one of those defeated girls who took her job-for-
life behind this desk with inspirational stoicism.

'How you going, Gordo? Just getting these orders sorted
for you.'

'Yeah, good, Zoo.'

Zoe fluttered her velvety eyelashes, the most intact reminder
of her youth. She no longer had much else to flutter. She glanced
up and transparently thought something similar of Gordon.

'Didn't go too well for you in there,' she said while rolling an
old-fashioned stamp across an inkpad and impressing each paper
with the authority of the law. 'Bloody Dog. Friends like him, who
needs enemies?'

The whole town, Gordon thought. The whole bloody town.

'What's the damage?'

'You didn't have any hope, you realise. That new access legislation tilts the balance in favour of the developer.'

'A man's property is no longer his castle,' Gordon said, wishing
he'd remembered to say that in court. Then he counter-wished it;
it was a line from a movie. Tim Phelan would have done him for
plagiarism, and he'd have lost the moral high ground.

'Not that it's technically your property,' Zoo Plankton said,
her bland expression masking her pleasure at knowing Gordon's
business.

'Okay, okay,' he said, glancing over his shoulder for his
stepmother-in-law.

'Regulations are going to be relaxed even more after the next
council merger,' Zoo said. 'That's the rumour we're hearing.'

'I thought you'd already merged. Isn't this one of the supa-
councils now?'

'That was eight years ago—you really are behind the times.'
Zoo leant forward between the glass partitions separating her
from the two other council employees who had heard the same
rumours at the same council-subsidised lunchtime Pilates class. She
presented Gordon with a confidential squeeze of cleavage. 'Word
is we're getting a *maxi*-merger. It'll send everything to custard.'

Gordon wondered if it was humanly possible to make things
any more custard-like than they were. But this was local government; there was always a new digital-age way to fuck things up.
Beyond supa-custard was *maxi*-custard. Was it the hand of fate:
we in our little pocket of preserved paradise had been lucky for
too long, and the blind flesh-eating bug of cosmic injustice, having
overlooked us, had now found time to tidy up loose ends?

'There you go,' Zoo said, withdrawing the cleavage and substi-
tuting a payment slip. 'You're lucky Archie represented himself.
The only cost against you is the ninety-four dollars the application
cost him. Card or cash?'

'Can I put it on a plan?'

Zoo sniggered, as if he'd made a good joke. But the one thing
about him that Zoo didn't know was that, as light as the penalty
was (and, to look at the bright side, a massive win over the theoretical cost of a solicitor's meeting), Gordon, after a check of his
online balance on his phone, realised he only had seventy-one
dollars in his cash account and a twenty in his wallet. Sam's
advances through the Bluebird Building Society were taking
longer to clear than they used to. And then he had to account
for seven dollars—what the fuck, it had just ticked over to fourteen!—in parking.

'I'll take care of it,' said a voice behind Gordon.

'You sure, Dog?' Zoo Plankton looked embarrassed on Gordon's behalf. His bills being picked up by Kelly's squeeze. What would the girls at Pilates make of that?

'On Mrs Chidgey's behalf,' Dog said. 'She is listed as a co-respondent.'

And, Gordon thought, she sent you to make sure I had no chance of winning.

'I guess it's not Gordon's property, is it?' Zoo said, pushing the form Dog's way. 'Technically? Given the wording of the title and the transfer deed?'

The whole fucking town, Gordon thought.

He was turning for the door when Dog said, 'Not so quick, Gordo. Leonie wants to meet you at the Hilton.'

'I've got my mother's birthday lunch at the country club.'

'That's okay, it's on your way, we won't take long,' Dog said with the air of a man who had already thought all this through. 'Give me a lift?'

To Gordon's surprise—after he had parked beside the bottle shop and followed Dog through the old pub that was now a boutique beer-tasting bar with adjoining VIP poker lounge, up the stairs to the private rooms that he remembered all too intimately from the days Noel Chidgey made most of his money from the Hilton's illegal activities and boys like Sam, Owen and Gordon spent their nights peeking through strategically placed holes in the walls—the top rooms had been gutted.

'Leonie's turning it into five-star accommodation,' Dog explained. 'Another small step towards civilisation.'

'Why didn't I know about this,' Gordon commented.

'Weren't you listening in court? You can't stop progress even when you do know about it, so you aren't much chance when you don't.'

'Maybe not, but you can stop progress being fun,' Gordon said.

'She is having fun, champ, that's the problem. She didn't send me in there just to save you money and embarrassment—you were going to lose anyway. It was because she is acting on your behalf.'

'You made sure I lost. How is that acting on my behalf?'

'A good renovation, such as Archer David's new pad, ups the property values for everyone; it helps Leonie, and it helps you. Everyone's a winner. I was just there to get you out of your own way.'

'Where is she?'

'Five minutes.'

Gordon tensed. He never looked forward to these little chats. Leonie's emergence as his unexpected ally, indeed his saviour, in his break-up with Kelly gave him the jitters. Leonie's generosity was a form of puppetry; he could feel the tug of the strings. He might be an instrument of Leonie's retribution against Kelly, but he feared that Leonie's machinations hid some obscure grander purpose in which he would end up losing everything he held dear. Dog had scared him by mentioning the Chinese agents and asking about the contract; even Zoo Plankton had made him nervous by saying, with the knowingness of the council employee who has access to paperwork, that The Lodge was not 'his property'. If he ended up being a party, even unwittingly, to The Lodge being pulled down, he could not live with himself.

Dog's phone rang. 'Leonie,' he said and went onto the balcony, leaving Gordon to inspect the new hotel rooms above the Hilton.

Though the floorboards were unsanded, the walls had been painted and some black-and-white photos hung as decoration. Gordon identified luminaries of the Bluebird Surf Life Saving Club. There was Tony Eastaugh, the original Bronzed Aussie, hands on hips in a one-piece lifesaver swimsuit, cap on head, reel at his feet, gazing into the distance for a distressed swimmer to save or a little boy to perve on. Uncannily, Tony in the photograph was the spitting image of today's Sam.

Gordon moved along the posed portraits and staged action, lifesavers pretending to be on the job. The star was Noel Chidgey. These mid-century men were generically square-jawed and heavy-browed, but something stood out about Gordon's father-in-law, his effing ineffable ownership of nature, a confidence around the ocean that spoke of more than just physical assurance. That confidence had been lost in Gordon's generation, who knew too much tragedy: too many drownings, overdoses in the dunes, assaults, thefts, crimes petty and major. Too many cliff jumpers. The men in these photos, while as craggy as Mount Rushmore carved heads, were innocents. They looked at Bluebird Beach and saw disorder in need of command. Gordon saw only threat and loss and the last-ditch possibility of salvage.

Dog came back in, still holding his phone to his ear, inspecting Gordon inspecting the photos.

Ending his call, Dog said, 'She's been delayed a few minutes, said to apologise for making you wait.' He paused at the photo of Chidgey. 'They thought he was a traitor when he married her.'

'Half of those old diggers ended up with foreign wives,' Gordon said. 'It was hardly a betrayal of White Australia.'

They scanned the rows of lifesavers in march-past. With their anachronistic little caps, some of them were ninety percent chin.

'Yeah nah, not that,' Dog said. 'He was a traitor for marrying a woman who had her own ideas. It was like he was cheating the system. He'd made his packet, and then he went and married someone with twice his brains.'

Leonie was not the standard-issue trophy wife, that was for sure. Her skill was less in fighting expectations than confusing them. She had been the financial controller of a girls' private school when she met Noel Chidgey, but no Australian school would have employed a thirty-six-year-old non-white foreigner at her due seniority, so she had quit the profession, taken on Old Bluebird in their cannibal game of property development, and eaten them up. Old Bluebird couldn't figure her out. Her sex, colour and accent seemed a three-card trick she was playing on them.

'How are your parents, anyway?' Dog said.

'Yeah, good chat, but I really have to get to lunch.'

'How's Victa?'

After Ron's second stroke, Dog nicknamed him, rather insensitively, after the brand of two-stroke lawn mower.

'Plugging on in the nursing home,' Gordon said tightly. 'But Mum's strong as an ox.'

'Why isn't Victa having treatment for his kidneys?'

'After two strokes, he wouldn't be able to survive a transplant.'

'Dialysis?'

'That was his choice,' Gordon said. He had been putting out this answer for twelve months, ever since the shock of his father's diagnosis had been followed by the second shock of his refusing treatment. Ron had been told that as his renal failure set in, he would gradually slip away, sleeping more each day, losing energy and eventually expiring without pain. 'That'll do me,' Ron had announced, not entirely without pleasure, to Gordon and Norma.

Most important, there would be minimal interruption to his routines of television, cards, drinking, eating, driving and ordering Norma around. Gordon had almost admired his father's reconciliation to his fate. There was something uncharacteristically Buddhist in refusing western health care. But recently, it emerged that this was a mischaracterisation of Ron's intent. After his admission to the nursing home, Ron's repeated escape attempts, verbal attacks on Norma, offers to take over the carriage of Gordon's property disputes and demands to drive to Chester Dam and the country's other great engineering projects had revealed that he was not reconciled to his fate at all. The truth was that he had refused western medical treatment because he possessed the unshakeable belief that he was the one-in-a-billion miracle patient who would not decline in its absence, who would not get worse in the usual way, who would not die. It was the opposite of him reconciling himself to his fate, as anti-Buddhist as you could get. Which was, if disappointing, at least consistent.

Once Gordon had come to realise this, his father had made sense to him again.

'Good old Victa, gotta hand it to him,' Dog said without feeling. He followed Gordon out to the room's Juliet balcony. Below, teenagers were arguing with the security staff about being allowed in without ID. Politely, the uniformed Tongans were standing firm, but if the teenagers really wanted to press their point, they would leave in an ambulance.

'Christian bouncers, I used to think that was a contradiction in terms,' Gordon said. 'Now. Just tell me. Why does Leonie want this meeting?'

'Maybe she wants some thanks for paying your court costs.'

'How far away is she?'

'Couple of minutes.' Dog looked at his phone.

'Yeah, well, maybe you can thank her for me. I can't be late for this lunch. She can meet me at The Lodge later. She does still live there, on paper.'

'She might move into this place,' Dog said. 'She was saying how those stairs to The Lodge would kill her hips. She said she might install an electric chair—is that what they call it? No, an electric chair is something else.'

Nobody knows what it's called, Gordon thought, but everyone can see themselves riding up and down in one. Then again, an electric chair would be an idea.

'Okay, I'm off.' Gordon moved towards the door.

'It's the Chinese agents,' Dog said urgently. 'She's with them now. Ken Grainger. Or Cara. Or both! The only thing that can bring them together: Leonie and a big sale. Fuck, I didn't want to be the one to tell you.'

'She's selling?'

'She's threatening.'

Gordon felt the floor give way beneath his feet. He, Kelly and Ben, and Lou too, lived under the illusion that they were a family trying to sort out their future. But they were really just Leonie's toys: effects of what she had done, what she could do, what she might do next.

'Mate, she can't help herself,' Dog said, wringing his hands as if he had nothing to do with it. 'She goes on all the time about how when she first came here, this beach was full of bigots and misogynists, and most of all it was full of bigoted misogynists. But none of them was as bad—those old crusties were all hypocrites one way or another—none hated her quite as much as Noel's little princess. She wants to drive Kelly out of her mind. Moving you in together, she's fucking with you.'

'Kelly has always said Leonie's some kind of evil genius.'

'But it's not the main game. She's going to sell the whole thing out from under you. It's the end of your lifestyle, pal.'

Gordon tensed. 'I wouldn't call it a "lifestyle".'

'She's not going to let you save The Lodge. That's why she sent me to court to bugger up your case.'

'I didn't need your help doing that.'

'The old lady doesn't leave anything to chance. She needed to make sure it went her way. She's going to do up the Hilton and sell it all, lock, stock and barrel, Hilton and Lodge, to the Chinese.'

'So what does she want from me?'

'Don't ask me, champ. That old duck's five steps ahead of all of us.'

Gordon thought: She is only a few years older than me and yet she's old. We're all old. She's a powerful old woman and I'm the sad old deadbeat whose fate is in her hands.

Dog's phone beeped. He read the text message.

'Go to lunch, Gordo.'

'Huh?'

'Leonie's cancelled. Enjoy the arvo. Enjoy every minute in this place like it's your last. Tell Victa I said g'day, and tell Norma happy birthday from me,' he said, giving Gordon a look to say he wished he could find better words to express his condolences.

The fall

'THIS IS NICE. THIS IS JUST HOW I LIKE THINGS.'

As she raised her glass to her birthday, Norma Grimes scanned the faces around the circular table: Gordon, Ron, dear sweet Ben, Lou, and so lovely of Kelly to come, even if Norma had had to bribe her. Really, she'd had to bribe them all. They weren't a large family or one given to ceremony, but she could still marshal the forces of guilt and a free lunch to get them to come and toast the birthday girl. Ron took a sip, though he wasn't meant to. The waiter came and served him roast beef with gravy and buttered potatoes, a dish as rich in prohibited items as a crime bust. Ron underlined his naughtiness by smothering it all in salt, and raised his glass of red to Norma.

Gordon watched her from a position of braced self-defence. He detested the country club, this den of middle-class complacency, and had tried to wriggle out of coming, but his mother had hit him with the magic words: 'It's probably Dad's last, you know.'

So Gordon was in, as to his surprise, was Kelly, over whom Norma also exercised some mysterious emotional hold.

His gift of the vase had been met with the mildest pleasure, as if Norma had known of both its chequered provenance and his original plan to give it to her as a token of apology for his recent neglect. 'You're not easy to buy for,' he'd said as she rotated it in her hands and summoned up a grateful expression. What, he'd thought, do you give a woman who's had a gutful of everything?

'I cannot remember feeling such total wellbeing,' Norma said now. 'It's not just having my family together, though that is nice enough after the difficulties of the past year. It is being able to host you all in this club where so many good things in our lives have occurred. We were married here, we celebrated our fiftieth anniversary here . . .'

'Not to mention all your competition wins!' came a female voice from another table. Norma nodded hello to her friends in the dining room, her real audience. The other diners were not part of her birthday celebration, though she had strategically staged the party on a day when she knew they would all be lunching. Marg was here, and Barb, as well as Pat, Peg and June. Pam would be in later for nine holes, and Gay would duck into the office later to say hello to Pip. Norma let her eyes rest on the view through the window, over the balcony to the eighteenth hole. The pond, the flags, the grove of cypresses flanking the first tee. The tennis courts and the bowling green. 'You can imagine paradise,' she said, 'or you could join the Bluebird Country Club.'

From two tables away, Barb was raising an eyebrow that congratulated Norma on bringing her flock together. What a success! Ron's poor health and difficult behaviour were well known in the club, and Norma had surmounted both. The girls at the other tables were experts in surmounting male obstacles, and Norma felt their approbation. But what they would really be noticing was Kelly and Gordon. Had Norma been able to reconcile them? She hadn't been secretive about her plans to hook Kelly into the club and get her interested in golf. Even a Chidgey could be civilised at some point. But no, the real coup was to get Gordon into a collared shirt, showered and shaved and looking so, if the girls were not mistaken, clean.

Gordon saw himself reflected in Norma's satisfaction. He had to respect her for training herself not to focus too much on his state of mind. Or Ron's. Or, most of the time, her own. She was a model for pressing forward without an inward glance. She should be celebrating *that*.

Her little speech finished, Norma walked around the table. Ron had been bickering with her before, during and after the luncheon, but about what, she could not now remember.

Lou stood to offer Norma her place. Brushing her offer aside, Norma chanced her weight on the arm of Lou's chair, leant across Ron and laced her hands around his neck. Seeing the urgent need for a counterweight, Lou quickly sat down again.

'I'm sorry, sweetheart.'

Norma aimed a kiss at Ron's cheek, but he moved at the wrong moment and she got the bandaid beneath his ear. She took his chin between her fingers, turned his face to hers, and kissed him on the mouth.

'I know you are, pet.'

'So, so sorry,' Norma said, before kissing him again on the crown of his head. Beyond Ron's shoulder she could see Gordon, rigid with awkwardness, horror, confusion—but did she care?

And beyond him, the eyes of Marg, Barb, Pat, Peg and June, startled but then soothed to see the warring Grimes canoodling again, back to their old tricks. A kiss was all Norma needed, all Ron needed, all the world needed to spin right again. In these little hinges of respite, there could be joy. Life was composed of moments, you realised at a certain age. Sometimes the clock would pause and let joy in.

Gordon resumed his brace position.

'So . . .' Ron drained his glass and smacked it down on the white linen tablecloth. 'Enough nonsense. Who wants a game?'

Whenever Gordon was alone with his mother, he suffered an existential dilemma. As soon as he had collected her in their golf cart, she took off like a greyhound jumping out of the gates on a one-breath monologue about her friends, her doctors, her opera, her golf, her bridge, her doctors, her overflowing diary, her superabundant consciousness, her doctors. His mother was a social being, in the deep sense that she existed in her relationships with others. It was a strange sensation, to feel like an offstage actor summoned only for these moments. As he struggled to listen to Norma, Gordon wondered if he even existed when he was not with her.

'He was a Chogie.' She was talking about a doctor. At least, Gordon, whose attention had drifted, assumed she was talking about a doctor.

'And after he'd gone out, I said to your father, "Where's he from?" And your father was in one of those moods. He said, "Perth." And I said, "Where is he really from?" And he said,

"Just south of Perth." I said, "Do you have to be like this?" He was all innocence, of course. So I said, "Where's his *family* from?"'

Gordon re-lost the thread as they followed the other two carts down the fairway. Kelly and Ben were in one, Lou and Ron in the other, under the strict condition that Lou not allow Ron into the driver's seat. Only Norma, Ben and Kelly were playing. Norma had given Ben a junior membership of the club and then, astoundingly, she had made a gift of an associate membership to Kelly after her split with Gordon. What was that about? Gordon wasn't capable of asking.

Of the three non-players, Lou had never picked up a golf club, Gordon had sworn off it, and Ron was not permitted. Gordon wished that he and not Lou was driving his father, but Ron had kicked up a stink about not being allowed to drive, and Gordon had offered him Lou as a compromise. Ron needed a vigilant chaperone, and the old man had an unaccountable affection for 'your rug-muncher'.

While his mother spoke, Gordon kept a close eye on his father. Just that morning, a ninety-two-year-old resident of the nursing home had been caught crawling through a hedge wearing army camouflage. You couldn't make it up. The peaceful suburbs of leafy northern Ocean City were actually a gulag of prison camps filled with elderly male inmates intent on freedom but prevented by their individual misanthropy from cooperating to organise a mass breakout. If only they knew how many of their kind harboured the same obsession, they could start a revolution.

'Did I tell you how long it took me to find a parking space at the home?' Norma went on. 'Did I tell you' was purely rhetorical. Whichever of Norma's conversations were not about Asian doctors were about parking, the two subjects being subtly connected. 'I was so flustered I pressed the wrong lift button and went to the Alzheimer's floor. I can't tell you how awful it is. Dr Tang told me that one of the . . .'

Gordon had gone there once too, a mistake he had not repeated. Ron's floor, Banksia, was identical to Eucalyptus, Boronia and Grevillia, whereas Acacia, the Alzheimer's floor, had fences around the beds and locks on the rooms.

'. . . but Jada came and rescued me,' Norma said. 'The staff on the Alzheimer's floor are Indians too. Isn't she lovely!'

Gordon was used to trailing around after his parents in damage control. He liked Jada and had more than once speculated on what would happen if he asked her out for a coffee. But he was too scared—of his parents finding out, of the gossip among Jada's co-workers, of Jada turning him down.

'I don't know what they're feeding him,' Norma said, rattling through her agenda. 'They're told no protein, no sugar, no fat, but of course they do what they please. Just up here, will you? Not so close!'

As he parked the cart according to Norma's instructions while she got out to putt on the green, Gordon's mind wandered back to the morning's events. If Leonie was going to sell The Lodge from under him and Kelly, why had she given Gordon his one-third share in the first place? Was he nothing to Leonie but an instrument of spite? What kind of monster would let him in there, knowing how much he treasured The Lodge, knowing he would bankrupt himself trying to save it, only to rip it away from him? Gordon remembered Dog saying Leonie was five steps ahead of him. True: there was some key part of the puzzle he was missing, some leap that might enable him to scale those five steps, even get ahead. It felt like his ability to grasp her strategy was blocked by some fundamental character flaw. That old shadow at the door, standing between him and the other side.

Which reminded him of his mother.

He got out of the cart and held the flag while the others had their putts.

'You've got good pretty quickly, Mum,' Ben said after Kelly sank a twenty-foot putt.

'Thank you, darling. I'm taking lessons from the assistant pro.'

'Wait, what?'

'I'm taking lessons.'

'Pity Dad doesn't play.'

'Yes, it's usually men who give up their marriages to go and play golf.'

It was perverse that Kelly had accepted Norma's long-standing offer, designed to bring her closer to the Grimes family, just as she was distancing herself from them. But she had her reasons, Gordon thought. An assistant pro? That wasn't perverse; that was sick. He watched a smile come to Kelly's lips as, having plucked her ball from the hole, she tossed it nimbly from hand to hand.

'Wait, what?' Ben said.

Kelly said nothing, and Ben didn't understand her meaning.

'Dad hasn't given up on your marriage,' Ben said.

After Norma putted out, Gordon walked her back to her cart, passing Ron and Lou in theirs.

'You've got to oversteer,' Ron was telling Lou. 'The small steering wheel, the small tyres, it's not like a normal car.'

'Thanks, Ron, I'm getting the hang of it.'

'If you'll just let me show you. One hole?'

Lou shot Gordon a pained smile. 'I don't know what the equivalent of losing your licence is on a golf course, but if I let your father get behind the wheel I'm pretty sure I'll never be allowed back.'

'Do you care?' Ron interrupted, jealous of Lou's attention.

'No. But I'm still not letting you drive.'

'Are you lot all like this?'

'Like what?'

'Determined to drive. Or is it just the ones who are the man in the relationship?'

'Maybe I'm just the man in *this* relationship.'

'You know, we've had a few through our family, quite a few surprising ones.'

'A few what?'

'Lezzos. Going right back. Only, they didn't talk about it in those days. You have to join the dots, but there were more than anyone knows.'

'Fascinating, Ron, but you'll have to back off a little, I don't like the way you're grabbing at my handbrake.'

⌒

They were at the fifth tee when it happened. The players had to leave their carts and walk up a steep set of stone stairs to hit off, and then descend a flight on the other side of the tee box to where the cart paths looped around to pick them up. Coming off the fourth green, Ron approached Norma after she tapped in, and shuffled her under a spreading coral tree for a private conversation. Gordon and the others were pretending not to watch, but Norma's voice carried across the green.

'I can't, Ronald! I just can't!'

Norma, for all her gregariousness, was as emotionally sturdy as an eggshell. She burst into tears more often in a day than Ron had in his life.

'I've told you!' Ron was roaring. 'You don't need to!'

Kelly looked to Gordon, but the argument was too old for him to get involved in. The bargain of his parents' marriage had been the traditional one: Ronald took care of Norma by providing, and Norma took care of Ronald by giving him undisputed authority. Ronald had trained Norma as nursemaid and surrogate mother as well as wife; but alas, he had trained her too well, and when her fear of him falling over and cracking his head open got too much—when she nursemaided him to the verge of insanity—Ron had decided he did not want that kind of attention anymore. What he wanted now was a second kind of servant: one who would remain invisible until called for. Gordon wanted to say to Ron, *After fifty-six years, you want to renegotiate the deal? Bad luck, fella.*

Gordon also wanted to tell his father: *You have those kinds of people right where you're living: they're called staff.*

But every time he got mad at his father, his mother did something insufferable and his sympathies lobbed back to Ron. Maybe his dad could live at home, if his mum were not so over-protective. It was exhausting. In trying to take both sides, Gordon found himself unhappily on neither.

Kelly was at his shoulder. 'You have to do something.'

Gordon walked across the fourth green, taking Ben as protection.

'Grandma, Grandpa, there are people behind us, we have to move on to the next hole.'

Norma and Ron stared at Ben as if he had just landed from Mars. Norma's attention was diverted by Barb and Peg, who sallied up to the apron of the green in their cart. With a well-bred muttering, Gordon's parents shuffled on, Ron bent over, Norma chittering along beside him. There was something beautiful, Gordon thought, in the way his mother was clutching his father's arm; for once, neither of them trying to *win*. Back at school, a religious education teacher had once told Gordon's class that they should act all the time as if they were being watched by God. Gordon had never been convinced. But now he thought, if only his parents could act all the time as if they were being watched by the membership of the Bluebird Country Club.

Perhaps, Gordon thought later, Ron had engineered that encounter on the fourth green to create confusion on the next hole. Norma took her driver out of her golf bag and climbed the stone steps to join Ben and Kelly on the fifth tee. Below, on the cart path, Gordon saw that there were only two drivers—Lou and himself—and three carts. He asked Lou to drive Ron down, while he, Gordon, would take his cart and tell Kelly to collect the third cart. But there was a communication breakdown somewhere, and when he parked his cart at the bottom of the path beneath the tee, Gordon turned to see Lou driving up alone.

'Which is that?' he said.

'It's Kelly's.'

'So where's yours?'

Alarm broke over them simultaneously.

'No, no.'

Gordon began running back up the cart path towards the turning circle.

'No running on the golf course!' Norma called as she laboured sideways down the stairs.

'Dad's been left alone with a vehicle!' Gordon shouted. His mother's hand went to her mouth.

Gordon's first fear was that Ron would speed off towards the clubhouse, the exit, the street, all the way to Chester Dam. Had Gordon been thinking straight, he would have understood there was no cause for concern on that front: a golf cart could be chased down by an ambulant human, and in any case the electric Bluebird Country Club carts automatically switched off beyond the course's gates.

Ron's necessities were darker than escape.

As Gordon rounded the corner of the path, he saw his father, wild glee carved into his face, steering the cart right at him, pedal to the floor. The tinny electronic motor whined like a killer mosquito. Gordon jumped into the groundcover beside the path. His eyes went to the tee box. He could see no-one up there. He shouted a warning anyway, even though he knew what was unfolding. For once, he was ahead of the game.

Whether Ron timed his run in the cart to coincide with Norma's arrival at the bottom of the stairs, nobody could say in a court of law, but Kelly, Ben and Lou thought they saw him bunch his shoulders and take aim. He met Norma the instant she stepped onto the cart path. Though it wasn't travelling at great speed, the front wheel of Ron's cart carried several hundred kilograms of downward momentum. When it clipped Norma's knee, a sickening crack was heard above the engine's protests.

Gordon, who came upon the scene last, having dug himself out of the foliage and chased after Ron's cart, mustered all his strength, all his stubbornness, all his power to deny time and character and reality, to shut out the idea that his father might have done this on purpose. With an effort of will that gave him an instant blinding headache, Gordon thought back to the club-house, Norma's arms around Ron's neck, laughing and blowing kisses and enjoying the kind of immoderate bliss he had rarely been allowed to see as a child.

And never when he was an only child.

Norma must, he concluded with hope in his heart, have tripped. Fallen without cause, but not without consequence. She hit her head against a rock wall and landed hard on her hip. She already had replacement hips on each side, and her left femur, sandwiched between concrete path and titanium prosthesis, made that terrible shattering noise. She was out cold. Gordon fell to his knees and cradled her head. A grey mouse swelled where her eyebrow had hit the wall.

The cart was upside down, having rolled into a drainage ditch beneath the tee box. Lou and Ben climbed in to fetch Ron, but he was able to crawl from the wreckage under his own steam. He pushed away their assistance and, dusting sprigs of native rosemary off his shirtfront, shuntered up to where Gordon was holding Norma.

'Oh, what a bloody idiotic thing to do, what on earth was she thinking,' Ron said. 'Broken hip—for an old person that's the beginning of the end.'

THIS
PART

THIS
PART

Bird's eye

Five steps ahead? They flatter me.

    It is a little-publicised burden of being an evil genius that we are never happy. Some of us dislike being called evil. I am the other: I object to being called a genius. Their thinking me evil represents a failure of their courage, which is no news. But I cannot stand them calling me a genius. I am blunter than I used to be, duller than I think I am, and less calculating than they take me for. For them to think that of me is a failure of compassion. It is lonely up here.

    Ask me what is inside their heads, and all I can do is echo my legal adviser: I don't fucking know. *Bluebird is what it is, and these people are what they are. Up here in the sky, I can only take them as I find them: on the wrong side of history, worth one good look before they go. Ronald is out for the count, and here goes Norma, and oh boy, is he right about a woman's hips being the beginning of the end.*

    First the hips, then the entire race. Twenty years from now, these will be the lost Australian Incas. And they don't have a clue. Except for Gordon, who knows maybe too much about being on the wrong

159

side of unseen forces. Yet what does he do? His sincere belief that the world is turning to shit has paralysed him, turned him into history's limp bystander. He's going down big time, and yet he's still going to separate his rubbish and walk rather than drive, he's still going to feel bad about not seeing his mother more often, he's still going to fight for his doomed Lodge because, you know, why can't you do the right thing inside your little helpless man-sized soul?

And I love him for that.

And so does Kelly, so does Ben, so does Lou, so does Sam, so do his cronies. They can't help it.

But to love Gordon is not to know him, and to inhabit his days is to get no closer to what I must know.

What the fuck is wrong with him?

Alas, he won't tell me, and loving him is an obstacle to knowing him.

As Norma might say, Enough about me; now what do *you* think of me?

I must change my avatar. I am no scavenging seagull, no pred- atory hawk, no death-loving vulture. Certainly I am no ugly wicked witch—all this (indicating the work I have had done) did not come for nothing!

To know Gordon, I must know them. I must stop trying to influence events and instead observe and record. I must remove my emotions. I must spy into their souls. I must venture boldly into foreign lands. I must be the mechanical eye in the cerulean Bluebird sky.

I am no evil genius. I am but a humble drone.

Cricket

WHAT BENJAMIN GRIMES COULDN'T TELL ANYONE, MORE THAN he couldn't tell them how often he wanked or who he thought about while he did (seven to eleven times a week, Japan Ned, Tonsure Man, occasionally Dog's wife Sally, briefly the six-time state champ and back to Japan Ned), was that he still believed he would play cricket for Australia.

The awake part of his brain-life knew this was impossible. At cricket practice, baking in the outfield of Father McInally Oval, fluffing yet another catch, not bowling or batting because he needed to be saved from himself, Ben had enough self-awareness to keep private his conviction that he would one day wear the Baggy Green. But there was a more exciting part of his brain-life that felt like the climax of a movie. Everyone—the school, the beach, the whole country—is standing at the Ocean City Cricket Ground waiting for the next batsman . . . and down the steps of the historic Members' Stand strides Benjamin Grimes, number three for Australia. He has seen it and felt it and smelt it and heard it, down to the last detail. He has been there. It just remains for the world to catch up.

'Grimy, what ya doin, ya spaz?'

Ben returned from playing for Australia to see his teammates glaring at him and Coach Stoyle in teapot stance. Ben ran to where the ball rested in the gutter and hurled it back to the pitch. Or halfway, which was as far as he could get it. Daniel Abottemey, anticipating Ben's hopelessness, came to fetch the ball before underarming it with a snap of his wrist to Mr Stoyle, who caught it one-handed, as if they needed to put on a demonstration of hand-eye coordination to reassure themselves that they were not Ben Grimes, and furthermore that Ben Grimes was only allowed here because it was school policy to hand every willing cricketer a place in the Firsts, given that there were only twelve cricketers across years nine, ten, eleven and twelve in these benighted days for the gentlemen's game.

Centre wicket practice continued, far from Ben. Daniel shouted orders to bowlers and batsmen. Mr Stoyle, in his permanent uniform of polo shirt and shorts over absurdly muscular calves that Ben had occasionally imagined wrapped around his neck, murmured tactical intimacies to Daniel. Cricket was a cerebral sport. Even out here in the lowlands of deep fine leg, floating out of position so that you could get some shade from the Father McCarthy eucalyptus grove, you had to use your brain.

Ben was worried about his dad, and how their family troubles might impact on his ambition to play for his country. He had seen Lou slipping packets of cash Dad's way. He had heard an argument about money between his mother and Grandma Leonie. He saw Dog, of all people, leaving bills on the microwave. He knew there was something going on between his dad and Sam.

His Grandma was in hospital, which had to be terribly expensive. It added up to nothing good. And Ben knew that to have any hope of playing for Australia, you needed the full ongoing support of your family until you were old enough to get an agent and sew up your corporate sponsorships. There was a pathway, but the first steps needed cashed-up parents.

The over was over, and Ben ran to fine leg at the other end, covering one hundred and fifty-five metres when nobody else had to change position by more than thirty. The batsmen were a right-/left-handed combination, so Ben also had to run sixty-two metres when the strike changed. If he forgot, he could rely on a bark from Mr Stoyle.

Mr Stoyle was a bit of a legend in the school, having played for the state back in the day. He had thick centre-parted blond hair and a sporty manner that could make Ben just about melt. His father said Mr Stoyle was a phony. He had looked up past state reps and, whaddaya know, no Stoyle. Ben knew that his father's aim, in popping the coach's bubble, was to help him feel better about the constant snubs. But Ben believed, like all the boys, in Mr Stoyle's legendariness. He had played for the state. Just like Ben was going to play for the country.

'Righto, bring it in!'

Mr Stoyle called an end to practice. Ben, as usual, was the only boy who had neither batted nor bowled. Today they were down to nine so there were no excuses. Joel and Jai Evans and Caleb Carney had told Mr Stoyle they were practising with the Bluebird Cricket Club adult high-performance squad, but Ben had seen them go surfing. He didn't dob them in, because Joel, Jai and Caleb were the top three in the batting order. Mr Stoyle put an arm around Ben's shoulder and said, 'You know, a cricket team is only as good as its twelfth man. Whoever tells you it's about the stars, they don't know their cricket.' This, Ben knew, was a direct jab at Gordon, who had confronted Stoyle a few weeks ago to ask why Ben should keep giving up his Saturdays and Monday and Thursday afternoons for this time-devouring game that he rarely got a turn to play. Mr Stoyle replied: 'Ben is a key man in our team because he loves it.' Boo-yah! Dad clean bowled by Stoyle, golden duck! But now he understood why Dad was being like this: he was hiding his embarrassment at not being able to offer Ben financial support. He was trying to turn Ben off cricket to cover this embarrassment. Ben felt terrible for not understanding until now.

The boys filtered from the park. Daniel, flicking his dark hair out of his eyes, collected his personal kit bag and dragged it by the wheels, joining Mr Stoyle for a confidential walk towards the teacher's car. Daniel only lived a few blocks away, but as captain he was often chatting with Mr Stoyle about selections, tactics and higher-order issues such as Daniel's pathway. Ben envied this intimacy, but it was a captain's privilege; a man's privilege: Daniel, his muscles and his beard were on the enviably far side of a post-pubertal transition that loomed before Ben like a high wall.

Ben picked up his gear: a second-hand kit, too-small gloves and box, borrowed pads and helmet, and no bat—how could you be a cricketer with no bat! He was still such a kid. There was no way he could ask Dad to buy him one. He slung the kit over his shoulder, with his school bag in the crook of his elbow, and made for the gate.

'Eh, check this out.'

If Ben was the regular twelfth man, Zane Dwyer was number eleven in the pecking order. Ben was the talentless cricket tragic, clinging to this team with invincible enthusiasm, while Zane was in cricket as a more or less permanent detention. With his history of delinquency and crime, coming from a well-known family of 'unfortunates', Zane's participation in cricket was Roman Catholic educational charity in action. The teachers, unable to cane him as they had been educated to do, subjected him to a virtual house arrest of compulsory extracurricular activities to stop him consorting with fellow criminals. Assuming there were no criminals in the cricket team.

Whereas Ben was forever hoping to get a turn, Zane was usually avoiding it. But cricket did offer certain opportunities to Zane, such as the one he was sharing with Ben now.

'Oh no, that's Jai's!'

Ben was staring dry-mouthed at the youth-size Gray-Nicolls bat Zane was sliding out of his unbranded nylon carry bag.

'Joel's,' Zane corrected him, eyes flickering.

'Same diff. You nicked it?'

'Joel hardly uses it, he's always borrowing *Daniel's Spartan*,' Zane said, putting on a Daniel voice, which he made interestingly effeminate. Zane was on his knees, rummaging in his bag. Ben felt drawn into some dark enterprise.

'They'll kill you.'

'They won't even catch me,' Zane's voice said from the depths of his bag. He came out with a grin, a handful of Puma stickers and a Stanley knife. Sitting cross-legged with the bat across his knees, he began digging at the edges of the Gray-Nicolls stickers.

'What are you doing?'

'Ever heard of rebirthing?' Zane said. 'New Puma bat, all yours for eighty bucks.'

Zane's hatred for the 'ruling class', as he called the more popular boys, was so ferocious that he would take any risk to spite them. This included promising Ben he would 'fix your little problem' of never getting a bat. Ben had only thought Zane would punch someone, not steal Joel's Gray-Nic.

'Are you nuts? They can literally expel us!'

'Nobody'll know,' Zane assured him. He had the Gray-Nicolls face sticker off, and flipped the bat to work the red stripe off the back. 'Your cricket heroes do this all the time. They pocket a million bucks a year to use some Indian brand, and what they really use is their old bat, just change the stickers.'

Zane loved to impart his worldly knowledge of adult fraud. He always had some story about famous people being hoaxers. Zane intended his cynicism to give Ben a kind of armour against the bullshit that was thrown at him. If everyone was living a double life, Zane said, everyone was equally vulnerable.

'I don't know,' Ben said, wavering. He hated fear, all the more now it had moved into their home. In his mother, sometimes he saw the fear so naked he didn't know whether to hug her or run away from her. Why should fear rule a grown-up's life? His father's fear had mutated into sadness, which was worse. Fear kept you running, Lou said. Sadness stopped you in your tracks.

Looking at the bat, now a cleanskin, Ben felt both fear and sadness. Zane was sizing up the Puma stickers. Ben's mouth went dry with need. Everyone had called it the magic stick when Jai went on a run of four straight half-centuries. Jai had grown out of it, which was why he used one of the three Spartan bats supplied to Daniel as part of an elite junior sponsorship program and bequeathed his own bat to Joel, whose average rocketed from the thirties into the eighties. If Ben had that magic Gray-Nic stick, it could be his first step towards playing for Australia.

'Course you know,' Zane said, seeing through Ben just as he was seeing through the plastic backing of the Puma stickers, 'this is how we shove it up the man. Here: brand-new Puma stick.' Zane presented the bat to Ben. 'You can pay me later.'

Ben's hands, as if they weren't part of him, reached out and held the bat in a correct grip. Damn, it felt right. 'Where am I going to get eighty bucks?'

'Make it sixty,' Zane said, as if that was solving the problem. 'Your grandmother gives you an allowance—what is it, two-fifty a term? Take it out of that.'

Ben cursed himself for being dumb enough to tell Zane about Leonie's allowance payments. That slip of the tongue had already cost him a scooter, a skateboard and a ripstick. He didn't know if he felt sorry for Zane or was terrified by him. When he paid for Zane's mobile phone plan, he realised he was both.

'They'll see the cherries,' Ben said, inspecting the bat face. 'They'll know it's the magic stick.'

'You want to play for Australia, you've got to know how to use sandpaper,' Zane said, with a *do I have to explain everything?* roll of his eyes.

'I can't pay you,' Ben said. He needed to save his allowance money to give his dad. It was his one hope. Dad was short of cash, and Ben could pool his allowances to help tide him over. Everyone was pitching in. They'd get Dad on his feet again, and in time he would be able to pay Ben back by supporting his efforts to play for Australia. But if Zane kept taking all of Ben's spare cash, he'd be stuck.

'Sure you can,' Zane said with a whiff of impatience, as if the matter was settled.

Oh, and Ben did want this bat. He was already sliding it into his kit bag, under his ratty old pads. 'I'll look after it for you till we give it back to Joel.'

'Okay, just look after it for me then,' Zane said, knowing from habit that the first stage in getting Ben to agree to a theft was to make him think it was a loan. 'If anyone asks questions, you're hanging on to it for me.'

'For Joel.'

'Joel doesn't have a Puma,' Zane reminded him. 'He's got a Gray-Nic.'

They walked along Trevally Street towards Bluebird Beach, Zane heading for the bus stop that would take him to his housing commission block two suburbs away.

'I don't know why you play,' Zane said. 'They're such cockheads. With Coach Stoyle sucking on their dicks.'

Ben blushed. He didn't know if this kind of talk was homophobic abuse; it was more that Zane's insinuations that the tough boys in the cricket clique and their coach were a gay circle-jerk crew supplied Ben with fantasy material that he couldn't quite un-imagine. He couldn't help hoping, which became suspecting, that Zane, with his ability to see through social facades, was not issuing an empty insult but revealing a secret.

'How's it going between you and Daniel anyway?' Zane asked in a gentler tone. Regrettably, Ben had told Zane that he was pretty sure Daniel was bi-curious. There were too many of the familiar signs of struggle. For Daniel, who lived in that busy heterosexual intersection of cricket, footy, surf club and his dad a big wheel on the council, the journey towards honesty was going to be rocky. Ben wanted to help him. He had tried to start the conversation with Daniel in the surf, where it seemed possible to talk as equals, but Daniel splashed water in his face and paddled away, muttering about fucken faggots and their kinky parents.

'I only wanted to help,' Ben said.

Every day started with the intention of wanting to help someone, and ended not the way he hoped.

'Course he's gunna heap shit on you,' Zane said. 'He's dangerous, man, he'll do you damage.'

Ben knew about damage. Once Mr Stoyle had brought it to the principal's attention that Ben was being bullied because he had 'something wrong with him', the school's pastoral response was to stage 'healing conferences' between perpetrators and victim, 'truth sessions' where everyone had to 'own' their actions. Ben discovered that the only person who ended up owning anything was the victim, who came out of the meetings with one hundred percent ownership of his pain. Dad had confronted Mr Stoyle about the bullying. 'Oh, they eventually get the message and leave,' Mr Stoyle said. Dad had walked away satisfied, until he realised that Mr Stoyle meant the victims.

This was how Ben knew he was not a victim: he had not left the team.

'I met a guy Up North,' Ben told Zane. 'We talked about my mum and dad and my step-grandma and my god-sister and how we're all living together.'

'That's some fucked-up shit,' Zane said, meaning Ben's family, though he could have meant Ben being with a guy. Ben's mind went back to the heart-melting poignancy of that night Up North, how he'd cried and laughed with the boy about the weirdness of their families.

'You suck his cock?' Zane asked.

Ben would never work out why he opened up to Zane, the most blatant homophobe. It had been amazing, after the long struggle to admit who he was, to actually kiss a boy. It seemed like a world-historic event, it should be on the TV news. But he couldn't tell Zane. Kissing was too soppy. He would sooner have lied and said they'd had sex. 'We're Snapchatting each other,' he said.

'Fuck, man, if I had Snapchat, I'd have fourteen chicks on the go!' Zane said. 'Fourteen!' He marvelled at his theoretical virility. Then he spat on the street and said, 'Fucken phones, I'm down to zero balance.'

Zane knew these practicalities better than Ben. But maybe that was part of receiving nothing, as opposed to receiving everything. Zane was the only kid Ben knew who was not given a phone by his parents. Ben lost his phones at the rate of one a term. On the bus, at school, at cricket, at the beach—he'd lost a phone in every locality on the seaboard. His mum, keenly protective since the split, kept buying him a new one without telling Dad. 'I only want to know where you are,' Mum had said, as if that was a good thing. His dad, not knowing what Mum was doing, also bought him new phones. Whenever he had a spare, Ben passed it to Zane.

'I can't afford to get you another plan,' Ben said.

'Forty bucks for the magic stick and I can top up.'

'No, I'm serious. I can't pay for the bat. I have . . . money problems of my own.'

'You're shitting me!' Zane grabbed him by the shoulder. Ben flinched, thinking Zane was going to hit him. 'You serious? Okay, I can work with that.'

'What do you mean?'

'We'll sell it on the black market. Split the proceeds fifty-fifty. I reckon I can get two hundred for it.'

'But . . . you can sell it anyway; you nicked it. You don't have to split anything with me.'

Zane's hand had moved from Ben's shoulder up to his neck. It was gripping him with a force Ben could have taken for tenderness if it was not hurting. But maybe Zane didn't know the difference. His eyes had turned soft.

'I didn't nick it, remember, I borrowed it,' Zane said. 'But listen, you've been good to me. A mate's fallen on hard times, we help each other out. I dunno what you need the cash for, but if you're asking *me* for help, you must be fucken desperate. Tell you what. You use this bat—it'll get you a game for sure—and when you're done we'll get four hundred for it, no worries! Two hunjee for you, two hunjee for me!'

Zane clapped him on the shoulder, friendly but too hard. Ben was rubbing the pain out when they turned into Fishman Avenue, the long flat stretch that led to the beach past the derelict fire station and Bluebird Surf Life Saving Club.

They paused at a strange sight. Daniel, who lived on Fishman, was standing on the footpath in front of his house, with his cricket kit at his feet, by the side of Mr Stoyle's Toyota Celica Sports. They were in agitated conversation with Daniel's father, Principal Oxenford and Ben's mother. None of the adults looked happy. Ben gave his cricket bag a shake, to shuffle the stolen bat deeper under the pads.

'Outta here.' Zane, who had no desire for adult contact, jogged up Pelican Street. He was a real athlete, Ben thought, watching him vault over a low brick fence. If I had Zane's body, I'd play for Australia for sure.

To dodge the adults might attract their attention, so Ben continued down Fishman. The stolen bat burnt in his bag, and when Ms Oxenford and Mr Stoyle turned their eyes on him, he felt like he was going through an airport X-ray. His arms and legs fizzed. He dropped his face. Their discussion fell into a tense silence.

'Ben, how are you?' Mrs Oxenford asked.

Ben stopped and looked at her flat-heeled shoes. 'Good thanks, miss.'

'Coming home from cricket?'

He looked up at her. The question seemed strangely loaded. Of course he was coming home from cricket. Coming home from cricket was what Mr Stoyle and Daniel were doing.

'Wait, what?'

'I beg your pardon,' Daniel's father corrected him.

'Yes, miss,' Ben said, dropping his eyes again. He heard Mr Stoyle clear his throat impatiently.

'How's your dad?' Ms Oxenford seemed determined to hold him there.

'What?'

'How's your—'

'Yeah, good,' Ben said, looking at his mother. Kelly was staring at her golf shoes, which she carried in her hand. She was wearing golf clothes, but looked as guilty as if she'd been caught in her underwear.

'Please give him my regards,' Ms Oxenford said. Ben could hear her smile shaping her words. 'And I'm glad you're enjoying your cricket.'

Ben remembered Ms Oxenford's role in persuading his dad to let him play, reminding Gordon of the benefits team sports could provide during the difficult teenage years. 'It's so hard to get them to participate in anything at this age,' she'd said, 'you should be grateful that he's giving you the problem of wanting to play. We don't often get parents so . . . determined to stop their teenagers doing sport.' Ms Oxenford had gone to school with Dad at Bluebird High. After that meeting Dad said to Ben, 'Amazing that she's so pro-sport now, after what those jocks did to her.' He wouldn't tell Ben what he meant, but Ben had always been grateful to Ms Oxenford for swinging the argument. He would thank her publicly when he made the Australian team.

'Let's go home,' his mother said, setting off towards The Lodge.

Behind him, Ben heard the conversation restart in a calmer tenor. They were making arrangements to 'discuss this further'.

'What was that about?' he asked.

'Nothing to do with you.'

They continued in silence. Ben felt uneasy about the conversation he had interrupted, uncomfortable about the hot cricket bat in his bag, unhappy about his dad's lack of money, and unvirtuous about the fact that he hadn't visited his grandmother in hospital this week; but always, these days, he felt awkward with his mum.

'How's things, anyway?'

They were crossing the vacant lot behind the fire station. A public right-of-way ran through the lot, where the community had begun a herb and vegetable garden. Ben's mum, after brooding for a few minutes on whatever had been discussed back there on Fishman, stopped at the garden.

'Wait, what?'

Unlike Gordon, Kelly didn't repeat herself for Ben. He heard what she said, it just took time to sink in. She loved him and, in the circumstances, indulged him, but she had her limits.

'Good,' Ben said.

Kelly bent down to the corten retaining wall separating the herb and vegetable beds by produce and 'owner'. The community gardeners had initially staked twee painted signs such as GIVE PEAS A CHANCE and DON'T STOP BELEAFING, but more recently the messages had become a more tersely proprietorial MEG + JANE or PETE + LIZ, and the council had put up an explanatory notice saying visitors were welcome to 'enjoy' the garden, meaning look but don't pick.

Ben watched his mother pluck some sprigs of rosemary, dill, coriander and parsley.

'Mum, you can't do that.'

'I'm cooking pasta tonight. Wouldn't you like some fresh flavours?'

'It's against the spirit.'

Kelly considered him for a moment. 'It's a community space, right?'

'Wait, what?'

'It can only be a true community space if the produce belongs to the community.'

Ben wished his mother wasn't so smart. He hated getting into philosophical arguments with her.

'The signs,' he said helplessly.

'Which have been put up by Daniel's horrible father and his council. Next thing, they'll be putting out tenders for lockable fences.'

'Because of you,' Ben said.

With handfuls of four types of herb, Kelly pushed herself to her feet and brushed the dirt off her knees.

'If I can't enjoy the garden, it's a private space, which couldn't be legal.'

'If everybody did what you do, why would the gardeners plant anything?'

'Ah, but everybody doesn't do what I do.' She grinned. 'And I only pick a few leaves here and there; it's not like I go for the carrots and tomatoes.'

People called Ben's mother a cheat. It seemed worse than the other things they called her, because it was true. She'd cheat community gardeners out of their herbs. He didn't want to say anything, though. Her hobbies, like Bikram and Pilates and golf, were meant to calm people down, but in Ben's experience, exercise wound his mum up like a prize-fighter. When she had her golf shoes in her hand, she always came home looking for an argument.

'You sound like your father,' Kelly said as they resumed walking. 'Always the moral high ground.'

Ben thought it was pretty rich of his mother to talk about morality, but he didn't have the words to take her on.

'Why can't Dad be happy?'

Kelly let that sit between them all the way past the fire station and the BSLSC to the bottom of the stairs to The Lodge. She thumbed a text message. Ben knew she was asking Gordon if Dog was in the house. Poor Mum, he thought. Poor Dad.

Not getting any response, Kelly started up the stairs. At the first landing, she stopped.

'You might not believe this, but it's all I've ever wanted.'

'Wait, what?'

'What as in you didn't hear me, or what as in you want to know what I want?' Kelly waited until Ben looked her in the forehead. The sun was going down behind his back. 'I've only ever wanted your dad to be happy. But I've come to the realisation lately that it might not be possible.'

Ben followed her up the stairs, wishing he could say something. He could smell the herbs in her hand. Too smart, she was; so smart she could be mean without knowing it.

Honest

KELLY LED BEN UP THE STAIRS, EDGING SIDEWAYS PAST ARCHER David's mini-excavator, which was parked in a narrow no-man's-land between The Lodge's laundry and the new development. Holding her golf shoes, Kelly took extra care with her footing. She was fit, thanks to daily Bikram and this bizarre new golf thing, but Norma's accident had reminded her that past a certain age you were one slip-up from becoming that inner self you devoted your days and nights to reversing, postponing, or at least arguing into submission.

These wobbly wooden steps from the beach brought to mind the places she would rather be. She wanted to travel—somewhere landlocked like Mexico City or Udaipur or Madrid. The Himalayas. It didn't matter as long as it was a million miles from the ocean, high and freaking dry.

Butterflies rose in her stomach as she came to the side door to see a portrait of the men in, or on their way out of, her life: Gordon, his phone with her neglected message on the card table, was shuffling saucepans around the kitchen with a towel slobbishly over his shoulder. (How many times? How many freaking times?) Dog, at the jigsaw puzzle, was annoying the shit out of Josie, Tonsure Man and Red Cap. Jesus. And she had to walk in and pretend this was her home.

She skirted around the deck and followed Ben to the balcony, where he was avoiding the crowd inside and mind-surfing the waves below. 'I don't want to go in either,' she said. 'Fancy a spot of coordinate geometry?'

You had to have something you did with your son. Doing maths with Ben made her want to strangle him half the time, but it was better than only sharing an interest in whether he had cleaned his room.

'Wait, what? I've done my homework.'

'You're in year eleven, darling. If you've done your homework, we do revision. It'll be fun.'

Ben returned her brittle friendliness with a withering microsecond, his standard length of eye contact. You couldn't say he was unable to express non-verbal emotion. He could, with impressive economy. She occasionally wondered if the vacuum left by Gordon's passive acceptance of the whole break-up/infidelity thing had drawn out Ben's latent hostility to her, and therefore done his emotional development a favour.

A blessing in disguise, then.

Freaking good disguise.

He turned away from her and went down the external stairs. Which, she had to concede, was what she deserved.

'Okay, no geometry then,' she said, as if they had come to an agreement. She entered the living room, where the notice the men took of her inverted her needs. Ben, who she loved more dearly than life, had run away from her. Dog, who she generally wanted to punch or fuck but at this moment to show the door, gave her a blandly pleasant hello and competitively tap-tapped a jigsaw piece between Red Cap and Josie. And Gordon, for whom she had a perplexed overhang of strong but complicated feeling, greeted her with a relieved smile and a sign language offer of dinner.

'I'm looking for guinea pigs,' he said.

'Wasn't it my cooking night?' she said, throwing a savage look at the guests, meaning Gordon was supposed to have kicked them out by now.

Returning to the kitchen, he swung through the saloon door like Steve McQueen sorting the place out, only he was going the wrong way. He picked up an expensive pot holder and wrestled for control of a vast quantity of fettuccine. The fancy pot holder was, she noticed, one of those fuck-off Eastons gems. Once he'd explained these out-of-character purchases, she fell a little bit—a tiny, tiny bit—in the general vicinity, the hazy insinuation, back in love with him.

She dipped a finger into the sauce, let out a gasp of pleasure, and picked up a spoon to go in again.

'Haven't you been fed this week?' Gordon asked.

'I just get so hungry after golf. Where did you learn to make an arrabbiata like this?'

'Thank you,' Gordon said. 'Only you could make a compliment sound like an accusation.'

'You must be having an affair,' she said. A proper arrabbiata. Next it'd be a haircut less than ten years behind fashion. And then shoes without socks, and she'd be dead to him.

'I brought some goodies.' She tossed her gleanings from the community garden onto the benchtop.

Gordon gave them a snooty look and said, 'You know I don't deal in hot herbs.'

'Of course not. You thumb your nose at the lifeguards, you go to court over some bullshit with the neighbour, you're the saviour of Old Bluebird.'

'Unlike pilfering community herb gardens, which is really sticking it to the man.'

'Oh, you drive me mad,' she said without feeling. For lack of anything else to do, she began to run the tap to wash up, but then, remembering that she might look like a wife and mother, dropped a handful of utensils with an over-dramatic splash and stripped off the rubber gloves she had just put on. Her throat tightening with some kind of dirty emotional bomb, she moved to the window.

'This is an inch thick in salt scum,' she said. 'How can you enjoy the ocean through that?' But she knew the answer: Gordon saw the world through salt-covered glass. And he had an abiding affection for scum. 'Don't you have some buddy who cleans on the cheat?'

Gordon's eyes widened. She wondered if she had said that or thought it. So Freudian. Was it Freudian when you came out with shit like that?

'Cheap,' she corrected herself.

'How's Ben?' Gordon said mercifully. 'He did all right in his maths exam, thanks to your help.'

'Thank the Vyvanse.' Kelly raised an invisible glass in a mock toast.

Gordon made a face. Since Ben had been diagnosed with mild attention deficit hyperactivity disorder at the age of nine, Gordon had fought a rearguard action against the medical recommendations that paediatricians and Kelly thought were simple common sense. For six draining years of their marriage, the arguments had sat as entrenched as the Western Front, a few inches gained one month only to be given up the next, the defender always at a natural advantage to the aggressor. Pure attrition, fought over the same patch: Ben's all-precious membrane of self-esteem. Gordon argued that the Vyvanse pills were low self-esteem in a bottle. Kelly countered that Ben's self-esteem was already taking a battering from the daily reminders that, due to his sparrow-like attention span, he was limited intellectually and ostracised socially. The ship of his self-esteem had sailed, she said. When Ben, at fifteen, finally asked if he could give the pills a try, Gordon surrendered. So now Ben was swallowing a daily dose of slow-release dexamphetamine. The doctor had said with professional slyness, 'It's only a trial, and if it doesn't work, you can stop it.' Kelly had used enough ampheta-mines over the years to know that they worked. Oh boy, did they work. Ben's attention and school results improved, his popularity rose a notch, and he could now almost catch a cricket ball.

'You can't say he always takes my side,' Gordon said, reading her mind. 'Does he talk to you about it?'

'The Vyvanse?' Kelly shook her head, her aggression dissi-pating into forlornness. 'He used to, but now he doesn't talk to me about anything. Listen to this. I ran into Jude Oxenford on my way home this afternoon. She was talking to Stoyle and your mate Frontal. Jude says it's a real problem. Kids on uppers halve their doses and make some cash.'

'Dealing ADHD drugs? Jesus. Not Ben, though?' He gave her a stricken look, silently asking her, if the answer was bad, to please lie.

'It seems not, but he's one of the few boys who aren't. They live in a different world, Gordon. Ben hit puberty and we turned one hundred. We're losing him.' Life sometimes seemed like one long struggle to reverse time: Bluebird time, family time, Kelly time, her-and-Ben time. She was nostalgic for their mother-son intimacy even before it was fully gone. 'And he's losing us.'

'You know he reckons I should move Up North and leave him with you,' Gordon said. 'I felt gut-shot.'

'Thanks for the vote of confidence!'

'You know what I mean.'

'He sees things, you know? You're the only one who wants to be living here. I'm stuck because I'm stymied by fucking Leonie—who won't come near the place, by the way, she's scared the floor's about to cave in. Lou's here until she gets her life back on track. And our son spends most of his time camping in that men's toilet downstairs. Do you think it's healthy for him to be sleeping in a bunk room with you and Lou, and me a wall away?'

'I know it didn't come the way I wanted, but I've always wanted to live here. Why should I be the one to leave?'

Kelly smiled in irritation. She could always rely on Gordon to dodge the subject and focus on this bloody house. Seeing the bright side for some men wasn't optimism; it was cowardice.

'Yeah, living in The Lodge, dream come true.' She waited for her annoyance to subside. Their son wasn't dealing Vyvanse. Small mercies. 'Ben only wants you to be happy. You should be the one to leave because you're the one who *can*.'

'Who says I'm not happy here?'

Kelly moved to the saloon door and watched the jigsaw players, who could have been something particularly dire from Cézanne. She knew how to tag an emotion with a great painter's name—*Merci beaucoup*, Workers' Education Association night courses! She had to look outwards at this stage of life, and the art appreciation classes she'd taken up distracted her commentary from, in this instance, 'Look at those fuckwits stuck in their rut' to 'Aha, Cézanne, something like *The Absinthe-Drinking Jigsaw-Playing Desperates*'. Art appreciation made her feel not only sophisticated but transgressive. She would soon move on to abstract expressionism, and those people, those blobs of paint, would be stuck here forever. Although, or perhaps because, she had grown up in Bluebird as the only daughter of the village chieftain, Kelly had always thought of Bluebirders as 'those people'. They'd always suspected that she looked down on them, but they didn't know why, as they couldn't tell the difference between entitlement and entrapment.

'Have you been seeing that new hairdresser?' Josie squawked up the slope of the floor at Kelly, who self-consciously touched the back of her head, undercut two days earlier. Red Cap and Tonsure Man were ignoring her because they had no interest. Dog was ignoring her because he had too much. She reckoned.

'Which one?' Kelly asked unenthusiastically, trying to recall if any of her recent Tinder dates had been a barber.

Josie was giving her a look that was either fed up or startled. It was hard to tell with Josie, her affect was so mixed up since her brain surgeries. Kelly thought: A face straight from Van Gogh, equally confused and confusing, a handful of pieces missing.

'She's Indian,' Josie said significantly.

The men shifted. Kelly could have sworn Dog took the moment to rearrange his block and tackle inside his board shorts.

Kelly couldn't think of which of Bluebird's two dozen working hairdressers in four competing salons Josie might be talking about, but that was irrelevant because Josie was really talking about her, about Kelly. These moments were always aggravating, more so as she got older. Months and years could pass without her being reminded of the colour of her skin. She was not Indian, of course; she was Australian. But to a certain generation of Bluebird people, birth could not wash out your 'real' origins. No matter where you were born or to whom, Josie deemed it important that you knew 'another' Indian person on the beaches, just because, well, you lot might want your hair cut by your own kind. Kelly had been teased as a curry-muncher, of course, but a long time ago. People forgot. Or you saw the same people for so many years, day after day, that you assumed they forgot. The deadening of your senses protected you. And then someone like Josie or Norma would come out with shit like this, which made Kelly think that the whole thing was a charade and the moment her back was turned they would all be referring to her, particularly when her infidelity to Gordon came up, as 'that Indian'. No matter how long you lived with them, you never forgot that one time you caught them putting on an accent and a head-wobble. She supposed they saw their racial prejudices as evening the score, a fair exchange for the fact that she was Noel Chidgey's daughter and part-owned this fucking house.

'Do you know her?' Josie persisted.

Red Cap muttered something to his mother, which caused her chin to drop into the wattles of her neck. Josie refocused on the jigsaw, as if that were dignity.

'Carn, Kel, where's ya sense of humour?' Dog said, tap-tapping another piece, as pleased with himself as when he relocated Kelly's sweet spot at that party. (Hint: after the champagne, the coke and her incandescent rage at turning fifty, it would have been harder to miss than to find.) She noticed how the others set aside their annoyance with Dog. Life in this little reality refuge had to go on, that was the important thing with those people; nothing changed even when—particularly when—everything had changed. Their collective genius was for transmuting *everything* into *nothing*. As far as they were concerned, Dog was getting up their noses because he was the irritating prick they knew, not because he'd rooted Gordon's missus, who was a curry-munching up-herself filthy rich daddy's girl, so what did it matter. Indifference, a fair go, being laidback, whatever you wanted to call it, was a collective effort mighty in its tenacity. Even her husband, now hovering over the jigsaw players with that goofy grin. Most of all her husband.

She had to get out of here. But—oh shit, she couldn't. She lived here. She had to get *them* out of here. But she was outnumbered. Again.

'I've lost it,' she replied to Dog's question. 'Someone let me know if you find it.'

She slapped the diagonal pine feature wall and stomped downstairs, out of the house for—what, a romantic walk on the beach, hand in hand with herself? And who should she run into but another of them, Gordon's omigod-daughter on her way up from a board session with her *salon de clubbie refusées*.

Admitting defeat, Kelly slumped onto the driftwood log that served as a bench on the patch of lawn and watched Lou come up. The girl was built like a wheelie bin, but in her one-piece swimsuit all that wet muscle looked kind of sexy. Kelly remembered Dog saying he liked athletic women. 'You can really wrestle with them,' he said with relish. But then Dog liked every kind of woman; you could always do something with them. He wasn't fussy about looks. It was meant to be one of the lovable things about him.

'You look like you're running for your life,' Lou said. Kelly felt mildly offended—Lou did not know her well enough to say something so insightful—and saw herself getting up and walking away in a huff, only to trip down the wooden stairs and break her freaking neck. All in preference to being so see-through.

'I'm stuck here,' Kelly said. 'What's your excuse?'

'What makes you say that?' Lou said with a frustrating pleasantness. At times, Kelly thought, Lou could be Gordon's daughter. A goddaughter, for God's sake: it wasn't that she disliked Lou, it was more that she didn't understand the point of her.

'How was training?' Kelly asked.

'You know, that's the most hospitable thing you've said to me in months? Just because I've kind of taken Gordon's side doesn't mean I'm your enemy.'

'Don't they mean the same thing?'

'Not with me.'

Overcome by a bulge of shame, Kelly ordered herself not to cry. Hearing that Lou did not consider herself her enemy gave rise to an equal and opposite force: the intuition that Lou might be her friend. To her surprise, Lou, who had shown her nothing but wall-eyed contempt since moving in, sat beside her and raised her arm, like a drawbridge to the firmness of her shoulder. A shoulder to cry on. And she had plenty of it. Kelly eyed it like a pillow, and then, wearied by all the hours of conversation she could abridge with just one gesture, let her head rest on it.

Lou patted the top of Kelly's head, in the unnatural but polite way a non-animal person would stroke someone else's pet.

'I know I came in late on all this, so tell me to mind my own business,' Lou said. 'But Dog? Really? What was in your head?'

'You don't want to be in my head,' Kelly said, her voice wavering. She had nobody to talk to.

'Wouldn't you have spent all these years thanking your luck? I know how it ended with him, but didn't you dodge a bullet? And it's so long ago! Why would you go back there at . . . at your age? When you have revenge sex, you're not meant to have it with the person you're taking it out on.'

At her age was what explained everything. Lou just didn't know it yet.

Kelly watched her hand chipping pieces of bark off the log and moving them across her lap, as if arranging samples. 'When you get to my age, your unfinished business becomes more important than your happiness or whatever.'

Lou scratched her armpit and paused, it appeared, to extract a sea louse.

Kelly sat upright, dusted the bark off her lap, and began to tell Lou what had happened, if only to disabuse her of the idea that the sex meant anything. The sex was the least of it, the revenge even less. At times, with anyone younger than twenty-five, it could seem like you had to explain the entire human condition in order to get to square one.

She was the one who had acted like a crazy woman, upending their lives, but, if only Lou could understand, Kelly was only a kid too. She was a kid when she'd made her decisive choice, marrying on the rebound from a devastating public humiliation, literally left at the altar by literally her childhood sweetheart. Talk about a cliché pile-on. She felt the return of every corpuscle of blood and fury that had flooded her neck and shoulders, all her bare parts and her covered parts, waiting in the church, the dread certainty of what was unfolding. She knew it the moment she walked up the aisle. It was out of order, the bride first. Where was Dog? Oh, probably gone outside for a nervous smoke. Why didn't anyone stop her? Instead of saving her embarrassment, her fuckwit father had made her enter the silent church, all those people's faces on her. Maybe he was thinking he could still pull it out of the fire; but not even Noel Chidgey's indomitable will could conjure the groom.

Or maybe he did, just his timing was off. And his aim. Dog's best man—the first face to smile at her, completely detached from the horror as if he were a halfwit, floating in some kind of reverie—was Gordon Grimes. A groom was waiting for her, not the one she was in love with, but the one she would marry, same place, same set-up, eight months later.

'You fell for Gordon just like that,' Lou asked, or rather stated.

But then—flash forward, where did her life go!—thirty years' worth of unanswered questions had collapsed into one night at her and Gordon's joint fiftieth at the Hilton. Bluebird, sunset . . . all these deadshits' idea of perfection. She only had a few steps to travel back to that fork in the road. She wondered if anyone really changed. She would have been surprised to look in the mirror and see that she was not twenty and made up for her first wedding day . . . and here was her long-lost groom . . . well, not exactly long-lost, recast as family friend, married father of two and all that, legal practitioner, man about town blah blah blah, historicised as if none of it had happened to *her*. And primed on resentment, reflection, a refillable flute of Veuve and the three quick lines Dog had beckoned her for in an upstairs room, what else was she to do but grab the impending midlife crisis before Gordon took it first?

'What a mess, and all of my own making.' For once, she couldn't blame Gordon, her late father, her lamented stepmother, her brother, or even Dog: in that trip through time, all her nemeses had evaporated, leaving only herself. It had been strangely liberating, to be the sole author of her misfortune. At last she owned something.

Appearances lied. She was still a kid. But she couldn't expect Lou to understand that.

'Do you know how we got caught?' Kelly asked.

Lou shrugged one of those slabby shoulders, like she only half wanted to know, and only so long as it didn't heap further humiliation onto her poor godfather. Good old Gordon, Kelly thought, everyone's favourite victim.

'I suppose Dog was boasting about it.'

Kelly shook her head. Dog wasn't a bragger. He must have slept with three hundred girls before Kelly, and another three hundred before he ran out of gas. Sal, the woman he married, was simply the one he happened to stop at. His mates, including Gordon, used to make legend of the Doggy Love Magic. But Dog himself? Never said a word for or against any woman. He maintained a code of silence in his promiscuity. You could never say he respected women, but he did respect the privacy of the bedroom.

'It was that fuckwit Eastaugh,' Kelly said.

'Sam? Gordon's surf buddy?'

Kelly bit her lip. This would be news. Fettuccine arrabbiata was one thing, but *surfing*? Gordon's refusal to surf at Bluebird symbolised half the problem with their marriage. Now he was surfing again? He must be having an affair.

'Not Sam, his father. The old perv.'

'Tony? This won't sound very nice, but there's something about the colour of his artificial leg that gives me the heebie-jeebies.'

Kelly felt a surge of warmth in her stomach to be the wise older woman. She did have something to offer, even if it was only thirty-year-old gossip.

'You don't know anything about the people you've landed with,' she said.

'I don't suppose I do.'

'Old Tony walked in on us. Or we walked in on him. Dog and I were in the main bedroom of the Hilton, and the old bloke had gone into the ensuite before us. We were pretty sure the coast was clear because we were in the room for a while before we did anything. Okay, we were doing lines. Having a giggle. But you can't account for the old and their toilet habits. Tony had been in there, quietly doing his thing, or trying to do his thing, for a long time. Eventually Dog and I were, you know, when Tony burst out of the ensuite. Dog wanted to run. Tony still scares them; he takes them back to when they were little boys. And Tony pushes his reading glasses up on his nose and goes, 'Gotchaz!' I hadn't spoken to the old coot in years. I thought he'd lost his marbles. But apparently not.'

Lou was shaking her head. 'Caught in a bedroom at a party? How old are you, sixteen?'

Kelly felt some relief; she had never had to spell out the gory details. 'Tony told Sam, and Sam shirtfronted Dog. Told him he would take out his front teeth if he didn't man up and tell Gordon. I never really got that.'

'Got what?'

'Why it was so important to Sam to break up his best friend's marriage.'

'Maybe he thought he'd be doing Gordon a favour.'

'Well, that would be consistent with Sam's attitude to me, so yes. I just don't get why he would want to hurt Gordon and Ben. I mean, who made him God?'

'He's a fireman.'

Kelly thought: Girl, you really don't know shit about these men.

'Of course, Dog never had a clue. He just told me to ignore Tony, no-one would listen to him, and Sam wouldn't follow through. Dog had to take Sally home—Tony wasn't the only person at the party who was legless. So it was left to me. Sam was dead serious. Dog was wrong there. Sam gave me the chance to confess or else he'd tell Gordon. I had to show courage. And what the hell. I understood that there would be no point to what I had done *unless* I told Gordon.'

She had made her confession to Gordon while they were alone at the end of the party, companionably cleaning up.

'I felt relieved to have it out there.'

'Really?'

'I just thought at last someone had *done* something. Have you ever had that feeling? No, of course not. It's like a vice has been tightening millimetre by millimetre, year after year, since the beginning of time, and if you don't do something your head will explode. It doesn't matter what you do, as long as it's something.'

'I don't know.' Lou was shaking her head. 'You had an okay marriage. Do people your age really split up because someone's rooted someone else? Aren't you a bit beyond that?'

'This is what I'm trying to tell you. Marriage to Gordon was killing me.'

'But to sleep with Dog to end your marriage? It's like suicide by cop.'

'Divorce by Dog.'

Still under the influence of the coke, she had hoped to explain it all, rationally, to Gordon, and find common ground. Surely he had been feeling the same oppression in their marriage? But she had miscalculated. Her satisfaction in confessing only lasted until she saw the collapse of Gordon's face. He had not responded as she'd hoped. He spent the night at the firehouse. When the coke wore off, she realised she had mistaken nostalgia for vindication.

'Fireman to the rescue,' Lou said.

'Sam and Gordon have a . . . unique history together.'

'I'm sure they do.'

You don't know the tiniest fraction of it, Kelly thought.

They watched the last of the light fade over the ocean baths. Kelly ached to leave Bluebird, even more now than when she had blown up their marriage. Once she'd understood that she would not be forgiven, she'd expected to be cast out. Which was fine, and perhaps what she really wanted. So why the fuck hadn't that happened? Fuck Gordon and, in particular, fuck Leonie. Fuck, fuck, fuck her, and once she's truly fucked, fuck her again. Fuck her.

'Gordon does forgive you,' Lou said. 'He thinks it's more important to save the past, warts and all.'

'I've given him a few warts.'

'So what about Dog?' Lou wrung her hands as if she wanted a neck to put between them. 'Red Cap and his mum can't cop him, Ben and I can't bear the sight of him, Sam wants to murder him. So why is he still allowed to keep stinking the place out every day?'

Kelly was shaking her head. Lou still didn't understand the first thing about it.

'What am I missing?' Lou said.

'It's Gordon. The more Bluebird vanishes, the more essential it is to him to preserve The Lodge. It's like he's one of those model battlefield obsessives, and every person in this house is one of those little painted soldiers. For him to be able to preserve it, the people aren't allowed to change. What happened between Dog and me *must not have happened*. Do you get it? That is Gordon's sole reason to get out of bed each morning. To obsess over his model of the past and stop anyone tampering with it.'

Kelly was panting with the effort of compressing a lifetime— her lifetime—into this last moment before a chill mist fell over the lawn, and she and Lou walked up to the house and became their normal selves again.

'I want him to smash Dog's face in,' Lou said.

'That's not Gordon's style, but he does have his little revenge acts.'

'I wish I could see them.'

'Oh, you just need to know where to look. You know those imported coffee cups you use? The French tablecloth? The pot holder? The odd little senseless splurges from Eastons that bob up in the kitchen?'

'I thought they were things you get,' Lou said. 'Through your work.'

'I wish!' Kelly smiled. 'No, Gordon takes rides on the Fast Ferry every few days. Sometimes he just goes to OC and back without stopping. Sometimes he drops into Eastons to pick up something really, stupidly expensive.'

'Gordon's the last person in the world I can imagine doing that.'

'It's not him, but he has to.'

'Why?'

'Because the night of the fiftieth, he found two charge cards in the bedroom where Dog and I had been. One was a Fast Ferry pass, the other was an Eastons store card. Dog had been using them to chop lines on the bedside table. When old Tony caught us, Dog left his cards behind. Later that night, Gordon trousered them. Dog knows he has them, and Gordon knows that Dog knows, but these guys being as emotionally retarded as they are, Dog won't ask for them. To ask for them would risk having the conversation they can't face. And Gordon won't hand them back. And so whenever Gordon feels like he needs to get a bit off his chest, he rides the Fast Ferry to Eastons and buys something outrageous. It's the most he can bring himself to do.'

'You make him sound insane,' Lou said.

'They think they're saving the world. What can be more insane than that?'

'Gordon is their hero. They so desperately want him to win.'

'Gordon.' Kelly swallowed, contemplating whether to stop talking now. 'He can't win.'

'Why not?'

Kelly stared for a long time at the sandstone cliff face on the far side of Bluebird Bay, above the ocean baths. Last year, some kids had graffitied a chubby blue tag to the very rock where it happened. After forty-two years, just a coincidence. Maybe it was more surprising that nobody had graffitied it until now. She squinted to try to read the stylised lettering.

'He's never been the same, really, since what happened to his brother.'

'Gordon has a brother?'

'Had. A long time ago. They were kids. The brother died over there, where that graffiti's on that rock. The more time goes by, the more I think it kind of got Gordon stuck. Stuck here. Stuck back then.'

'How?' Lou asked.

'How what?'

'Did the brother die.'

'They were kids. Gordon was eight, the other two were twelve.'

'Two?'

'Sam. He and Owen were best friends, Gordon used to run along after them. They were playing—up there—see the graffiti on that rock? Owen went off.'

'Went off?'

'Slipped. An accident.'

Lou's face shut down. She sighed and looked out over the beach, showing no interest in continuing the conversation. Kelly felt physically dirty, as if she had been caught betraying Gordon once again. Was Lou judging her? Maybe not. Maybe talking about family deaths hit Lou's off switch. Too much for her. Too much, Kelly thought, for all of us. She inhaled into her sacrum. She wondered if she would keep betraying him, again and again, until he *woke the fuck up.*

'At least that was the official version,' Kelly said. 'There was another ...'

'Why?' Lou was glaring at her.

'Why what?'

'Why are you telling me this?'

Lou's words echoed like a voice crossing some forbidden land between dream and memory. Kelly pressed her hands under her arms to stop the fierce shuddering that rushed through her.

'You asked if I fell for Gordon just like that,' Kelly said. 'I'm telling you.'

The night of her wedding—her intended wedding, her aborted wedding—came vividly before her eyes. She was curled on a bed, hiding from the audience, her face smeared with mascara and humiliation, and Gordon, in his ridiculous tuxedo, was the only guest with the courage to come and knock on her door. The others pretended they were protecting her, but they were avoiding her. She was cursed. And maybe Gordon had seen this too, which was what had prompted him to share his own curse. He told her about the afternoon he had been playing with Owen and Sam on the cliff. Everyone knew this about Gordon; it gave a solemn dignity to his silences, his passivity, his *absorbency*. He carried the load of Bluebird's pity; with her wedding-day humiliation, he saw that it was a load Kelly now had to carry too. After he had been narrating the story for a little while, he had appeared to break into himself, pierce some locked inner door. He told her that he and Sam had lied about what happened to his brother. 'You lied?' Kelly said, lifted out of her misery into that of a little boy sitting beside her. Gordon nodded. His face looked turned inside out. He went into some kind of a trance, mumbling about his last sight of Owen . . . 'that look on his face as he went' . . . 'yeah, like satisfaction' . . . 'that naughty grin he always had' . . . 'got him in so much trouble' . . . 'his arms out each side, like Christ' . . . 'he went backwards' . . . 'I can't forget him smiling' . . . 'still don't understand' . . . 'never forget that smile he had' . . .

'But why?' Kelly had asked, her cancelled wedding a distant memory. 'Why did Owen take his life?'

Gordon blinked at her as if she had slapped him out of his state and he had no idea where he was. 'I didn't say that.'

'You said he was smiling when he jumped.'

'I never said he jumped.'

'So what did happen?'

Gordon had seemed, then, to shake himself from his dream, to backtrack, to unsay what he had said. Kelly pressed him, but he would not discuss it. Nor would he raise the subject, or allow it to be raised, ever again. Their silence became their glue. The intensity of that fixing between them, the sharing of their misery, had hardened into a bond she had thought would last for life. By coming to her that night of her humiliation, by opening up, even if momentarily, and showing her that she was not alone in her pain, Gordon had won her.

'And that's how I fell in love,' Kelly said.

Lou took her hand and squeezed it. 'I get it,' she said.

A triumphant noise broke over the balcony. Dog was yelping happily. Josie was arguing.

'Don't they have homes to go to?' Kelly said with a weak laugh, feeling rocked and shamed but also relieved by Lou's response to what she had said. 'You don't want to be here.'

'Shouldn't I be the judge of that?'

'This place has a darkness,' Kelly said, but Lou's eyes reflected the darkness onto her, and she decided she could go no further. 'It's not going to be good for you.'

'I don't need you to tell me that,' Lou said, and rewarded her with a softening, almost a smile, that felt all the more precious for being so hard-won. 'Let's get rid of that mob.'

As she followed Lou's shoulders up the stairs, Kelly thought: So this is the point of an omigod-daughter.

'Eh,' Kelly said.

Lou stopped, her feet caught on separate steps.

'You're teaching him how to make those Italian dishes, aren't you? Did you get him surfing again?'

'Nah, not me. He's probably having an affair.'

The prodigal stepson

TWO AFTERNOONS LATER, A SATURDAY, BEN WAS WALKING UP the hill from The Lodge to the Bluebird Hilton. His cricket game had finished, and his dad had asked him to come along to visit Grandma Norma in the rehab unit of Capri hospital, where she had been moved from the orthopaedic ward following the operation on the hip she had broken at the country club two weeks earlier. Ben sensed that his dad wanted him as a buffer: Gordon always got on better with Norma when Ben was between them. To sweeten the deal, Gordon had offered Ben the chance to drive the car and get some of his L-plate hours up.

It must have been grandmother day for Ben's dad, because first he'd had to go to the Hilton for a face-to-face with Grandma Leonie. Of the many plates Dad had to keep spinning, Grandma Leonie was the one he couldn't let drop, and worst of all, Dad told Ben, she knew it.

Ben felt sorry for Grandma Leonie. Everyone except his dad seemed to really hate her. During their trip Up North, Dad had confided, 'Your Grandpa Noel deserved some fun in his autumn years, and in my mind there was nothing wrong with the old boy having some on his way out. Don't tell your mother I told you that. But he never got much fun. Leonie once told me that if she put a jelly bean in a jar for each time they made love before their marriage, and took one out for every time after, she would still have got indigestion on beans.' It took Ben a while to figure out what Dad meant. 'But she gave him better than fun,' Gordon went on. 'And better than nursing. She gave him sound financial advice.'

As he walked up the hill, Ben was in a good mood, as his team had won their semi-final, qualifying for the final against Cobcroft Boys' High. Ben had been twelfth man. Luckily, the match had finished before an unseasonal sou'-easter swept in torrents of rain. It had turned into one of those afternoons when Ben's dad snuck out for a surf thinking nobody knew. Dad would be pissed off he had to do his duty to the grandmothers instead. Ben sped up to a jog to reach the Hilton before he got drenched.

In the public bar, early starters clustered around the prime stand-up table beneath the television screen to watch a two-year-old repeat of a pro surfing event in Portugal. As none of them remembered who had won, they placed bets, kidding each other about inside information. Ben exchanged nods with Snake and Tonsure Man.

The stairs smelt of sawdust. The renovation zone seemed empty. He wandered through the stripped, bare-board rooms and entered the prize corner suite. The windows were rattling, but the gun-barrel vista of Bluebird Beach and the sea was going to make Grandma Leonie's renovation a winner.

'Not bad, eh?'

Ben swung around. 'Wait, what?'

There were no shadows in this bright half-painted room, but a man who seemed able to make darkness around him hobbled out from a previously unseen corner, sweeping a flop of grey-bloomed chocolate-coloured hair out of his eyes. He was dressed in shapeless trousers and an XXXL jumper.

'You don't remember me?'

The hand he offered Ben seemed boneless. He wrung it in pain.

'Two broken metacarpals. But you should see the other guy.'

Ben didn't know what to say. This strange man's glassy eyes focused over Ben's shoulder.

'Hey, Gordo.'

'You've always been big on the surprise entrances.' Ben's dad entered the room behind him.

'My presence was requested by your stepmother-in-law,' the strange man said. 'The puppeteer snaps her fingers, we come running.'

'Want to go downstairs?' Ben's dad asked, looking rattled. 'I'll buy you a drink.'

'I'm not allowed.' The man ducked his head and crossed the room to sit on a sawhorse. Gordon perched on the windowsill, negotiating a clear space. Ben felt like a bug that had flown into a spider web in the thickening air between his dad and this man.

'Doctors or publicans?' Gordon asked.

'Both,' the man said with a cough. 'My meds interact with alcohol. Probably bullshit. What they don't realise is that if I was worried about the interaction, I'd just give up the meds. But yeah, I went into the front bar last night and drank lemon squash and still got banned. Or it might have been the enforcement of a pre-existing ban. Ah well. And this is Ben, right? Lucky he got his looks from his mother.'

Ben's dad appeared to have only just noticed him. It was like this man had eaten up Gordon's field of vision.

'Hi, mate. How did your cricket go?'

'Wait, what?'

'How did your cricket match go?'

'We won.'

'You said hello to your uncle Carl?'

'What?'

Gordon shot a worried glance at this Carl man. This Uncle. Ben could see the words spoken by their eyes.

'He only beat you by a minute,' Carl said. 'Not long enough for me to do him any permanent harm.'

Ben had heard about his mum's brother, but he couldn't remember the last time he'd seen Uncle Carl. What stuck in his mind about his uncle was that his mum said you never knew if you were meeting good Carl or bad Carl. In care or out. Dangerous or safe. Ben had heard the old men telling stories about Carl Chidgey. Lots of stories.

'You're looking . . . all right,' Gordon said.

'Appearances are the first victim.'

Gordon smiled. 'I've never known if the shit coming out of your mouth is famous quotes, lines of poetry or your own invention.'

One of Carl's shoulders rose and fell inside his jumper. He let his hair-curtained eyes settle on Ben.

Seeming to want to divert Carl's attention back to himself, Gordon said, 'You still . . . still living in the city?'

'Needed my passport stamped, coming back here. If I had a passport,' Carl added.

'Where did you stay last night?'

Carl smiled privately and nodded at the floor. To Ben, he looked like some putty-nosed, puffy-faced, prematurely aged, mumbling drug casualty. But to his dad, Ben knew, Uncle Carl still carried the glamour of what he had been: the most handsome human alive, the prince in the sawpit. Gordon had spoken mistily of Carl sweeping into parties in a navy greatcoat, Gitanes at his lips, book of Mallarmé in his hand (truly), impossible European model on his arm. 'Carl's charisma somehow protected him from being beaten up as a wanker,' Ben remembered his dad telling him. 'We all invested hope in him. The one lobster who would be allowed to climb out of the pot. Dux of our class, popular, gentle, gorgeous, idolised by girls in three school districts and beyond; what could possibly go wrong?'

To explain the difference between *that* and *this* Carl was, Ben sensed, to hold life in your hands: history, the former self and its shadow, the tightrope an adventurer such as his uncle had had to walk (and fall from); the mysteries of chemistry.

'My mother broke her hip,' Gordon said, ending the silence. 'My dad's in a nursing home and making a pest of himself.'

Ben could see his father being softly intimidated by Uncle Carl. Gordon was sweating and stammering like a nervous kid.

'My sister really fucked you all up, didn't she?' Carl said. 'I should never have let her inflict herself on you.' To Ben, he added, 'Sorry, *mon ami*. Clearly not everything she's done is a failure.'

Gordon raised his hands haplessly. 'She's not the cause of every problem.'

'Did your old man do it? That's what I heard.'

'Do what?'

'It was an accident,' Ben interrupted. If Uncle Carl, the last tendril of the Bluebird grapevine, had 'heard' that Grandpa ran over Grandma Norma on purpose, then this must have been what the community had decided. Ben didn't want his dad brooding on that.

'Leonie also told me you're milking the property market while taking an implacable stance against it,' Carl continued. 'Hypocrisy always played well in this place.'

'Ben, do you want to go downstairs?' Gordon suggested.

'He's old enough to be part of the men's talk,' Carl said. 'Aren't you, *mon ami*?'

'So what are your plans?' Gordon asked, yielding to Carl without a struggle.

Through the corner window, Ben saw a car pull a U-turn in front of the Hilton and park beside the bottle shop. A carnelian red Prius. He saw Grandma Leonie get out. It didn't seem right. Should he tell his dad?

Ben looked at Uncle Carl, who was smiling privately. 'My step-mother has run my life ever since my father stopped running it. What do you think I live on? It's the price for forgiveness. And for this.' He waved a hand to indicate the little of Bluebird they could see through the rain. 'We get to be children all the way.'

'Nobody ever ran your life,' Gordon said.

Ben had heard the legends. When the rest of the Old Bluebird crew came of age and began to catch up with Carl Chidgey— screwing around and screwing up—he disappeared. Gone travelling was the official explanation, though Grandpa Noel had disowned him and Ben's mum could never bring herself to convincingly play the concerned sister. Grandma Gladys was dead from cancer and Carl was dead to Bluebird. Some time Up North, some in the

Northern Territory, some in places unknown, a shocking amount of it in OC. Rumours of a medal from Ocean City Uni. Nobody saw him. Bluebird had cast Carl out. Ben looked at him. He was their broken dream.

Grandma Leonie's high heels tapped out her approach up the stairs. Something in the energy holding Carl together buckled. Ben was shocked to see a placid, amenable, needy smile take possession of his face. The threat slackened. Whether through twelve-step programs or jail or dependence—on pharmaceuticals, on Leonie—it was suddenly obvious that Uncle Carl had been broken, or broken in. Ben hated himself for the momentary wish that Uncle Carl had died, young and romantic, when he had the chance.

Then he wondered if Uncle Carl looked at Dad and wished the same.

A phone trilled. Ben heard Leonie answer it. Her voice faded as she descended the stairs.

Carl shoved his paws under his thighs and hunched over the sawhorse, as if the only way to stop his hands from committing a crime or shaking uncontrollably was to pin them with his full weight. His eyes on the floor, he said, 'She told me you can't keep relying on her goodwill.'

The way Carl said 'goodwill' made Ben dizzy. The red Prius outside. Daniel's father had been working on Grandma Leonie. Or with.

'She told you that?' Gordon croaked.

'She's on the title, Gordo. If you're doing the wrong thing in The Lodge, council can hold up the Hilton approvals. She can't risk you stuffing it up for her.'

Ben went to the window and looked out. Grandma Leonie was leaning into the red Prius.

'If she wants to stop us doing the wrong thing, she only has to ask. She can buy us all out tomorrow if she wants. Kelly'd be stoked.'

But Ben got it before his dad. He saw it all.

'Uh-uh.' Carl shook his head, eyes on the floor. 'She's spent so much keeping you and Kel and Ben together, she doesn't want to move you out. She just wants to avoid her own interests being impeded.'

'How am I getting in the way of her interests?'

'She has to get her name off the title of The Lodge. That way, whatever you're doing won't affect her redevelopment here at the Hilton. She likes you, believe it or not. She even likes your old man, you know? She keeps going on about "family values". Won't shut up about how too many families are falling apart, how badly things turned out for you and Kel, how this was her big chance to help. She talks a lot about Ron, how he shouldn't be left to rot away in that nursing home.'

Oh shit, Gordon's face was saying. Oh shit shit shit shit.

'She's already exchanged the title,' Carl said. 'Settlement happens in six weeks. Family first.'

'She can't.'

But, Ben understood, she already had. She had set loose an electronic rabbit inside Gordon's future; the greyhounds of his objections were racing to catch it, but they never would. The rabbit always won.

Carl joined Ben at the window. Grandma Leonie was getting back into the Prius.

'Looks like she's left it to me to break the news,' Carl said. 'She's not coming up.'

'She can't do this,' Gordon said.

'I think we know she can do anything she wants.'

'If my dad moves in, one of us is going to kill each other.'

Carl started to say something, then stopped. 'Who said anything about your dad?'

Gordon's breath caught in his throat and even in the instant before he turned to Carl, who was now wearing the broadest smile his ravaged face would allow—or it might have been a painful wince—Ben's dad was realising he had jumped to the wrong conclusion.

'Don't be silly, Dad,' Ben said. 'Grandma Leonie hasn't sold to Grandpa.'

Now Uncle Carl was looking at Ben.

'Why did everyone tell me your kid was slow on the uptake, Gordo?'

The man in the ironed shorts

THE ENCOUNTER WITH UNCLE CARL HAD SHAKEN BEN'S DAD. Often, when disturbed like this, Gordon became jittery and talkative. As they drove to Grandpa's nursing home, Gordon told Ben some more about Uncle Carl.

'He came back to Bluebird once before. Briefly.'

Ben tried to focus on the road. It was like his dad was speaking to himself. Ben felt as if he had crossed into a land of myth and legend.

'I became editor of the *News* when I was twenty-eight. You'd never believe it, but your dad was considered something of a success back then. In my "peak".' Gordon laughed grimly. 'Carl called me to apply for a position as a subeditor. Amazing, that Carl would ask something from me. But we had a proper back bench: eight subs, night workers, rebel aristocracy. During the day they were artists, poets, musicians, cartoonists, designers, defiantly independent—though they were all doing drugs, so I guess they weren't as free as they said. You'd have been amazed at the types. They had their secret language of style, brilliance, dexterity, a folded glassine mini envelope. They left me flapping. They disdained us daytime careerists. They arrived late in the day and remade the paper. They were like wizards; they wrote headlines, they rewrote all the stories, they tore strips off reporters for splitting infinitives or leaving modifiers dangling. The paper you read was the subs' paper, not the reporters' and certainly not mine.

'So I gave him the job. What choice did I have? Three years Carl was back here. And then when the advertising collapsed and newspapers had to rationalise or die, or rationalise *then* die, the first to go were the subs. We marched them out with insulting redundancies. Carl was too proud to take the package.'

'What happened then?' Ben hardly dared to speak.

'I hoped he would flourish—the still-employed are always the quickest to see a silver lining for the unemployed. I thought that now he'd been freed from a job, at last Carl could release his genius. Only later did I understand that those years on the subs' desk, his early thirties, were Carl's prime. Mine too.'

'That's not true, Dad.'

'I thought everyone would see me as the villain for sacking the subeditors,' Gordon said, without having heard Ben. 'I braced myself to become public enemy number one. I'd sold my soul to the man, and then retrenched all the brilliant people. But it turned out everyone thought Carl and the subs were a pack of arty wankers. No more over-clever headlines and cartoons! The locals were glad to see the back of them. Hooray for Gordo!'

'See, you were the good guy.'

'I slogged away for another thirteen years subbing the *News* on my own. I was shithouse, excuse the language. No danger of any clever anything. And eventually, when I was on the receiving end of my own termination letter, people were good enough not to remind me that what goes around comes around.'

'But what happened to Carl?'

'We don't really know. Jail, rehab, psych wards. Lot of fights. At least he didn't die. For most of that legendary subs' desk, when they fell out of their jobs, heroin was there to catch them.'

'That's horrible.'

'He's not well, you know? Better a beautiful corpse than what he's turned into.'

'Better for who?' Ben said, feeling guilty for having had the same thought back at the Hilton.

'Good question, Benny, good question.'

They arrived at the nursing home. While Gordon went inside to fetch Grandpa, Ben mulled over his story. It made sense of why his dad always seemed to think he'd let Bluebird down. The old chieftains had built it up, and sons like Gordon and Carl had let it go. Ben, who knew how failure felt, wanted urgently to give his dad a hug and tell him it wasn't his fault, no matter what those mean old men said. Some fathers were hardwired to see their sons as useless, whatever they did. Ben felt grateful that Gordon wasn't that kind of father.

He couldn't wait for his dad to bring Grandpa out. He had to hug his dad now, to save him from the old chieftains. He went inside and caught the lift to Banksia floor, only to find his dad in Grandpa's room with one of those very chieftains. Gordon was looking like he had been shot in the stomach.

Snowy-haired Tony Eastaugh sat with his plastic leg across his knee in Grandpa's comfortable armchair. Mr Eastaugh was a man Ben had always put a mental force field around. To kids in Bluebird, he was this peg-legged creature from the black lagoon.

Ben's mum wouldn't hear the man's name mentioned, for reasons of her own. Ben didn't ask. It was obvious that you didn't go near Mr Eastaugh. Ben's dad couldn't avoid him, due to his friendship with Firie Sam, but whenever his name came up Gordon changed the subject. Grandpa regarded Tony Eastaugh as a drongo, a dickhead, with insinuations of worse. So why was he in Grandpa's room, chuckling over a glass of stout like an old crony?

'What's he doing here?' Ben said by way of greeting his grandfather, who brandished a beer in one hand and a brown envelope in the other, as if choosing between known and unknown quantities of good fortune.

Tony Eastaugh looked Ben up and down from under his reading glasses.

Gordon was holding a beer bottle. At first Ben thought he was drinking too, but Gordon had confiscated it from Grandpa. 'If I can't decide the company you keep, I can save you from destroying your kidneys.'

'See what I mean?' Grandpa addressed Tony, who glared savagely over the top of his glasses at Gordon. 'The minute you do something they haven't controlled, they can't handle it.'

Gordon indicated the envelope. 'What've you got there?'

Grandpa shot a look at his new mate. 'He wants to know what I've got here, Tony.'

Ostentatiously, like it was the jackpot in a game show, Grandpa went to his clothes wardrobe and slid the envelope under his stack of checked shirts, all washed, ironed, folded and delivered by Grandma in the days before her accident. Since then, at a loss over who to order to do his laundry, Grandpa had reverted to wearing the same Wallabies fleece day after day, although, Ben noticed, it was beginning to accumulate an archaeology of food stains.

'Wouldn't he like to know?' Tony growled.

'Okay, have your fun,' Gordon said. 'You ready to go, Dad?'

'Enjoyed your visit with Leonie?' Tony Eastaugh asked with a nasty grin.

'She couldn't make it,' Gordon said.

'She's got him by the short and curlies,' Tony rumbled to Grandpa.

'Beware of foreigners bearing gifts,' Grandpa said with a vindicated air, even though he had never discouraged Gordon from accepting Leonie's share in The Lodge, and in fact had told him to grab it with both hands.

Ben was looking from one old man to the other, still unable to comprehend why these two were sitting together as if they shared a beer every other day.

Tony raised his glass—*you can't take this from me*—and chuckled, pushing his spectacles up over his eyes to show he was done with anyone further away than the length of his arm.

Ben stepped forward. 'Come on, Grandpa, let me get you to the car.'

'Nice boy,' Tony gurgled behind Ben's back.

In the lift, Ben remembered he had meant to give his dad a hug. But he couldn't do it in front of Grandpa.

～

Ben had never seen an old person so keen to get into a hospital. His grandfather, he had to conclude, was a strange individual who became stranger with every passing day.

The first night Grandma had been in the hospital, they couldn't get Grandpa to leave the ward. Due to the pharmacopoeia that she subsisted on, from methotrexate for her rheumatoid arthritis to cortisone for her chronic pain to temazepam for her insomnia, the surgeon had decided that Grandma needed a full flushing-out before he could operate. So Grandma lay in the emergency department suffering not only the pain in her broken hip but full-blown withdrawals. And, to make matters worse, Grandpa stayed by her bedside all night telling stories about 'all my fellow inmates at the nursing home who are sent here to die'.

Even when Grandma had her surgery the next day, Grandpa insisted on waiting for her until she came out of intensive care.

'I don't know if this is a good idea,' said Gordon who, with Ben, had spent the night sleeping in waiting-room chairs. 'She'll be pretty groggy from the anaesthetic.'

'If you're getting tired,' Grandpa said, 'you go home and get some rest, just leave your car here with me.'

'It's okay, we'll stay.'

Ben realised that by threatening to get behind the wheel of a car, Grandpa could make Dad do whatever he wanted. Grandpa was still the boss, more than ever now that he was convinced he was a prisoner.

Over the next fortnight, Gordon had had to bring Grandpa every day, as much to stop him finding his way there himself as to give him and Grandma time together.

As Ben drove now, his dad was chewing the insides of his cheeks in the back seat. Gordon was usually an adequate driving instructor, but he got nervous when Grandpa was also in the car.

'Dad, why were you with Tony?' Gordon asked.

'Your father was a terrible driver at your age,' Grandpa told Ben brightly. 'Hopeless! He failed his test three times before his mother organised paid lessons. The instructor was a defrocked priest. Whisky blossom as red as his beard. He became enraged at

Gordon's driving. He got out and slammed his door so hard that the glass pane dropped through the cavity and shattered. Remember that, Gordon?'

'I just want to know what you were up to with a man you've despised for forty years.'

'Wouldn't you like to know? Change lanes here, son!'

'No, it's a solid white line,' Gordon said.

'Change *here*, I said!'

Confused, Ben obeyed his grandfather.

'How many more hours' driving do you need before you get your license?' Grandpa asked.

'Another sixty-five.'

'At this rate, you'll be an old man before you qualify.' Grandpa looked into the rear-view mirror. 'This must be very inconvenient for you, Gordon. You'd be better off leaving the car with me.'

Gordon gave a weary sigh and didn't ask Grandpa again about Tony Eastaugh.

⌒

The patients in the rehab unit were older than in orthopaedic. Grandma wore her own clothes instead of a hospital gown, which cheered Ben a little. When they arrived, she was primed for a monologue on one of her favourite themes.

'All Chinese,' she broadcast into the hallway. Gordon got up and shut her door. 'The surgeon, the anaesthetist, the emergency doctors, the nurses—and, what you'd never guess, also the physio and the occupational therapist!'

'Mum, you can't say that,' Gordon murmured.

Grandpa was in an armchair beside Norma's bed, reading the Saturday *Herald*.

'Oh, all right.' Norma waved a dismissive hand at her moralising son. 'They're all *Eurasian*. That better?'

'How are you feeling, Gran?'

Gordon had once told Ben he would like him to referee all the arguments in their family. And once he'd done that, fix the Middle East.

'Awful, my love.' Grandma tried to push herself up on her pillows. 'Just awful. Bored out of my brain.'

'Is there anything we can do?' Ben asked.

'Oh, there's so much that needs doing at home.' Norma rattled off a list of insurmountable problems: the cleaner had to be paid, the newspaper delivery had to be reinstated in preparation for her return, a pharmacy bill was falling due in a month, and she needed her diary as well as her iPad. And her fleece, she added, giving Ron's a once-over. 'Didn't I tell you to give your washing to Jada? Have you been wearing that *every* day?'

'Can't trust them,' a voice said from behind the *Herald*. 'This is a valuable souvenir from the year we won the Bledisloe Cup. I let them take it to the laundry, the next thing it'll be for sale in the *Trading Post*.'

'I'll take care of it all,' Gordon said, though Ben knew Grandma would decant her chores one at a time to maximise the time his dad was on call. 'Including his washing.'

Norma burst into tears. 'It's just so awful, the way our lives are turning out!'

While Ben put a cold washer to Grandma's forehead, Ronald remained absorbed in his newspaper.

'You all right there?' Gordon said.

'Fine, thanks. Capri won last night.'

'You want to help at all?'

Ron's paper came down and he studied Norma. 'The boy's indulging her. Her mood is medication-induced,' he added as if Norma weren't there—speaking like a doctor—and resumed reading.

Ben gave Grandma a tissue. She was able to wipe her nose and dab her eyes, but her legs were 'excruciating' and 'the Chinese' were not keeping up her pain medication. To divert her, Ben said, 'I took a classic catch at the game today!'

'I thought you were twelfth man,' Gordon said.

'It was during warm-ups. Mr Stoyle has to pick me in the eleven now.'

'He will, my love, and you'll make a century,' Grandma said. As Ben had guessed, she could be picked up and swept along with any new subject, and her certainty in his dream to reach the top rung of the cricket career ladder, when he hadn't even clawed his way up to the bottom, was one of the things he loved about her.

'I tried to get out of the way, but it came so hard it got stuck in my elbow!' Ben said. 'Dad said I couldn't catch a cold.'

'And you've proved him wrong,' Grandma said. 'Gordon, you should be proud of Ben for telling it the way it happened. Most boys his age are such awful blowhards. I don't think you're slow.' Grandma patted Ben's hand. 'I think you're *pure*.'

'I am proud,' Gordon said to Ben. 'As long as you didn't get hurt.'

'Daaad.' Ben put him on a rack and stretched him out to three syllables.

Gordon had confessed to Ben that he feared cricket balls too. 'I'd feel safer if you were getting whacked around in rugby league. Bigger boys know when to stop hurting you, but a cricket ball doesn't.' Yet Ben wouldn't be turned off, and now that he'd taken his first-ever catch, accident or not, he was fully on the hook.

'Daniel hugged me so hard he pulled me onto the ground,' Ben told Grandma, a cloud coming over his face. 'Then he realised everyone was looking, and he got a bit angry at me.'

'Was Daniel's dad there?' Gordon asked.

'Yeah, but he wasn't watching. He was talking with Mr Stoyle. Mr Stoyle's a good coach,' Ben told Grandma earnestly. 'He played for the state.'

'Well then,' Grandma said, 'I'm sure he recognises your talent.'

'We're in the final,' Ben said in a small voice. 'If he picks me it'll be amazing.'

'We'll be there,' his grandmother said. 'With bells on.'

'And Mum?'

'I don't know, pal,' Gordon said.

'Of course she will!' Grandma blurted, with a significant look at Gordon.

'And Uncle Carl?'

Before Gordon could reply, Norma said, 'Don't tell me that awful piece of work is back hanging around.'

'Must be some financial inducement,' Ron said.

'Is he into cricket?' Ben asked.

'Well,' Norma concluded disapprovingly, 'he is *very* Indian; it came out stronger in him than in Kelly.'

'Anyway!' Grandpa said, folding his *Herald* with a snap. 'You won't need to rely on Gordon to drive you, pet. I am taking leave from the nursing home, and I shall become your primary carer. Don't worry about anything. I can come and go in your car, save these poor boys the trouble.'

'Oh, don't be ridiculous,' Norma snapped. 'You can't even take care of yourself, and I can't look after you. How do you expect to look after me?'

Grandpa waved away her objections. 'I'll do the shopping, I'll drive you to your appointments.'

'You'll do no such thing. You'll go back to the nursing home and Gordon will look after me.'

Grandpa said to Gordon, 'Give me five minutes with your mother.' He issued a little get-lost whistle and flick of his hand.

Gordon took Ben along the corridor to a snack machine. For most of his life, Ben had not been able to hear when his stomach told him it was full, and, like a labrador, he would eat until food was pulled away from him. This too had been a source of family friction. His mum thought he should see a doctor, while his dad thought he had to learn self-control. For all that, his dad took pleasure in the ability to patch over awkward moments by buying him a sneaky chocolate bar.

'Kit Kat?' Gordon scanned the vending machine. 'Fanta?'

'Wait, what?'

Gordon nodded to the machine.

'No, not hungry.'

'You all right?'

Ben picked his nose and stared at the product as if seeking an answer.

'When I came out, do you remember what you said you admired most?'

Gordon nodded. 'Your guts. I said you'd proven yourself to be tougher than the toughest opening batsman. Here.' He opened his arms for Ben to walk into, so he could give—if not quite receive—a hug. He let his eyes fall shut, his mouth in a half-smile.

Ben did not walk into his arms.

'Hundred percent, guts,' Ben said. 'You and Grandpa, you and Dog, you and everyone. Even Uncle Carl. You let them pick on you.'

'What's this all about, Benny?'

Ben fought back tears. 'I always knew that I had an uncle but I'd lost him. Mum sort of dropped hints, Sam mentions him every so often, but you never talk about him. Now he turns up today and you tell me you didn't really lose him, he just went away. You never did anything wrong, but you walk around like it's all your fault. Where's *your* guts, Dad?'

Ben sought eye contact, but Gordon stared into the vending machine, a cold look on his face. Ben felt unbalanced.

'Let's go back.' A crack ran through Gordon's voice. 'And if I were you, I wouldn't say anything about uncles to your grandparents.'

As Ben watched his father walk down the corridor, he felt he had made an enormous mistake. He had injured him in some unthinkable, unknown way, and Dad was not going to give him any chance to figure out what he had done.

⁓

When they got back to the room, Grandpa was making his way to his armchair after poking his nose into Grandma's medical notes, and she was shouting at him about using his walker.

'So he's told you Carl's moving in with us?' Gordon asked Norma.

'I can't see how he's going to fit. What on earth is that awful— that awful—*Leonie*—up to?'

'Leonie believes in family,' Grandpa said. 'It's one of their traditional values.'

Misinterpreting Ben's querying look, Grandpa added: 'I would love to go for an outback road trip. Do you like camping, fella?'

Ben asked his grandmother if she wanted water. She nodded, and Ben evaded the situation by ducking out to the nurses' station.

'I'd love to see Chester Dam one last time,' Grandpa was saying to Gordon when Ben came back. 'You wouldn't deny that to your old man, would you? While your mother isn't using the car?'

'Oh Lord,' Norma gasped. 'You think my hip is the best thing that's happened to you, don't you? Your big chance!'

Ben still refused to believe that Grandpa had run Grandma over on purpose, but he couldn't unhear the rumours. He studied his grandfather for a hint, but Grandpa was reading his newspaper. He couldn't be that crazy, Ben thought. Just crazy enough to take off in the golf cart, but not so crazy as to *aim* at Grandma. In-between crazy. Not a complete maniac. Surely. Still.

'Dad, you can't drive,' Gordon said and looked at Ben as if to ask, Stopping my father from driving: what is that if not gutsy?

'Have you forgotten how awful those trips to Chester Dam were, you silly man?' Grandma said. To Ben, she continued: 'The great engineering sites of New South Wales! Don't look at me like that, Ronald; those trips brought out the worst in you.'

'The best,' Grandpa countered. 'Nothing made me happier than planning and logistics.'

'You mean your intolerance for anyone not doing things precisely as you wished! He turned those trips into a misery. Once'—she turned her face to Ben—'he stormed out on us in the middle of the night. He drove three hours in the direction of home before he became ashamed of himself and turned around to come back and pick us up.'

'And regret it to this day,' Grandpa said. 'No offence.'

'None taken,' Gordon murmured.

'The coming back,' Grandpa clarified, 'not the storming out.'

'Still none taken,' Gordon replied.

'He was hopeless, absolutely hopeless,' Grandma went on. 'The disappointment wasn't his tantrums. We expected those, didn't we, Gordon? It was that for all his engineering principles and his military control, he couldn't even erect a tent or set a campfire! Don't deny it! It's true, isn't it, Gordon? I ended up having to do it all. Absolutely hopeless!'

'What about the rug-muncher?' Ron said. 'Will she take an old man for his last great adventure?'

'You mean Lou,' Gordon said.

'She like camping?'

'Ronald, please!'

'She looks like she does. A mannish thing like that.'

Norma paused from sucking on the ice cube that Ben had brought her, spat it into her paper cup and said, 'She'll never find a man, the way she dresses.'

'She doesn't want to find a man,' Ron snapped.

'Of course, that's what I meant,' Norma said, the pair of them finding common ground. 'Can't you do something for her?' she asked Gordon.

'I think she's getting by quite fine without my advice.'

'I don't care if she's pink, purple or albino,' Ron said. 'I want to know if she'll come to Chester Dam.'

'Okay,' Gordon said. 'It might be time for us to leave.'

'I need to use the facilities.' Ron wobbled to his feet. 'My final camping trip and no-one will come with me. This might be the last chance. You never know with kidney failure.'

'Oh Lord, what can we do?' Grandma said the moment Grandpa had shut himself into the bathroom. In a small voice she said, 'You don't think I'm bad for not taking him home?'

Without waiting for a reply, she answered: 'I just can't look after him! I can't even look after myself!'

A squall of tears came and went. Ben gave her another ice cube.

'Thank you, my darling.' She looked at Gordon as if noticing him for the first time. 'And you: what hope do you and Kelly have if that awful Carl moves in? Oh, that Leonie, I could wring her neck!'

'Kelly's not going to cop it,' Gordon said. 'She'll be working on a plan.'

'I hope it involves all three of you.'

'She can make her own decisions, Mum.'

Norma's eyebrows congregated in thought.

'I never liked the idea of you marrying into the Chidgeys,' she said. 'But now I find I want nothing more than the two of you to be back together.'

Ben watched his father's face for the effect of this comment. But Gordon was tapping his watch as if to check why it wasn't moving faster.

'And what are you going to do about money?' Norma demanded.

Ben's grandparents had never let go of the belief that Gordon's finances were their concern. They always wanted to know how he was paying his bills. No reassurances could stop them. They never offered to help. They just wanted to know. Ben felt a rush of unhappiness flare across his chest.

'I'll work something out,' Gordon said.

'No, you won't!' Norma declared. 'You have no hope! No wonder Kelly won't come back to you!'

'Shall I check on Grandpa?' Ben asked, reminding them that this was a conversation he shouldn't have to hear.

'Grab your grandmother another cold washer, would you, my love?'

'I'll do it.' Gordon got up and listened at the bathroom door. Silence.

'If he's waiting for me to clean him up, tell him he'll be waiting a long time!' Norma said.

'Dad?'

No answer. Gordon cracked the door.

'Dad? Oh bugger.'

Gordon turned to Ben.

'Mate, you stay with Gran. He's done a runner.'

︶

A runner was a relative term for Ronald Grimes. Gordon found him in the lobby being helped into a wheelchair by a staff member who said he had fallen while making for the exit.

'He's okay?' Gordon said.

'Don't be stupid,' Ron interjected. 'I'm like a cat, I always fall on my feet. It's one of my many gifts.'

Gordon wheeled him back towards Norma's room.

'So have you contacted the JPA?'

If Ron had a question for Gordon, it tended not to be because he wanted an answer, but to somehow assert his autonomy. A few years back, when Ron had 'got right into the internet' and harboured dreams of becoming a late-life local government lobbyist and pamphleteer, he had asked Gordon, who as a newspaper editor might have had some expertise, for advice on desktop publishing units. Gordon, quietly chuffed at being asked—for advice! By his father!—did two days of research before preparing a tailored solution: Apple Macintosh computer, QuarkXpress WYSIWYG software, ImageWriter printer. And Xerox paper. So Ron went out and bought an IBM computer, Publishing Partner software and a second-hand HP printer. He'd got a deal. When Gordon mumbled about having wasted his time on research, Ron said, 'I did take your advice. I got Xerox paper.'

'Why are we going back?' Ron asked now, his eyes on the exit. 'Hospitals depress me. Too many old people.'

'You were desperate to visit Mum, remember?'

Ron checked his watch. 'I want to go!'

'You've just made that clear,' Gordon said. 'But I need to fetch Ben, and maybe it would be nice if you said goodbye to Mum.'

'I have to go back so she can keep bullying me?'

Gordon was so startled by this that he lost the strength to keep pushing the wheelchair.

'*Mum* bullies *you*?'

'You've got no idea. You're her son.'

'I'm your son too.' Gordon got him moving again.

'You were always on her side. You were never any good on camping trips; it was your brother who took after me.'

Gordon pushed the chair faster. The sooner they could get this finished, the sooner he could breathe.

'That's why I want that rug-muncher of yours. I can see her putting up a tent. Does she like engineering projects?'

'Lou has enough going on.'

'Chasing little girls around the beach, no doubt. It never stops. Just when they get on top of the dirty old men, it's the lezzos, hiding in broad daylight.'

Gordon wheeled his father silently back to the room. When Norma saw Ron in the wheelchair, her face fell.

'Oh no, what's he done?'

'He's fine, just had a stumble,' Gordon said.

'You silly man!'

'I want to leave,' Ron said.

'You can't drive!' Norma said.

'Who says I want to drive?' Ron replied with a look of pure innocence. 'It's fifteen minutes until dinner. It's your son who's making me late.'

Norma looked reprovingly at Gordon. 'Why won't you take the poor man to his dinner? There's nothing of him.'

Gordon told his mother he would settle her bills, fetch her things, pay the cleaner and do Ron's laundry.

'The cleaners need cash, and I don't know where they live!' she cried in a panic.

'That's all right, I'll pay them next time they come.'

'They need to be paid! I can't let them—'

'Mum, I'll take care of it.'

'Why do you always talk over the top of me?'

'That's right,' Ron said. 'Thinks he's so smart, always talking over the top of you.'

'Please,' Gordon said.

'Oh, you think you know it all,' Norma moaned. 'I'll end up having to pay them myself.'

'He's hopeless,' Ron said. 'I kept telling you we got the wrong one back, and you always treated it as if I was making a joke.'

'Okay, let's go, Dad. Come on, Benny. See you later, Mum.' Gordon bent over his mother to kiss her forehead. She turned her face away. When Ron came to kiss her, she offered him her tear-smudged cheek. They cuddled for a moment, burbling sweet nothings, urging each other to stay well. They shed tears: Norma predictably, Ron outrageously.

'There, see?' Ron said to Ben as Gordon wheeled him out. 'Your father has some use after all. He's the one problem your grandmother and I agree on.'

Ronald Grimes made it back in time for dinner. He shucked off Gordon and Ben without a thank you and tucked into his low-fat creamed potatoes with French beans and hard-boiled eggs. He would miss the cooking here; in his opinion it was a big improvement on Norma's.

At the next table sat Neville Coyte, a buffer in blue blazer and club tie. Every single bloody meal. Above the table, Neville looked every bit the bowling club president and law firm partner Ron had kept at a safe distance for donkey's years. Below the table, Ron knew, Neville was clad in stained pyjama pants and nappy. Poor old bugger. Eyes up!

The biggest headache about the nursing home residents, he'd found, was that you knew too many of them. For some reason his power of attaching faces to names was improving as the rest of him went down the crapper. But because they were familiar, he could also recall why he had never had anything to do with them. There was a woman from next door he couldn't stand. There was a man he'd had a nodding feud with over a long-ago parking dispute. What he remembered with the greatest clarity was his lack of interest in their lives. Not before, even less at this late date.

Neville Coyte was, at least, a gentleman. Ron had retained him for a transaction once. No complaints about Neville, provided you didn't mind closet poofters. And best of all, a heavy stroke had silenced him, so Ron didn't have to put up with complaints, reminiscences or aimless observations. Neville just sat there, his rheumy eyes expressing a placid despondency that Ron found agreeable.

'Do you like camping, Neville?'

Ron scooped up a mouthful of creamed potato. Even better if they'd allow him a sprinkle of salt.

'I'm planning a trip to Chester Dam. My wife would turn it into a journey to hell. Gordon is absolutely hopeless at everything he turns his hand to. They wrecked all my camping trips.'

Neville Coyte's eyes appeared to be welling with sympathetic tears.

'There's a grandchild, but he's no good either. I'm thinking about trying this big strong broth of a girl, useful around a camp-site. And a lesbian, so I wouldn't have to worry about her having a crack at me, and Norma getting jealous. What do you think? You ever have anything to do with poofters of the fairer sex?'

Neville was dabbing a monogrammed handkerchief at his eyes.

'I know, Nev: you can't rely on anyone. Not even to stay alive. It's just you and me from here on in. Good day to you.'

Ron shuffled back to his room, where he would sit for the evening in front of the ABC. He liked to fall asleep to *Letters and Numbers*. That girl who wrote up the answers kept him going. Her and this trip to Chester. He'd get the car, he'd find a travelling companion, he'd drive to the camping store for a primus stove, and then off into the blue yonder. It sounded like a plan.

Yet he couldn't drift off. Something was buzzing around his head like a blowfly trapped between panes. He shuffled to his single wardrobe, bent down to the drawer that was filled with a short-sleeved, collared, checked cotton shirt for every occasion—red check on navy, navy check on white, white check on grey, grey check on tan, tan check on red—and slid out his secret.

He shut his bedroom door. He was safe: Norma was in hospital, and Gordon wasn't coming back. Anyone else didn't matter. The staff, Chogies from India or wherever, he didn't count as sentient beings. They couldn't be, to do the things they had to do for those old people.

The brown envelope opened like an enchanted castle.

Norma had been at him for months to make his room 'homey': another tactic to make herself feel better about dumping him. Put up photos, stack your books, bring in your stamp albums, anything to distract you from her perfidy. But Ron wanted the very barrenness of his prison cell to make a point to visitors. Nobody should form the impression that Ronald E. Grimes JP accepted his fate!

He'd got Tony Eastaugh to visit him. When Ron snapped his fingers, that old crook knew to come running. Sometimes the deeds you had done and the debts you were owed still counted. Tony had forgotten much else, but he knew not to cross Ronald E. Grimes JP. Ron had known Tony would have the photo. He just had to play nice for that old pervert, sweet-talk him into finding it. Tony'd gone into his album collection and pulled out the photo first go. Of course he did. Never know your luck when you stick your hand into a dark place. Eh, Tony?

Chester, said the caption, and the exact date. Why had these men recorded meaningless events so assiduously? Ron couldn't imagine why any of them had ever thought these memories would one day assume any importance. Like Tony, like all of them, his entire life had been an exercise in sorting, separating and categorising rubbish that would all be thrown in one big pile into the one incinerator. The world had gone mad—nobody valued anything anymore except dirt and land, dirty land.

What an idiot, Ron thought as his eye settled on his son in the photograph. Good job Ronald Grimes was not a quitter. The one job he'd been dying to walk out on was as a family man. But he'd stuck at it. *Chester.* Did he really want to go back there? What if the place reminded him of things he'd rather forget? He'd have no choice but to live through them again.

Gordon—it wasn't the disappointment; it was the loneliness. A son should be the one person in the world you could talk to. No, he'd never got over it. He and that boy were lonely. Bugger this life. The only person who really grasped the truth was himself. Pity he wasn't better company.

Such thoughts acted like a warm bath on his mood. He gazed down on the photo. How he loved those hydroelectric dams. They were the only reason for going on holidays: the wonder of engineering. Marvellous. A reason to live: the ingenuity of mankind in the cosmic void. There was him standing proudly by the dam, as if he was the owner. A crease ironed into his shorts.

Hang on. That wasn't him. Oh bugger, of course, this was '79. That's right. That bleak sad season. The mourning after.

He had a solution. A fix for his problems and the boy's. He could be Ronald E. Grimes JP again, man of influence. He would have their respect. He would pull them all out of the fire. They would need him again.

He just had to keep it in his head.

He let his eyes fall on the photo. It was the first year after they lost the boy. They'd taken the holiday with some other families, as a cushion against themselves. He and Norma and Gordon wouldn't have to be alone. The Eastaughs and their boy. The town clerk. Their little circle of Bluebird, holding him and Norma tight.

You wouldn't want to be out at Chester Dam and find yourself alone.

Who had taken the photo? The irony was, it must have been himself, with Tony's camera. Recording and labelling, their life's work.

Norma, Tony and his wife, the boys, and the town clerk. The stone wall of Chester Dam resplendent in the background. The ghost boy in their frowning faces.

Ron wouldn't be seen dead in shorts with an ironed crease.

The country club

THREE WEEKS LATER, WAITING FOR HER MOTHER-IN-LAW BY the rose garden of the Bluebird Country Club, Kelly Chidgey Grimes wondered how she had lived so long without golf. She limbered up with her rescue club, feeling the eyes of a passing herd of gentlemen members. It didn't matter that most of them predated the Cretaceous. Today was a glorious Ocean City late-year Thursday. Social golf day. On weekends, when the younger predators were on the course, she drew a higher quality of eyeball with her pleated tartan mini and pink sleeveless top. Golf fashion for men was a contradiction in terms, but one of her incredible recent discoveries was that golf clothes could make women look hotter. It didn't hurt that the standard of competition was not the highest.

Kelly's competitive urges had been bottled up for too long. She played golf to win, she manipulated her handicap to give herself the best chance of success—she was a serial 'burglar' off a twenty-eight mark—and damn it, if women golfers weren't so boring and would take her hints for a little flutter, she could monetise the thing. Men, who would gamble over each shot let alone each hole, were more fun.

She revelled in the irony of splitting with her husband in mid-life to take up golf. Like any club, Bluebird was full of male members who, having acquitted their obligation to provide for their children, faced the deep existential crisis of western civilisation: my wife or my golf clubs? On the other hand, a wife who left her husband and threw herself into golf: that got their attention.

'Yoo-hoo!'

A hand waved in the corner of her vision. An involuntary groan escaped her. She looked around to see if any of the members copping an indiscreet eyeful of her tanned calves had heard her. She slipped her rescue into her bag and strode purposefully to the car park, where her soon-to-be ex-husband mooched beside his mother, who was folding herself into a motorised cart.

'You can't come any further!' Kelly hissed. 'Look at you!'

'What's the problem?' Gordon said. 'This is my best T-shirt.'

He was wearing Stranglers merch—he'd taken Ben to the concert, for God's sake, a skinful of legalised misogyny—untucked over paint-spattered jeans and Blundstones. If he wanted to give the club an up-yours and show what a slob he was, she wasn't going to gratify him by listing the clothing regulations he was breaking.

'I've told him to make himself scarce,' Norma said. 'Go on, shoo!'

Gordon bowed mock-ceremoniously and dragged his feet back to his car.

'We tried,' Norma said.

Kelly wondered if Norma was reflecting on the end of the marriage, Gordon's dress sense, or her inability to get him interested in golf. Or just Gordon in general.

'He used to come and caddy for Ron, but that was as much as he could take,' Norma explained. 'I think he was scared of the way Ron carried on. He nearly burst a foofer valve. Gordon never forgot seeing his father in that state. You should have seen his swing; it was like an octopus falling out of a tree. Every now and then he would hit a ball miles down the centre of the fairway, and that convinced him his swing was fine. You couldn't tell him that the straight hits were the flukes and the wild ones were the entirely predictable outcome of that swing. Oh, that poor man was not built for golf, but he couldn't give it up. Now. Jump in?'

Kelly tried to stay relaxed while listening to Norma's monologue. Norma, once talking, was hard to stop. It was going to be an enjoyable social round (Kelly's determination speaking), but a long one (reality). Norma drove them around the front of the clubhouse to the first tee. Kelly ducked into the pro shop to have a little chat with Ricky, one of the assistant professionals who had been giving her some late-afternoon swing lessons.

'Good to see Norma back on the horse,' Ricky said with a double-entendre grin that Kelly couldn't quite decipher. She got the flirty undertone, she just didn't get what it had to do with Norma.

'She's only just out of hospital,' Kelly said. 'She's not able to play yet.'

'It was the talk of the club,' Ricky said. That grin again. 'Good that she's fixed—more than I can say for the old cart. It was a write-off.'

'Thank you, Ricky, I'll see you later.'

'Can't wait.'

The only reason Kelly hadn't asked Ricky to meet for a drink at the Hilton was that she still had enough remnant self-respect not to fulfil every cliché of the divorced woman. Not an assistant golf pro, surely. Instead, she dated twenty-two-year-old surfers off Tinder. But Ricky was cute.

Kelly's drive off the first tee sailed long and true. Whether the whistles from God's waiting room were in praise of her shot or her tartan skirt was immaterial. She curtseyed to the men hovering about like cows at milking time, jumped into the cart beside Norma, and they sped off. She imagined rheumy eyes lingering nostalgically.

'I know I've said it before, but thank you so much for all this,' Kelly said. 'It's such a special place. It's kept me sane.'

'Soon I'll be on the course again,' Norma said. 'I have an appointment with Dr Kim on Friday. He's Korean. He was telling me he's a member at Royal Ocean City, which was quite an eye-opener. I didn't know they let them in.'

'Orthopaedic surgeons?'

'Stop it, you know what I mean.' Did it make Norma less racist to utter these comments while not caring about, or even seeing, Kelly's own colour? Long ago, way back at her wedding, Kelly had heard Norma blow her top at one of her friends in 'defence' of Kelly. 'She's not Indian!' Norma had cried indignantly. 'She's Anglo-Indian!' Kelly and Gordon had shared the joke for years. Where did you even start?

While Norma spun a lazy Susan of conversation through her favourite subjects—her time in the hospital, doctors and medicine, Asians, golf clubs, Ron—Kelly let her mind drift. If she could switch off, she'd enjoy the afternoon. Norma would not be able to play for months, and Kelly wondered if it was cruel to invite her to the club, like forcing a dog to sit at the window to watch people eat, but Norma had accepted with a Uriah Heepish gratitude that anyone would invite her out for anything.

So they were grateful to each other, Norma for the day out and Kelly for—her divorce dividend! Of course, it wasn't intended that way. Norma's offer had been a standing one for twenty years. This club was the centre of her social life, and she couldn't understand why the next generation wouldn't embrace it. Gordon had flat-out refused. In Gordon's view, the country club was populated by the 'worst of the worst', Bluebird's 'petty bourgeois ruling class', a protected zone for retrograde values. He'd rather die than join, which was saying quite something given the people he hung around with. Until recently, Kelly had been indifferent. Her father had been captain of the club, but her mother was a golf widow and Kelly grew up resenting the game. She fell in behind Gordon's more principled ideological opposition—he also deplored the misuse of water and other scarce environmental assets to maintain a golf course—until, in a moment of perverse adventurism after their marriage unravelled, Kelly had gone to Norma and said yes, she would take up her offer if it was still open. For Norma's part, disapproval of Kelly was overridden by the all-cleansing properties of golf. Golf was good. Golf might redeem even Kelly. Golf might turn her into a white woman. As Norma paid for Kelly's enrolment, subscription, tuition and swift development from beginner to competitive bronze-grader, Kelly had felt her mother-in-law soften. Whatever else Norma thought of her, Kelly was now a golfer, which endowed her with a respectability that could somehow be squared with the rumours that she was screwing half the town.

Kelly hit her second shot into a bunker but got into the hole in five. Her mother-in-law massaged her hip while wearing a tragic face. As she steered through a culvert to the second tee, Norma said, 'You're not in a very chatty mood.' Norma, who left little room for dialogue, sometimes remembered there was another person present.

'I was thinking about Gordon,' Kelly said. 'We could have enjoyed this together, shared a hobby. Aside from Ben, we had no interests in common.'

'Ron and I travelled widely to play golf. Scotland, America, South Africa, Hawaii. Some beautiful courses. Even in Asia.'

'I'd like to travel. But it's so expensive.'

'You'll have to find someone to go with; golf travel is too sad for singles.'

Kelly bit her tongue. If she wasn't careful, Norma might offer herself.

'Ron and I were so lucky,' Norma continued. Kelly didn't feel that Norma had been all that lucky. Being shouted at by an angry engineer to go find his balls? Not to mention the other. But Kelly had to keep impersonating the daughter-in-law Norma wanted, so she replied, with a damp smile, 'Yes, you were.'

She hit another nice straight shot off the second tee. Norma was lost in reveries about what a good husband Ron was, an exercise in rewriting history that became more comprehensive the more Ron's health deteriorated. The doctors estimated that the old man only had a few months. His kidney function was down to one or two percent. Miraculously, his rage to get out of the nursing home to drive his car to Chester Dam was intensifying. Meanwhile, Norma, who had seemed destined for an activity-filled last phase of life once she reached the safety of widowhood, had become unexpectedly gloomy after breaking her hip. She had recently confided in Kelly that she lay in bed some nights thinking she was about to die. 'I just feel so flat, there's nothing left in me.'

Kelly had nearly burst into tears. So flat, nothing left. God, the poor woman was living the last two years of Kelly's marriage.

'Your father was a wonderful golfer,' Norma went on. 'I don't suppose your stepmother had much interest.'

No, Norma would be fine. She was just waiting for Ron's demise to clear her diary. And good luck to her.

'Leonie didn't mind him being out of her way,' Kelly said. 'She was busy reorganising his business affairs.'

'It's funny how things turn out. You know, Ron and I never thought that much of you, but I'm a mother and I can't bear seeing what that horrible *Leonie*'s done to you people. It's all about the money with them.'

Kelly scuffed her second shot into the creek crossing the fairway, then took a penalty stroke and scuffed her next into the creek too. There goes a good score, she thought. Her mind was addled by what Norma had just said. Or not addled, because it was predictable that Norma associated a younger second wife with money-grubbing, but disordered because Kelly couldn't quite work out how to weave that subject into the request she had for Norma.

'Yes, it's a funny little place,' Norma was saying. 'You think you live in a big city, but really our lives have nothing to do with Ocean City, do they? Here's you and me, playing golf together, and there's my son and your stepmother, plotting over real estate. Funny little village.'

'I don't think Gordon is plotting.' Ever since she had known the Grimes, Kelly had felt bound to defend Gordon against his own parents.

'They're always plotting,' Norma said, leaving it ambiguous whether 'they' were Gordon and Leonie, or Leonie and her fellow foreigners.

Kelly picked up her ball without finishing the second hole, and promptly drove her third tee shot out of bounds.

'You've completely lost your swing!' Norma cried. 'And once you lose it, it's impossible to get back.'

'We might stop after nine.'

'Absolutely not! Let's just enjoy this special place. I'm going to miss it if I can't get back to playing.'

'I'm sure you'll play again.'

Condemned to four hours' hard labour, without the prospect of a good score to compensate, Kelly checked her phone messages. Nothing. They were due to finish at six. Four would be better, giving her time to prepare for her Tinder date with the barista from Caffe Emporio (the other fun fact about divorce was that it had turned her into a bloke; an extremely busy, lecherous, youth-obsessed bloke). But if there wasn't too much traffic on the course, they might get eighteen holes in by five-thirty. She just had to execute her mission without murdering the old duck.

In line with the illogic of golf, once Kelly gave up on her round, she began to play well. The day really was spectacular, she had a wild night planned, and Norma's voice had become white noise, eaten up by the cicadas and the breeze.

'Well, as long as you're happy with who you are,' Norma said on the fifth hole, apropos nothing.

'Sorry?'

'Marriage is like golf. Most of the time it's an enormous disap-pointment. It brings you to tears of frustration. It's not good for your health, it drives you out of your mind, and you spend most of your time wanting to give it up. It's hell on earth, really.'

'But?'

Kelly waited, but Norma had sunk into a brown study, contemplating the disappointment, the tears, the madness and the hell on earth. Why was she now re-revising the history she had already revised? Kelly realised they were at the same curve of the path, below the tee box, where Ron had run Norma over.

'And?' Kelly said.

Norma, looking at the stone wall on which she had hit her head, blinked back tears.

'And . . . but?' Kelly repeated. 'You had such a good marriage!' Wasn't that what Norma was saying a few holes ago, or had her happiness gone the way of a golf swing, here one minute gone the next, impossible to get back unless you gave up on it?

'You've paid your fees, so you might as well stick at it, and if you walk off the course in the middle of a round you will get a reputation,' Norma said, her facial expression suggesting she was as surprised as Kelly by the extended metaphor that had just issued from her mouth.

By the seventeenth tee, Kelly was marvelling at having held herself together so well as the dutiful daughter-in-law for three hours, while still doubting she could hang in for another two holes. But she had to. Just as Leonie had Gordon locked into The Lodge, Norma had Kelly locked into gratitude. She and Gordon shared this in common, still: they were in too deep to get out. The tyranny of the older generation! Kelly might have to be polite to Norma for another ten years. Fifteen! Was she mad? Had she finally gone stark raving mad?

'Fuck,' Kelly said.

'I beg your pardon?'

'No, it's all right.'

239

'You know, if anyone hears that language, you'll be out of here quicker than Jack Spratt.'

'Was he a member?'

As Norma muttered to herself, Kelly's eyes returned to what had caused her expletive. She had hustled through the round so quickly, they had come up the back of a foursome, among whom, she noted from his bright red polo-shirted gut overhanging his Bermuda shorts, was the so-called love of her life. Worse still, he was playing with his wife. Kelly noted that when Dog was at the beach, he sucked that gut in like he was Charles Atlas, but when he was with Sally, he literally let himself go. Would he have been better at fifty if he'd hung around another five minutes and married Kelly at twenty? Or was it marriage that did this to him?

'What are you waiting for?' Norma asked. 'You've been like a cat on a hot tin roof all day and you don't want to hit now?'

'Just washing my ball, Norma.'

'I've got to get on—I have plans, you know.'

'Me too, but we're going to hit up onto them.'

'Oh, never mind them, they'll let you play through.'

'Just a minute, I need to clean my clubs.'

Deliberately, Kelly put each of her irons through the abrasive scrubber beside the tee box. How long could she stall? She didn't want to look at the foursome in case Dog was waving her through. If she had to talk to them, she might throw up.

And she had to have the conversation she had brought Norma here for, the conversation she had been twisting and turning all day to avoid.

'It's been a lovely afternoon, hasn't it?' Kelly sat in the cart.

'What are you doing? If you don't get ready on the tee, they'll never call us through.'

'I have a question for you.'

'Oh Lord. If it's about your "single life", honestly, dear, I've got no time for that.'

For a moment, Kelly considered telling Norma about the twenty-two-year-old baristas and twenty-one-year-old surfers with their milf fetishes. There really was a lid for every saucepan. If these young boys liked fifty-year-old women so much, there must be others who were into seventy-seven-year-olds. Gilf fetishists? There was everything else. Maybe it was something Norma could bear in mind as she dealt with the lonely nights post-Ron.

'What are we going to do, Norma?'

'I think you should just hit, they'll see you. They're so slow! I might have to report them to the club.'

'About what Leonie's doing.'

This was the moment, Kelly thought with a skip of her heart. Norma would either shut her down or let her in.

Norma was staring ahead at the green. Her lips were agitating.

'How long is it now?' Norma said. 'Till things start moving?'

Kelly guessed, from the catch in Norma's voice, that she wasn't talking about the foursome. She forged ahead. 'It's three weeks to Leonie's settlement with Carl.'

'He was always a ne'er-do-well. And I've noticed your brother and Ben are beginning to spend an unhealthy amount of time together. He let Ben drive his car to visit Ron the other day.'

'That concerns me,' Kelly said. Since Carl's reappearance, he and Ben had struck up a furtive rapport, which had accelerated when Gordon had asked Carl to pick up Ben from school some afternoons. There were slabs of after-school time when, through pure inattention, Kelly and Gordon could not account for Ben's whereabouts. For all they knew, he was with Carl right this minute.

To steer Norma away from the subject of her maternal inadequacies, Kelly said, 'It's not just the danger of what happens when Carl moves in. You know that if Gordon stays in The Lodge, the way things are going, he will be homeless within six months. He's eating the house.'

'Eating the what?'

'Drawing down against his equity. He thinks nobody knows, but most of Bluebird is doing it. They're all using their increased home values as a piggy bank. Which is okay for them, because when they run out of the capacity to borrow, they'll sell up. And they have cash flow of some sort. But Gordon's got no income to pay it back, and he's not allowed to sell, so he'll get into negative equity soon, if he's not already, and he'll be stuffed. Bankrupt. Leonie will be finished with the redevelopment then, and she'll be able to buy Gordon out for one dollar. The share will have been revalued upwards—there's no other way Gordon could have kept borrowing—so Leonie will have made all that profit for free. That was her plan all along,' Kelly said, as if she had known from the start, when in fact she had only just worked it out as she was saying it. Leonie had seen how Gordon's weakness for The Lodge could work in her favour. It was a masterly scheme. Leonie might have enjoyed using Gordon's ownership to fuck with Kelly, but only up to the point where it served her financial interests. And then she would pounce.

'Oh dear, Ron was right,' Norma said.

'Ron knows?'

'He always said the boy was an idi— . . . was easily led. But can't Gordon just get a job?'

Kelly gazed at Norma over the rim of her sunglasses.

'All right, all right,' Norma said.

'Once Leonie's finished with him, Gordon will have nothing. Where will that leave Ben? With Carl?' Kelly pressed on. 'My brother has more problems than you can poke a stick at. Do you want Ben living in those circumstances?'

'Well, he'll always have his mother. That's all a boy needs.'

Kelly swallowed rapidly, unsure if she was more shocked by Norma's disloyalty to Gordon as a father or saddened by Norma's love for Gordon as a son.

'I—I don't want to sound selfish, Norma, but you know what it will be like. I have no other way of saying this. I don't think I can hold out any longer. Ben ought to be with Gordon in The Lodge, where they're both happy. As for me, I—'

'Take it from me, there's a point in a woman's life when she's had a skinful of standing aside and quietly letting things happen without speaking up,' Norma said distantly.

Kelly swallowed back her surprise. Her mother-in-law never stopped speaking up. Had Norma ever done anything in her life quietly? And yet this was the truth, wasn't it? Was Norma's incessant talking her disguise for a life of *quietly letting things happen*? This was what she seemed to be saying. Kelly was paralysed, for a moment, by Norma's self-awareness.

'So yes,' Norma said. Kelly caught but ignored the flash of gold in the corner of Norma's brown eyes, the hint of the fox within. 'What *are* we going to do?'

Kelly felt such a blush of solidarity at that 'we', she had to force herself not to hug the woman. Norma would hate that. To feel a positive emotion was forgivable, but to demonstrate it at the country club was beyond the pale. Kelly took a deep breath and imagined herself stepping into an icy sea.

'May I ask you something? You're the only person I can ask. It's not for Gordon or me, it's for Ben. He needs a safe place to live. You and I want the same things. For Ben.' Kelly hated herself, just a little. 'I wonder if you have considered taking an interest in The Lodge.'

A new expression was coming over Norma's face: hard to read, but . . . fierce.

'Have you spoken to Ron?' she said.

'Ron?'

'For all our lives, Ron has looked after the finances. Women of your generation sneer at us, but I *liked* it that way. I felt *safe*. I know that makes me a traitor to our kind and all that, but you have to understand, this was the way we were brought up and we were happy with our roles.'

'Of course, but as you said, maybe it's time to stop letting things happen.'

'Without speaking up,' Norma said.

'Without speaking up,' Kelly repeated uncertainly. 'You don't need Ron's approval for financial decisions now. You have an enduring power of attorney. You pay his nursing home bills. You hold the purse strings.'

'Do you think I'm bad?' Norma said suddenly. She was wiping her nose with a tissue.

'Bad?'

'For not having him at home?'

'Why would anyone think that?'

Kelly's mouth turned dry with panic. Just when she thought she had her mother-in-law on track, Norma flew off on a tangent about Ron, how he was safe in the nursing home, how the Pakis were good people underneath it all, how they loved him in spite of the way he treated them, how he would live longer if only he stayed where he was and stopped bothering her about driving.

Kelly didn't know how to answer. No—she knew how to answer. She only had to reassure Norma, tell her that everything she had done was right. But she had to think strategically.

'By everything you've done, you have saved that man's life,' Kelly said with great solemnity.

'He hasn't been well with his kidneys, and you only know the half of it.'

'I can imagine what you went through for all those years,' Kelly felt giddy, as if she teetered on a precipice. She waited for Norma to speak.

'We have not had an easy life,' Norma said finally, and fixed Kelly with a cold vulpine eye—the mother-in-law eye that had never lost its power to intimidate her.

'I know that . . . there were so many unanswered questions about Owen . . .'

'Owen fell.'

'Okay, right, okay.' Kelly felt as if she was in her own grave, and a ghost had just walked across it. For years, she had puzzled over what Gordon had meant when he said he and Sam had lied about Owen's death, and that Owen had died smiling. Gordon had slammed that door in her face. Norma—whatever she knew— was no different. This family, she thought . . . and they reckon my side's fucked-up.

'I don't want to be pressured,' Norma's voice resumed normal service. 'I know you think I'm weak, but if you're proposing what I think you are, and if I did have the wherewithal, and if Ron agreed to it . . . See, I have to ask him. He's not long for this world, but he's not gone yet.'

'What do you think I'm proposing?' Kelly said.

'That we buy Gordon out. Oh, don't look at me like I've just landed from Mars. I might be the financially illiterate dependent spouse, but I'm not stupid!'

Kelly almost laughed. You had to hand it to Norma. Beneath the helpless 'traditional housewife' was a cunning, street-smart operator.

'That is what you're proposing, isn't it?' Norma went on. 'Ron won't like it. But Gordon will never sell. You know how stubborn he is, and how much he loves that place. I can't see how we would convince him, even if he is going to end up bankrupt.'

Kelly took a deep breath. She had one card left to play. 'Not Gordon.'

'Not Gordon?'

'Carl. My idea is that you buy out Carl.'

'Your brother?'

'There's a window of opportunity. Leonie can't finish her redevelopment of the Hilton while she has a controlling share in The Lodge. That's why she's selling her voting share to Carl until the Hilton is finished. But it's a sham. To buy his share, Carl has needed to borrow money, and guess who he's borrowed it from?'

'Leonie.'

'Right. It's barely even legal. When it's safe for Leonie to own The Lodge again, she will transfer back her voting share from Carl, she'll get Gordon's share for nothing, and then she'll be able to sell The Lodge at the new valuation. Huge profits for her.'

'And Gordon's out on the street.'

'Because he's over-borrowed.'

'Oh, that boy.'

'But when they settle three weeks from now, until the Hilton redevelopment is complete, Carl will have Leonie's voting share. We—well, you—can buy him out. I can see how we might make him do it.'

Norma's mouth formed a tight line. 'Why would Carl double-cross Leonie when she's done him this favour?'

'I know my brother's relationship with cash. Moth, meet flame.'

'But what would I do with The Lodge?'

'Anything! You are in total control. You can secure Ben's future!' And, Kelly thought, you can dissolve the deed of trust and screw Leonie royally, mother-in-law to mother-in-law, and let me out of there. 'You can save The Lodge; you can save *Bluebird*,' she added, wondering if she was laying it on a bit too thick.

'Oh, what a mess!'

'Sure is,' Kelly said, almost marvelling at her chicanery. She exhaled. She'd had a rough plan in her mind, but it was only while spelling it out for Norma that she realised how many loose ends were in there, and now she was wondering if it all stood up to analysis. But that wasn't the point. The point was that Norma was now contemplating the consequences, which was halfway to making it real.

'Just awful!'

'Not half as bad as if Leonie gets her way. Bad for Gordon, bad for me, but, most of all, absolutely awful for Ben.'

'Well,' Norma said stiffly, straightening out her attire as if to walk onto a stage. 'I'll think about it. But you know, you could help me a bit more.'

'Me?'

'I think you know what I mean.'

'Oh?' Kelly said into her collar, glancing up at the green. She took her club out of her bag and walked onto the tee to set up her shot.

'Well, isn't our number one priority Ben?' Norma's voice reminded Kelly of a domesticated animal peering through an open gate at the alluring, terrifying wilderness. No doubt about it, Norma didn't like it to be seen, but she still, at seventy-seven, had a desire for freedom. 'What is hurting Ben is—is, well, I think you know.'

Kelly's practice swing stopped halfway through.

'You want me and Gordon to . . .'

Norma squeezed out a nod. 'I believe in helping those who help themselves.'

'Oh, Norma.'

'I would do anything—anything—to see you and Gordon try to make a go of it again. He's been through so much in his life.'

Kelly studied her mother-in-law. In all the time she had known her, they had never until today broached the subject of what Gordon had been through 'in his life'.

'And you too,' Kelly said. 'With the *accident*.'

'And us too,' Norma agreed, gliding past Kelly's emphasis. 'Perhaps a little kindness wouldn't go astray?'

'You drive a hard bargain.'

'Surely not that hard? You managed for so long.'

'I'm not sure he even wants me back.'

As she stared at Norma across the tee box, Kelly wondered why neither of them had given a thought to how Gordon would react to their schemes. How had he made himself such a bystander in his own drama that his mother and his wife should decide his fate like the dictators carving up Poland? What passed between her and Norma now, it seemed to Kelly, was the mutuality of hope: despite so many of their actions, they both did love Gordon, and love would be enough to make up for everything else. Such as the action they were about to agree on.

'It's marriage,' Norma said. 'Like golf. You're in too far to get out.'

As Norma looked at her, Kelly felt an overpowering pull of, if she was not mistaken, sisterhood. It was a play of such vicious cunning—Norma would consider Kelly's plan, but only if she got back together with Gordon—the woman was a disguised devil, so Machiavellian that Kelly could only admire her. It was a cunning that came from suffering. When she looked into Norma's fox-golden eyes, Kelly saw the toll in happiness that Norma had paid, as a woman and as a mother. Against that toll, what Norma was asking from her was a tiny fraction.

'You've outplayed me,' Kelly said.

'Well . . .' Norma batted her eyelids.

'But I guess nothing can be perfect.'

'I used to think we had a perfect little family. But you live with what happens, not what might have happened.'

Kelly hadn't planned to end the conversation like this. In the way she had war-gamed it in her head, she would have brought Norma to a certain point and then let gravity take its course, let Norma feel she was in control, allow her plan to become Norma's plan. But Kelly now saw that she was a child playing against an adult. It *was* Norma's plan. Norma's pain, greater than Kelly's could ever be, was her fuel. Kelly had not only been outplayed, she had been outlived. It was Norma who was ending the conversation, at the point of her choosing.

'I'll do my best,' Kelly submitted.

'Ultimately it's about Ben's welfare. Now, I think you should play your shot.'

Kelly hit a beautiful five-wood onto the middle of the green. Norma was quiet, for the first time that day, as they drove down the cart path by the little dam. Kelly remarked on the pretty lilies floating in the water, but Norma said nothing. As they drove up the rise towards the green, Norma said, 'Who's that waving?'

'I don't know, I've got to go and putt.'

'Here, she's coming this way. She doesn't look happy. Maybe she's hooked her ball across into the dam. Oh, she's calling out to you! Kelly?'

But Kelly was crouched over her putt.

Sally Gilsenan's voice came closer, and here, now, Kelly heard Dog trying to calm Sally, and oh God, another husband-and-wifer on the golf course, it was so embarrassing when couples fought—but Kelly remained bent over her putter, thankful as never before that the etiquette of golf gave you countless places to hide from conversation, and one of those sacred zones, for better or worse, was when you were over your ball on the green, putting for a birdie.

Safe spaces

BEN MUST HAVE DONE SOMETHING WRONG, BECAUSE THERE could be no other reason for getting sent to the principal's office. He told himself to keep his mouth shut until he had figured out what he had done. There was always a chance that by speaking too soon and denying one misdemeanour, he might accidentally admit to a worse one, such as denying he'd given money to Zane Dwyer only to reveal that he'd stolen that cricket bat.

As he waited in the anteroom outside Ms Oxenford's office, he wondered if it was about him and Daniel. Why had Ms Oxenford been outside Daniel's house with Ben's mum, Daniel's dad and Mr Stoyle?

It was very confusing. Most days, he wished he hadn't come out. He'd got up and made a speech about it during Rainbow Week, following the lead of his classmates Johan Fraser and Gabe Cubbin, who had come out in the previous year's Rainbow Week, and the even more eagerly accepted Nate South, who experienced a seamless transition to Natalia. Kids took pride in their tolerance.

Diversity was cool. Or it was until Ben's coming-out, which fell flat: someone seemed to have decided that they could only take so much, and Ben took them past the unspoken limit. He regretted the robotic nature of his speech, repeating the key words and slogans he had been taught to conquer his nerves. But his speech had sounded cold and insincere, like he was trying to get attention. Ever since, he had been a target for the giggles, open taunts and bullying that had been bottled up during the embrace of Johan, Gabe and Natalia—who also picked on him for jumping on their bandwagon. He didn't get it. It must have been something about him.

He heard Ms Oxenford's footsteps approaching the door from inside. She had a real heart, and he had considered taking his troubles to her, as she was a friend of his dad's. But she was also the principal, too high up to really be able to help.

'Ben. Won't you step inside?'

Ms Oxenford's white hair was not old-lady white. It was short and stylish, contrasting with her bright red lips and whisky-coloured eyes. She was way too pretty for a principal, and Dad said she could have been taken for Annie Lennox in her tailored black Mao suits. Ben had googled 'Annie Lennox' and thought, yeah, kind of, not really. Ben wondered if his dad liked her. He'd gone to school with her. He could have married her, and then, wow, she'd have been Ben's mum. Which could come in handy right now.

Inside Ms Oxenford's office, Ben's heart stopped beating. Uncle Carl was slouching by her window in his dark grey duffle coat. It was thirty degrees outside; why did he always feel the cold? His hair hung over his eyes and he was so intent on the carpet that Ben looked down to see what was there.

'Wait, what?'

'I've been explaining a couple of things to your uncle about the pick-up zone,' Ms Oxenford said in a brittle tone that Ben knew was covering up for something heavy.

'Wait, what's it got to do with me? Last period doesn't finish for twenty minutes.'

'It might be best if you went home with your uncle now.'

'Am I expelled?'

'Of course not! I'm just sending you home as a favour.'

Among the many things Ms Oxenford didn't get was that adults' favours to teenagers were not favours, they were curses. Ben didn't want to be singled out for preferential treatment, no matter how well-intentioned. Since that coming-out speech, his dream was to get through school without anyone noticing him, so that when he ended up playing for Australia, they wouldn't recognise him as Ben Grimes from St Pat's. He would be a whole new person. A man.

'Then I haven't done anything wrong?'

'Why, have you done something wrong?'

'What?' He blushed. Did she know about the cricket bat?

'I'm joking, Ben. It's lovely that you have your uncle back in your life,' Ms Oxenford said. 'Boys need positive male role models.'

Ms Oxenford was often off sick with unspecified medical problems. Ben wondered if you could give yourself a medical problem from stretching the distance between what the world was and what you want it to be too tightly.

'Wait, what? Yes, miss.'

Ben looked at Uncle Carl. Why was she talking like he wasn't here? From under his hair Carl shot Ben a look too quick to read.

'And Ben?'

'What? Yes, miss?'

'Maybe your uncle can explain why you're getting an early mark.'

Ben made for the door. Carl was still at Ms Oxenford's window. Ben waited for a minute but then, confusingly, Ms Oxenford closed the door on him. Had he been given an early mark or not? The principal's assistant wasn't here to clarify. He couldn't go back to class—there would be too many questions to answer, too much attention grabbing—so he sat tight.

Uncle Carl had been back in his life for four weeks. Ben would have liked to travel home independently, but one afternoon he was bailed up by kids who stole his wallet, leading to Ms Oxenford decreeing that he be collected by an adult unless he was going straight to cricket practice. Uncle Carl didn't live at The Lodge yet, and was sleeping on the floor of one of the rooms in the Hilton during the redevelopment, but Ben's mother was crazy with work while Ben's dad was on the run doing things for Grandma and Grandpa, so it had been kind of good timing that Carl was around to do pick-ups. Ben's uncle had become part of the furniture, dropping by The Lodge most days to hang out. And he had a car. And he was all right. He knew a lot about the world outside Bluebird, which was more than Ben could say of his mum and dad; no offence, but compared to Carl they hadn't seen anything.

Hearing raised voices, Ben put his ear to Ms Oxenford's door.

'Are you going to report it?' he heard. Oddly, it was not Uncle Carl asking this question but the principal.

Uncle Carl's reply, soft and spongey as his skin, was inaudible. Carl's voice often sounded like it was caught behind cheesecloth at the back of his throat.

'I offer you an unconditional apology on behalf of the school,' Ben heard Ms Oxenford say. This was weirder still. Apology for what? The exterior door to the principal's anteroom squeaked and Ben jumped. Escorted by the principal's assistant, looking dishevelled and resentful, was Daniel.

'What are you doing?' the assistant, Ms Agostini, asked Ben.

'Wait, what?'

'What are you doing?'

Ben mumbled something.

'What?' Ms Agostini said.

'I've been told to wait here.'

Ben was staring at Daniel, whose eyes were on a square of carpet just like the one that had preoccupied Uncle Carl.

'Is your uncle still with her?' Ms Agostini asked.

Ben nodded.

'We're going to have to wait somewhere else,' Ms Agostini said to Daniel, and nudged him towards the exit.

'I think they're almost finished,' Ben said.

'Safe spaces,' Ms Agostini sang. 'We have to provide a safe space for the student and the . . . the other.'

Ben's life could be summed up in this image: a vast network of safe spaces connecting all seven billion people on earth, and him standing alone on the outside, in the last remaining unsafe space. Daniel gave him a baleful glare and turned to follow Ms Agostini.

'Daniel?' Ben said.

Daniel swivelled. Ms Agostini was giving Ben evils.

'R U OK?' Ben hoped Daniel could hear it was letters, not words.

Daniel gave him a horn sign. Ben blushed with happiness.

A few minutes later, Uncle Carl shambled out of Ms Oxenford's office.

'What did you do?' Ben said.

'Tell you later.'

Uncle Carl tried to step past him. Ben moved into his way. If Ben knew anything, it was that Daniel and Uncle Carl had to be kept in separate safe spaces.

'Um, can we wait? Ms Oxenford might want to talk to us again.'

'She doesn't.'

'What?'

'She *doesn't.*'

'Oh. Um . . . ?'

Ben counted to ten in his head and tried to look ill, but Uncle Carl charged into the corridor. Phew, Daniel was nowhere to be seen. They made it to the school gate, but Ben had caused so much delay, the bell rang just as they got there and boys began barrelling out. As Carl searched his pockets for his car key, Ms Agostini came up, deep in conversation with Daniel. Uncle Carl's face twisted, he mumbled to himself, then he advanced towards Daniel and Ms Agostini.

'You don't want to make things worse, Mr Chidgey.' The principal's assistant was holding up a flat palm like a stop sign.

Ignoring her, Carl said, 'You weak little cunt,' his throat thick with emotion. What did Uncle Carl and Daniel have to do with each other? Ben was outside a pretty important loop here.

Daniel did not respond with his usual smart one-liner. Instead, he cowered behind Ms Agostini.

'Please,' Ms Agostini said, 'just take Ben home, and we'll deal with what happened through the proper channels.'

Uncle Carl was such a balled-up mass of intent that Ben thought he was going to launch himself through the air at Daniel. But a car pulled up, and Ben saw Daniel's father, Mr Abottemey, pointing his phone camera at Ben, then at Daniel, then at Uncle Carl and Ms Agostini. Carl pulled Ben away. Mr Abottemey continued pointing his phone at them.

Once they had made it into Uncle Carl's Camry, Ben said, 'What happened?'

Carl gave a dry chuckle. 'When we were kids at Bluebird High, your headmistress was the same interfering busybody she is now. Born for that job. Always looking for "solutions" to "problems". She had so many solutions, she had to go around inventing problems.'

'Is there anything wrong with that?' Ben didn't want to be on Ms Oxenford's side, but he couldn't see what Carl was getting at.

'To a man with a hammer, everything looks like a nail,' Carl said. 'And if you're a nail, everyone around you looks like a hammer.'

'What happened?'

'Not everyone is a "problem".'

Ben frowned out the window. Uncle Carl had this habit of not taking him directly home. One day they went to the high rock ledges at Cliff Street, another day up the bush tracks of Capri National Park. Carl liked bushwalks. Another day, they had driven an hour to Fairview Lighthouse, Ocean City's northern limit. Carl talked in long circular spools, and Ben tended to switch off. It wasn't that he didn't like his uncle's conversation; it was just that he lost the thread of Carl's thoughts, which scattered into a confetti of poetry, philosophy, religion and personal reminiscence. But Ben enjoyed the excursions, which saved him from sitting in that damp smelly basement to do his homework.

They were stuck in the Capri afternoon traffic.

'Fuck off!' Carl said to the cars.

'Were you a "problem" today?' Ben asked.

Carl waited until the traffic moved again.

'I was wondering how I was inside the office of Jude fucking Oxenford. A new low, that's for sure. She decided not to report it. I think this was breaking the rules.'

'Report what?'

'I was involved in an assault on school grounds,' Carl said.

'You assaulted Daniel?'

Carl wheeled into the council car park and took a ticket at the boom gate.

'Where are we going?' Ben asked.

Rather than answering Ben's questions, Carl applied his full concentration to fitting his Camry into a space marked out in the 1970s (as Ben had heard his dad complain), which was now shrunken to obsolescence between a Skoda Yeti and an Audi Q6. Carl and Ben had to squeeze themselves out. Ben was gentle with his door so as not to hit the Yeti, but even so he startled a guy inside who was rolling a joint. Ben heard Carl's door bump the Q6. Carl let out a honk of laughter.

Descending the stairwell, Carl resumed his theme. 'Jude was scared of me.'

'Wait, what? You can't hit Daniel, and you can't hit the principal.'

'I haven't hit her since we were six years old. No, she was scared of me taking action against the school for not providing a safe environment. Isn't that hilarious?' Carl said without humour. 'Took me fifty years, but I've finally been expelled! You'll have to come to the car to meet me.'

'You shouldn't be wandering the grounds anyway.'

'I wasn't.'

Carl stalked across the Capri pedestrian mall and said no more until they were at the ferry wharf. Afternoon commuters streamed both ways. While Ben opened the turnstile with his transport card, Carl vaulted over the gate like a delinquent fifteen-year-old. Ben's heart missed a beat but the staff were not looking. He followed Carl onto the old ferry that had just emptied, up the internal stairs to the enclosed outdoor viewing deck at the bow. Carl sat on the slatted wooden bench and crossed his legs.

'I'll be late home,' Ben said.

'Anyone gives you shit, they'll have to answer to me,' Carl said, then slapped Ben's shoulder. 'Joking!' Ben could never tell when Carl was joking, or lying, or performing.

Carl was still ruminating on Ms Oxenford. 'I was an outcast at the Bloodbath, and she was always the one being "nice" to me and "bringing me into the group". You know the type.'

Ben nodded, because he liked Carl's confidential manner, but he didn't know the type. 'Nobody brings me into any group.'

'They end up as school principals,' Carl ploughed on. 'Keen awareness of the pecking order. They eat that stuff up. She used to try to tee me up with depressed girls, her way of "fixing" me. A good lesson in the total hopelessness of future life. You know she doesn't like being touched?'

Ben was trying to be mature in a men's conversation, wondering what his dad or Firie Sam would say, but he couldn't keep up; he was gawping at his uncle like a fish.

'That's why she's never paired up,' Carl said. 'She has this, like, medical condition, somethingophobia.'

'That's so sad.'

'Could be sadder. She could have ended up an unemployed junkie loser. Instead she never left school. When you get to my age, you realise that everything you've ever done has been governed by what you're most scared of. For one person, not naming names, you're scared of boredom. Your safe place is drugs. For her, she's scared of a lot of stuff and the solution, the safe place, is school. If she offers to help you, run like your hair is on fire. If she asks you to her office, just name, rank and serial number, no further cooperation. She will make you think that she is your friend. She is not. Copy that? She is not your friend.'

Carl went to the cafe on the lower deck. Ben knew how dire the food offerings were, and was unsurprised when Carl came back with a bottle of water and a bad smell on his face.

'Some of those doughnuts have been there since I was a kid,' Carl said. 'I recognised the pineapple one. I said, "G'day, old mate," and it moved. Its soul was in there. *Let me out!*'

Carl drank some water and offered it to Ben, who didn't like to share drinks. It wasn't that Carl was especially germy, though he didn't look very healthy either. He was a vegan, which suggested he looked after his body, but then he had confided in Ben that 'one hundred and five percent of reformed heroin addicts are vegans', and again Ben felt he was out of his conversational depth.

'Yeah, so, *mon ami*, you really want to know what went down?' Carl said.

Ben made a noncommittal movement. He didn't know what he really wanted to know.

'That weak cunt took a shot at me,' Carl said. 'I was outside the gate, just minding my own business, waiting for the bell. Doing nothing at all. And then—I don't know why that piece of shit wasn't in class, he was loitering with a couple of his boofhead mates—he comes up and starts abusing me. You know, *You useless junkie fuck, you piece of shit, my dad's told me all about you.* You know the drill.'

Ben knew a variation of it.

'The old me would have taken them on, just for the buzz. Some days the only way you can get your hands on strong painkillers is in an emergency ward. But I'm a shadow of my former self, huh. So when they begin crowding in on me, I figure my best chance is to move inside the school grounds. There are things they can't do inside. So they're, like, pushing me up against the fence, doing that bully thing, taunting me to take the first shot so they can "retaliate", and I just pivot on the fence and throw myself over. I end up arse over turkey, but I'm inside. But so then they pile over after me, and I'm shitting myself. Fifty years old and running from the bullies to the principal's office. Never did that when I was a kid.'

'He's bi-curious,' Ben said.

'What? Who?'

Ben nodded. 'Daniel.'

'Who says?'

'What?'

'Who says he's bi?'

'Bi-curious. Since I came out, everyone's been really mean to me, and Daniel's been sort of leading it. That's how I got the hint. Then I keep seeing him looking at me. So I went to him in the holidays and said, "Listen, I know how hard it is to keep it to yourself, but I'm just telling you that if you want to talk to anyone I'm here for you."'

'Ha. And how did that go for you?'

'What? Yeah, not good.'

'Maybe he's homophobic just because he hates fags. Doesn't mean he is one. If being homophobic makes him a fag, that means every bloke I went to school with was a closet fucken poo-puncher. Maybe he was looking at your dick because he wanted to see what a fag dick looks like. You're a weird kid. See what I mean? Hammers and nails.'

'One thing I have is a good gaydar. Better than yours.'

'Horseshit. I've got a NASA-certified fagdar. It's been used by law enforcement agencies. You fags have the worst fagdars. It's simple confirmation bias.'

'*You're* probably a closet gay.'

Ben wondered if he had gone too far, but Uncle Carl said, 'Well, I've been there and given it a crack, so, yeah, whatever. Worth investigating but not for me. Okay, does that mean I'm a poof? You tell me.'

'Maybe you're bi-curious like Daniel.'

'I hardly know the kid, so I'm not going to get into a debate about it. I'm just telling you what happened. I turn up to fetch you from school, and that kid and his goons decide to beat the shit out of me. What's become of the Bluebird we used to know?'

Carl cackled. There was so much about the adult world Ben couldn't figure out; why should Grandma Leonie complicate it even further by letting Uncle Carl, the most confusing adult of all, into their lives? Ben could see a massive bust-up coming; it was written on everyone's face. He didn't care about The Lodge, they could shove it. He just wanted his family—him, his dad and his mum, and Lou—out of harm's way.

When they arrived at the ferry terminal in the city, Ben got up to disembark but Carl wouldn't move. They were going to stay aboard all the way back to Capri, the full loop. Carl reached into a pocket of his duffle coat and pulled out a thick, beaten-up black paperback. Ben sat down again and watched him reading. The print was microscopic.

'What's the book?'

'*Don Quixote.*'

'Donkey what?' Ben said.

'*Don Quixote.*' Carl flashed the cover: a painting of a knight, carrying a shield and a lance, on a horse. A short fat guy in a white shirt sat on a short fat horse beside him.

'Is it good?'

A private smile crossed Carl's face. 'Put it this way, a man I once knew said it was brilliant and beautiful but it only has one thing wrong with it, which is it's completely unreadable.'

'It took you fifteen minutes to get through one page. Why don't you stop?'

'My mate, when he got to the end, burst into tears.'

'He was angry at the time he'd wasted?' Ben felt like adding: *He'd gone nuts?*

'No, he was weeping tears of pride that he'd managed to push through despite everything the author threw at him.'

After thinking for a few seconds, Ben said, 'Your friend sounds weird.'

'That's not why I'm reading it. I've had enough pain in my life.' Carl patted the cover and slipped the book into his pocket. 'It was written in 1615, in Spain. A long way from here and now, a long way from us. But you know what? It's all about your dad.'

'Wait, what?'

'It's about a man who dedicates his life to preserving the ways of the past. He thinks everything used to be better than it is now. He's on a one-man crusade to stop progress.'

'Is that the knight, or the short guy?'

'That's your dad,' Carl said.

'Does he win?'

'Who?'

My dad, Ben wanted to say. 'The knight. Does he stop progress?'

'I'll tell you when I get to the end.' Carl laughed, but it was a mean laugh, like he already knew the answer. 'What I know is, he should listen to the short guy more often.'

'Who's the short guy?'

When Carl turned his eyes on Ben, they were sad and old. 'Your dad, he doesn't have a short guy. Your dad needs his brother, *mon ami*.'

'My dad doesn't have a brother.'

'You need a different uncle.'

'I only have one uncle!'

Carl faced away from Ben again, set his view on the far shore of the harbour. Capri Wharf was looming.

'Sure, Benny. Whatever you say.' Again, like he knew better.

Now Ben was getting mad. He didn't mind Uncle Carl messing with his head a little—Carl couldn't help that—but sometimes he went too far. Sometimes when Carl got all mysterious like this, knowing too much about too many things, being so wise and so wasted, he seemed to be trying to hurt Ben, who could see a similarity, how Carl and his mum were more alike than they cared to admit.

'I don't believe you,' Ben said.

Carl raised his eyes. 'Which bit? The knight or the uncle?'

'About Daniel and his mates trying to beat you up and you running off to Ms Oxenford's office. I don't believe that story.'

'Why not?' Carl said. He wasn't offended. Ben had his interest. Which told Ben he was right.

'Because I've been beaten up by that crew, and that's not how they operate.'

Carl arched an eyebrow and nodded. 'Well done.' He looked squarely at Ben. 'Now are you going to tell me what really happened?'

Ben couldn't tell Uncle Carl what had happened, he only knew what hadn't. There were a billion things that hadn't happened, and hidden among them was only one thing that had. How was he supposed to find it?

Carl said a few things about how the one sure way to lose sight of the beauty of OC was to live here. 'Blindness from overuse of the eyes,' he said. They didn't discuss Daniel again, or what had really gone down at school, or Ms Oxenford, or Gordon and his mad quest and the uncle Ben didn't have. Ben didn't want to shut down against Carl, but he felt his heart muscles clamping like an oyster closing its valve.

As the ferry pulled into Capri terminal, Carl closed his book but slid out the bookmark, which Ben noticed was an envelope.

'When do you see him next?' Carl asked.

'Wait, what? Who?'

'Young Frankenface. Your fag pal.'

'Daniel? At cricket practice tomorrow.'

'Do me a favour? Give him this.'

Ben looked through the window in the envelope.

'You pay him to beat you up?'

'Very funny. Just give him this and bring what he has for me.'

Now Ben knew. Out of all those billion things. He should have guessed.

'How much is in here?'

'Never you mind,' Uncle Carl said. 'Just do it for me.'

A gear in Ben's brain slipped into place, the teeth of two cogs meshing. It happened so infrequently, this feeling gave him a rush like falling in love.

'How much?' Ben repeated.

'I don't want you involved.'

'Not involved, just be your courier? How much for how much? You don't tell me, you are so busted. I'll tell Ms Oxenford the truth: that you and Daniel staged a fight as a cover-up when you were about to get caught doing a drug deal outside the school. That's what it was, wasn't it?'

Carl considered saying a few things, but gave Ben a defeated smile. 'Five hundred for three bottles.'

'Wait, what?'

'Just take the money to Daniel and get my bottles, right?'

'I don't think so,' Ben said, but he didn't give Carl back his money. Carl had said it himself: Ben wasn't as slow on the uptake as everyone thought.

Ben put the envelope into his pocket and started talking.

⌒

The next day, Ben found Daniel in the cricket nets rolling his arm over, supervising spin bowling practice. Daniel would never know how much it hurt to watch this when you would give anything in the world to be able to carelessly bowl a perfect leg-break; Ben could practise for a year and never execute a delivery that Daniel bowled without thinking.

'Hi,' Ben said, impersonating a normal boy. He remembered the horn sign.

Daniel caught a ball, another carefree display of coordinated ease. He smelt of aftershave—not the cheap brand that Ben wore after his monthly attempts to de-bumfluff his jawline, but a flavour you wanted to eat.

'What's up?' Daniel said.

'I was speaking to my uncle. He told me what happened.'

'He did?'

'He said you and some guys beat him up.'

'We did?' Daniel took a few skips to catch a ball.

'I didn't believe him,' Ben said. 'It didn't ring true. And, um, you wouldn't do it anyway. You've got the surf carnival at Bluebird coming up on Saturday. It'd be silly to get into a fight four days out.'

'Well that's good.'

'So, yeah. And there'll be parties afterwards, and you'll probably want some cash.' Lou was planning a fundraiser at The Lodge; maybe, Ben thought, he could tap Daniel for a donation.

Daniel studied Ben as if weighing up how much to tell him. He lobbed the cricket ball to Ben, who tossed it from hand to hand, as he had seen the good bowlers do, and windmilled his arms in a warming-up motion.

'Carl sent me here to finish the deal,' Ben said. 'He's given me the money.'

Daniel looked at him again, in a way that stripped Ben naked. His balls tingled. Daniel was keeping a secret. He was right about Daniel; it didn't matter if it never came out, but he was right about him.

'Mate,' Daniel said. 'Want a bowl?'

Ben looked down. 'I'm in my school shoes.'

'Borrow my spares.' Daniel nodded towards his kit bag, lying open a few steps away. 'We're the same size. You've got big feet for a little guy. You're going to be huge when your growth spurt hits.'

Daniel cruised to the bowling crease. Then he turned to Ben and said, 'Hey. You do enough bowling. Want a bat? Use my gear.'

Ben's pulse went to two hundred. He could bat? He looked down the practice net. They were only bowling slow. They could humiliate him—they would humiliate him—but they couldn't hurt him. He sat beside Daniel's kit, wrenched off his school shoes without untying the laces, and put on Daniel's spares as reverentially as if they had belonged to Steve Smith. He sensed, from past experience, that he was falling into a trap. Being welcomed was the first step to being belittled. But he wanted so much to bat.

Ben would have blurted something about the bat he and Zane Dwyer had stolen, but he was in too much of a hurry to get into the nets. He was not humiliated; in fact, he batted his best ever. It might have been Daniel's bat, gloves and pads (and his box, which Ben wore underneath his underpants, next to the skin, he hoped without Daniel noticing; but so what if Daniel did?). Wearing Daniel's gear gave him the confidence to step forward and hit the ball truly, even to dance down the pitch. He was only dismissed six or seven times in fifteen minutes, which for Ben was a remarkable success rate. Only after he came down from the heights of the session—Batting! Daniel's gear! Hitting the ball! Daniel's *box*!—did Ben remember what he had come here to do.

He sat beside Daniel's kit bag and unstrapped his pads, removed his gloves, replaced his shoes. The last piece of Daniel's kit he removed was the box.

Daniel was standing over him.

'Okay, the stuff's in the inside zip pocket of my kit bag,' Daniel said. 'Don't let anyone see. You got the envelope? Just put it in the zip pocket and swap out the stuff.'

'Two hundred for three bottles,' Ben said. He couldn't meet Daniel's eye. His heart was racing.

He heard Daniel snort. 'It's five.'

'Five bottles? Even better.'

'Five hundred, doofus. For three bottles.'

Ben took the envelope out of his school shoes. Those shoes were so uncomfortable.

'Don't wave it around!' Daniel hissed, cutting his eyes from side to side.

'It's two hundred,' Ben said. 'You want five hundred, bring ten bottles.'

'What the fuck?' Daniel's voice was cracking with disbelieving laughter.

'And you'll take the deal,' Ben said. 'Two hundred bucks is two hundred bucks—pretty good for stuff you get for free.'

'That fucker. Tell him no deal.' Daniel paused, meeting Ben's eye. Ben saw fear. 'What's he doing trying to reneg?'

'Okay, no deal,' Ben replied with a smile and pocketed the envelope.

'Shit, okay, gimme the two hundred. Arsehole, I thought he was desperate.' Daniel clicked his fingers impatiently and beckoned for the money.

'Nope.' Ben patted his pocket. This felt so good, he almost got a stiffy.

'Whaddaya mean? I'm the man!'

'Sorry, Dan. He's got a new man.'

The sunshine that kills us

THE FOLLOWING SATURDAY, BLUEBIRD BECAME A PLACE OF worship as host beach for the statewide surf carnival. Viewed from The Lodge, the carnival made glorious wallpaper. Kelly threw open the windows to let in the shouting and the whistles and the starting guns and the cheering. The Lodge reeked like the bottom of an ashtray emptied into the stale dregs of a glass of beer aerated by middle-aged man fart. It needed health.

She stood on the balcony with Gordon, drinking passable cappuccinos that he had somehow learnt how to make on the La Marzocco. Definitely seeing, or planning to see, a woman, she thought.

'What a shit show,' she said.

Kelly had never been in the habit of attending the surf carnival, though she had found new objections to reinforce the old. The BSLSC had evolved from the hostile beast of her youth into a corporate advertising exercise, safe and soulless. A bank sponsored the marquees, a law firm sponsored Bluebird's surfboats, a tech start-up sponsored the lycra racing outfits, and a management consultancy sponsored the royal blue banners tautened by the early-arriving nor'-easter. The BSLSC was now run by identikit executives who won their positions based not on time served but on their ability to raise revenue. Each brought their gift of corporate social responsibility to the club's true business: the competition on the beach was merely a cloak for the race between clubs to poach each other's assets.

'It's not like I would defend the old ways,' Gordon said, sharing her thoughts, 'but I miss a surf club being a place where you went to learn how to help others survive in the sea.'

'And how to avoid nasty old men,' Kelly added.

'But then, we're nobody's target demographic.'

From the stairs, Carl materialised, swaddled in the duffle coat in which he slept, ate, lived and, for all Kelly knew, bathed.

'Leonie's coming,' he said without preamble. 'Wants to take us to that.' He inclined his head, vaguely, to the beach.

'Who's us?' Kelly said. 'What's that?'

Carl shrugged one shoulder. 'She'll be here in a couple of minutes.'

Kelly felt her mind racing away. The notion of Carl, who had nurtured fantasies of blowing up surf carnivals since he was ten years old, strolling down to take in the sunshine and crowds, maybe suck on a pine-lime Splice while walking the dunes with Leonie, knocked her off balance.

'We can't let her up here,' Gordon said. To Kelly's questioning look, he held up a marble he had taken from his pocket. 'The slope of the floor. It's down to nine seconds. She'll have a fit. Call her, Carl, we'll meet her at the beach. The young ones are down there getting ready.' Lou had been given dispensation to enter her surfboat crew as a 'Bluebird II' team, and Ben was helping her to organise the girls.

Carl mumbled something about coffee.

'Perfect!' Gordon said shrilly, pushing Carl towards the staircase. 'It's much better at her cafe.'

He punched Leonie's number into his phone and handed it to Carl while he went to his bedroom for a sunhat.

Alone with her brother, Kelly said, 'I haven't seen Gordon move that quickly since he was offered redundancy from the paper.'

'She's not answering.' Carl handed back the phone to Gordon, who had re-emerged with three hats. Carl refused to wear one.

'I'll text her, tell her we'll catch her down there,' Gordon said.

Kelly had forgotten how a carnival in full swing could trigger an involuntary surge of pleasure. Colours flew like flags of the world. The names of the beaches brimmed with a certain magic: Manly, Maroubra, North Curl Curl, Whale Beach, Bronte, Avalon, North Narrabeen . . . Despite her inner revulsion, she could still be stirred by the rollcall. And then there were the out-of-towners: Thirroul, Old Bar, Merimbula, Tuncurry—music to Australian ears. The beach was a study in organised mayhem. Events were lost in the gigantism of the carnival, as if the racing were incidental to the choreography. There was no scoreboard or central focus, so a visitor would never make head nor tail of who was winning. And yet somehow the clubs knew precisely where they stood and who they wanted to destroy. From the outside, it was sunshine and colours and bodies and logos. Health and service glimmering in their perfect corporate mirror. From the inside, it was kill or be killed.

Kelly felt Carl's suffering as they wove through the crowd to the Beach Cafe. This put her in an even better mood.

She caught sight of Leonie in a yellow shell jacket with red trousers. You could stick her in the sand and order the board riders to stay south. She was twittering to Paolo with eye-hurting brightness. Carl glowered. Her brother didn't like foreigners; he had invented his own niche of bigotry. He had a liberal, cosmopolitan, artistic, intellectual bent; he deplored racism against First Nations and his fellow People of Colour, he was a bare-knuckled defender of his LGBTQI+ friends, he would chain himself to an old-growth tree rather than see it cut down, and yet the things Kelly had heard him mutter against Brazilians, Jews and Southern Europeans were pure Old Bluebird. Watching the two Italian baristas, Carl's lips were rippling homicidally, as if he cared so much about his stepmother's honour it was worth taking a kitchen knife to Paolo's throat.

Some dickhead at the front of the queue was simpering, 'I've just spent three weeks in Rome and never got an Italian coffee as good as yours.' Lucio looked unconvinced and Carl shaped to hurl the dickhead into the nearest banksia tree. Kelly informed the dickhead that the coffee here was Australian-grown and brewed to a 'local recipe' and the Italian boys were just window dressing, and in any case they were as straight as the day is long, so the dickhead was barking up the wrong tree.

The dickhead was about to bite back, but then Gordon said, 'And the queue starts over there,' with such cold-eyed ferocity that the dickhead reconsidered and trudged meekly to the end of the line.

Kelly said, 'Nobody messes with the politeness police.'

'Just a right way to do things,' Gordon said. 'You think I might get a customer-facing job in crowd control?'

'Why were you in such a hurry to get out of the house?'

'Honest?'

Kelly smiled. 'No time like the present.'

'I can't keep up, everything's falling apart. It's not just the floor. The steps might collapse under her. The knob on the banister might come off in her hand. She might trip on the Shitfuckerpoobum and break her neck.'

'You're worried about accidents?'

'I'm ashamed. I love that place, and I'm letting it go to rack and ruin. I can't let her see what I've done to it.'

'It's not you, Gordon. It's time. Look at what it's done to all of us.'

Carl was bumbling past. 'Gotta get out of here, can't stand their fucken dago coffee anyway.' He headed for the aluminium grandstand improvised at the northern side of the surf club, reserved for competitors' families. Kelly followed him, leaving Gordon to deal with Leonie. As she followed Carl up the steps of the grandstand, Kelly thought she heard someone say, 'Is he still alive?'

She sat behind her brother, who was shivering in the thirty-degree heat under his duffle coat. Leonie, takeaway cup in hand, took up a position at the base of the grandstand and put on a show for the beach sprinters. Did she care who won? Kelly wondered if Leonie could ever have imagined herself, in her fifties, on a strip of sand on the edge of this island continent, cheering nonsensically for children diving into sand to grasp pieces of hosepipe.

'Why does she want us here?' she asked Carl, whose shivers spasmed violently.

'Laying the pelts of slaughtered beasts before the peasants. Here are your princes, at my feet.'

'You're such a fucking wanker,' Kelly said.

Her eye was caught by a smile, apparently for her, from the front row. Jude Oxenford was on her way up, getting away with a sundress in broad white and navy diagonals, grinning from under a pizza-sized straw hat and Jackie Onassis sunglasses.

'Mind if I sit down? Oh, hello, Carl. Long time no see.'

Carl gurgled something dismissive, or French. Jude, accustomed to surly teenagers, nodded understandingly. Carl walked to the end of the top deck and turned away from the beach, finding something interesting to look at in the parking lot behind the BSLSC.

'I hear your goddaughter's been given permission to race her surfboat crew,' Jude said. 'That's exciting!'

'Wouldn't have happened in our day,' Kelly said. 'And she's not my goddaughter, she's Gordon's.'

'Can you imagine the old crusties!' Jude laughed, and put on an old Anzac rumble: 'No, no, no—not properly registered. Girls! I don't bloody well think so!' She grinned at Kelly and said, in her own voice, 'Do you remember when the law stopped them from banning women from the upstairs bar of the BSLSC, so they re-designated the whole top floor as the men's changing room? If they couldn't maintain a rule to keep women out, the threat of old codgers walking around in the nude would do the job for them. There was some kind of genius in it.'

'They never let progress get in their way.'

'And we never realised how much we needed the patriarchy,' Jude said. 'It was our only defence against the future.' She nodded towards the empty mansions serried around the headlands.

'Are you here to keep an eye on your students?' Kelly said.

'I'd have no hope of keeping an eye on anyone! It's chaos, isn't it? I'd say organised chaos but I'm not entirely sure about organised. Those crusties had something going for them. A clip over the ear to put the kids in line instead of all this namby-pamby no-touching. Talk about herding cats. It's as bad as school. Is Ben participating?'

'He's water boy for Lou's Lezzos,' Kelly said.

'You can't say that.'

'I just did. So why *are* you here?'

Jude watched the south end, where surfboats were forming up for their heats. An ocean swimming race to a buoy off the north end was in train, while juniors were competing on rescue boards in the middle and the beach sprints were moving through their eliminations closer to the dunes.

'He's doing much better,' Jude said.

'Ben?'

'His teachers are saying he's working with more purpose.'

'He's on the paediatrician's speed pills, so maybe it's that.'

'Half the school is medicated, you know.'

'Pills to stop boys being boys is what Gordon calls them.'

'It's probably more than the medication,' Jude said.

'You mean us splitting up? It's given him some much-needed certainty, instead of wondering how long we'd last?'

'Stability is the thing. But are you really split up?'

Jude knew more than Kelly was comfortable with, but she also didn't know the half of it. If their finances deteriorated any further, and if Norma didn't take up Kelly's proposal, the instability of Ben's living arrangements might just be starting.

'Down there,' Jude said before Kelly could reply. 'She could teach my staff a few things about caring for kids.'

Valiantly, Lou was organising her eight-strong crew to wheel their surfboat trailer from the ramp to the southern corner. The girls were more disciplined than boys, but they were also occupied with talking to each other. The trailer had to stop when it ran over a very tall girl's foot.

'She's been an amazing mentor to him,' Jude said, eyes lingering on Lou and the girls' crew.

'Ben told you that?'

'Kids that age need one adult they can talk with.'

'It used to be me and Gordon.'

'Not many choose a parent.'

'Or the principal.'

'A role that's evolved since our day.'

'Right.' Kelly reached out to remove the Onassis sunglasses, which Jude permitted with as much ceremony as if Kelly were disrobing her. 'What's going on between Ben and Daniel?'

'Ben and Daniel? I think Ben arrives at school each morning aware that he has to watch every step. He's negotiating a maze of social factors. It's not easy for him to assert his unorthodox self while fitting in with a group that has a low tolerance for unconventionality. But we see the entire school as a safe space.'

'Again, in English?'

Jude took Kelly in, amused. She removed her sunglasses from Kelly's hand and replaced them on her face. 'Daniel's a complicated young man. But the road ahead of him is different. Ben has a mother and father who are supportive, a sister figure in Lou whom he can open up to, and a certain imperviousness to other people's opinions.'

'Others were accepted quicker.'

'He needs to understand that it's not required for him to evangelise. He feels sorry for Daniel and wants to help him, but what worked for Ben isn't necessarily the solution for Daniel.'

'Meaning it's harder for an alpha male with a knobhead father.'

'Maybe we should just leave Daniel alone. That's what I've been telling Ben. Celebrate your own growth, you're not responsible for anyone else's.'

It was an interesting perspective, Kelly thought, as she picked Ben out in the crowd, running plastic bottles to the girls for a last sip before they pushed their surfboat into the southern rip. Ben, scrawny-daggy in his loose white T-shirt and cricket hat, scurried about picking up the bottles the girls tossed onto the sand. Lou was barking orders.

'That doesn't bring me any closer to knowing what's going on,' Kelly said.

'Was it meant to?' Jude's smile was interrupted by the sight of Carl, a few rows away, beside Leonie, two fingers in his mouth, whistling support for Lou's team. Kelly had spent her teens practising vainly to whistle like this. Carl's old charisma.

'As for that one,' Jude said.

'My brother?'

'I found him inside the school the other day. He had apparently been running away from some boys who were trying to assault him.'

'"Apparently."'

'There's more to it but I can't figure out what.'

'There's always more to it with him. Is there anything I can do?'

Jude considered, then shook her head. 'You and Gordon haven't been lucky with your brothers.'

'I'm not sure which of us was unluckier,' Kelly said, and regretted it. Her fucking levity. Her fucking acid levity.

'I wonder if he's trying to reconnect with the self he left behind,' Jude said, eyes still on Carl.

'Too far behind.'

'Or if he's trying to find a way to survive all this . . .'

'All this good fortune.'

Jude smiled. 'All this sunshine and health!'

'The sunshine that kills us.'

'I think it's killing your brother right now. Look at the poor guy.'

Carl shone marble-white in his heavy coat, like a Soviet agent given the wrong weather information. He seemed in some kind of waxen fever, cold and overheated at once, about to congeal.

'Don't think Leonie's put Carl in The Lodge to help his recovery,' Kelly said with genuine sadness. 'Once he's served his purpose she'll turf him out.'

Jude looked surprised at her vehemence.

'I'm not Carl's keeper,' Kelly added. 'I can't even keep myself. I need to be shedding, not accumulating.'

'What you need and what you do are separate things. It's what I keep telling your son.'

A gunshot started the intermediate girls' surfboat race. The swell was not large, but the relentless short-period nor'-east wind chop threw the boats to left and right as they attempted to bash ahead. These summery conditions made the race a lottery. Lou's crew did well going out, making the most of their draw, and were in the top three as they rounded the buoys. Leonie was jumping up and down in her ridiculous yellow and red, while Carl, ghost-pale, spread his arms as if summoning a migration. Down on the sand, Ben and Lou clasped each other.

'Are they going to win?' Jude asked.

Gordon, who had joined them, shook his head. 'It's zero sum. The rip helps them on the way out, but it'll stuff them on the way back. No waves breaking inside means no push.'

Sure enough, once the girls' boat turned back to the beach, it began to bob as if the crew were rowing against a river. What the rip had given, it now took away. They staggered in behind nine or ten other boats. Capri won, their Amazon-like crew having gone methodically about their business. When you were that superior there was no need for excitement. Those girls must have been chewing steroids with their baby formula, Kelly thought; they were bigger than Gordon and not yet sixteen years old. Among Lou's crew, Kelly could see the disappointment even from a distance. Outside their tearful circle, Ben slumped. The usual reality check. Bluebirders were world-beaters, as long as they kept the world out.

'It's tough,' Jude said with feeling, and the way Gordon put his hand on her knee, his eyes moist, got Kelly wondering if she was the woman he was seeing. Jude hated being touched, everyone knew that. She placed her hand on Gordon's and gave it a tender pat before lifting it off. Perhaps he'd discovered a last chance to get to know this woman he had known all his life. Habit, over-familiarity, neglect and inaction killed more lives than cancer. Kelly's stomach churned.

Carl and Leonie were climbing back up the bleacher. Leonie looked personally offended by the surf crew's failure, while Carl was waxily inscrutable. Kelly cast her eyes to the south, where Ben was trying to convey the girls' boat back to its trailer. The very tall girl was crying, hobbling on her sore foot. Kelly pondered running down—to help Ben or, better still, to run straight past to the wooden staircase and up to The Lodge, there to lower the blinds and curl up in bed.

She went to say something to Jude, but the other woman had slipped away. In her seat, preventing any hope of escape, was Daniel's father. Kelly at first failed to recognise him out of his council manager's beige-on-beige. Dripping wet, Frontal wore a tight Bluebird rashie, a lifesaver's skull cap, and a pair of the bicycle-style shorts now favoured in surf clubs over budgie smugglers. His attire, like the page at the back of an opera program, was a billboard of sponsors' names.

'Why is Leonie in the neutral area?' Frontal said. 'We have a VIP box.'

'Go down and ask her,' Kelly said.

'I'd lose my seat for the senior boys' race. They're good things.'

Frontal was dressed as a club marshal, but he might as well have been a competitor in the event for proud fathers. Daniel had graduated to the senior crew despite being two years younger than the other boys. Bluebird success, having taunted Frontal all his life, had arrived ahead of time for Daniel. There was something miraculous in it: Frontal disappearing to Greece for five years and coming back with this son, like a prize from Troy. And yet it was love, only love, Kelly admonished herself. She had to be more like Jude: more forgiving, more adult.

'Which one is Daniel's boat?' she asked.

Frontal thrust his arm across her towards the Bluebird I crew, where Daniel towered over the eighteen-year-olds. 'These boys are raised on good food and exercise, raw talent and hard work! No genetic advantages!' Frontal attempted a self-deprecating laugh, throwing his hands open to show his less-than-prepossessing physique.

'Are you marshalling?' Gordon asked.

'Not for Dan's race! Conflict of interest!'

Whistles were blown and the senior boys dragged their boats to the tideline. Unlike Lou's girls, the Bluebird boys' team was in the middle of the beach, in the top-seeded position, where they would have to contend with the battering chop on the way out but would receive assistance on their return.

'You paid your rates yet?' Frontal said out of the side of his mouth.

Kelly looked at Gordon, who shrugged.

'We haven't?' she said.

'Here's what you don't get,' Frontal said, directing a fixed smile at the ocean. 'I know you don't want to see someone like me as your friend, but the sooner you realise I have your interests at heart, the better you'll be. If your rates go overdue another cycle, you get a mandatory inspection. And you know what that means.'

'Now's not the time or place,' Kelly said.

'Sure, sure,' Frontal replied. 'We're here for the boys.'

'And the girls,' she added.

What was insulting was not that Frontal thought he was doing the right thing; it was that they were fifty years old and having to answer to this knobhead. Whatever happened with The Lodge, they had to get out of here. Gordon was kidding himself. He was no hero of conservation; he was a slave to circumstance. Frontal might be its weak-chinned face, but their real nemesis was an impersonal, inescapable force. Frontal's power manifested not in pieces of paper, but in the arm-twisting muscle of gravity. Gordon's unreasonable hatred of this pathetic individual diverted him from the truth, which was that he had, long ago, lost the battle.

He had lost. Kelly had to make him see that.

'Never mind the way out, you just watch them come home,' Frontal murmured, as if passing on a last-minute betting tip.

The starting gun cracked. Kelly noticed Daniel nearly falling off the side of the surfboat as he jumped aboard. Frontal winced, but soon the boys were stroking in unison. The wind chop threw the boat, but the sweep was able to maintain their line. They were in fourth place as they rounded the buoys. Frontal leapt to his feet.

The heavy wooden surfboats had to round two buoys about fifty metres apart, making their course a triangle. This design was to ease congestion, but at both buoys the crews were cutting across each other. There seemed to be no rules. The tactical battle was said to thrill purists, but it was a slightly terrifying convergence, Kelly thought, of testosterone and teak at sea. Fortunately, it took place far enough out for the spectators not to take fright. Otherwise, surfboat racing might have gone the way of bare-knuckle boxing.

Bluebird I emerged from the melee in second place, ahead of Manly and Capri but trailing Old Bar. Frontal cupped his hands around his mouth and screamed support, his voice cracking; he seemed more concerned that Bluebird beat the hated neighbour Capri than win the race. Halfway to the shore, Old Bar caught a crumbling wave that slung them further into the lead. Bluebird was left behind this wave and slightly ahead of the one behind, which was caught by Capri. Sixty or seventy metres from the sand, Old Bar held a handy lead while Bluebird was fighting to hold second place ahead of a fast-closing Capri and Manly.

Accounts of what happened next would differ. There were no television cameras, and phone footage from the beach was fragmentary. The Bluebird sweep would allege that his boat had right of way ahead of Capri, while Capri would claim they were stopped from passing by one of the Bluebird rowers pulling his oar from the water and smacking a Capri rower in the jaw.

The Bluebird and Capri boats came together with a crack that splintered the breeze. Rather than bounce off and stroke for home, as usually happened in these close battles, both crews became primarily interested in belting each other. It appeared to Kelly that Daniel was the first to leap from his boat and board the enemy's, brandishing his oar like a pirate. But she couldn't be sure. With their swimmers stuffed up their cracks, all the rowers looked much the same. Teenage boys were jumping from boat to boat and using their oars as weapons. A larger wave overturned both surfboats. Then Manly careered into the middle and all three crews went under. Spectators turned away from the beach sprints and the girls' reel towards the surfboat chaos and let out alarmed cries. Old Bar hit the shore, crew abandoning boat and sprinting for the finish line. Maroubra went into second place and Windang into third, while the Bluebird, Capri and Manly boats were hull-side up, the rowers a jumble of froth.

The beach was dune-to-shore in lifesavers, but a strange paralysis set in. The confusion was overwhelming. Frontal was one of the first to move. He shouted Daniel's name, ran to the water and porpoised out between the oncoming surfboats. Soon others were following him. It was unclear how many of the boys from the Capri, Manly and Bluebird crews had surfaced. Anyone who knew about surfboat races—and anyone who didn't—saw the peril. Rowers could be knocked unconscious. Capri and Bluebird were still brawling. Witnesses and combatants would say that the worst injuries were not from oars or boats hitting the crews, but from testicles twisted under the water.

Shock pulsed through the crowd. Following the deputy general manager of the council, trained lifesavers swam towards the overturned boats. The crew from last-placed Bondi jumped from their craft to help rescue the Bluebird, Capri and Manly boys. The voice on the loudspeaker was yelling indistinctly and adding to the mayhem.

'*Oh, the humanity.*' Carl was by Kelly's side. 'The eternal cycle. Here we are again.' Hunching into his duffle coat, he walked down the bleacher and, against the tide of people streaming onto Bluebird Beach, made his way up through the car park towards the Bluebird Hilton. Leonie gave Kelly a glance indecipherable behind her sunglasses and hat, and tripped after Carl.

'Where are Ben and Lou?' Kelly asked Gordon.

'They were taking up the girls' boat, last I saw.'

'I don't want him playing the hero or going anywhere near those boys,' Kelly said with such feeling that Gordon gave her a searching look. 'Can you go find him?'

In the water, the upturned boats had drifted beneath the cliff's edge. Kelly saw a flurry of water in the place—she looked up from the water to the ledge—precisely where, on another windy day, Gordon's brother had gone off.

Gordon rushed down to the beach where marshals and guards formed a human retaining wall to stop unqualified people from entering the water. He ran around in a rising panic, searching for Ben.

Kelly needed to tell someone: a boy lost his life beneath that ledge.

She could now, from this angle where she had not been in years, read the fat graffiti.

'Ha,' she said, involuntarily.

It expressed the full extent of their imagination. It meant nothing. It said:

BLUEBIRD

As if they were dogs, and all they could bark, all they had to say to the world, was: 'Dog. Dog.'

Injured rowers were being carried to the beach. Lifesavers were shoving each other off their feet to save lives. Some rowers were bleeding and one, in a Capri cap, was carried unconscious by severe-faced professional lifeguards, laid on the sand and tended by paramedics. Marshals manhandled the crowds to make space for an ambulance. Clubs were told to form up for a headcount. From the reassembling Bluebird I team, one crewman was still unaccounted for.

The water was as empty as if there had been a shark alarm. Officials were shouting orders while among those conditioned to obedience a sense of anxious dread had set in around the blue-faced Capri boy with the paramedics, the missing rower from the Bluebird team. Everyone knew. This was a beach where boys died.

'Mum!'

Ben rushed into Kelly's arms, his thin shoulders shaking, T-shirt sucking his skin.

'Mum, it's Daniel.' Ben's voice was muffled against her chest.

Lou came up behind Ben, shaking her head gravely.

Kelly wanted to lick up Ben's tears, steal his pain, keep him in her arms, shield him, leave him pure. This was all she wanted to conserve. Not The Lodge, not Old Bluebird. Just one boy.

'Where's Gordon?' Lou asked.

Kelly pointed. Two ranks of tanned bodies emerged onto the sandbank in a marching formation, rising out of the water like pallbearers. Frontal staggered, half-drowned, at the head of the cortege. Gordon waded behind him.

The men were carrying a body.

'No,' Ben said.

'My love.' Kelly hugged him and tried to cup her hand over his face, but Ben ripped himself away.

'No, no, *nooooo*!'

The carrying party came up the beach. Spectators and carnival participants massed on the sand, thousands more on the dunes and in the car park. Around the high-rise buildings on both headlands, balconies were crowded. Cars were jammed into the bluffs and car parks.

At the centre of this amphitheatre, the carrying party stopped. Kelly heard a moving silence, and then the beginnings of—what— applause? People were clapping these heroes who had brought in Daniel's body.

'Wait,' Ben said. 'What?'

Above the heads of the funerary procession, a fist was raised. Then a second. The fingers formed the horn sign.

Daniel wasn't a body; he was a hero. Set down on the sand, he rose in front of the thousands with arms raised. The survivor. The cheering gathered force. Frontal clasped his son's right hand aloft so they were saluting the crowd together. The marshals escorted the injured crews up to the BSLSC. Faces were smeared with emotion: they had witnessed a dead boy brought back to life! His father had saved him! Kelly felt the tremors of the hero's welcome engulfing Daniel and Frontal, and within herself, a great swamping wave.

'Kel.'

It was Gordon, soaking wet and gassed.

'I thought they'd lost him,' he said.

Kelly was about to say something cynical about the Abottemey family, how they had, typically, staged their own coronation, pulled off a tricky bait-and-switch on the crowd by reviving Daniel from apparent death. What a scam. But as she looked at Gordon, she saw a grieving old man, his features furrowed, his complexion an atlas of sickly colours.

'It's all right,' she said, clasping his hand. It was wrinkled from the water. She understood. 'They didn't lose this one.'

Gordon tried to speak but had to clear his throat, in a harsh self-injuring gouge, before he could get a word out.

'We've lost,' he said. 'We've lost.'

Kelly gripped his hand between both of hers and rubbed those wrinkles as if she could make him smooth again. She could find no words.

'Wait, what? No!'

Kelly and Gordon looked at their son.

'We haven't lost yet!' Ben's eyes glittered. Kelly caught the reflection of light from Daniel's resurrection. 'We haven't lost yet!' Ben repeated, and as they climbed the stairs to The Lodge, no matter how many times Kelly asked him to explain, this was all he would tell her.

The fundraiser

SAY WHAT YOU LIKE ABOUT KIDNEY FAILURE, LOU THOUGHT as she looked up from her work to see Gordon bearing his father down the stairs from Cliff Street, it lightens the load. Ron's arms were laced around his son's neck, his ever-optimistic overnight bag hanging from his shoulder. It might have made a noble portrait of filial love, except that Gordon looked so pink with suffering, he might have been taking a run-up to throw the old man the rest of the way.

'Hurry up!' Ron said. 'It sounds like my kind of fun down there.' The bass in The Lodge's music system was making the wooden staircase dance. 'The joint is hopping!'

As Gordon set his father down on the top landing and rubbed the kinks out of his back, Lou slid out from beneath the padded medical chair connected to the beginnings of a mechanical pulley system.

'Hello there,' she said. 'You're a bit early for me.'

'Sounds to me like we're late!' Ron said.

'I never saw you as the party type,' Lou said drily.

'Since when was there an age limit?'

'Not functioning yet?' Gordon nodded at the StairLift, a parting gift from Leonie to The Lodge before her share was transferred to Carl. The StairLift had been delivered a few days earlier and Lou, ever-practical, had decided to try to install it herself to save on costs.

'It's not as hard as I thought,' Lou said. 'I was really hoping to get it working before the fundraiser.'

'Sounds like the mob didn't need it to get themselves in,' Gordon said.

'No, but they might to get themselves out.' Lou studied the instruction booklet. 'How are you, Ron?'

'I'm looking forward to when this chair is in—I'll be able to get in and out whenever I please.'

'Dad,' Gordon said.

'She's a marvel, this *girl*.' Ron glared at Lou as if daring her to take offence. She wouldn't bite. He turned back to Gordon. 'Look at everything she's doing for you. This fundraiser is her idea, isn't it? You certainly have everyone pulling out all stops for you, son. Ever feel inadequate?'

Gordon's hands wrung themselves. He drew a breath for patience, his well-practised *I am speaking to one of my parents* breath.

Lou had seen a change come over Gordon in the hours after that morning's aborted surf carnival. He had brooded alone for two hours on the balcony, rebuffing Kelly's invitations to talk, until he announced that he couldn't bear the thought of Ron dozing in front of the ABC while they were throwing a party. No matter how badly they behaved, Gordon said, you had to look after your parents. But now that he had fetched Ron, he looked queasy with remorse. Typical Gordon, she thought.

'It's generous of you to bring him,' Lou said.

'The generous one is Leonie.' Ron gave Gordon a cheerful slap on the shoulder. 'Driven by a pure love of family. This is what we of the older generation are here for,' he said to Lou. 'I've offered to fix everything, but he's too proud. Not too proud to get you working like a slave, though!'

'I have to force him to let me help,' she said.

'Your mother-in-law is an excellent businesswoman and, just quietly'—Ron leant closer to Gordon, his eyes darting, shooting what he intended as a lubricious wink but coming out more like an attack of palsy—'older ladies like younger men. Always have, but now it's allowed. Look at your wife, chasing boys young enough to be her sons.'

'You're out of your tree, Dad.'

'There were always wealthy old biddies around Bluebird, don't let anyone tell you there weren't,' Ron went on. 'I was stupid not to put my mind to it when I had the chance. You know what the worst thing about being my age is? There are no more older ladies.'

'Your "mind", you're calling it,' Gordon said.

'No need to be crass,' Ron said in an offended tone. 'If I'd married one of those old biddies, she'd have fallen off her perch within a few years. Brutal, but short. And then I'd have been on easy street. Turns out I married one anyway.'

Lou rolled her eyes at Gordon. Just when Ron had exhausted all the ways he could appal her, the old fellow came up with another.

'Norma's three years younger than you, isn't she?' she said.

'Leonie's not that much older than you, son,' Ron pressed on, undeterred. 'And there are parts of her that are quite a bit younger.'

'If she's got an eye for young men, I doubt she'd take much interest in me. Anyway, she's not doing this'—Gordon nodded gloomily at the StairLift—'out of generosity. She's just making improvements to get the place ready for market.'

'No, you're right,' Ron said. 'Blow it, I thought I'd figured it all out for you. Ah well, you could always get a job.'

'Whenever I feel sorry enough for Dad to do him a favour,' Gordon said to Lou, 'why do I feel like I'm walking into a trap I've walked into before?'

'Because those who ignore history are condemned to repeat it!' Ron said triumphantly. 'Didn't they teach you anything in school?'

Cheers rippled up from The Lodge. Gordon raised an eyebrow at Lou. 'Who's in?'

'Who do you reckon? Dog, Red Cap, TM, Sam and his dad, Snake, the old ladies, the surf crew. I've got a good repeat crowd from my other fundraisers. And a whole bunch I've never seen, up from the carnival. They're playing blackjack. Carl's set himself up as dealer. You better keep an eye on him, Gordon. He's not quite right.'

'Not for money?' Gordon said, thinking Frontal would have him now for running a casino.

Lou winced. 'You reckon that mob has money?'

'Pontoon!' Ron cried.

'Anything I can do?' Gordon asked Lou.

'I might take a break; I probably can't get it done tonight.'

'Good,' Ron interjected. 'I can sleep over!'

Gordon bent to pick his father up again, but something grabbed in his back and he lowered him to the landing.

'Hopeless,' Ron said.

'I'll take him.' Lou gathered Ron up and cradled him like a child.

'Thanks,' Gordon said.

'A pleasure,' Ron replied, hugging Lou's neck and pressing the side of his face against her chest.

'Not you,' Gordon said, trying to conceal the pain pulsing in his back.

'You don't like camping, do you?' Ron asked Lou. 'Or have we already discussed that?'

'You've already discussed that,' Lou said.

She got Ron to the bottom of the stairs and he shuffled into the house. On the doorstep, she gave Gordon a kiss on his cheek that told him all he needed to know.

'You're leaving,' he said.

Lou bowed her head. 'I promised I'd get the girls' crew to the carnival and watch Ben's cricket final. But then, yeah.'

'I'm sorry.'

'What are you apologising to me for?'

'I've failed you. I hoped to offer you a better place than the one you left.'

'Fuck's sake, Gordon, open your eyes. If you don't think you've got me to a better place, just for once in your life Open. Your. Fucking. Eyes.'

⌒

In the living room, the assembly paused their blackjack to cheer Ron's arrival. His popularity was inexplicable to Lou. Nothing but rudeness and contempt towards this crowd, and here they were, warming the house for him. Their sun-blasted Bluebird amnesia granted him a kind of emeritus status. He wasn't a cranky old misanthrope; he was Old Bluebird returning to its sacred land.

Carl was displaying an unexpected facility for handling the crowd and the card game. The Velvet Underground's *Loaded* was belting out of the stereo. His eyes glittered and he rambled briskly while dealing the cards. Lou figured he was dangerously high. She'd seen these types back home. A quiet, withdrawn, sad, helpless, gentle Carl was a good Carl. An exuberant, bullish, super-capable Carl was one step from the precipice.

Fuck, she thought. Home. Not here. Home is where your shit is waiting for you. Bluebird wasn't her shit; it was all theirs.

'Faites vos jeux! Rien ne va plus!' Carl called, and the ladies snickered. Red Cap, Snake, Dog and Tonsure Man were playing, while Josie and her older sister Lucie were spectating. Tony Eastaugh reclined in an armchair, his plastic leg elevated on a vinyl pouf, drinking something brown from a jam jar, while Sam was outside with Chook and Macca, plus, judging from the numbers, sundry Chookalikes and Maccalikes. Ron, itching to take over as dealer, made for Carl. Lou stepped into his path.

'Be careful,' she said, eyeing Carl. 'He's not predictable.'

'I can handle that wanker,' was Ron's reply.

Lou laughed, despite her resolution never to laugh at anything Ron said.

'You behave. Here's a chair, sit with your new best friend. Maybe you can talk him into going camping with you.'

'Whatever you say, boss.' Ron sat with Tony behind the card players. Tony squinted over, then under, and finally through his reading glasses.

'Ron,' Tony began their conversation.

'Tony,' Ron finished it.

From the side table next to the armchair, Ron picked up a manila folder of documents and began leafing through it. When it came to personal effects, Ron's view towards Gordon was what's yours is mine and what's mine's me own.

'Do you mind?' Gordon assumed the folder belonged to his ill-organised paperwork—distributed between the armchair, the kitchen bar, the card table and the bunk room—which he was rushing about to gather up from wherever guests might settle.

Ron gave a dismissive shrug and put the folder back down, leaving his hand on it as if to say that he would nose through Gordon's private business in his own time.

Lou asked Ron if he wanted a cup of tea. 'I'll have what he's having,' he said, nodding to the amber fluid in Tony's jam jar.

Gordon followed Lou through the saloon door to the kitchen, where she poured a Toohey's Old for Ron and drained the longneck.

'You really reckon Leonie's preparing the place for sale?' she said.

'That's my information.'

'And that's not a good thing for you? The freedom you and Kelly would have?'

Gordon shook his head. 'All a sale would do is clear the debts I've incurred since I've been here. And The Lodge would be gone to the developers.'

'We'll make some money tonight. I've set up a GoFundMe page.'

'If I knew what that was, I'm sure I would be appropriately grateful,' Gordon said. 'But it's drips going into the top of the bucket while I've got a massive hole in the bottom. Even Ben's claiming he's got some plan.'

'Ben?'

A female throat cleared behind them.

Lou turned to see Jude Oxenford bearing a box overflowing with books. At fifty, this chick would have beaten Annie Lennox in an Annie Lennox lookalike contest. Lou liked her for her intelligence and insight, and because she genuinely cared for Ben. It was Lou who had first asked Gordon if he was 'interested' in Jude; they were always chatting. But no, he'd said, he wasn't interested in that way, meaning *she* wasn't interested in that way. Gordon talked with Jude because she had a brain, and because, both having grown up here, there was so much he didn't need to explain. He was comfortable with her because he knew her inside-out. Poor Gordon, Lou thought with an inner smile as she caught Jude's eye; some things were too close to his nose for him to see.

'I forgot to tell you at the carnival, I've been keeping these aside for you,' Jude told Gordon. 'I didn't know that upgrading your library was worth this much celebrating.'

'It's not the first time I've discovered I'm throwing a party after it's started.'

'Ah, the "organic" nature of social life.' Jude gave Lou a complicit smile. 'I remember it being like this.'

'Organic, like fungus. It lies in wait for the right conditions and ingredients,' Gordon said. 'Lou organised it as a fundraiser, but as I was about to tell her, if we raise too many funds we'll have council on our case insisting I make the house safe or some bullshit like that. You've met, haven't you?'

'Of course.'

Jude reached across the sink, gave Lou a pert smile, a strong handshake and a flash of perfectly-formed collarbone.

'Why so many books?' Gordon asked.

'Oh, just cleaning out at home.' Jude nodded towards the blackjack game. 'Is this Old Bluebird? What you have solemnly vowed to preserve?'

Gordon gave the card players a weary smile. 'I made my brother-in-law chief librarian but he seems to prefer croupier.' He looked down at the box of books Jude was sliding onto the melamine table: Poe, Steinbeck, Melville, Hemingway, Bellow.

'I hope you like them,' she said. 'Are you a reader, Lou?'

Lou finished Ron's beer.

'Carl will love these,' Gordon said. 'He's taken it upon himself to hector our borrowers to stretch their minds, tells them that if you are what you read, their brains are pap. You should hear what Red Cap's old lady has to say about that the minute his back's turned.'

'Nobody likes a know-it-all,' Lou said, her eye on Jude.

'Somehow he thought it would work the other way,' Gordon said.

They contemplated the game. Carl's hands were spitting out cards so fast the players were having trouble catching them.

'Carl calls this place the Bureau of Missing Persons,' Gordon said, 'because if anyone can't be found where they should be, they'll turn up here.'

'Poetic,' Jude said.

'Yeah, but it's from a book. Every word Carl says comes with quote marks.'

'So what will you do with him?'

'The question is what'll he do with me.'

'You might become a missing person yourself.' Jude nodded pensively. 'He on his meds?'

'Taboo subject. Every day we get through without an incident, I chalk it up as a win.'

'He's okay?'

'You know how it is.' Lou, having opened another bottle of Old, edged Gordon aside. 'The bit where he's okay comes before the bit where he's in a police station. Or a hospital ward.'

'And Ben?'

'Wait, what?' Lou said.

Jude smiled in recognition.

'Downstairs,' Gordon said. 'Knuckling down with his school-work. Or something.'

'He must really want to avoid these people,' Jude said. 'Has he said anything about Daniel?'

'Are you going to tell me what happened at school?' Gordon smiled. 'Or are you going to keep faking it with me?'

'There's some white male privilege speaking,' Jude said to Lou. 'Gordon's allowed to fake it, but we're not?'

Lou and Jude smiled each other into silent submission. Eventually it was Lou who couldn't hold on. Jude was a school principal; she won staring contests against harder cases. Dropping her eyes, Lou levered up a clump of Hemingways and, from beneath, picked out a Wharton.

'Gordon could never have made the hero of a man's story,' Lou said, scanning the back cover of *Ethan Frome*. 'Men's heroes have motivations to act. Gordon makes excuses not to. A man's hero is compelled by his desire to surmount obstacles and negotiate complications. All Gordon wants is the status quo.'

Jude nodded at the book in Lou's hand. 'He belongs with Edith, not Ernest.'

'Hello?' Gordon said. 'Is your hero still in the room?'

'With the rainbow that landed up his arse the day he was born,' Jude said to Lou.

'And all the fortune he's pissed away.'

'I'm just another Bluebird battler,' Gordon said.

'If you could grow up in Bluebird and still consider yourself a battler,' Jude said, 'I congratulate you for achieving a feat of unseeing that would be admirably stubborn if it wasn't so pitiable.'

'You feel pity for him?' Lou asked.

'Only for them.' Jude tilted her head towards the living room. 'The inherited blindness. The quickness to disown privilege. The pride in the chip on the shoulder. The fetish for underdog-ism. The strident ordinariness.'

'What do you tell the kids?' Lou asked, unable to hide her interest. 'Be conscious? Don't pretend you're ordinary?'

'There's a moment, just before they become adults, when they listen. That moment is what I live for.'

Lou now tried to meet Jude's smiling eyes, but blushed shyly. If this was some kind of contest, all Lou knew about it was that she was losing.

'So?' Gordon asked with a feeble tremor, like a third wheel. 'How about you tell me what happened with Carl? Isn't that what a teacher has to do for a parent when there's some issue involving their child?'

'Not since the last century.' Jude frowned. 'I'm sorry, Gordon, I'd really like to be able to tell you, but I would only be able to do so in a safe space where the student and his parent also had the opportunity to participate.'

'I am the parent. And the student is downstairs hiding from this party in the basement like I'm hiding from it in here. You want to come down and set up a conference?'

Jude gave him a steady, serious stare. 'You and Ben are not the student and parent who have the problem.'

'Oh.'

'Right.'

'Frontal.'

Jude nodded. 'The issue is between Daniel and Carl. That's why I can't talk to you about it.'

'It's none of my business, even though we both know it is.'

Jude gave an apologetic shrug. 'Have you thought about asking Kelly?'

'She's not here,' Gordon said. 'I don't know what she does with her evenings.'

Jude rolled her eyes. 'She is looking good these days, even if I say so myself.'

'Want to stay a while?' Lou said.

Jude sighed in the direction of the living room, where the uproar was swelling and falling in sharper peaks as more alcohol was added. Japan Ned had shown up, along with the five-time state champ and her husband, as well as more surfers from the beach, who had washed off downstairs and followed the scent of free beer.

'I don't really fit in with the old crowd.'

'Sure,' Gordon replied. 'Well. Thanks for the books.'

'Here.' Lou was holding out her longneck to Jude, whose hand reached out and accepted it autonomously. 'It's not a microphone,' Lou said, and Jude drained it with three bobs of her upturned throat.

Gordon left Lou and Jude in the kitchen and went into the living room, where the volume had risen another notch. Red Cap's mother had spotted Dog 'up to a bit of jiggery-pokery' with the cards, against which Dog, backed up against the diagonal pine feature wall, was indignantly defending himself. Carl was shuffling, staying out of the argument with an intense preoccupation that Gordon tried not to find suspicious. Tonsure Man had drifted away to the clothing bins, where Ron had stationed himself, ostensibly to help Tonsure Man's sartorial choices but probably to talk him into handing over Red Cap's car keys 'for safekeeping'. Gordon took orders for drinks and poured some beer and G and Ts into more or less clean glasses, jars, mugs and vases.

'Settle, petal,' Dog was saying over his shoulder to the card players as he followed Gordon. 'Eh, the governor in his mansion! How's things? Tell you what,' Dog continued without waiting for an answer, 'I saw Kel the other day at the golf club. She's not bad!'

Gordon's eyes narrowed in the search for double meaning, but Dog seemed to be presenting face value. Not for the first time, Gordon contemplated the utter failure of his scheme to kill Dog with kindness. Quiet retribution, the appearance of forgiveness, was meant to drive Dog onto his bad conscience, and he would writhe in agony every night until his guilt drove him to repentance, apology, and finally reparations. The truth was that Dog had that most stupendous Bluebirder's gift, the knack for oblivion. That shit was yesterday. Today's another day. All good, champ. All, all good.

And Gordon suddenly saw himself the way Dog saw him: not as a nice person, not as a friend too noble to act from petty vengeance, but as a poor miserable prick incapacitated by a pain so profound that it whited him out. With pain like Gordon's, survival could only be found in forgetting. Oblivion was Gordon's lifelong habit and their great shared talent; why should it stop now?

'She was playing with your old lady, of all people,' Dog was going on. 'Good that Norma's getting around with that broken hip. She was in a cart.'

'I know, I dropped Kelly off.'

Dog aimed a head-twitch at the balcony. Red Cap and Snake protested about the disruption to the card game. Dog told them to continue without him, which Carl was already doing, flicking cards with Vegas wrists.

The sun was setting over Bluebird Beach, empty but for a huddle of kids in the south corner sharing a joint. Reminded, Dog produced a thing that looked like a second-hand toothpick from his board shorts pocket and sparked up. He offered it to Gordon, who declined.

'I live in hope,' Dog said. 'Hey now, I wanted to ask you something.'

Gordon grimaced. 'You mean tell me something. That I don't want to hear.'

'You know she's been rooting one of the assistant pros? How tacky's that.'

Dog's outrage seemed, outrageously, genuine, bereft of any memory of his part in Kelly's fall from respectability.

'Sal took a piece out of her,' Dog said. 'I mean, Kel's a free woman, but you've got to draw a line. There was a bit of how's-your-father, and who should get involved but your old lady. Norma stood up and gave Sally a big poke in the chest and said if she knew how to satisfy her husband none of this would have started! Mate, you'd have been proud of the old bird. Who'd have thought she'd be sticking up for Kel?' Dog paused, only now thinking through the tactlessness of what he was saying. 'Naturally, I made myself scarce.'

'That's what you wanted to ask me?'

'Nah, champ, just thought you'd like to know.'

'What did you want to say?'

'Well—' Dog took a drag on his joint like it was a theatrical punctuation mark—'I was down at the local court the other day and who should I run into but old bugalugs.'

'Bugalugs.'

'His nibs here.' Dog tossed his chin to the side.

'Sorry, I'm not that quick.'

'I was down there for a mention for a client who's been caught up in this banking inquiry.' A well-publicised royal commission into the banking industry had, unlike other royal commissions, resulted in actual criminal proceedings, albeit against junior rogue traders, cowboy loan officers and mortgage brokers whom the banks cut loose with no-one to represent them but bottom-feeders like Dog.

'Turns out, one of my client's close friends is old mate here.'

'If you don't tell me who you're talking about, I'm going inside. I'm meant to be keeping an eye on Carl.' And Ron, he thought. And Ben. And, as he heard Jude Oxenford's laughter from the kitchen, Lou.

'Champion, you've got your hands full with that one,' Dog said. 'I thought you had a complicated home life before.'

'What do you mean?'

'Carl's out of his gourd. Are you sure he's not on the juice? I don't think it's going to last, mate.'

'I don't think I will either.'

'That's what I'm trying to get to if you'll stop interrupting me.' Dog interrupted himself with a succession of deep drags. He was about to flick his roach away when Gordon stopped his hand.

'Just make a bit of an effort,' Gordon said.

'Sure, sure.' Dog put the roach into the pocket of his board shorts. 'But anyway.'

'Bugalugs.'

'Him!' Dog rammed a thumb at the side of the house. 'Do I have to make it any clearer?'

Gordon followed the direction of Dog's thumb, which seemed to be aimed at the bushes.

'That fucking weasel who took us to court!' Dog's voice broke.

'David Archer? I took him to court, if you want to be technically correct.'

'Yeah, Archer David!' The joint hadn't done much to dampen Dog's natural excitability. Gordon sometimes wondered if cannabis was so woven into the fabric of Dog's metabolism that he didn't get stoned anymore. He practised law, he'd kept his marriage together miraculously, he played passable golf, he surfed most days—there were few of the obvious harms associated with thirty-five years of daily smoking, so maybe there were equally few of the benefits. Maybe he smoked to maintain a steady state, and it had no more psychoactive effect than a cigarette. Exasperatingly, he always came back from his health checks with a clean bill.

'Archer David's involved with my client, who let slip that our old mate's quietly put his place on the market.'

'I doubt it. He hasn't finished his renovations.'

'Well that's the thing: he's not going to finish. He's having to sell quickly because he's going to be implicated in this action. And he's having trouble finding a buyer.'

'I suppose that can happen when they do it quietly. But they eventually get what they want.'

'You're an incurable optimist,' Dog said without irony, 'but you're wrong. The market's tanked. Have you noticed Ken Grainger's listings round Bluebird?'

'No.'

'That's because there aren't any. Nothing's selling. They're either taking places off the market or doing private off-market deals that they're not talking about because the prices are rock bottom. Something weird's going on in China. The moneymen know something. Shoe factory output numbers—I'm not sure what it is but it's set off a fucken real estate Armageddon.'

'I haven't heard anything.'

'That's because you wait till it's on TV, which means you're hearing about it six months after the fact. Which is why you were such a shit journo.'

'I was a popular journo.'

'Exactly. If you were better, nobody would have liked you.'

Gordon had to give Dog that point. Whenever Gordon got near a genuine news story, he considered who it might hurt. His reflex response had been to forget what he'd heard, or tip off one of his colleagues, even a rival newspaper. Gordon had no competitiveness, only a fail-safe instinct for the quiet life.

'Anyway,' Dog went on, 'if you listened, you'd hear the screams of chickens running around with their heads cut off. Old mate next door is going to cop a million-buck hit.'

'I thought he ran a successful multinational business. T-shirts or something.'

'Yeah, right. Successful fraud.'

Dog winked, to suggest he knew more than he was letting on. But his wink meant nothing. It was just his face, in the Orwellian sense that at fifty he had the one he deserved. Dog deserved to look like a man who was conning you. Gordon wondered: do I have the face I deserve?

'Okay,' Gordon said. 'Sounds like good news. Collapsing real estate market might save what's left of Bluebird.'

'What's your equity situation in this place?'

'I don't know. Sam can tell you.'

'Sam,' Dog said, mulling this over. 'Sam.'

'What about Sam?'

'Oh, nothing.'

'What?'

'Nothing. Anyway, all I'm saying to you is that when word gets out that there's actually some serious shit happening in those shoe factories, it's gunna be the bonfire of the fucking vanities out there; propertyapocalypto. Did I just make that up? Fuck I'm good. Half the bankers in town are going to jail, half are going to lose their jobs, and the other half are bringing down the hatchet on lending.'

'That's three halves. I'm glad you're not a banker.'

'That would have made me a *perfect* banker,' Dog said. 'Here's what I'm saying. Whatever you and Sam have been cooking up, or whatever he's cooking up on your behalf, I'm warning you, you're rooted. Best-case scenario? The bank will revalue the house and you'll be up to pussy's bow in negative equity. No more draw-downs, no more fancy living, no more parties.'

'That's the best case?'

'The worst case is that Sam ends up being represented by me.'

'Sam?'

'As soon as the voting share changes hands next week from Leonie to Carl and the title search produces actual documents, Sam's lending practices will be on the record. It's a domino effect, buddy. That's what I'm telling you. You reckon Leonie's handing The Lodge to Carl just to protect her position in the Hilton? Champ, you know her better than that. There's always wheels within wheels.'

They paused to watch the circle of kids on the beach shake the sand off their blanket and leave. They were laughing and pushing each other. Innocence: Gordon tried to remember that.

'I knew you were going to be telling me something,' Gordon said.

'Come again?'

'You said you wanted to ask me something, but I knew you'd be telling me something.'

To Gordon's surprise, the kids on the beach were heading not up the sand path to the top car park, but southwards along the shoreline, towards the jump rock and the base of the stairs leading to The Lodge.

'Oh no, I did want to ask you something,' Dog said.

'What's that?' Gordon's mind whirred through a sequence of fantasy questions Dog might ask him.

Why, after how I stitched you up in court, do you listen to a word of my so-called legal advice?

Why haven't you thrown me off this balcony for what I did to you?

Why don't you max out my Fast Ferry and Eastons cards—why do you make such pitiful token purchases when you could really get me in the shit with Sally?

And one last question.

'Fuck! Holy fucking fuck!'

Dog was smacking at his thigh. He ran down the external stairs to the shower, swearing noisily. His unextinguished roach had ignited his board shorts. His pants were on fire.

Gordon leant over the rail.

Dog howled in pain. His board shorts and shirt were soaked. 'Fucken fuck this!'

There were only one or two times in a life, Gordon thought, when you felt you had the power of magic.

Dog saw him leaning over the rail. Perhaps he didn't like the smug look on Gordon's face. Perhaps he had remembered what he meant to ask.

'Why are you letting everyone else fuck up their lives trying to help you? Eh, champ? What makes you so special?'

Gordon turned his back on Dog and went into the party to look for Sam.

The cliff

GORDON TAPPED SAM ON THE SHOULDER.

'A word?'

'Brother, I thought you'd never ask. Outside?'

'Not here.'

Under a fingernail moon they crossed the beach and climbed the rocks behind the ocean baths and the 'marina', a shed and concrete ramp for launching shit-tin dinghies. It was still there, the marina, long after they'd stopped the boats.

Sam was limping from a fin-cut to the arch of his foot he had sustained while surfing. They climbed past the RSL, which was undergoing a renovation paid for by three towers of home units and townhouses in construction on its adjoining land. No words were needed for where Gordon was taking him. It was years since they had been to the sad place, the bad place. In the old days, they used to come up each anniversary, to sit and let their legs swing off the ledge, feeling the pull. Sam felt that pull again now. They stepped across the narrow sandstone bridge from the tip of the headland. The moon lit the rocks. Sam sat beside Gordon on the ledge. Their blood pooled in the bottoms of their feet. Sam rubbed his aching fin-cut.

'So it's true?' Gordon said.

Sam confirmed Gordon's fears. All too late, Sam had figured out Leonie's plan. She had guessed that Gordon would eat the house and that Sam would enable him by stealthily revaluing his share. She would buy Gordon's debts for one dollar, and his share of the trust would, thanks to Sam's dodgy valuations, be worth three times what it was when she gave it to him. That extra couple of million would then finance operations at the Hilton.

'What if I find another buyer? Leonie can't make me sell to her. That'd be like . . . slavery,' Gordon said hopefully.

'You're a holy fucken fool, Gordo. We're all cheering for the holy, but sometimes it looks like the fool is winning. If you'd read your contract, you would know that it gives Leonie first and last option. You can't sell to anyone else. It's a two-million-dollar fraud at the expense of the Bluebird Building Society, made possible by my weakness for my mate,' Sam said. 'And of course I'm not going to report it, because that would implicate me.'

'So Leonie wins.'

'Doesn't she always? It's like a slow-motion Attenborough doco,' Sam said appreciatively. 'Insect caught in the spider web—that's us.'

'We're fucked.'

'And just when we thought the world had run out of ways to fuck us, council's approved the redevelopment of the firehouse. We can lodge an appeal with the Land and Environment Court, and good luck with that if you don't have fifty grand. Groundworks start in three months. They're knocking the joint down. Gordo, there's nothing of Bluebird left to save. We should probably be amazed that it lasted this long. Still! Check out this view.' Bluebird Bay glimmered beneath their feet. 'The world is good, yeah?' Sam spat, and watched his golly arc down into the dark ocean.

But this was the place for beginnings, not endings: they had tacitly conspired all those years ago to dedicate this place to the future. Here, Sam had become Gordon's brother.

'So why did you bring me here?' Sam asked. 'You reckon this is a good place to hear bad news?'

The breeze carried noise from The Lodge across the bay. The rest of Bluebird was empty mansions with robot lighting. The Lodge, one happy bulb, was all the illumination left. Gordon said nothing.

'Don't you think it's weird that Ron and Tony are talking to each other?' Sam said. 'Well, when I say talking to each other, I was looking at them in the party and Ron was doing all the talking. But then I noticed that Dad was doing all the talking too. Both gabbing over the top of each other, deaf as posts. Talk about strange bedfellows. What do you reckon that's about?'

Gordon looked distant, as if he was asking himself, *Why did I bring him here?*

'The future, I reckon,' Sam answered himself. 'How is it that they're more invested in it than we are? No choice, I s'pose. No way they can talk about the past. Camping trips, eh. What else is there to look forward to? Ron's probably figuring out how to pinch Dad's car keys. You know, the one part of me that actually looks forward to the firehouse being knocked down and all the shit hitting the fan is that I'll finally go somewhere Dad can't find me. I'll shoot through—if I don't end up in jail—and the old man will get put into care. Goodnight, nurse.'

Gordon's face looked like it was full of fish hooks, each weighed down by a lead sinker.

Sam put a hand on his shoulder and asked, 'Do you think about him as much as I do?'

Gordon breathed through his nose.

'I've got it down to two or three times a day,' Sam said. 'I often think we'd have been better off if we all went our separate ways, got shot of him, started again. It's like when he went over, he had a hand around each of us. Just like this property crash. Everyone in Bluebird's got his hand around the next bloke's ankle. One goes down, we all go down. You know what I'm saying? It's been forty-two years, but he won, didn't he? He took us down.'

'I just love Bluebird,' Gordon said.

'Shit, brother, there's no fucking statute of limitations on what you've put yourself through for his sake. You're loving Bluebird to death. And why? Because we fucked up and it's up to us to make it good? What if we can't? How many years before we admit defeat?'

'I feel lucky every day to wake up in The Lodge,' Gordon said.

'You sure don't look it. Fuck, man, you want to speak in clichés? Let me give you one. Saving The Lodge won't set you free. Only the truth will do that.'

Gordon patted Sam's hand and lifted it from his shoulder, got to his feet, backed away from the ledge and crossed the sandstone bridge. Sam, with a frustrated sigh, limped behind on his wounded foot. They walked the beach under moonlight. The kids with the picnic blanket had disappeared. The Lodge was hopping, music flooding the bay: Carl had gone the full Hendrix.

As they re-entered the party, Sam relieved his dozing father of his empty beer jar. Ron was still sitting beside him, reading

Gordon's mail. The last of their kind, Sam thought. Leaving us, the good sons, to repay their debts. I've only ever wanted to make it all right again. Could there be so little mystery? And what would it mean if the one good man in this place was the one who ended up in jail?

Sam dropped the beer jar back into Tony's lap and strode across the crowded room with a fierce look.

'Gordo.'

'Come again?' Gordon cupped a hand to his ear. Carl had turned '1983 (A Merman I Should Turn to Be)' up full-bore. Those kids from the beach had come in: boys from Ben's school, a couple of stoned-looking girls.

Sam enclosed Gordon in a hug.

'You want another cliché?' Sam's voice was rough, savage in Gordon's ear. 'I love you. And no matter what happens, you don't owe me, I owe you. I love you. I love you, Gordo, I fucken love you.' Sam felt Gordon shaking. He tightened his hug so he couldn't see Gordon's face. 'But you're fucken killing us all.'

Fight night

BEN HAD NO TIME FOR PARTIES. IN THE WEE-SMELLING Boardroom, he took up his stance in his cricket kit before the full-length mirror Lou had rescued from a hard rubbish collection. Pads, thigh pad, box, gloves, helmet, magic stick. Zane had told him they might get five hundred for the Gray-Nic. Ben would use it in next Sunday's final, which he had to be picked in as they were down on numbers. The two injured boys from the Capri surfboat crew were in the St Pat's cricket team—yay! He would make a huge score with the magic stick, and then he and Zane would quietly clean up on the black market. A signed collector's item! Ben could then add his share to the nine hundred dollars he had already socked away from his recent enterprises. The community would pitch in together and save Gordon, save The Lodge. Then, Ben could refocus himself on playing for Australia, and one day in the future, his dad would wonder what all the worry had been about.

He tapped his bat on the concrete, played a handsome straight drive, held his pose in the mirror. 'Classic shot from Grimes, that,' he murmured.

Just then he heard a surf ski slide down the other side of his wall and crash into the concrete.

'Bugger!' Ben heard his dad say.

In a rush, Ben hid his bat, got out of his cricket gear, and slipped into a T-shirt and board shorts. Luckily, his dad didn't appear until Ben was dressed and the cricket stuff was hidden. Gordon continued to swear and fuss about, scraping surf equipment on the hard floor.

'You okay, Dad?'

'Yep, yep, fine.' In a strange way, Ben's dad looked like the one who had been caught in the act.

'How's the party?'

'Noisy,' Gordon said. 'I wouldn't mind hiding down here too.'

Ben was leaning against his desk in an unnatural posture. To do something with his hands, he picked up the expensive Seiko alarm clock his dad had bought at Eastons. It was a yellow box, like the timing boxes used at the finish line of the Olympic Games, but it was a pointless gift. Ben had several alarm clocks. The Seiko model was the type of thing you would buy to impress a twelve-year-old. Ben recognised it as the simulacrum of a gift, not a real thing. Its meaning lay somewhere off to the side. Gifts were symbols of gifts. Life was a dreamlike symbol of life.

Beneath the Seiko clock was Ben's envelope, with the nine hundred dollars he had saved. He made a decision: he was going to give Dad the money now. He had not come up with a story to explain why he had nine hundred dollars, but the stricken look on Dad's face showed him that the time was right. Dad needed money, but more than that, he needed good news.

Ben reached for the envelope.

'Oh, your friends are upstairs.'

'Wait, what?' Ben's hand froze.

'Your friends. Upstairs.'

'Friends?'

'Daniel and some others,' Gordon said casually, as if Ben had friends who turned up every day. 'They came up from the beach.'

'Oh. Okay.' Ben decided to leave the money till later. He took his hand away and ran it through his hair. 'Does Daniel look all right?'

'Miraculously unscathed,' Gordon said.

'I know you don't like me hanging with him.'

'I just want you to be careful. Whatever you think of Daniel, it might not be your job to bring him out. You're going to like a lot of other boys in your life.'

'I don't *like* him. I just want to help him.'

'And I only want to help you to be better than me at fifty. And better than your grandpa at eighty. I don't think I can achieve any of that. But I do think I can help you to be safer than me at sixteen.'

Gordon opened his arms. Ben stepped forward to be hugged. An enormous crash above their heads ruptured the moment.

As Ben made for the stairs, Gordon said, 'And, mate? Sorry, when's your cricket final?'

Ben ventured a smile. 'You forgot the date, or you didn't realise I'd be picked in the team?'

'Both, to be honest.'

'Sunday.'

There was an outburst of shouting. Ben's eyes popped.

'Oh no—is Uncle Carl . . . Where did you say Daniel was?'

'Yeah, up there.'

Ben took the stairs three at a time. His father, as usual the last to join the dots about what was going on in his own house, shambled along behind.

It took time for Ben to make sense of what he saw at the top of the stairs. The newel from the staircase had come off again and was in his hand. The blackjack game was in an uproar, with Josie, her sister Lucie, Tony Eastaugh and Grandpa, of all people, screaming incoherently at each other. The card table had been upended. Grandpa was hurling cards like lost betting tickets. Tonsure Man was trying his best to calm Grandpa down, while Tony Eastaugh appeared to be delivering a chairman's speech, his prosthetic leg wobbling, calling the meeting to order, but nobody was listening. Lou and Principal Oxenford were observing from the kitchen, detached and amused, over the saloon door. Dealer Carl was nowhere in the exploded card game—because Dealer Carl was out on the balcony, where the real action was. Kids and surfers were yelling and pushing each other and two stoned girls were screaming. Daniel was throwing punches like an out-of-control millwheel. Dog was somewhere at the bottom of the pack.

Just as he didn't know how it began, Ben couldn't work out how it ended. Unlike movie fights, real fights are over the minute you've realised they have started. Daniel and the kids disappeared from the house amid more yelled threats. Red Cap's mother was shouting at Carl, while Tony Eastaugh was calling 'Order!' at Dog, who was wiping blood off his mouth.

Ben felt something crunch underfoot. He looked down: a Kyoto teacup lay in shards. From the crack in the next floorboard, a jagged half of a beautiful saucer protruded.

'Just get out!'

Ben looked at his dad.

'The lot of you, get the fuck out of my house! Go on, fuck off, the lot of you!'

Ben had never seen Dad like this, in a hot rage, waving his arms, yelling and screaming. He wasn't disturbed to see Gordon crack up. He was proud.

Getting them out took longer than the fight. People were reacting in bizarre ways to Gordon's outburst. Josie had the temerity to shake her fist at Lou for not having finished installing the StairLift. Red Cap had words with Gordon about using that kind of language to his mother and aunt. Japan Ned told Gordon it was going to be 'Shit out tomorrow', flashed his white teeth and flung out an unreciprocated high-five.

Even when Gordon had rearranged Grandpa in an armchair with a Scotch, Carl on the balcony with a cup of tea (Big W mug for him), and Lou had escaped into the dark with Principal Oxenford, Ben couldn't figure out how two fights had broken out simultaneously. Eventually he pieced together that Grandpa, who had been quietly watching the card game, had hobbled behind Carl to get eyes on the dealer's side. Grandpa then announced that Carl was cheating. Carl said Grandpa was giving signals to Josie, who was passing those messages to Red Cap. To this counter-allegation, Josie had become confused by the detail and taken maximum umbrage, not at Carl but at Tony Eastaugh, whom she had known all her life and didn't think a lot of. Tony said some things about Josie's marriage, which had ended with the death of her husband some nineteen years earlier, information which was freshly injurious. When Red Cap defended his mother's honour, Tony said some more choice words about Red Cap's teaching career and threw the first punch—at Tonsure Man, who had been standing by innocently. Tony seemed to mistake him for someone else.

Carl, whose enthusiasm for the card game had evaporated, had shuffled outside to take cover from the fiasco. Nothing was guaranteed to upset his fragile equilibrium more than old people in a bar-room brawl. He didn't like being accused of cheating either. But what threw him right out was seeing an adult giving kids drugs, which was what he literally stumbled upon outside, after tripping on the Shitfuckerpoobum and falling into Dog, who was offering a joint to Daniel's friends. Carl spoke to Dog about pushing dope to minors and, on the way through, about fucking his best friend's wife. This in turn led to Daniel telling Carl that he had no high horse to get on. Who threw the first punch was now beyond relevance.

Carl was trembling and sweating. 'I'm a bit shaky,' he said to Ben.

'Generally, or tonight?'

Carl's tea mug knocked against his teeth with a Big W clink. He lowered the cup and looked at the white line of froth on a broken wave in the moonlight.

'Neither.'

A noise interrupted them. From inside, Lou was rapping urgently on the sliding door. At her side was Principal Oxenford, who still smiled like she was watching a TV comedy, and behind them was Ben's mum, hair piled on her head, dressed like one of the Bangles. Ben wasn't sure if he felt caught and guilty or left behind and innocent. Kelly's panic-stricken face moved to one side; behind her stood two blue-shirted police officers. To Gordon she was silently mouthing, 'What the fuck?'

'Officers, welcome to The Lodge,' said Ronald Grimes, hobbling past Gordon. 'How may I assist you?'

Shameless

KELLY WONDERED IF POLICE CAME IN GIRL-GIRL PAIRS OR OLDER woman-younger man. Every other kind of couple in the world was recombining but not the police. In The Lodge's living room stood the standard twosome: older plod, junior woman. Kelly didn't know either one. Long gone were the days when the men who carried out the busts were your schoolmates' dads.

'Are you the owner of the premises?' Plod asked Gordon, who glanced at Kelly, Carl and Ron and said, 'Long story.'

'That's a yes?'

Gordon nodded. Dog had one word of advice regarding cops: 'lawyer'. But Kelly had seen Dog hiding in the garden with his weed stash, and Gordon was too exhausted to bother with strategy. He was on the wrong side of everything—history, for a start, but not, if he got lucky and made the right moves, the law.

'If it's a noise complaint, I'm sorry, it's over now.'

The cops' eyes were spraying the room: broken chairs, an upturned couch, a card game decidedly past its best. The newel-less banister tilted. A slat of the diagonal pine feature wall was missing, as were two of the louvres in the saloon door. The macramé curtain on the kitchen window was in tatters.

'Who lives here?' the policewoman asked, jotting notes.

'Me and my son,' Gordon said. 'My goddaughter's been here a few months.'

'And me,' Kelly said. 'And as of next week, him.' She indicated Carl, who was vibrating in the balcony doorway, stomping down the aluminium Shitfuckerpoobum.

'Who's he?'

'He's my brother.'

Both police officers gave Carl a hard look. While Plod was wafting an expensive-looking digital device—his iPlod?—the junior partner, equipped with analogue recording materials, continued writing notes on her pad.

'Me too!' This was Ron, raising his hand. 'There's no electric chair, so I'm in for the long haul. My daughter-in-law will make up a bed for me.'

Kelly gave Gordon a look of raw horror. Gordon shook his head and said to the police, 'My dad lives in a nursing home down in Capri.'

'Did live,' Ron maintained. '*Did* live.'

'Please don't take advantage of a difficult situation. I'll be taking you home later.'

'See'—Ron appealed to the police—'how they treat me?'

Ron interested the police less than he should have. They took a moment to confer, their eyes on Carl, who responded by pushing through the silent group with his empty tea mug, rinsing it in the kitchen, and returning to the balcony. He appeared to step out of his way to give the senior policeman a shove.

'How long has he been here?' asked iPlod.

'His mother was the owner, and she's gifting it to him,' Gordon said.

'It hasn't gone through yet,' Lou interjected.

'Stepmother,' Kelly said.

'It's going through, don't worry,' Ron said.

The police were looking from character to character as if they had missed the start of a play.

'You got a tricky situation,' iPlod said to Gordon. His partner continued jotting.

'You don't know the half of it.'

'Right,' iPlod said. 'Anyway, we did get a noise complaint but we came to deliver this. Not strictly our job, but the station's often doing the courthouse's work. Cost cuts, you know.'

He was holding a urine-yellow envelope in a significant way. Gordon decompressed. They were not getting busted for the fight. Dog's pot smoke had blown away. Carl had not decked one of the cops. The night was looking up.

iPlod regarded the assembled company and looked momentarily like Poirot about to deliver the solution. But he sighed heavily and said, 'Good luck with the family and that.'

'I'll show you out,' Kelly said.

When Kelly came back, Gordon had opened the envelope. She stood at his shoulder and read the council letter demanding a statement of occupancy: how many people were living in the premises, how many bedrooms, what were the purposes of the dwelling, was any commercial business being undertaken. Please provide details. (Even, Kelly thought, if the answer is no?) The letter mentioned fines, costly improvements, unspecified legal action, or eviction if the building's purpose under zoning laws as a residential dwelling with a maximum occupancy had been violated. It had Frontal's fingerprints all over it. No, that wasn't very deductive: it had Michael Abottemey's signature at the bottom of it.

'Frontal's made his move.' Gordon handed Kelly the letter and started to right the chairs and couch.

'I don't know what to say,' Kelly said. 'This place looks like fucking *Animal House.*'

'Language,' Ron rumbled.

'And how are you?' Kelly asked sourly. 'Isn't it about time you went home?'

'I told you, I'm staying the night,' Ron snapped, throwing an air punch in Kelly's direction.

'Leave the cleaning to us,' Lou said to Gordon. Jude Oxenford was on her knees, gathering up the shards of the broken Japanese china. 'You take your father home. Are you parked above or down? Are you under the limit?'

'I'm fine,' Kelly said. To Gordon's inquiring look she added, 'Dud date.'

As Kelly and Gordon lifted him out, Ron began to bleat about illegal evictions and how he would call the police, if not on the phone then at the top of his lungs. But the poor fellow was so weak, so heartbreakingly light, that they were able to cart him down the stairs without breaking a sweat. By the time they got to the beach, Ron was unconscious.

'Well that was a success,' Kelly said.

'What a debacle.' Gordon had to stop to pull up his falling-down trousers. Ron lay in a heap at his feet.

'It's been coming ever since Carl showed up.'

'Let's get this one buckled in.'

Gordon picked his father up and recommenced towards the Car With No Name.

～

While trying to keep her eyes on the road, Kelly turned towards her father-in-law, who was burrowing through the glove compartment. Gordon was in the back seat, staring out the window.

'Don't waste your time,' she said. 'Only an idiot would keep a second key inside the car.'

'That's why I'm looking.'

They were almost at the nursing home and Ron was going through Gordon's things with the persistence of a truffle pig. Kelly, who had lied about being under the alcohol limit, proceeded slowly, as if to drive below the limit of visibility.

Ron smacked the glovebox shut.

There ought to be some kind of criminal offence, Kelly thought, for being Ron Grimes.

'What are you smiling at?' Ron said.

'How Gordon took you to The Lodge, where you had a lovely time, not that he needed to, only because he felt sorry for you, and yet already you're plotting to steal his car.'

'What else would you expect me to do?' Ron said.

'Can we do a drive-by delivery at the nursing home?' Kelly looked in the rear-view mirror at Gordon, who was still disengaged. 'I can slow down below twenty, and we just chuck him out?'

'You've really made a mess of your lives, haven't you?' Ron said.

'Do you have a point,' Kelly asked, 'or are you just taking pleasure in the bleeding obvious?'

Ron was reading a caravan park brochure from Up North that Ben had left in the glovebox. Ben, Kelly knew, had an overdeveloped curiosity in real estate to go with his premature anxiety about his parents' finances. He had picked up the brochure as an encouragement to Gordon.

'Onsite vans,' Ron read. 'All those losers who couldn't keep up with the city, flattering themselves that they're "refugees". As if they'd escaped from a war instead of their own uselessness.'

'If it pleases you, I won't call myself a refugee,' Gordon said.

'So you are thinking about it!' Ron exclaimed. 'I told your mother you would let us down.'

'He's already putting everything on hold for you and Norma,' Kelly said.

'And what would "everything" be? Curing cancer? Stopping global warming? You'd be saving the world right now, except for your responsibilities to your dear mother and father?'

'No,' Gordon said, 'just putting off moving Up North to live in a caravan like all the other losers.'

For all the pitfalls in conversations with his father, they tended to force Gordon to blurt out a truth he didn't recognise until he said it. Kelly wondered if that was Gordon's bail-out plan—an onsite van, eating his heart out over his beloved Bluebird. She couldn't see it. Whether he knew it or not, he had to go where the love was, and what love did he have in his life? Ben and Lou, who would leave him. His parents, sort of. Herself he did love, she guessed, out of habit. He wasn't *in* love with her anymore. Unrequited passion for your own spouse carried too heavy a discount. He loved his friends, but only in that they were woven into that texture of beach and village which was the stuff of his life. And this was it: if he did have one love it was Bluebird. He couldn't leave. He was stuck with it.

'You going to throw me out like a bag of garbage, or just sit there half drunk?' Ron was saying. They were in the forecourt of the nursing home. The reception area was lit up behind the glass front doors, which were activated by the four-digit da Vinci code. 'Oh no, you're too good, aren't you? You wouldn't hurt an old man, no matter how much he provoked you. What a pair of heroes.'

'Ron . . .' Kelly wanted to tell her father-in-law the truth. *We won't hurt you because we can't trust ourselves not to kill you.*

Ron was nodding as if agreeing with Kelly's thoughts. 'I'd have more respect for you both if you came and smothered me in the night. It must be tempting. With these retirement home fees and God strike me pink, the taxes on getting old! We're spending your inheritance as fast as we can. We're worth a lot more to you dead than alive. Come to think of it, if we really wanted to help you out, your mother and I would take the injection right now. You thought of that?' Ron stroked his chin, speculating for the first time on fatherhood as an act of self-sacrifice.

'Constantly,' Kelly said.

'Good girl!' Ron smacked her thigh. 'Because if you're waiting for us to die so that you can inherit something, think again. Once I'm gone, Norma will live another fifteen years. Take my advice. Don't do anything for us in the expectation of a pay-off.'

'Thanks, Ron, we can reassure ourselves about the purity of our motives.'

'Too much purity if you ask me,' Ron said.

'What does that mean?' Gordon asked, and looked immediately like he wished he hadn't.

'I'm not stupid, son. All these years, I'm trying to get you to bite back. You won't even ball up your fists against me in self-defence!

We know what it is, and believe it or not, we know you're not piss-weak, but whatever strength you've got, it's the self-destructive kind, I'll tell you that. You've spent your whole life trying to make it up to us. It's been terrible to see.'

Kelly's throat felt like a westerly wind had blown through it. Ron Grimes was speaking to Gordon honestly about what had happened to their family. If Gordon opened up in response—if he and his father could *share*—she could die happy.

She tilted the rear-view mirror to see Gordon's face. He looked like one of those computer-generated images of what a new US president would look like after two terms in office. He looked thirty years older. He looked like Ron.

'It's been pretty terrible for him to live,' Kelly said.

'Shame is a worthless currency,' Ron said. 'No matter how much you have, it can never be enough.'

'What else could he do?'

His face lit by the nursing home's glowing porch, Ron was glaring through the windscreen like a death's head. 'He could have been more like his father. You've always called me shameless. You think it's a bad thing? It's not, it was the only way forward. I've set Gordon an example that he never cared to follow. He's wasted his life—*your* lives—trying to make it up. Stuck in the past, boy, that's always been your problem. Try living for tomorrow. It's not too late. And for the love of God, contact the JPA!'

Gordon got out of the car and for once Ron was compliant, waiting patiently for him to unfold his walker. Kelly saw the nurse, Jada, receive them in the foyer. Jada, Gordon and Ron had a brief smiling conversation. Lies for lies.

Kelly took another look at that caravan park brochure. Gordon should go. Bugger the parents, bugger the obligations, bugger

Bluebird. There's no dignity in this life. Listen to your father. Be shameless. It's not too late.

She returned the brochure to the glovebox and pulled a U-turn. Gordon got into the car and they drove back past the home. Ron's bedroom window was lit up. So was the downstairs lobby, bright enough to show the old man, eighty years old, overnight bag on his arm, furiously punching the inside keypad. He smacked the double-glazed door. It was this—the image of utter failure in that lit-up goldfish bowl—that brought a smile to Kelly's face. Gordon began laughing. He wound down his car window and howled at that silent man on the other side of the glass, striking it like a bird flying into an invisible pane.

'Sucked in, you mean old prick, they changed the code today!' Gordon shouted, and Kelly doubted Ron could have heard him, but as she dropped the car into gear and squealed off, she thought she caught a glimpse of the old man giving them a thumbs-up.

One for the road

KELLY AND GORDON SAT ON THE DECK OVERLOOKING BLUEBIRD Beach, mortally fatigued, minds racing too fast to sleep. Gordon had told her about the earlier part of the evening, before she got home. All those plates he had been spinning were falling to the ground. Lou was going to leave by Carl's settlement date, once she'd got the StairLift installed. Something was going on between her and Jude Oxenford. Ben's involvement with Daniel had Gordon on high alert. There was the fight, or fights, and the still unresolved acts that had provoked them. There was Carl, there was Carl, there was Carl. There was Dog's information about David Archer, aka Archer David, and the collapsing real estate market. There was Ron, there was Ron, there was Ron.

There was his conversation with Sam, but he did not tell her about that.

There were unseen forces closing in. Maybe not unseen: there was, in his hand, Frontal's letter.

'At least I know how to deal with this one,' he said.

From between two deck boards Gordon prised a matchbox—must have been Dog's, dropped during the fight. He lit the council letter.

'If Frontal wants me, he knows where to find me.'

'Hey, lighting fires is illegal.' Kelly pulled a doob from her handbag and lit it with one of Dog's matches. 'Oh well, if you insist . . . You don't mind?' she said, the kind of politeness that had come into their marriage once it was over. She watched Gordon flick the last ember of the council letter over the rail. 'Have you seen the new blue post the council has put in down at the top of the path?'

Gordon shook his head. 'Post?'

'The list of things you can't do. They had to extend it to fit in all the pictograms. It's taller than me. It looks like an Egyptian obelisk.'

Gordon said, 'The Dog. No Dogs.' A reference to a photo they had taken of a pub, years ago: the pub was called The Dog, and next to it was a sign saying NO DOGS. It had become one of their thousand points of private language. They shared a mellow chuckle, the unintended consequence breaking over them: they couldn't mention Dogs anymore without a second wave of remorse. Maybe, Kelly thought, of all the things that had been lost, that was the worst of them, the innocence of their language.

'I heard you had an interesting encounter at the golf club,' Gordon said.

'Oh?'

'With Sally Gilsenan.'

'I thought you were going to say with Ricky the assistant pro. That was my dud date tonight.'

'You can have all the assistant pros you like. After thirty years of me, I'm not going to begrudge you a bit of fun,' Gordon said. 'Actually, I don't mean that. I'm saying it because I want to sound grown up.'

What had their sex life dwindled to? The unspoken contract, since early in their married life, that she would never say yes and he would never say no. There might also be a question of what he deserved after so many years of that.

'Yeah, Sally,' she croaked through her smoke. 'She wanted to take me down, right there on the seventeenth green. She was blowing up about the charges on Dog's Eastons card. She reckoned it was me! And then your mum stepped in.'

'I wish I'd been there.' Gordon looked at her and grimaced. 'Not really.'

'Don't underestimate your mother,' Kelly said. 'She's still got a few surprises in her.'

'Such as?'

Kelly gave an enigmatic one-shoulder shrug, rearranged the spaghetti strap that had slipped down her upper arm, and blew smoke at Bluebird Bay.

'Let's just say that not looking after your department store charge cards ranks pretty highly in your mother's scale of no-nos. It wasn't "You ought to keep a closer eye on your husband", it was "You ought to be ashamed of not keeping an eye on your Eastons card". But hey, your parents have been through a lot.' She sharpened her eyes at Gordon, who ducked his head. 'We do need to talk about it, darling. You, me, Ben.'

'Do you think Carl's okay?' Gordon said to shift them off his fucked-up family and onto hers.

Kelly dragged smoke into her sacrum. The window into Gordon's soul had cracked open back there with Ron. Maybe Ron deserved credit. But it had snapped shut again. Good old Gordon. That's all right, she thought. We'll get there. The three of us.

'My brother? If you mean what part of the cycle he's in, no, I don't think he is okay. This is how it starts. He's fine for months, and then something sets him off and you can count down the days until he gets locked up. You know,' she said, contemplating her roach, 'when he says that smoking so much weed has no effect on his mental state, we've always laughed at him. It's like, you idiot, you really are in denial. But I can see what he means. If you took the weed away from him, he'd still go through the cycles, the triggers would still set him off. Who knows? It might even be good for him.' To congratulate herself on her insight, she took another drag.

'I didn't think he was smoking,' Gordon said.

'He's smoked every day since he was fourteen. He's secretive about it, but if he stopped smoking he'd be hanging from a tree. It's the other stuff interacting with it that causes the problems.'

'He started the fight,' Gordon said. 'It was all about Daniel again.'

Kelly waved a cloud away. 'That boy's too slick.'

'Jude Oxenford said I should ask you why Carl's been told to stay away from the school grounds.'

'Do you really want to know?'

'I want to know how it affects Ben.'

'It doesn't affect Ben.'

Kelly reflected on something else she missed about Gordon. For all their surface dissimilarities, he and she saw the world in fundamentally the same way. The overwhelming relief of being with him was how little effort it cost her to share. Like both of them being able to take one look at a kid like Daniel and think the same thing.

'Daniel's a lot slicker than his father,' Gordon said.

'Frontal's never got over that chip on his shoulder towards us Chidgeys, so I kind of feel I know where I stand with him. The kid's different. He's everything Frontal wanted to be, and he knows it. Adults want children to be polite, but it's the polite ones you have to watch. I find it easier to trust kids who can't string a sentence together.'

'I've disliked Daniel since I first laid eyes on him in second grade. I never feel that way about kids. Why would I distrust him at first sight?'

'What does Lou say about disliking Dog instantly? Saves time.' She flicked her roach over the rail and looked at Gordon with her hand over her mouth. 'Whoops, that's an eighty-buck fine, it says on the post!'

'Better hope Frontal isn't down there. He can do us a lot of damage.'

'To which you've just responded by burning his letter. Where was the letter-burner in all those years we were married?'

'We *are* still married.'

'Gordon Grimes, you are full of surprises!'

She surprised herself by saying this. So often, during their married life, she found herself desperately missing Gordon even while he was with her. They each found their sandwich-generation roles so onerous, and themselves so unsuited, that very often the only person with whom either of them shared any understanding was the one member of their family they had freely chosen. During a rough patch with Ben a couple of years earlier, Gordon had lain in Kelly's arms and confessed: 'I don't want to be a son, I don't want to be a father, I only want you.' She loved him for saying that. And then, a year on, she thought she had not loved him anymore.

She went into the house. It was tempting to go to bed and leave him to the ringing of her last words, but she re-emerged with two fresh bottles, the lids unclipped. She slammed down a third of hers and wiped her mouth on the back of her arm.

'Fuck it, Gordo, you're so bloody frustrating. If it's such a joy for you to be here, why do you spend all day whingeing about how shit it's become?'

'I'm a full-time nostalgic. I whinge, therefore I am.'

'Fuck!' Kelly made a wild face and pulled at her beer.

'I've been trying to find a way to talk about it with Ben,' Gordon said. 'How having been given all these advantages, you're under pressure to make the best of it. You're as lucky as anyone who ever lived. So at the end of each day, you think about how you've reached another sunset having pissed that luck away. What do you say in the end? *I lived at Bluebird Beach. Fuck, I was lucky. Fuck, I did so little with it.* See? I feel that pain every day. Otherwise . . .'

Kelly was looking at him as if, after all this time, he had given her something worth listening to. 'Otherwise?'

She became freak-outishly aware, for a chilling moment, of his male presence, an arm's length down the balcony rail. There was such a thin skin between this world and an alternative where they were slipping their clothes over their heads. But not that thin. No, it was a double-brick cement-rendered steel-reinforced wall, going by the name of sanity. Problem was, she was feeling those alternatives to sanity more and more. They spiked through the fabric like spear grass. Was it a sign of mental decay? Was that what she and Dog had given in to that night of the fiftieth—not lust, or fantasy, but an attack of senility?

'Otherwise you don't think about it, you just take it as your birthright,' Gordon said. 'No peeping below the surface. And that's the life of a dumb animal. Which is what most people here were like when we were growing up. Still are.'

'You're not really nostalgic, though. You hate the old Bluebird.'

'Some of it's got to be worth saving.'

'At what cost? You really want to spend your middle years sucking up to my lunatic stepmother? Do you realise how self-defeating that is? And how it affects Ben?'

She had him there. Here, there and everywhere. Where did she not have him? Any longer, and she would have him handing in the keys tomorrow, fleeing Up North, where there could always be, for Ben, a nice room that wouldn't double as a shower-toilet.

'So tell me,' he said, weariness glugging up his words. 'What do I do? If I leave here, that's the end of it. Bluebird becomes just another place. Leonie will sell up and you'll leave. I can't do it, Kel. I know Ben comes first, but Ben's going to leave one day. That's what kids do. You're right. He doesn't love the past like I do. Doesn't love this place. Nor does Lou. They go before we're ready.' He swallowed back a lump. 'They've got their lives ahead of them. Dad's wrong about living for the future. My life—mine is behind me. It's the part that's behind me that I want to save.'

Kelly upended her beer bottle over the rail. It spattered on the kikuyu grass like a balcony piss.

'And you can't leave your parents, because of—that part that's behind you. That you can't save.' She was glad he couldn't see her properly in the darkness.

'Happy families,' he said unhappily.

'You're a good man, I get that you feel your obligations, but you're in truly fucked-up shape. You think you're protecting Ben and staying here to be a good son to your parents and, oh yeah, preserving Bluebird and The Lodge, but you're not, you're just going crazy in your little cage, walking round in circles like you have been forever.'

Suddenly he looked so tired, she wondered if he *was* asleep.

'The cage is me. Why would I want to leave me?'

'Because you're breaking the heart of everyone who loves you!'

She flicked a hand at him and looked over the beach, as if what she hated might give her peace.

'If I could do anything to make you happy with me right now, what would it be?'

She looked at him sadly. 'Let your anger show. Smack me in the face. And then I can go to sleep.'

Sleep. She pictured Gordon's cramped little bunk; it must have been reaching out to him like a plushly petalled flower.

He shook his head. 'I'm not angry with you.'

'Then why? *Why* aren't you angry with me?'

Gordon's face dropped. She didn't need an answer. He didn't know. He just didn't know. Did his ability to forgive say something terrible about him? Was she saying that his forgiving, non-violent nature was his great failing? The poor guy wasn't just confused about her. He was confused about himself.

'I've been tormenting myself over my feelings about you for quite a while, Gordo. But you know? In the end, once I'd dug over the entrails for the thousandth time, I ended up asking myself what I have no answer for. It's why you fell out of love with me.'

'I didn't,' he said helplessly. 'I didn't.'

'That's what you're not getting. That's where you're dishonest. That's where you're nowhere near the beginning of honest. You've spent so long practising what honesty is meant to look like, you've forgotten how to *be* honest. With yourself, with me. With anyone. Everyone thinks you're the most honest person, and you've come to believe that as well. That's why they're all on your side. Including our son, you've tricked him too. But it *is* all a trick, that's what I'm trying to get you to see. You are the least honest person. The least!'

'I'm so sorry,' he said.

'And that's another lie.'

It never failed to surprise her, the free-floating nature of strong emotion. Here he was, about to burst into tears with the shame of recognition, having been exposed by Kelly as the scared little lying Bluebird boy he'd always been; right on the brink of tears, and yet the tears, like a rain cloud looking for a slope, floated across him and lit on her instead. His tears were coming out of Kelly's eyes.

The fingernail moon had come out from behind a shelf of cloud. Not a fingernail really. More a sickle.

He bent over the rail and looked down at the grass. 'I'm still the same litter Nazi. Your roach is one thing I don't want to see floating in the waves.'

Kelly was quick to her feet. In his face like a boxer at weigh-in, she blocked his way to the stairs.

'Kel.'

'One for the road?'

'I'd have thought you'd had enough.'

She shook her head emphatically. 'Ricky blue-balled me. Just a kid. Didn't know what he was missing out on.'

'Why? Um, I don't know why I asked that.'

Kelly pulled a face. 'He has an early tee time tomorrow.'

Her hand was in his, her middle finger tracing circles in his palm.

'No—why? Why this? Me?'

'Ask no questions, hear no lies,' Kelly said smokily.

'The walls are too thin,' Gordon said. He was already negotiating. He was already lost.

'Why don't we go down and see where that roach fell.' Kelly gripped his wrist.

'I don't get it.'

In his eyes, she could read his mind. He was seeing himself floating with her down to the lawn.

'Gordon. Just'—she laughed—'let's just shut the fuck up.'

⟶

It was the deal of a quarter-century: when Kelly asked, Gordon was not to refuse. He went with her, feeling that this might silence his gasbagging mind, but it didn't, in the end, he realised as he lay awake four hours later, alone on his bed in the bunk room, so close to the springs of the bunk above that his breath bounced back into his face, the sound of Kelly's snores next door perforating the asbestos wall; no, it didn't take any of his troubles away, it only added another.

LAST
PART

LAST
PART

Bird's eye

Dear oh dear. When I said I wanted to do something for Family, I didn't mean anything so tangible as bringing Gordon and Kelly back together. I'd assumed Gordon's questionable personal hygiene would cancel out whatever animal sexual pull he and my stepdaughter still exert on each other. What on earth have I done? Have my actions brought them into alliance against a common enemy? (Though I wouldn't like to be called common.) I can only hope this was an aberration, a mutual lapse in consciousness, or taste.

Talk about shooting myself in the foot! They fear me, they think I control them, and yet when you look at what I have done, each of my moves has backfired. My proxy over The Lodge is in the most unreliable hands, the value of my properties is in freefall, and my foul stepdaughter is—for one night at least—sleeping soundly.

I blame Gordon. The man is a cripple. He carries an inner injury of unknown origin. They are trying to help him, but he will not allow himself to be helped. Maybe, in the name of love, he has a buried urge to bring about their demise. Maybe he has some kind of inherited

343

death drive. I have long held the suspicion that his unconscious will is to love Bluebird, The Lodge, his family, the lot of them, until they die from it.

Who am I to stand in the way of a tribe so hell-bent on their extinction? My lawyer suggests, only half jokingly I fear, that I declare terra nullius over The Lodge and claim it as uninhabited. The man is a scoundrel, but he reads my mood.

I am a migratory wild seabird. I can do nothing for them. Time flies. My season has come.

Such a tease. But this is not the outsider's story. This is the story of those who are in the middle yet on the margin, the hole in the doughnut, so close to the centre that they have fallen into the void.

Allow us old birds our jollies.

Time for us all to set ourselves free.

A misunderstanding

KELLY CHIDGEY GRIMES, LATE TO RISE, A LITTLE ROPY FROM the previous night's turn of events, tripped over a body face-down on the floorboards between the clothing bin and the lending library. The head was sheltered by a Cluedo board. The body was clad in a black Hurley tank top, a single adidas Stan Smith runner on the left foot, and a pair of madras pants bunched around the knees. No underpants. Kelly moved the Cluedo board to see the face and to unsee the rest.

'Cnut.'

He rolled over, to show the front side of his head. It was weeks since Cnut had been sighted. Everyone assumed he would turn up again. Cnut's history, nutshelled.

'Wake up.'

Kelly switched on the La Marzocco. Cnut probably had a real name, she thought, but Bluebird had no curiosity. This place named its own names.

'When did you turn up?' she asked.

Groggily, Cnut scratched his bald head, or bald face, whatever you called it, and held a scrunched-up piece of official-looking paper with a Bluebird Building Society logo, which he now read with as much puzzlement as a pirate who had passed out with a treasure map in his hand. Kelly's first task: fill this guy with enough coffee to get him out.

'Forecasters are bullshit,' was Cnut's wisdom for the day. And: 'Bankers too. Never trust anyone.'

Kelly untangled the hem of her morning-after caftan from where it had got caught up in her underpants and made coffee. One footstep at a time. Her phone rang: Norma. Kelly's headache spiked. She popped a Berocca and went out to the deck. She gazed down at the beach, wondering where Gordon had gone and whether it would be better for her to be at home when he came back, while offering periodic murmurs of assent into the phone so that Norma could sustain the suspension of disbelief that she was being listened to.

'. . . who has a lovely unit at Edendale, though I believe you have to pay for absolutely everything. John Nolan was the solicitor there when they set it up, and he said—you know John Nolan, his daughter was Ellen who was at school with you until she was hospitalised with . . . was it nodules? No, it was the other one who had the nodules, Ellen had the . . .'

Boy, could that woman talk. Her streams of consciousness would divert at the least provocation onto a tributary of over-detailed, excruciating mundanity. Since forming her country club bond with Norma, Kelly had come to forgive the idiosyncrasies. At heart, Norma was well-meaning, burdened with antiquated views and half a century of marriage to Ron. But couldn't she just say something in five words, not the available five thousand?

'. . . and so Doctor Chun, who's Korean, told her she had a spongiform growth on one of her . . .'

If Kelly listened closely, Norma's storytelling had what her teacher at the Workers' Education Association would term a certain modernist mastery. She held six or seven different parenthetic asides in motion, ultimately tying off each loose end before returning to the main theme. But shit, she took so freaking long to get there. And unlike, say, James Joyce, her talent was wasted on her material. Kelly shook herself out of it. This wasn't art; it was therapy. The talking filled a need for self-soothing. What hadn't struck Kelly until recently was the depthlessness of that need.

'. . . eczema, which began bleeding when she scratched it . . .'

Less hungover, Kelly might have fancied going down to the beach, which had fallen eerily quiet after yesterday's drama, in her new bikini. She usually enjoyed flaunting herself to the club-bies, making up for lost time. She had been the property of men since she was fourteen. After becoming single, her character had not changed but its mode of expression had. The same fuck-you, but whereas before it had involved concealing her body, now it involved showing it off to the rollcall of boys and man-boys of Bluebird (actually seven, but it seemed a lot more) with whom she had had relations since splitting with Gordon. Was Gordon included in the seven? She had to work that out, do a recount. What was going on between them? What had she done? Why did she feel so helpless and weak this morning, like she was waiting for him to come home and dictate their new terms of engage-ment? Her fuck-you was all bluff, she now realised. She was as full of shit as any man.

Norma was talking about the general manager of Ron's nursing home, 'who has a doctorate but he's not a real doctor, I think it's in theology'. From there she progressed to an abscess she was developing on her thigh and her upcoming visit to the dermatologist, to which Kelly would of course drive her.

Lou was climbing up the steps from the beach. Pinning her phone between her ear and her shoulder, Kelly raced to her bedroom to replace her telltale caftan with bra, T-shirt and shorts.

'I have to go.'

'Well. You don't have to be like that,' Norma responded as if denied her right to free speech. 'You're always in such a hurry. Sometimes I think you're only interested in what you can get.'

Every now and then, Norma came out and said what she thought. It took her so long to get there, it always felt like an ambush.

'I'll call you later, Norma.'

Inside, the front door closed behind the departing Cnut, and Lou was bearing down on the La Marzocco. 'Coffee?'

'I've already had two,' Kelly said.

'So that's a no?'

'What harm could another do?'

'That's the shot.'

The girl's quiet strength intimidated her. Kelly felt as solid as a house of cards. Lou's wholeness and youth felt like an open threat.

'How have your crew recovered?' Kelly asked.

'I'm devo. The main thing is to make sure the girls are disappointed too. Maybe not as much as me.'

'I guess you have to be tough if you want results.'

'Sure,' Lou said without conviction and brought Kelly a vastly superior coffee. They stood at the Shitfuckerpoobum. The day wasn't pleasant, with the nor'-easter belting in, but it was sunny and warm and sometimes you just had to cop the freaking gloriousness.

Forcing herself to enjoy this place was the rent Kelly paid for living here.

'I heard what happened,' Lou said.

For a flash, Kelly thought Lou was referring to her and Gordon. They had taken precautions, getting dressed and sneaking about afterwards like teenagers, and Gordon had gone back to his own bed before disappearing early this morning. Surely Lou couldn't know—and if she did, had she told Ben? Kelly was so worked up, she wanted to scream.

'To?'

'To Daniel.'

Kelly relaxed, but was also caught off balance. To her inquiring look, Lou went on, 'There's an investigation into the surfboat crash. Some footage on Facebook. It's not conclusive, but the Capri crew are making statements that it wasn't an accident.'

Lou showed Kelly her phone. The mainstream news coverage of the surfboat crash, which had been themed as a tragic accident wrought by the terrible power of an ocean angered by climate change, had altered to commentary about uncivilised testosterone-charged teenage boys and the sad deficit of male role models.

'Daniel's been suspended from school while the clubs look at the footage and decide whether to refer it to the police,' Lou said. 'His father's been packed off from council on a mental health break.'

'That was a quick response on a weekend.' And you've got good information about the school, Kelly thought.

'Shows there could be something in it.'

'I'm sure Jude is on top of it,' Kelly said teasingly.

Lou did not react.

'Do you think Daniel started it?' Kelly asked.

Lou gave her a what-do-you-reckon look.

'He's either headed for jail or a bravery medal.' Lou finished her coffee and turned for the front door. 'I'm going to finish installing the StairLift, I'm going to see Ben play in his cricket final next weekend, and then I'm off. You probably knew.'

'I didn't,' Kelly said, suddenly wishing she could take back all the negative things she had told Lou, all the bitter sisterly wisdom.

'You'll miss me, right?'

Kelly didn't know if this was a late assay at solidarity, a hug while walking out the door. Would Lou understand what Kelly had done last night, or see it as another crime against Gordon?

'Gordon's going to miss you,' Kelly said. 'Not to mention Ben.'

'You were right. This place is doing me no good.'

'I thought you enjoyed it here. The crew, the games nights, the clothing bins, the library—you've been a breath of fresh air. For everyone,' she added.

'It feels like I've only caused trouble,' Lou said. 'I raised nearly three grand, but Gordon won't take it.'

'He doesn't mean to be ungrateful.'

'He said it would get him in the shit with council. Everything I've done to help, I've made things worse. The place is so beautiful, but you don't let anyone else in.'

Kelly bridled, to disagree and defend, but a second thought overtook her: Lou was right.

'I'm sorry,' Kelly said.

'Not your fault.'

'Where are you going?'

'Somewhere people don't know each other so well.'

Kelly had never disliked Lou. It was more that the strength of Lou's dislike for her had come between them. But maybe that was just another misunderstanding.

'That night we talked, you told me a lot about yourself, but you never answered my question,' Lou said. 'Why you did it.'

'Did what?'

'You know.'

Kelly let out an animal groan that made Lou look directly at her.

'You said it yourself. It's what comes from living here too long. You never grow up, you never grow out of it.'

'Well, now you understand why I've got to leave,' Lou said. 'In case I'm wrong, and I become one of you.'

The news

FRONTAL CROUCHED ON THE DUNE IN FRONT OF THE TOP CAR park and peered through his binoculars at The Lodge. Local surfers such as the five-time state champ, Sam Eastaugh, Snake, Chook and that Japanese mate of Gordon's had passed him on their way down to the beach and offered a greeting. The wild look in his eye warned them off further conversation. They'd heard enough on the coconut wireless. Best give him his space.

He had seen Gordon leave The Lodge early that morning. He fixed his glasses on that death trap and let his thoughts roam. Had Gordon's old *Bluebird News* still existed, it would have been enjoying its finest hour. Since that mobile phone clip had come out, allegedly showing Daniel starting a fight and capsizing the Capri boat, national television crews had descended on the village. Slow news day or what! The Surf Life Saving Association state president, the head of the ambulance service and the local member of parliament issued statements, while random pedestrians trapped on Capri's main street had spoken colourfully for the cameras.

The news bulletins were filled with inarticulate ravings from an older surfer about 'onshore conditions', and that Japanese guy was quoted saying that on the day of the carnival it was 's--- out'.

Frontal and Daniel had been given time off from work and school to deal with the issue, but there official responsibility ended. Daniel had disappeared, and now Frontal was squatting in the dune grass of Bluebird Beach, binoculars on The Lodge. He spied Kelly, whom Gordon had never deserved, climbing the stairs to Cliff Street. Still looked great, still wouldn't give Frontal the time of day. For Kelly, read the whole world. Gordon the deadbeat was always forgivable; Frontal the servant of the community, never. Gordon gets the girl. Well, fuck you very much, Gordo.

Was all that old shit coming back again?

He knew he'd never had a chance with Noel Chidgey's daughter. She and Doug Gilsenan formed a royal couple through high school. She was The Prize, and Frontal was A Bystander. He sublimated his crush on Kelly into a higher feeling: his duty. He only ever came out with his feelings to Kelly once, when he confessed, in year twelve, that if only she were a Christian like him, she would be the perfect human being. Frontal blushed at the memory. Kelly had accepted the compliment in her usual way, laughing it off. 'Nobody can be perfect,' she said.

She sure wasn't. Gilsenan dumped her at the altar, and she fell into the arms of the luckiest loser. Gordon Grimes would have done everyone a favour if he had died as a teenager, like his brother. As things turned out, Gordon earned an undeserved tragic glamour, the overhang of Owen's accident. To Frontal's frustration, Gordon, who had cruised through an untouched life, delivering nothing more than he had promised, who was both remembered and, because he hung around, forgotten, won

The Prize. What a fucking injustice. While Frontal had taken the best possible revenge—he excelled in economics and joined Capri Council as a graduate cadet; he became an elder in the Bluebird parish committee and vice-president of the surf club; he had *gone away*, something the Gordons of the world never had the balls to do, and been afflicted by his own personal tragedy, which *nobody cared about*—Gordon had remained here, a local hero. Local dero more like it. Somehow Gordon ended up in The Lodge. And now, as Frontal's personal observations last night had disclosed, Kelly was sleeping with him again! Fucking Gordon!

He focused his binoculars. Kelly went up the high stairs to where that lesbarista, the whatever she was, worked on that mechanical chair for invalids. They stopped and talked. Laughter. That'd be right: celebrating Frontal's downfall. Kelly continued up the stairs, disappearing behind Archer David's now disused mini-skip.

How in fuck's name did they get away with it? As his father had told him, only a corrupt pre-war council could have let The Lodge get built. If only a deputy general manager had the retrospective powers to reverse historic offences. Never mind, he thought. A dish best served cold.

He arrived at a decision. They were violating Bluebird, they were desecrating it, they were injuring him, they were laughing at Daniel, and he would make them pay. Sure, he would be living down to everything they thought of him. He didn't care. He just didn't care. They would recognise his authority if it killed him.

'Eh!'

Frontal's binoculars were tugged roughly from his eyes. The body on the other end of that rude hand belonged to the person he most loved in the world.

'You doing a recce for us?' Daniel asked, the 'us' alerting his father to his companion. Squinting against the sun, Frontal thought he must be mistaken: the most unlikely, the last chum his boy should ever have.

'How's it hanging, Frontal?'

Carl Chidgey was not, from appearances, presently in a psychotic state. Small mercies. As long as Frontal had known the guy, there were only two gears: the mellow, harmless, probably stoned Carl, and the incoming headbutt. Whichever Carl this was, what on earth was his Daniel doing with him?

In response to his father's unasked question, Daniel glanced at Carl, whose eyelid twitched.

'I got bored at home,' Daniel said.

'It's all good, *mon ami*,' Carl said. '*Tout va bien.*'

'It's fine, Dad,' Daniel said.

It wasn't fine. It couldn't be fine if Daniel was with this man. It was so ingrained in Frontal's nature to know the lines of relationship among everyone in Bluebird, his internal motherboard melted down to see his Daniel creeping around the beachfront with Carl Chidgey like a pair of criminals planning their next enterprise. What was wrong with this picture? he thought. What was *right* with this picture?

He saw Daniel wondering the same about him: peeping through his binoculars, same park, same suspicious odour. He'd caught them out, yet it felt like they had caught him. A jagged lump rollicked around inside his gut. Standing over him, these two men were tough. They were purposeful. They were up to no good.

Frontal nodded towards The Lodge. 'Is that where you're going?'

Another glance between Carl and Daniel.

'Do you want us to?' Carl asked.

All I want, Frontal thought, is to put a world between you and my son. For Daniel to go home and for you to go to hell.

'I'm moving in,' Carl said. 'Nice, eh?'

'That will exceed the occupancy regulations,' Frontal said, rising to his feet and feeling that a bracing discussion about zoning might bring him back to himself. His knees were killing him and his head spun from getting up too quickly. He put his hand out. Daniel steadied him, and then let go.

'Hey, Dan', Carl said. *Dan? Since when is my boy your 'Dan'?* 'Why is your old fella so uptight?'

Frontal was taller than Carl Chidgey. Carl had always seemed to loom over him, but now he had a slump, a stoop, and his physique seemed both puffed out and shrunken, as if he had put on volume while losing density.

'You have no business being with my son,' Frontal said.

Carl sniffed as if conceding an immaterial point. Another quick exchange of looks between Carl and Daniel brought Frontal's blood to the boil. This drugged-up thug was owning his son, like the old men of this beach had always owned the boys.

'I guess he's old enough to make his own decisions,' Carl said.

Frontal gaped at Daniel, who opened his mouth to explain, but Carl interrupted: 'Gotta fly. Good chat, Frontal. Enjoy your mental health break.'

Frontal watched them walk away. He tried to call out to Daniel, to reel him back, to stop time, but the words dried in his throat.

'You idiots,' Frontal said as his binoculars dropped from his hands and bounced on the dune grass. 'Dear Lord, please forgive those fucking, fucking idiots.'

Sisters

KELLY WAS THINKING, AS SHE STOOD AT THE BOUNDARY FENCE the next afternoon waiting for Ben's practice to finish, that it was remiss of a hate-saturated world not to have found a word for how much she hated cricket. Teenaged boys so pleased with themselves, the pock of the ball on the wooden bats, that nitwit Ryan Stoyle strutting around on his little legs, harvested a disgust that had germinated during childhood Saturdays sitting uncovered in the sun waiting for her father to finish playing, then after his retirement waiting for him to finish umpiring, and finally, after he became club president, waiting for him to finish presidenting. Cricket rejuvenated her, if rejuvenation meant turning her into a bored, sulky young girl. Best that Ben never understand what a sacrifice it was for her to be here.

Seeing him so keen, practising in his full Saturday whites when all the other boys looked like they had just got out of the surf, darkened her mood further. Kelly had seen enough cricket to appreciate how hopeless he was; he couldn't catch, he couldn't throw, he couldn't bowl, and he seldom got a turn to show that he couldn't bat. She and Gordon had failed as parents in not steering him away from this unwitting torment.

The other boys couldn't be bothered teasing him. Fortunately, Daniel wasn't allowed to be here. Only that delinquent Zane Dwyer talked to Ben, leaning close to his ear. Rather than protect her boy from being bullied, Stoyle let it sort itself out. The Bluebird way.

'Hello there.'

No other adults would bother watching their sons practise, even with the final coming up. But no other parents were in quite the fix Kelly was in. She had lost him this year. She didn't expect his forgiveness, but she didn't expect him to hate her. Now he would blame her for Lou leaving. Like everything, it had to be Kelly's fault, and Ben would work his way backwards from there. God help her if Ben found out about Saturday night.

From the corner of her eye, she could see Jude Oxenford nodding. 'Do you think they like cricket because it gives them a safe place to hide?'

So why have I spent half my life watching them? Kelly asked herself, and then turned to Jude. 'I can't see why Ben would be hiding among the boys he needs to get away from.'

'Maybe he doesn't want to get away from them.'

'Maybe,' Kelly said. She respected Jude for taking on the world's shittiest job, but sometimes her familiarity crossed a line. Jude's close interest in Ben didn't reassure Kelly. In fact, it creeped her out. Jude had creeped her out since they were twelve years old. Gordon loved her to bits, for a start. And look at her, carrying off a short dress and a Status Anxiety handbag on a strap across her chest. No doubt about it, the toll not taken by not having children really began to not show when you hit fifty.

'You must be under a lot of pressure with the Daniel thing.'

'Tell me about it.' Jude was smiling. 'I've got everyone from the school council to Ryan Stoyle leaning on me to make him available for the final. The boys won't even look at me.'

'And why can't you?'

'Daniel himself.'

'What do you mean?'

'I sat with him for two hours this morning. I'm not sure that he wants to come back to school, or the team. I'm leaving the suspension in place to protect his dignity, if you like.'

'Ben wants Daniel to play,' Kelly said carefully. 'He wants life to be normal.'

'Or maybe Ben's more competitive than you give him credit for.'

'Credit? If you'd grown up in my world, the less competitive he is in sports, the prouder I am of him.'

Jude lapsed into the kind of silence that, Kelly felt, expressed superiority more than submission to Kelly's knowledge of her son. When did this fucking cricket practice end? Stoyle was hitting high catches. Ben was fetching balls from the boundary gutter. Kelly checked her watch.

'You know the issue with Daniel is not really the surfboats,' Jude said. 'That's just a convenient cover. It's more about . . . the other.'

'Daniel's growing a conscience?' Kelly asked. 'He'd better not tell his father.'

'His father?'

'Well, you'll remember when this came up a few weeks ago, Frontal persuaded you to sweep it under the carpet. A pretty silly place to talk about it, though, out on the street where anyone could see you.'

Jude studied her seriously. 'Things have moved on since then.'

'Moved on?' Kelly squared up, her mood punchy. If Jude wanted to step into the ring with her, she was welcome. The woman thought that just because she was one of the modern breed of 'caring' school principals, she owned your child. Fuck her. Precisely that: fuck her and fuck this shit.

'When I met with Daniel, he was very upset. He'd been with your brother all day yesterday, and they'd had a . . . discussion.'

'We know what their "discussions" are about. Carl's been scoring speed pills off Daniel. Big news.'

'Kelly, when this first came up, you asked me one thing. To tell you if Ben became involved. Yesterday, Carl and Daniel went up to The Lodge and visited him. Did you know that?'

Kelly felt a hot flush spread on her chest. 'I had a lot going on yesterday.'

'Well, when Daniel and I sat down together, he wanted to give me something.'

Jude opened the black handbag at her hip and took out a white pill bottle with an apricot-coloured lid. She held it close to Kelly's face.

'Those are the ones,' Kelly said defensively, fighting a nauseating swell of dread. 'Daniel's pills.'

'Read the name on the prescription. These are the pills Carl has been buying.'

Kelly watched her hand reach out and take the bottle. She didn't need to read the prescription. She clasped the bottle so hard, she could have annihilated it.

'I suggest you, Ben and Gordon have a talk,' Jude said.

'What business is it of yours?'

'None at all. In fact, Kelly, I really couldn't give a damn about any of you anymore.' Jude removed her sunglasses and put on a smile which, outrageously, stripped another five years off her. 'I've handed in my resignation from St Pat's, effective next week.'

'You?'

'Too much Bluebird.'

'Where are you going?'

Jude seemed set to say one thing, then changed her mind. 'Somewhere very different. So, you're right, you and your family are none of my business anymore. I wish you luck.'

'You're leaving us with this?' Kelly shook the pill bottle. 'You're fucking doing a runner? You coward, you're so sanctimonious, but you were always too scared to put yourself out there, never took a risk in your life. You just stand on the sidelines and leave everyone else to deal with the mess.'

Kelly's stomach sank. She was a bitch. She was the same schoolgirl who put down other girls because she had the guy and they didn't. Fuck. She didn't know what to say. Jude was looking over Kelly's shoulder. And Kelly could see, reflected in those ludicrous sunglasses, a man stumbling towards them in the clothes he'd been wearing all weekend, looking like a hobo.

Jude said, 'Speaking of mess. He's all yours.'

Vyvanse

GORDON HAD SPENT TWO DAYS TRYING TO OUTRUN HIS OWN thinking. Saturday night had left a line of questions at the door of his brain like secured creditors. He and Kelly had done enough talking before, but when it counted, *after*, they had been too busy covering their tracks to discuss the consequences of their actions. Did the urgency about not letting anyone know mean that the event was only a one-off? He had no idea. Life with Kelly had always had an element of strategy, like a game to which he had come late and with a wobbly grasp of the rules. He had never quite got over the good fortune of having her fall in his lap, so when she fell out of it again, slipping down the shadowy side of memory lane with Dog, her behaviour had an aspect of the inevitable. But the other night she seemed to be saying that her world didn't revolve around her and Dog, it was her and Gordon. Or just Gordon. Strange, that your wife putting you at the centre of your story was the most unexpected trick for her to pull.

He'd managed to avoid her all day yesterday, and they'd gone to their separate bedrooms last night as usual. He'd lain awake, wondering if Kelly was going to do something, or if he was. Nothing. Wherever his mind raced, he really couldn't track what was happening. Himself and Kelly was just one fractal of an infinitely repeating pattern, a crowd of matters with common characteristics yet different particulars, about which he was equally ignorant. There was what Dog had told him about the real estate house of cards about to collapse all over them. There was the ongoing natural disaster of his parents. There was Lou's recent evasiveness, probably connected with Carl's imminent move. There was his constant sense of being pincered by Leonie's plans. There was Frontal's letter, which he had stupidly burnt. There was his problem with Sam. And then, back again like a dog to its sick, he thought of Kelly.

When he burnt Frontal's letter in front of her—a love offering? An act of abandon?—he was momentarily incinerating his reality, to float away and pretend no other shit was happening. Or had ever happened. That's what Saturday night had been: beautiful, magical, mutual amnesia. But then came the memory hangover. And as he approached Kelly on the boundary of the cricket field, another wave of remembering broke over him. Lost amid everything else going on, he had overlooked the one person in this entire fiasco whose welfare was paramount.

⌒

As he came off the cricket field, Ben was confused. This morning, his parents had been competing to offer him driving time after practice. First his dad had suggested he would take Ben for a full hour and a half. Then Mum, one-upping and pathetic, had said she was *dying* to spend time with him. The divorce dividend, yeah, right. And now it looked like they wouldn't have time to take him driving after all. They were heading back to The Lodge, both of them cloudy in the face after Mum had been in a heavy-looking conversation with Ms Oxenford. His dad drove and his mum rode in the passenger seat of the Car With No Name. Just like old times, their little family of three, nobody talking to anybody else.

'Am I in trouble?'

Bad sign: neither of his parents answered.

When they got home, Uncle Carl was lying on the couch, speaking aloud and jotting in his poetry chapbook, acting like he owned the place.

He did own the place.

At the card table, reading about himself in the paper while pretending to listen to Carl, sat Daniel.

Ben's mum stepped forward and placed on the card table, between the peanut bowl and a glass of water, a white pill bottle with an apricot-coloured lid.

'Wait, what?'

Ben wasn't confused anymore.

Uncle Carl was rabbiting on about surrealist literature, dropping names—Cervantes, Baudelaire, Mallarmé, Dali—that used to suggest an encyclopaedic knowledge but now came across to Ben as just the same ones over and over.

He wished he'd figured Uncle Carl out before.

Kelly said, 'Okay, enough three-unit English,' and Carl fell silent, chewing the insides of his cheeks.

The awkwardness making him itchy under his armpits, Ben said, 'I'm in trouble.'

Everyone looked at the Vyvanse bottle as if its time to speak had come. Kelly had taken one of the pink-and-white capsules out of the bottle and broken it open, fanning out its fine white powder on the card table like a burlesque dancer. Carl couldn't take his eyes off it.

'Darling,' Kelly said, 'you want Daniel to play in your cricket final, don't you?'

'Wait, what?'

'And you know why he's not playing.'

'Um, because he was suspended after the . . .'

'Time to come clean,' Daniel interrupted.

'You're not in trouble, my love,' Kelly said, but Ben wasn't taken in by her tender tone. He looked to his uncle for a signal. Carl was leafing through his chapbook. Daniel was sitting with his arms folded, offering Ben an encouraging nod.

'Wait, what happened?'

'It can't keep going on,' Daniel said.

'The jig's up, *mon ami*.' Carl's voice came from the dark side of his chapbook. 'Sorry, I guess.'

From behind his back Ben heard his father laugh, but not humorously.

'I guess you should be happy that everyone else knew about it before me,' Gordon said, bringing a camp chair and unfolding it next to Daniel.

'Just like when you edited the *News* . . .' Kelly said.

'You read it here last.' Gordon shot her a wink and gestured for her to sit in the camp chair.

Ben loosened a little to see this exchange between his mum and dad. They seemed friendly—not to him, exactly, but chilled with each other. That was new.

'I don't know what I'm meant to say,' Ben said to his father.

'What's the only hope you have of not making things worse?' Gordon asked.

'Tell the truth, I guess.'

'There you go.' Gordon's relaxed air had fallen away and his face was dark. He went and fetched another camp chair for himself. It didn't match the one he'd given Kelly.

Now Ben felt bad again. He desperately wanted Carl or Daniel to tell him what to say.

'Carn,' Daniel said. 'Spill it.'

More than his parents' urgings, more than Uncle Carl's surrender, more even than the incriminating bottle of Vyvanse on the card table, it was Daniel's encouragement that told Ben he had to speak the truth.

'Wait, what'll happen to me? If you get off, aren't I in the shit?'

Daniel shrugged. 'Nothing goes beyond these four walls. That was part of the deal.'

'What deal?'

'Just tell them, and I'll play in the final.' Daniel gave him another smile. 'You're a brave guy, Ben. You've come out in front of the whole school. You can do this.'

'You're happy that everyone thinks you're a drug dealer?' Ben said.

'I am a drug dealer. I just reckon they should know that I'm not your *uncle's* drug dealer.'

'And if I tell them, you'll play in the final.'

Daniel nodded.

'And nothing more will happen to me.'

'Glad you're thinking logically.'

'But why? Why are you wanting all this out?'

From behind his chapbook, Carl said, 'Think of the knight on the horse charging at the windmills, *mon ami*. He needs his short fat friend.' Carl lowered his book so Ben could see his face. 'Daniel and I came to a decision. Turns out the short fat friend is *you*.'

'Ben,' Gordon said. Ben looked at his stricken father. 'Everyone's spilt their guts. Your turn.'

Ben looked at the floor, sloping away towards the Shitfucker-poobum. He imagined he could see a pile of innards: his dad's, his mum's, even Carl's and Daniel's. He felt a suction in his guts, as if his own insides were trying to get out and be with the others', there on the floor.

He started out, unsurely at first, but they were patient with him. After his first couple of months on the trial, he said, he hadn't liked the Vyvanse. At first, it had helped his concentration and his marks, so he had gone along with it. But after the 'trial' ended and he was going to have to take it as a regular prescription, he didn't want it. It wasn't that the pill made him feel bad—it didn't have much effect anymore—it was the daily message that there was something wrong with him. 'If there wasn't something wrong with me,' he said, 'I wouldn't have to take something that only makes me feel normal.'

He glanced at his dad for approval but Gordon's head seemed about to fall off his neck, too heavy to withstand gravity.

'Why didn't you tell us?' Kelly asked.

'You had enough problems without me adding another.' He knew that after so many years of arguing over it, they believed they were doing the right thing, and the easiest course was to let them go on believing and not reopen that dispute. He already thought he was the cause of most of his parents' fights. Once things settled, he would raise it. But their problems only seemed to get worse, so he'd put the conversation off. 'I'd piled up five or ten bottles since I stopped using them. And then I started talking to Daniel.'

Daniel nodded, not to Ben so much as to the adults, as if he was the defendant in a trial and Ben his star witness.

It hadn't taken Ben long to find out that a third of the boys in his year took prescribed ADHD meds. Most were casual about it, but Daniel was different. Ben had never suspected Daniel needed to take anything until he caught him at cricket practice one day, shaking a pink-and-white pill out of the familiar bottle. Daniel had begged him not to tell anyone; it was his secret; he just didn't like people to 'identify' him as ADHD. Besides, Daniel said, he was only taking it on 'high-performance days', when he needed to sit an exam, or deliver a speech, or perform on the sports field or in the surfboat crew. Ben had been startled that Vyvanse could be a cheat drug; it had never worked that way for him.

Gordon and Kelly were looking at each other and shooting glances at Carl.

'Go on,' Kelly said.

'Wait, what? Where was I at?'

'Daniel,' Gordon said.

'Oh. Right. When Uncle Carl arrived to live with us, we had a lot of chats about it.'

Uncle Carl knew exactly how Vyvanse worked. He told Ben about the biochemistry of its interaction with brain function. Even though Ben now wondered how much was true, he fell under Uncle Carl's spell. His uncle cared in ways that his parents were too busy for. And his uncle approved of Ben stopping taking it.

'Which was what I wanted to hear,' Ben said.

'And yet you still didn't say anything to us,' Kelly said.

Ben pressed on. Uncle Carl, his self-appointed 'counsellor', told Ben that the lack of side-effects he'd suffered from coming off the Vyvanse confirmed that he was doing the right thing. He felt a little more tired in the afternoons, but that was how he was meant to feel. How normal people felt. If tired was normal, Ben wanted tired.

Then, Ben continued, Uncle Carl told him how beneficial Vyvanse could be for *his* health. He was getting off all sorts of harder and more life-threatening drugs, so a slow-release amphetamine ticked his boxes. It kept him alert and awake, and it improved his mood. Ben looked sheepishly at his mother, who was staring in disbelief at Carl.

'Okay, okay,' Gordon said, scowling in that way he had when he was trying to keep things straight in his head. 'What next?'

Now Ben was really scared. There were two ways this could go. One would result in everyone being happy and together, and the other could result in violence and shouting and life changing course, maybe going even worse than it already was. All this, in his hands.

'Just the truth,' Gordon croaked.

'Tell them,' Carl said. The room fell silent. He folded his chapbook in half, like he wanted to break it, and slipped it into the pocket of his duffle coat.

Daniel said, 'They won't believe us until it comes from you.'

Ben swallowed.

'You won't tell Ms Oxenford?' he said to his mother.

'Irrelevant,' Kelly said.

'Just tell us,' Gordon said.

'I don't want Daniel in more trouble,' Ben said. 'We need him for the final.'

His mother nodded. 'Just tell us.'

'Tell them!' Daniel cried.

Ben took a breath and said, 'Daniel never beat Carl up at school. That was something they staged because they were caught doing a deal. But Carl was never selling Vyvanse to kids. The *kids* were selling the drugs to *him*.'

'You really are one fucked-up bunny,' Kelly said to her brother.

'Newsflash,' Carl said bitterly and went to the balcony to smoke a cigarette.

'And so I,' Ben said, 'I told Carl I'd be his dealer instead. It was easiest. Uncle Carl could get what he wanted, he didn't have to go to Daniel anymore, and I . . . I could get what I wanted.'

'And I got shitty with Carl because he wouldn't buy from me anymore,' Daniel added helpfully. 'How fucked up are we?'

'What did you want?' Kelly asked Ben.

'I wanted . . . to help Dad.'

'When did you ever lack for anything from us?' Gordon's heart-broken face made Ben drop his eyes to stop bursting into tears.

'You wanted money, and you still didn't tell us,' Kelly said.

'You guys were already so stressed.'

Kelly took out a handkerchief and dabbed at her nose, her eyes pink against the dark tan of her skin. Since he was little, Ben had always been fascinated by this struggle within his mother's complexion. He had decided that it represented some deep truth: emotions were stronger than skin colour.

Gordon got up from his chair and approached Ben with a slight stumble, the gait of a much older man. He crouched and put his arms around Ben's shoulders. Because of the difference in their levels, Ben could not get his arms around his dad, so he kind of laid them on his head. It felt awkward to the max, but also, for that reason, okay.

'Show us, Benny,' his dad said. 'Show us what you were about to show me the other night.'

Ben let go of his father and went downstairs to the Boardroom. From beneath his Seiko alarm, he took the envelope containing the money he had collected. He went back upstairs and put it down on the card table in front of his mother and father, who were clasping each other's hands.

'Fuck!' Daniel said. 'How much is that, you sly dog?'

Ben waited until his dad looked him in the eye.

'Just got past nine hundred,' Ben said. Despite himself, despite the implosion of everything, despite the meaninglessness of what he had done, he wanted his dad to approve, to acknowledge that what he had done was useful. But his dad's eyes were as cold as stone and a million miles from here.

'Cash! Old school!' Daniel said. 'Hey, who's hungry? Want me to take a hundred and go get some Thai?' Now that he had got what he wanted, Daniel's mood seemed to have taken flight.

Ben's dad twitched, clenched his fist and shoved it into his pocket. Ben might have saved Daniel's place in the cricket team, but right now he did not want Daniel here.

'Can you go outside with Carl?' Ben said.

Daniel was about to chirp some reply, but he cut his eyes to Ben's parents and, with a sombre nod, went out to the balcony. Ben saw him share a hand-rolled cigarette with Uncle Carl.

'And don't smoke before the final!' Ben called.

To his surprise, Daniel gave the rollie back to Carl.

Ben's father looked more wretched, more abandoned, more lonely than after he'd found out about Kelly and Dog. A voice in Ben's head told him he could cry later, not now.

'He did this for you,' Kelly said to Gordon. 'Our son made himself a drug dealer because he wanted to *help you out*.'

Gordon's eyes met Ben's, then slid away. Ben willed his dad to maintain eye contact, just like his dad had always done with him. But Gordon couldn't.

'I'm sorry,' was all that came out of his dad's mouth.

'That's okay, Dad.'

'It's not okay.' Kelly wheeled around. 'Look at what you've done to our son, Gordon! Look what everyone's done to themselves, just to help you!'

'I've said I'm sorry,' Gordon rasped.

'You know very well that's not good enough,' Kelly said. 'You have to let our son into his own family.'

Ben looked from one to the other. They were talking about something else. His mum was right. Sorry was just a word. There *was* more, only Ben didn't have the guts to ask for it and, he understood now, as his mum stormed off to the kitchen with a great impatient angry scream and began to make dinner, his dad didn't have the guts to offer it.

Straw man

THERE WERE BELL-RINGER DAYS, WHEN EVEN BLUEBIRDERS accepted that they would have to share their crescent of heaven with outsiders. Days when the sky was a spray-painted dome and the sea a dreamy teenager's doodles. Out of the turquoise depths came tapered head-high rollers, steepening as they gathered force against the reef, wall after glassy wall. Snake was first out before the sunrise, Cnut had been up all night waxing his quiver, and Japan Ned's cry of 'Good out!' was minimalistically apt. Tonsure Man arrived at dawn with Chook, two Chookalikes and Macca, five Maccalikes and the four-time state champ. Days like this, your first job was to eat enough breakfast so you could stay out four, five, six hours.

Red Cap, massaging his ruined shoulder, perched on The Bench of Broken Dreams in the top car park, where he intended to remain until coffee hour at The Lodge. He exchanged greetings with Dog, war-painted and ready to take on all blow-ins, hauling his stand-up paddleboard like a ballistic missile on parade in Red Square. By the time the sun had decoupled from the horizon there were sixty surfers in the water. 'It's worse at Capri,' Red Cap said. 'Doesn't anybody work anymore?' he added, forgetting that he didn't work anymore. Dog nodded grimly and set out for battle.

Out the back the locals were buzzing: Gordo was in the waves! The four-time state champ and Cnut paddled past him, grizzling about how they'd just had to pinch a two-wave set off a cluster of hungry youngsters; they gave Gordon a down-to-business nod. Tonsure Man issued him a horn sign and set off for his special spot, north of the peak, the sneaky left-hander that would break when a set came with more east in it. Japan Ned flashed his high-beam teeth. Dog, erect on his paddleboard as if walking on water, was too preoccupied with domination to give Gordon more than a terse we'll-talk-about-this-later glance.

Gordon was sitting on his board, still waveless after twenty minutes, when Firie Sam paddled back after ripping the lip out of a six-foot right-hander running all the way to the front of the BSLSC. There was no need for comment on the likelihood that Gordon wouldn't have the stamina or hunger, not to mention the rudeness, to drop in and pinch a wave off the pack. His return to the water wasn't about surfing; it was about information.

Sam had knocked at Gordon's door in the pre-dawn and harangued him out of bed, bustled him into his wetsuit, pushed him into the Boardroom, manhandled him from The Lodge to the sea on the promise of 'I need to talk to you and there's only one place I can do it'. Now they were out here, Sam was avoiding the subject, as if worried that to speak might drive Gordon back into hiding and deprive him of this all-time day. Or maybe Sam needed to surf more than he needed to talk.

'Why were you sleeping downstairs?' Sam asked, sitting on his board and catching his breath after six duck-dives paddling out.

'Carl's moved into the bunk room. None of me, Ben or Lou want to share with him so we're all on floors in the other rooms.'

'Leonie's room?'

'Verboten.'

'Happy families, eh.'

'Don't I know it. Here's another for you if you're cheeky.'

Backlit by the sun, a steepling wall came through, breaking too wide for the mass of surfers close to the point but finding Sam in perfect position, as he often was. They called it experience, they called it luck, they called it judgement. Gordon called it time: Sam spent so many hours out here, it was statistically certain that he would get good waves, as long as he had the arms to paddle. But to endow him with magical wave-attracting powers made a better story.

'That was worth it for the look on Dog's face,' Gordon said when Sam paddled back out.

'Happy you're back on the horse?' Sam said, pushing up on his board and rubbing his right shoulder.

'Happy to get out of the house.'

'I noticed. You look like shit, by the way. Do you sleep at all now?'

'Not much. How about you?'

'I've got too much on my mind. Then the moment I drop off, some old bloke's taking a piss on the other side of the wall.'

'How is Tony? Does he know the firehouse is about to get shut down?'

Sam offered a noncommittal grunt and pressed a thumb into his sore shoulder. 'Fucken did something to the rotator cuff there.'

'Give someone else a chance to get a wave.'

'You going for this one?' Sam asked, eyeing an incoming set.

'Ha ha.'

'Right, see ya.' Sam paddled but couldn't make it. Dog, on his SUP, stole it off the pack and was careering through the traffic when Japan Ned, not normally a drop-in artist, decided to take off in front of Dog and pull four or five snappy turns, Dog screaming homicidally at his back about being on his feet first. The mob on the peak cheered for Japan Ned: any wave stolen from an SUP was cosmic justice.

'That was worth the price of admission, eh,' Sam said.

'I only agreed to come out because you had something to tell me,' Gordon answered. 'So I can't say it was worthwhile until I hear what it is.'

Sam looked cautiously from side to side and paddled further from the pack, past Tonsure Man and out to sea. He kept peering through his armpit to check that Gordon was following.

What seemed to Gordon like halfway to New Zealand, Sam sat up on his board.

'Yeah, well, what we were talking about the other night,' Sam said. 'I was right. We are fucked.'

'I know that. You might have to narrow it down.'

'We're fucked in the worst possible way.'

'Which is?'

Sam pinched the bridge of his nose and wiped his eyes. At first Gordon thought he was crying, but he was just wiping off the salt water and blowing his nose into the surf.

'I've left the bank,' Sam said.

'Season for change,' Gordon replied. 'Jude Oxenford's leaving town too.'

'Bet she didn't get marched out of her own home office.'

'Come again?'

'I've been put on compulsory leave while my loan book is audited and my computer and phone records are gone over. These goons came in on Friday and took over my desk. Can you tell me why all the detectives nowadays look like bank auditors, and the bank auditors look like detectives?'

'Jesus.'

'I won't sugar-coat it, brother. You are fucked and I am particularly fucked. If they're not complete morons, they'll find out that I've been lending you money against shares, which is illegal for a start. On top of that, I've been having those shares revalued fraudulently, and you weren't meant to be on my books anyway. Fucken banking royal commission—who'd have thought they'd get anything done?'

Sam's dry laugh petered out. His giant chin quaked. Being out in the ocean was protection against being overheard, but no protection against emotions that paddled out here with you.

'What's it going to mean?' Gordon asked.

'I could go to jail, brother. And I do not want to go to jail. Not for a white-collar crime, anyway.'

'I'm sorry. You were only trying to help me.'

'Oh?' Sam looked strangely disarmed by this. 'It wasn't only you. I've been helping out friends my whole career. It's banking. Nobody said you weren't allowed to be a decent person. Bend a few rules for the little bloke. Apparently I was wrong.'

Gordon thought: Some things cut deep from angles you weren't seeing. He felt bone-weary. It hurt his back to sit up on his board so he lay prone on his stomach. The muscles had gone out of his arms.

'What . . . what does it mean for me? Can I just sell my property—sell my share—and pay the debt back? Is that what happens?'

Sam grimaced. 'You haven't been listening. I said you're fucked. Did you see what that cunt Archer David got for his place? Forced sales affect all valuations in the area. Now that my stuff's gunna come out, they'll assess my dodgy revaluations and benchmark it back to market. You're deep in negative equity. You're headed for bankruptcy court, brother.'

'What about Kelly?'

'Kel's all right because her share was part of her father's probate and she's got no debt. And even if the terms of her father's will prevent her from cashing it in, at least she has an asset still worth something.'

'Thank Christ for that.' The weariness was like a smothering blanket. All Gordon wanted was sleep. 'What about Carl? Can he sell to someone else? Kelly had an idea that my mother could buy him out.'

After their truth session with Ben, Kelly had revealed her plan to Gordon, who thought it was so ludicrous, the idea of his parents borrowing money to save his skin, that he hadn't taken it seriously . . . until he was woken in the middle of the night by the terrifying thought that Ron might buy a share in The Lodge and move in with him. This turned into another reason he couldn't sleep.

'Yeah, Norma came to me,' Sam said, looking distant.

'Then it's true? How did that go?'

'Let's just say that if I want to get a medical degree from an Asian university, I've made a good start.'

'Did she get to the point?'

'Eventually I figured out what she was trying to ask, but it's no good. Leonie already had Carl's share locked in.'

'How?'

'Ever heard of straw man directors? Usually they're drug addicts and down-and-outs whose names are whacked on company documents to cover up for some hidden beneficial owner. In Leonie's case, the down-and-out she chose to be a straw director was her stepson. Carl doesn't even own what he owns. She does. He couldn't sell it to your mum, or anyone else, even if he wanted to.'

'I didn't even know that was legal.'

'It's debatable. She'll want Carl in and out, she'll want you out, and it's getting pretty urgent for her to get the Hilton development done and dusted.'

'Fark. Can she even do that?'

'I've told you. She had some pretty devious legal advice. You'd have to be a criminal mastermind to set things up like this. It's genius. She'll end up owning the lot again, but the key thing is that she'll have got her Hilton renovation done for free. All funded by the Bluebird Building Society's generous revaluations of The Lodge.'

They heard a banshee scream from the peak. A massive set wave came through, cleaning up forty or fifty shortboarders. Only a giant board sitting far out the back could have caught it, and here he was, paddle aloft, murder on his white-painted face, loose flesh hanging from his ribs, budgie smugglers tight against what could, if Gordon's eyes weren't playing tricks, have been a half-mongrel.

'No doubt about him,' Sam said, after they finished watching Dog ride the wave of the day through to the beach.

'Is there any way out?' Gordon said.

'Well, I s'pose if The Lodge suddenly blew up today, you could score. You've got a brief window while Carl's still on the title. The worst-case scenario for Leonie would be if you, ah, somehow, you know, if something happened to The Lodge before she gets the Hilton finished, then the land value would revert to you, Kelly and Carl.'

'If "something happened".' Gordon's mood plummeted. His stubbornness had fucked up so many lives. Sam, Kelly, Lou, his parents, Ben—they'd all suffered from a contagious disease that could be traced back to a single carrier. His sentimental stubbornness might even fuck up Leonie. Some consolation.

Sam nodded. Gordon saw the muscles in his friend's neck and chest contract and his hands stiffen, as if he could feel a tsunami on the horizon.

'We found out something about Ben yesterday,' Gordon said. 'He's been making money by selling his ADHD drugs to Carl.'

'I wondered why Carl's always needing cash.'

'What, he's been coming to you as well?'

Sam gave a shrug. 'I might have organised a credit card for him.'

'I made Benny give Carl his money back. To see what I've done to him, what he did for me, it's . . .'

Gordon could no longer speak. In the circular workings of his mind, he always arrived at this point, and then he could not speak or act or do anything, all he could do was wish he was in darkness, asleep.

'It's all pretty fucked,' Sam finished his sentence for him. 'But good on you for dealing with Benny that way. Someone in this joint has to be a decent father eventually.' He swung his board around and locked eyes with Gordon. 'You know what I mean, brother. It was the lie that set us free. Until now, I s'pose. Now it looks like it didn't.'

They found themselves staring at the place where Sam had first called Gordon 'brother'. And ever since, Sam had been true to that word.

'We've got to make a plan,' Gordon said.

Once, up on that cliff, it was Sam who had done most of the talking. While Gordon spoke now, Sam remembered that day. He remembered how, as he had explained what was going to happen, Gordon was mostly shaking his head—not in disagreement but in wonder. Now, it was Sam who was shaking his head, yes, in wonder. This was no Gordon he knew. Eventually, cautiously, under persuasion, Sam began nodding. This was better than the Gordon he knew.

'Well, that is a plan,' he said when Gordon was finished.

'What do you reckon?' Gordon asked. His eyes lit on the top of the prominent sandstone ledge at the northern end of the beach, above the ocean baths and the marina, with the graffiti:

BLUEBIRD

'I'm in,' Sam said now, as Gordon had said then.

'It's our only hope.'

'Hundred percent. But I've got one condition. There's something you've really got to do.'

Before Sam could explain, they were distracted by another commotion in the pack. For all the beauty and the glory of such a perfect big-wave Bluebird day, there would always come a point where sharing and patience and appreciation of this holy place reached saturation. Tempers had been unravelling, and now every set of waves was resulting in an incident. Gordon saw Dog, whose voice pierced the air, fall off his weapon. The rubber rope linking his paddle to his board had been pulled by a surfer, yanking Dog into the water. Gordon thought he saw Japan Ned on the end of the rope. There was splashing and thrashing like a shark attack, and angry shouting. Gordon paddled towards the beach, and a nice big wash-through took him in. He tried to get up off his belly and ride it standing up, but his arms had turned to liquid. He slid into the beach, put his board under his arm and set off for The Lodge. He didn't need to hear what Sam wanted him to do.

The right way

'JUST GO. *GO, YOU CLOT!*'

'Wait. What?'

'Stay where you are.'

'Goodness, will you shut up?'

'Don't call him that, Ronald.'

'What?'

'Let them go, Ben.'

'It's a roundabout, Ron.'

'Bloody useless, the lot of you.'

Ben's dad had given him one and only one piece of ironclad advice about learning to drive, which was that whoever Ben chose to be his teacher, he should never, under any circumstances, drive with more than one adult in the car.

Now he had three, all yelling at him. Ben would give anything to get his one hundred and twenty hours. Today he was paying full price. His head was still spinning from what had happened at home over the past few days. He needed to be somewhere alone to digest it. Instead he was *here*, with *them*.

Grandma and Grandpa were impatient to get to lunch at The Lodge. You didn't want to make them wait for lunch. Grandpa was in the passenger seat, and behind him Ben's mum was gazing out the window with a faraway look, taking meditative breaths and letting her eyes half close. Inviting the grandparents for lunch had been an impulsive decision of Mum's, on the rebound from the emotions of recent days. Ben could see how discombobulated his parents were, how shaken out of their characters. Dad had gone surfing in a big crowd, and Mum had invited Ron and Norma for lunch. Something was not right.

An exuberant Grandpa, who had packed an overnight bag 'in case I stay for some time', could not contain himself. He regarded himself as the superior driver in the vehicle and barked instructions at Ben. Even though Grandma wasn't trying to instruct Ben, she was trying to instruct Grandpa, which was just as bad. Then Mum, out of nowhere, would offer an opinion. Everyone speaking over the top of everyone else was messing with Ben's head.

'He has to give way to the right at a roundabout,' Norma said to Ron.

'Learn the rules, woman! He only has to give way to traffic that is already on a roundabout!'

Roundabouts were, even more than homophobic schoolkids, the bane of Ben's life. With his clear head, his Ben head, his no-Vyvanse head, he was coping with most challenges, but roundabouts scrambled him, and now Grandma and Grandpa were making it worse.

'Your grandfather is right,' his mum said, re-entering the conversation after taking a moment to reconcentrate her peace of mind in her sacrum. 'But he's also wrong.'

From the passenger seat, a snort.

'Wait, what?' Ben said, braking hard. Couldn't they talk about this later? But he couldn't tell them to shut up when they were all telling each other to shut up.

'Technically, you do only have to give way to traffic that's on the roundabout,' his mum continued. 'But practically, if the other cars are speeding into it from the right, you're best giving way to them.'

'Rubbish,' Ron said.

'Oh, do be quiet!' Norma said to Ron.

'I'm sorry, Ron, but what do you want?' Kelly asked. 'To avoid an accident, or to be in the right?'

Norma let out an amused honk.

'I just want to get there,' Ron said, growling in the direction of his watch. 'It's nearly twelve.'

'You can get to where you're going five or ten or thirty seconds late, or you can wait for someone to cut you out of the car on a roundabout. At least you'll have been in the right.'

'What?' Ben said, concentrating on getting through the intersection. 'I didn't understand any of that.'

'We'll talk about it when we get there.'

'We are quite late,' Norma said fretfully, undermining Kelly and, as usual, ending up on Ron's side. 'Are you sure Lou will have everything ready? You know Ron can't have any salt.'

Ben glanced in the rear-view mirror. The day wasn't turning out quite as Mum had hoped.

While Ben took a few shots at reverse-parking into a space on Cliff Street, Kelly got out of the car. Let him have Ron and Norma to himself. They could all have themselves to themselves. Norma's plan to buy Carl's share had fallen through, which meant there'd been no point in Kelly's sleeping with Gordon or patching things up. She couldn't do it anyway. They hadn't been able to talk about it, but he wasn't into it, she could tell. And if she couldn't get back together with Gordon, any plan to keep the three of them in The Lodge would also fall through. So be it. She had to save herself and get out of here.

Norma, holding her walking stick, climbed out of the car and latched on to Kelly's arm. Ron was roughly pushing away Ben's attempts to get him on his frame. Everything had to be a battle. Every fucking thing. A wave of exhaustion washed through her.

'We're not going down those steps,' Norma said.

Ben mouthed to his mother, 'You should have told them.'

'See?' Norma said to Ron. 'I told you they wouldn't let us in. Gordon's worried he won't be able to get you out.'

'No, it's just that the StairLift's not ready,' Ben said.

'You're probably right,' Kelly said to Norma, and let that hang there. If they wanted to be part of this family they could be part of this family, chaos and all. Kelly wasn't going to pretend anymore. 'I'll see who I can get to carry you,' she said, unclipping herself from Norma's grip before heading down the stairs.

Ron gave a dismissive lick of his lips and set off after her. 'I don't need their silly electric chair,' he said. 'Waste of money. It's for you, Norma, you're the weak one.'

Ben followed him. Ron said, 'Stop hovering, boy. You want to carry me down? Be my guest! And then you can do your grandmother!'

'Oh, don't be so stupid!' Norma wailed.

'I have plans to move in here permanently,' Ron announced, 'so the sooner the electric chair is done the better.'

Ron leant passively against Ben, waiting to be picked up. Ben froze. He had been distracted by other things, but now he grasped the new reality. His mum and Lou would leave him in The Lodge with his crazy father, his crazier uncle and his craziest of all grandfather. As the 'bearer', among other things. All his preoccupations fell away. Ben saw the future as an adult must see it, not as a series of events but as an unbroken plain stretching to vanishing point.

'Wait, what? Grandma?'

'What is it, darling?' Norma said, edging to the top of the steep flight of stairs.

'There was something Uncle Carl said to me.'

'Well, I don't know if you can believe what comes out of your uncle's mouth,' Norma said, ruffling his hair with her free hand, then returning it nervously to her walking stick.

'Useful as a hip pocket on a singlet,' Ron said. 'Are we going?'

'It's been bothering me, something he said about him not being my only uncle . . .' Ben stopped.

'Chop-chop,' Ron said. But Norma, reading Ben's face, was ahead of his words. Her eyelids and mouth began to pucker as if sucked inwards by a vacuum sealer.

'Sorry, forget I said anything,' Ben said.

He looked down the stairs for his mother. He felt very alone.

Norma's stick clattered on the landing. Her hands went to her face. It sounded like her fingers had voices, and they were all moaning. Ben put his arms around her.

'Look what you've done to your grandmother,' Ron said. 'Come on, are you going to carry me or not? Big strong boy like you?'

If Ben could have any wish granted, it would have been the power to grab his words out of Grandma's ears and stuff them back into his mouth.

Grandma's hands had come away from her face and now held Ben's. Her eyes were inside him. Ben didn't do eyes. They scared him. Of the three hundred and sixty points of the compass, the one Ben could never look at was the one occupied by Grandma's eyes, which were more blood than eye. More yellow than white. More white milk inside the gold than the gold. Ben was afraid of getting lost in that blood, that milk. He pulled himself out of her, pushed her out of him. He understood something about his father. If he loved Grandma, he had to lie.

'I'm—I'm sorry, Grandma. I was just doing a family tree project at school and I . . .'

'All right, I get the message,' Grandpa said. 'I'll go down myself.'

Grandpa set out, not with any great speed, but the transition was too swift. Blood fled from his head, or his legs. His bones dissolved inside his flesh. The way he fell made Ben freeze. There was a crack as his shoulder hit the balustrade. While Ben was rooted to the spot, Kelly, who was coming up the stairs from the house, ran forward to stop Ron tumbling down the flight. As he fell, the old man violently fended her away. Norma cried out. Hand to her mouth, she hobbled to where Ron was sitting. And this was the impossible thing: he had somehow fallen in such a way that his back had slid down the balustrade and his bottom had landed squarely on the decking, leaving him in an upright seated position, his legs and arms floppily at rest, like a children's doll propped against a wall.

'Grandpa!' Ben, coming out of a dream, crouched down and took hold of Ron's right hand.

The old man, his face like that of a corpse, cold and urinous, eyes rolling back, pulled his hand free.

Norma whimpered. 'I knew he would push himself too hard! Should we get an ambulance?'

As his mum looked for signs of injury, Ben wondered if this was the beginning of the end that he had heard so much about. But a jolt passed through the old man at the sound of the word 'ambulance'. He flailed. His eyes were on his grandson.

'Grandpa?'

Ron's lips peeled away from his ivory teeth. He looked so deathly that Ben had to close his eyes.

'I fall like a cat,' Ron said, his voice surprisingly robust. 'I've told you, it's one of my many talents.'

'Are you hurt?' Ben said.

'How many hours do you have to drive on your L-plates?'

'Wait, what?'

'How many—'

'One hundred and twenty.'

'And how many have you done?'

'Seventy-six and fifteen minutes. I have forty-three hours, forty-five minutes to go.'

'Your maths is improving.'

'I know.'

'I wonder how far you'd have to go to get it all done in one trip.'

'You stupid man,' Ben's grandmother was sniffing. 'You stupid, stupid, *stupid* man!' To Ben she said, 'Please don't ever live in the past, darling, that's what makes you old ahead of your time.'

But Ron was nodding at Ben with an inner smile, as if after a long struggle he had arrived at a satisfactory solution.

~

When Gordon came up from his surf, he showered and dressed in a fresh set of clothes for the first time in he didn't know how long. He buckled a belt and put on real shoes with laces. He combed his hair. Kelly might be pleased that he was showing signs of life.

In the kitchen, however, she didn't look so happy. She cursed quietly as she tried to get the La Marzocco working. Gordon was about to offer to help when he was interrupted by his mother, swinging through the saloon door.

'. . . and when it turned out to be a fungal infection, which Dr Choy—he's absolutely lovely, he showed me his citizenship certificate he'd just received—so he said . . . Oh, hello, darling! Don't you look nice!'

'How did they get you in?' he asked.

'Well, that's a lovely way to say hello!' Norma hobbled towards him and kissed his cheek. 'Once you get that electric chair fixed, your father and I will be able to come and go as we please!'

Lou shot Gordon an apologetic look and disappeared into the bathroom. One more day, her eyes said. One more day till I keep my promise to see Ben's cricket final, and I'm out of this madhouse.

Gordon wished he could flee with her.

Ron doddered through the saloon door without his walker. Norma greeted him lovingly, showing him off to Gordon like a new boyfriend.

'He fell at the top of the stairs, poor thing. But he lands like a cat!'

Ron kept a stiff upper lip, but his jaw trembled. Gordon remembered something Sam had said. It was the lie that had set them free. But that too had turned out to be a lie.

Norma declared, with a dewy smile in Kelly's direction, 'And I'm so glad you two are back together. It's so much better for Ben.'

'Er, yeah,' Gordon said, shooting a wary look at Kelly, who was now busying herself, in excessive detail, in the kitchen. Gordon wanted to tell her that he'd had nothing to do with it, this was just Norma joining wrongly numbered dots. Unless Kelly had told her they were back together?

Norma peered over the rims of her half-glasses. 'All marriages go through their ups and downs, but some things we need to put behind us. Your father and I are so glad for the two of you.'

You've been putting things behind you for the past fifty-six years, Gordon thought. If anyone was a living warning against the perils of persisting with marriage, it was his parents. Then he gave himself a mental slap. Imagine thinking of your parents like that. But as Kelly came out of the kitchen he experienced a zing of synchronicity, knowing that she had just had the same thought, and the feeling was akin to sexual arousal, so maybe what Norma was claiming, she was willing into being.

'I don't think I can do this,' Kelly said. Gordon hoped she was only referring to the coffee machine.

'Don't spoil things, we were all in such a nice mood,' Norma said. 'Let's go out to the balcony, Ron, it's a gorgeous view on a day like this. Kelly, have you thought about setting up the luncheon outside?'

Kelly put on her Munch's *The Scream* face, which, without the Workers' Education Association, would have been plain old wide-eyed horror.

'That might set the timetable back,' Gordon said weakly.

'We're happy to wait, aren't we, Ron?'

'No.' Ron busied himself by poking through Gordon's mail. 'Anything from the JPA here?'

'I'll set up the card table outside,' Gordon said, thinking, Just get through this hour and we'll deal with the next hour when it comes. 'How's the hip, Mum?'

'Dr Ting was very pleased with me. Did I tell you that his daughter knew the two of you from back in school days? I don't remember any Chinese at Bluebird High.'

Ron asked someone to make him a drink, which gave Gordon an excuse to put off moving the card table and slip back through the saloon door for a conversation with Kelly.

'We can get through it,' he whispered forlornly.

Kelly looked at him not with new eyes but old. He felt a guttering flame.

'Gordon, I—'

'Why did we stop?'

'Stop?'

'We were—together again—we were—doing something—and then we stopped.'

She gave him a once-over, taking in the revolutionary impact of his clothing. 'Maybe we were only kidding ourselves that we'd changed.'

'Change is what I'm ready for.'

'Gordon . . .'

'If I don't change now . . .'

He had been aware of a sound like a stomach rumble, easily ignored, a distant hubbub, male, somewhere else. Now an angry voice rose above others, above the sky and sea, above the conversation he was attempting to have with Kelly, above even the clamour of voices inside his head.

'What is that?' Kelly asked.

They joined Gordon's parents at the balcony rail. Down on the beach, in the south corner, not fifty metres below, a circle of heads, five or six deep, clustered around what looked very much like a brawl. The circle seemed to revolve, like hajjis at Mecca. Angry shouting from all sides, men at other men to *Stop, stop, stop,* and others exhorting *Fight, fight, fight.* Several of the watching crowd had surfboards under their arms. Men dived in and pulled other men out: slaps of flesh on flesh. A broken black paddle was flung onto the rocks.

Ben joined his parents and grandparents on the deck.

'It's Dog,' he said, a glitter in his eyes. 'Getting the shit beaten out of him!'

The noise abated and the crowd was thinning. Gordon made out Japan Ned, in a torn wetsuit, near the centre. Tonsure Man's head gleamed brown in the sun, and the inky back of Cnut's head shone a livid blue, its expression even more ferocious than usual. Sam was hoisting Dog out of the sand. It seemed that a lot of surfers had been involved.

Sam helped Dog over the jump-up boulder to the base of the wooden stairs. Blood striped the white of Dog's face paint. Lighter strands of red were wrapped around his torso like bluebottle streamers. He was clutching his eyes. The backs of his hands were red with blood. Sam, in his zipper vest, was carrying half of Dog's paddle. No sign of his stand-up paddleboard.

'I guess Japan Ned finally had enough,' Gordon said. 'Every man reaches his breaking point.'

Ben said, 'We all do, Dad.'

Gordon looked at Ben as if to answer the accusation—why don't you hate him too?—but he had nothing. He looked down into the crowd but they were just heads and shoulders, breaking up and wandering off, some into the surf and some up the sand, witnesses to Bluebird justice, long delayed, no longer denied.

Sam and Dog arrived at the kikuyu lawn below the deck. Dog's injuries were worse up close. His forehead was sliced open, as was the side of his neck and his shoulder.

'I need an ambulance!'

Dog's voice was wobbly and frantic. Beside him, Sam nodded, like a parent apologising for his overambitious upstart son who has just picked on the biggest kid in the playground.

Gordon turned inside to get his phone. Lou stopped him.

'No.'

She stood with her legs parted, square-on as a cage fighter.

'You're not helping him,' Lou stated.

'He's badly hurt.' Gordon turned to Kelly, who was leaning over the rail. Gordon could hear Dog calling up from the lawn, whining, 'Lemme in, will ya? Kel?'

Kelly watched Dog teeter on the grass, weighed down by nothing heavier than his half-paddle. Certainly not consequences. Dog was Dog, while Kelly was unforgiven. She was still furious with Gordon for not decking the bastard, but maybe it was up to her. She had slept with Dog so that Gordon would kick her out. She had slept with Gordon to spite Leonie, and also, maybe in her heart of girlish hearts, so that Gordon might wake up to himself and be a husband. But fuck that for a joke, she thought: enough sleeping with men to manipulate her fate. By doing nothing, these men had put it all back on to her. If her nature was unforgivable, then there was no point trying to hide it anymore.

'No,' she said. 'Not here.'

'Not here?' Dog pleaded. 'Meaning?'

Kelly shook her head. 'Not ever.'

Next it was Ben.

'You're not welcome here.'

Dog was still whimpering, like a—like a dog.

'I'm bleeding to death here!'

'Didn't you hear them, you silly man?' Norma said. 'You need a hospital! Or at least the clinic in Bluebird will be open; there's a very good young Asian doctor called Leung . . .'

'I need an ambulance, I've been assaulted! Look at me!'

Ron jammed his walker against the balcony rail, as if he would have liked to propel it over the edge. 'Didn't you hear? You're. Not. Welcome!' He turned to Norma and said, 'Waste of space, the lot of them.'

'Champion! Let me in!'

Gordon felt Kelly's and Ben's eyes, Lou's and his parents', as he looked at Dog, the blood drying black on his neck and shoulders, fresh and red over his sliced-up face.

'Hard for an ambulance to get here,' Gordon said. 'You're better off calling from the surf club.'

'I need attention!'

They had come to the end. Forty-five years, and this.

'Gordo, buddy, come on! Let me up?'

Gordon reached into his pocket and found his wallet. He flipped it open.

'Here,' he said. 'This is yours.'

Dog's Eastons charge card spun on the breeze, not quite light enough to float, like a surfer cutting back against waves of air, before landing on the grass at his feet.

'I don't want this!' Dog cried.

'Fuck off. Just fuck off.' This was Ronald, who turned to Norma and said, 'Sorry, pet, please excuse my language.'

Gordon was first inside, followed by Ben and his parents, with Kelly waiting for Lou before sliding shut the glass door. They could hear Dog calling, but now Sam was pouring his low murmur over the top like concrete over a nuclear accident, and they were receding, down, back to the BSLSC, where an ambulance could pull in. And then their voices were gone.

Kelly's arm was around Ben's shoulders.

'What about his Fast Ferry card?' she asked Gordon.

'I gave it to Carl.'

'Thanks, Dad,' Ben said.

'That's okay, mate. Should have done it before.'

'Like years ago?'

'Like years ago.'

Gordon looked at Kelly. She lowered her gaze.

'Never too late to change, Dad. Or undo old mistakes,' Ben said.

Gordon was still focused on Kelly.

'After lunch,' he said quietly. 'After we get rid of my parents.'

Kelly raised her eyes to his.

'I'll take you there,' he said.

She nodded. He didn't need to say any more.

The kick

THIS WAS THE BOYS' PLACE, A SECTION OF THE CLIFFTOP THAT could only be reached by a narrow path on a crest of sandstone that dropped away to the ocean on both sides. Tourists didn't know about it, and locals wouldn't dare come further. The path stopped at an overhanging ledge where you could look straight down at the water and chuck rocks or spit or even pee, watching it bend and scatter in the wind. If you leant right over the ledge you could see a little blowhole, which, in the right swell and tide and wind direction, captured a gout of water and spat it at you, even wetting your face if you were lucky.

Owen and Sam had guarded its secret until they brought Gordon here, to initiate him.

'Swear you won't tell,' Owen said, spitting into the palm of his hand and offering it to Gordon, who grasped it with pride.

That day wasn't right for the blowhole. The tide was too high, the swell direction too south, the wind too flukey. Owen had seemed pissed off. When Gordon crossed the narrow rock bridge to the ledge, Owen called out, 'Fall! Go on, little Gordo, fall!' He cackled. Sam didn't see the joke. It wasn't the place to gang up on the younger boy, but this was Gordon's memory of Owen: you could never tell which mask he was going to put on at the beginning of each day, what mood he'd be in, who he would turn into as the day developed, who he would turn on.

Owen resented having to babysit Gordon that day. He'd been crapping on about it to Sam. Gordon was too young to go into large surf, so Owen was under strict instructions to keep him in the ocean baths. But Gordon had gone climbing on the cliffs above the baths, which had given Owen the idea to show him the secret spot and dump him there.

From the top of the cliff, Owen and Sam saw how the surf was pumping. Owen decided they needed to get their boards. Sam hesitated, but Owen said to Gordon, 'You promise on your life to guard our secret?'

The wet palm of Gordon's hand tingled. He nodded.

'Spit brothers,' Owen added solemnly. 'You'll wait here and tell no-one.'

Gordon felt as if he had been entrusted with the keys to a secret kingdom. No way would he let Owen down.

The elder boys surfed for hours, and while he waited Gordon grew bored. He explored the crags around the ledge, and found a way of climbing down closer to the blowhole. He could grip the strong heather and fit his toes into the horizontal furrows in the sandstone. He got down to that under-ledge. The blowhole still wasn't quite firing, but you could get your face wet here. Owen would be pleased with him for finding a closer lookout.

When, a while later, he turned around to climb back up, Gordon couldn't find those ladder-like corrugations in the rock, which had grown slippery with the spray from the rising surf. The sky had darkened suddenly, and a squall of rain was blowing in. It all looked different from below. He knew he couldn't call out for help to any of the tourists hurrying back to their cars on the clifftop above—Owen would kill him—so he took some deep breaths, told himself to be calm, and sat on the lower ledge to wait.

The minutes dripped by. He began to grow scared that Owen and Sam had forgotten him, would never come back, or that he would have to alert the surf lifesavers or scream out to passing adults. Either way, he was going to be in a world of strife.

He paused at the higher ledge. Forty-two years. Where had his life gone? Fuck's sake, his father was right. They did get the wrong one back.

It didn't feel right to be here without Sam. Whenever they had come here together, Sam was the leader, resuming his older boy's stance. Sam was his big brother. He'd never trusted Gordon to be here on his own.

'Gordon.'

He turned to see Kelly and Ben following him, stepping decisively across the sandstone bridge. They were holding hands. Funny how a new perspective changes things. As a kid, and even as an adult coming here with Sam, Gordon had perceived that bridge to be as narrow as a tightrope. It fell away sharply on both sides. Now, he saw Ben and Kelly walking across it with relative ease.

The afternoon was gorgeous, the sky beginning to flare in bronze, the swell still running, surfers in the water, the breeze offshore. Still that bell-ringer.

Kelly and Ben were across the rock bridge. Gordon had nowhere to run, even if he had wanted to. Maybe it needed to come to this, the physical entrapment as well as the emotional. He could tell the truth or step off, after Owen, right here. He looked over the ledge. A whump of sea hit the hollow base of the cliff, and a jet of water spouted, falling on him like a heavy rain.

'Blowhole's working,' he said.

Kelly smiled, in spite of herself. She swept her wet hair out of her eyes.

'This is where your uncle Owen died,' she said to Ben. 'Your dad was only a little boy. Sam was with them. Afterwards they lied about it. They've been lying about it ever since. Haven't you, Gordon?'

Gordon shook his head. 'It's not what you think.'

When Owen and Sam finished their surf and came back to find that Gordon had left the secret ledge, Owen flipped out. He was furious at Gordon for quitting his special post, and he was scared of their father's reaction. Owen was always getting beltings from the old men. Mr Chidgey got into him over the mess he and the other boys always left at The Lodge. Mr Eastaugh targeted him at the surf club, convinced he was a bad egg leading Sam astray. Then there was Mr Abottemey, always showing up unexpectedly at their home late at night to talk to their dad. Mr Abottemey hated kids in general but singled Owen out, glaring at him like he was a personal enemy, responsible for all the juvenile delinquency that, in Mr Abottemey's view, was going to kill this place the minute he let his supervision lapse.

They shouted and screamed his name, but Owen and Sam couldn't find Gordon. They would be in the deepest of deep shit. Sam said they had to go back to the Grimes' house. Maybe Gordon had gone home. Owen argued that if they went home and Gordon wasn't there, his parents would call the emergency services, triggering a whole missing-boy drama and, as sure as night followed day, Owen would get a belting.

Just then, they heard what they thought was a nest of baby birds crying. Owen followed the whimpers to the end of the ledge. Sam joined him. They looked down. Gordon was sitting, his knees bunched at his ears, his arms around his shins, crying between his legs.

'Oi!' Owen called. 'What you doing?'

Gordon couldn't climb back up. He had been too ashamed, or too upset, to answer their calls. Owen laughed with relief: he wouldn't have to notify the adults and get in trouble for losing his little brother! Gordon tried to laugh along, but he soon realised Owen and Sam couldn't get to him. There was a sheer drop below him of about thirty feet to the blowhole. The ocean was smashing into the headland and spraying him. He was cold and drenched, and the rock face was like soap.

'I've got to get down to him,' Owen said to Sam.

'Let me go to the surf club.'

'If I can get down to him, I can get him up.'

'Don't, O.'

While Sam stood watch, helpless to change Owen's mind, Owen edged down to Gordon. They hugged briefly, but Owen was then faced with the dilemma of how to get Gordon back up. Gordon, snivelling and frightened, made it clear that he couldn't climb. Owen could make it back up himself, if he was lucky, but what was he to do with Gordon? Put him on his back? Gordon flat-out refused. He didn't know if he could hold onto Owen's back.

'I told you, you've got to let me get the adults!' Sam, also whimpering now, called from the top of the cliff face. 'My dad's at the surf club!'

At the mention of Mr Eastaugh, Owen grew belligerent.

'You get him, I'll never speak to you again.'

Owen continued trying to persuade Gordon to climb, and then he tried bullying him, finally promising unbelievable rewards, but Gordon was clinging to the rock face, cold and wet and hysterical now, bawling his eyes out in panic at the thought of moving.

'Wait!' Sam called. 'Lemme come down and help!'

'Don't be an idiot, you'll only get trapped too,' Owen said. 'I'll take care of it.'

Owen was Gordon's big brother. He would get him out of this. Nobody would know except them.

'We won't get in trouble,' Owen told Gordon with grim determination, as if trying to convince himself. 'We won't!'

After a long stand-off, with Gordon refusing to move, Owen lost patience, raised his fist as if to punch him, and dragged him onto his feet. They paused on the first narrow wet ledge of sandstone. Owen climbed around the seaward side and found a different way up, a fraction more gently sloped with a number of handholds in the outcropping rock and the heathery scrub. Owen was confident and capable. Owen was the best rower in the junior boys' surfboat crew. Owen's eyebrows were crusty with the salt from surfing eight-foot waves. Owen could do anything. Gordon never had another hero.

Owen hoisted Gordon roughly onto his back. He climbed up the face, nearly to the top. He grabbed a handful of heather, banking on it taking his weight and Gordon's. It would have, except Gordon panicked. This was what happened. Everyone knew it nowadays, from the number of ocean rescuers who drowned while trying to save others. The drowner always panicked. The drowner pushed the rescuer down. Survival took over and the drowner would become an animal, blinded by its own fear, and kill the one who had come to save them.

Through Owen's body, Gordon felt the bunch of heather tear out of its roots and come loose in his hand. Survival sent Gordon mad. He screamed and jumped for another tuft. Using Owen as his springboard, he made it to the flattening at the top of the cliff. As he jumped, his foot contacted Owen's temple. Owen was stunned for a split-second: just long enough to lose his second handhold.

For a moment, Owen stood with his toes dug into the cliff face. He was still connected to the land. He stood in a perfect vertical. His arms spread to either side, as if opening to embrace Gordon.

As Gordon saw Owen lean back into the wind, he thought he was playing one of those trust games, where you let yourself fall backwards and it's going to be all right because your friends will catch you.

In that embalmed shard of time, Owen's eyes met Gordon's. Gordon swore he remembered it this way: Owen was *smiling*. Seeing the smile, Gordon was certain it would be all right; Owen was not worried, Owen was happy. He was Gordon's beautiful blond hero. It was a game.

But there was something wrong with the angles. Owen's toes were still on the land, but his top half was in the air, away from the cliff. He seemed to be there for an age, arms out, peaceful, poised like Christ on the cross. He didn't panic. He didn't try to stop anything from happening.

Gordon: a life determined from eight years of age.

But Owen had been smiling, Gordon was sure his memory wasn't making it up. Why? When your dumbfuck panicking little brother has kicked you off a cliff, why, when you had a last chance to speak to him, *why did you smile?*

⌒

'Nobody believed him and Sam,' Kelly told Ben.

They were sitting on the ledge now. Gordon had been speaking for a long time, maybe half an hour, and the sky had turned black. Kelly and Ben could not see his face.

'They came back and said they were playing up here, and Owen fell. No other explanation. Of course that was what they would say. They were little boys.'

Gordon thought back to how Sam had held him at the top of the cliff, stopped him going to the edge and leaning forward to see where Owen was hiding, and then eased him into the lie so rapidly, so purposefully, that the myth had Gordon's loyalty before he knew what he was thinking. All Gordon was seeing, as Sam spoke, was Owen's smile. He was still half-expecting that the big boys were playing a prank on him. In a moment Owen would reappear from behind a bush, creep up behind and pretend to give him a shove, scare the shit out of him, and then Owen and Sam would be cacking themselves at the gullible little boy.

What eventually shook him out of this was Sam's white face and the dry spittle on the corners of his mouth. Sam was talking, talking. He sat the trembling Gordon on the upper sandstone ledge and said, 'We don't have much time, here's what we're going to do.'

Then Sam had purposefully listed all the shitty things that would happen if they told people that Gordon had kicked Owen off the cliff. Gordon's parents would die of grief. The old men would flog them both. Gordon would be put in a home. Bluebird would be over. That's what Sam had said: 'We tell them what happened, and Bluebird's over. Life is over. It's down to us, brother. It's all down to us. We were playing, right? And Owen slipped? Got it?'

And even though Gordon was only eight, he held a perfect understanding of the necessity of the lie. It was more powerful than a threat. He needed something to believe in, and if Owen was not going to jump out from the bushes laughing, this was the next believable thing.

'Why was he smiling at me?'

'I didn't see that.'

'Was he happy I'd kicked him? Did he want to go?'

Sam grasped Gordon's shoulders and shook them so hard that Gordon thought the big boy was going to pitch him off after Owen.

'Owen fell while we were playing stupid armies! It's not your fault! Listen! You did nothing wrong!'

'I'm not going to a home,' Gordon said.

'Right! You spread some crap about it being your fault, we might as well all *die*.'

Gordon looked down: his shorts were drenched with pee, its warmth turning to chill. It was the thought of leaving Bluebird that made him piss himself. And when he looked across at Sam's shorts, also wet, he knew he had to lie. In the distance they heard the ring of the shark alarm: an emergency. Already a surfboat was charging out through the waves. Someone had seen a floating body. He caught a glimpse of a piss-yellow mop of hair. Tony Eastaugh and the lifeguard crew were on their way.

'But why was he smiling?' Gordon asked again.

⁓

Gordon did not know what time it was. Clouds covered the stars and moon. He had done something unbelievably stupid, even by his own epic standards.

'I don't know if we can get safely back across that bridge,' he said, gesturing to the blackness behind him.

'Wait, what?' Ben said.

'It's dangerous.'

'It's okay, Dad.'

'Is it?'

'Sure it is. Let's go.'

'Is it really okay?' Gordon was not speaking about the safety of the rock bridge.

'My phone has a torch.' Ben got up and led. From the far side of the bridge, which he crossed easily, he shone the light to show Kelly and then Gordon the path. Without being able to see the drop on both sides, Gordon felt no fear.

The three walked in silence past the marina and ocean baths and down onto the sand, where Kelly and Ben took their shoes off. Gordon realised he had left home without shoes. They were almost across to the southern end of Bluebird Beach when Kelly stopped, her face in her hands, and moaned quietly.

'Kel,' Gordon said.

'I can't go up there.'

'You can't face Carl?'

'I can't face *you*.' She dropped her hands. 'You lied to me. For our entire life together. You told your first lie the night of my fucking disaster, and you've stuck with it ever since. Are you proud of that?'

'I never lied.'

'Gordon, you opened your heart to me.'

'I didn't lie. I just didn't finish the story.'

'This is so *you*, Gordon. You know what I went away thinking. You know what you left me thinking ever since.'

'Who else can I be?'

'Someone who tells the truth, you piece of shit! You told me about him falling backwards with the smile on his face. This was the most extreme moment of vulnerability—I thought for both of us, you and me, that night—and you left me with that image of your brother. You have been happy for thirty years for me to believe Owen took his life.'

'Not happy.'

She turned to Ben. 'I believed your father was getting something really heavy off his chest. It was obvious the boys had lied, everyone in Bluebird knew that. Playing armies and Owen slipped? But it was left alone. They were boys. I was the only person he'd told the truth to—which, I thought, was that Owen jumped. It made me special, to know the real thing. A secret shared is a secret halved, eh, Gordon?'

'Why would Owen jump?' Ben said.

Kelly stood wringing her hands. Quietly, she replied, 'Same reason kids are jumping now. Same reason all these cliffs are fucking graveyards. Who knew what happened to your father's brother? I don't know, because your father has never allowed me to talk about it. So it was left to me to think about it. And, you know, there were all these bad men around the place then. Rumours about Mr Abottemey, Tony Eastaugh, even bloody stupid Red Cap's a registered sex offender—I don't know, Gordon, do you want me to run through all the stories? Do you want me to talk about my own father? Or does it mean nothing now, because Owen didn't fucking well jump? Because you—you pushed him off? How is that meant to make us feel about you, Gordon? How's it meant to make *me* feel?'

She lunged at him with her fists. Gordon bowed his head and closed his eyes and waited for her blows to rain down. But Ben got his arms around her, first in restraint and then, as she dissolved into tears, in comfort.

'I hate you, Gordon!'

'I know.'

'If I hadn't left you already, I'd leave you now!'

'It was an accident, Mum. He didn't mean it.'

'I'm not talking about that—I'm talking about the lies! He did mean those! He did!'

'But he's telling the truth now,' Ben went on. Gordon felt a glimmer of hope, his beautiful boy, his last ally, until Ben, as honest as the attention-deficit day is long, continued: 'I just can't work out why he had to tell me.'

Gordon wished he was back with Sam. He was still a fucking liar. He wasn't confronting his past and telling Ben and Kelly because of any higher motive than that he had to get this done so that Sam would set them free. The condition of the deal. You bullshit artist. He wished he was back on the cliff. He knew what he ought to have done there. Here on the sand, he had nowhere to fall.

'All I know is that I've been going about things the wrong way, Benny. I asked what was the biggest thing in me that I could change, and this was it. So I decided to change it.'

This almost convinced him.

'Did you think about how that might affect me?' Ben said. A renewed, heart-rending sob escaped from Kelly. 'You think your secret shared is a secret halved? Maybe for you it is, Dad. What about me? Now I've got the secret too. What am I meant to do? Do I tell Grandma? Grandpa? Do I go and talk to Sam about it? What do I do with your secret? Did you think about that?'

'Your grandparents already think Owen jumped,' Kelly said.

Gordon fell to his knees and then onto his chest. Ben was right, Sam was wrong. Sam had thought it was as simple as setting free a memory he had kept bottled up, but that was not how it was. To recall Owen's death was to reach into a dark arsenal where it was one of many concealed weapons. All had been locked up, and there was no exactitude in what destructive force he might have reached in and brought out, no certainty about what else he might have jolted loose. Was it a memory anyway? When he had spoken to Kelly and Ben on the ledge, it felt more like an invention. A fact, possibly, but a fiction equally concrete. He did not know what he was playing with. He did not know what else was in there. Following Sam's encouragement, he had been hoping to make his family real in more than name, pushing that heavy guard aside, opening the gate of his little one-man compound and letting his wife and son in. He had shared his shame. He had killed his brother. He had told them at last. This was meant to fix him? All it had done was spread the burden of a story. Kelly and Ben were better off when he had kept himself in quarantine: a lifelong quarantine.

'I've made a mess of it.'

'You're fucking telling me,' Kelly said.

'I feel sorry for you, Dad. I really do.' Ben stepped forward, bent down and gave him a pat on the shoulder. 'But now I'm going up there with Mum. I need to get some sleep; I've got a big game tomorrow.'

Gordon heard Kelly's weeping and Ben's consoling murmur recede as they went to the jump rock at the base of the wooden stairs. Soon he could no longer hear them. He wondered if he could lie here until the tide came in and drowned him. He lay on the sand until the lights in The Lodge had gone out. Finally he pushed himself to his feet, brushed the sand off his back and his front, and walked towards the firehouse.

Boys

AN ANGRY SUN WAS LIGHTING THE EASTERN HORIZON FROM beneath the sea. Kelly went up the passageway past Archer David's house, which was empty, even the robot lights disconnected. A little like herself. She picked up the free weekly paper, the Saturday-delivered *Daily*, now so slender you could use it to pick your teeth. She read most of it while standing on the path. She bore a dull resentment towards the *Daily* for still existing, four years after the end of Gordon's beloved *News*, even if it was limping along as a kind of student paper, owned neglectfully by a multinational conglomerate, written and edited by unpaid interns. The paper's innards were held together by what must have been the last print display ads in western civilisation, all real estate except for one furniture shop run by an ancient retailer called Harry Love who must have believed this internet thingy was a passing fad.

Front and back pages carried a serviceable tabloid version of the previous weekend's surf carnival. Despite being late (hence its nickname, the *Weakly-Daily*), it covered the key events—the crash between Bluebird, Capri and Manly in the surfboat race, the winners of the beach sprints—with the breathlessness of being first on the scene, if not the first into print. Kelly's eye fell on a photograph of Michael Abottemey with Daniel, in cricket clothes, smiling for the camera. There was nothing about Daniel's role in the fight. It must have been in, and then edited out, but they'd forgotten to remove the photo and its caption, which said: *Happier times.*

'Hey.'

Kelly looked up from the newspaper to see Lou crawl out from under the StairLift.

'Just about got it working,' Lou said.

'You've been on it all night?'

'I'm desperate to finish it before I leave this arvo.'

'Gordon can finish it for you.'

'Pfft. He's not up yet? Still brooding on the future down in those Bluebird deeps?'

Kelly could feel Lou searching her face for information she didn't want to hear. She shook her head.

'He spent the night at the firehouse.'

'Guess I'll get back to work,' Lou said.

'You know you're welcome to stay on.'

Lou seemed ready to say something, but at that moment Cnut stumbled up the stairs, his only acknowledgment of either Kelly or Lou the profanity he let out when he nearly tripped on Lou's foot. Where had he come from? Had he been sleeping in some corner of The Lodge? Kelly thought: If Lou changed her mind and decided to stay, I would talk her out of it.

'I'll go get Ben moving,' Kelly said. 'You still coming to his cricket match?'

'Wouldn't miss it, even if it means I don't get this thing working.'

Kelly went inside and made coffee for herself and Ben. Like all her efforts in the kitchen, the result was less than the intention behind it.

She carried the two mugs to the Boardroom where she found him in a Z-shape on his mattress on the floor, his face to the wall.

'Cappuccinos, I'm branching out,' she said, but he wouldn't roll over. 'I thought you'd be up practising your shots?'

Fuck, she thought, I am sick of myself. Lou's right: we all have to get out of here. But she's also sort of wrong. Bluebirders aren't creatures of the depths. We are in the shallows, brackish little seawater puddles left in the rocks by a receding tide.

'Sweetheart,' she said, her hand on Ben's shoulder. 'I get it.'

She felt a sickness rising in her stomach. She sipped her coffee, knowing it would make her nerves better and worse.

The muscles of Ben's back were rigid beneath her hand.

'He can't help it, darling. He meant well.'

Damn him. Gordon had had years to grasp this nettle. He'd been content to fuck his life up rather than let his own wife and son in, and now he had let them in, it was too late. Anger surged in her, displacing pity. Gordon had had his chances. He'd sent them all spinning off in their separate directions. That was what his silence had come to. Kelly had always believed in speaking, in letting it all out. Not so much anymore.

'Darling. Please don't tell your grandparents about this. You know how they're always saying don't live in the past, that's how you grow old? Well, it might not be because they won't; it might be because they literally can't. The past is too painful.' She stroked his back. From his tension, she knew he was listening. 'You know, I always wanted to be an only child. I grew up thinking Carl was the worst thing that ever happened to me. I wanted to give you the gift I never had: no competition.'

'Dad says being an only child is the best.'

'You're lucky, that's what we both believe.'

Lying awake last night, Kelly had been more scared for Gordon than for Ben. At the bottom of it all, she knew Ben better than Gordon did. Ben was a repository for Gordon's fears about himself. Gordon was always terrified that Ben might do what he had contemplated doing, as if the generations only refined and advanced your worst impulses. Gordon was the most unlikely narcissist, but a narcissist he was; he wasn't seeing Ben as an individual, he saw him as a facet of his own fear, a ghost, a parable, a tying of historical loose ends. There had been a night, soon after the break-up, when Kelly and Ben had had a fight. He had stormed out in tears. While Kelly had calmed down, Gordon had been distraught with fear. They had the Find My Phone app, to try to locate the phones that Ben lost on a regular basis, but also as a tracking device. Kelly had told Gordon to relax, but he had cried out in fear and showed her the screen. The tracker had placed Ben in Bluebird Bay. Gordon had run full-tilt for the headland. He had been convinced that the argument had pushed Ben to the worst thing imaginable. It had turned out that the app was not perfectly accurate. He had found Ben, not in the water, but sitting on the cliff having a think. Gordon had been inconsolable.

Kelly held no such fears. She knew Ben spent time on Bluebird's clifftops when he wanted to be by himself, away from his parents, away from all the riff-raff that blew through their house.

Her mind went back to those days after Owen died. A teenager's funeral in Bluebird in the seventies was a rare event, before teenagers overdosed, before they jumped, before they dropped acid and thought they were Superman and flew from all the cliffs of Ocean City. When that epidemic hit, the families of those dead kids whited themselves out of Bluebird. But Owen's death belonged to the age of innocent accidents. Owen's death, like everything else here, good and bad, was absorbed. Tide went out, tide came in, new sand covered it. Families like Gordon's cracked on, shaped by their wounds, eyes only on the future because the past could kill them if they let it catch up with them.

Everyone in Bluebird knew there was something about Gordon, something bad that had happened. A brother? Yeah, a brother. Outside the Grimes family, herself and Sam and a handful of others, that was all Owen became: a shadow who never made it past twelve.

'It was never spoken of. Never.' Kelly was wiping tears off Ben's cheeks. 'You might wonder why your dad is the way he is. Why he's . . . stuck. Why he has this mission to preserve Old Bluebird. Why he can't see what's best for himself. And us. Why he makes all these bad decisions. Why he and your grandparents can't get on but can't let go.'

'Why you did what you did?'

'I often think it all goes back to your dad's brother.'

Kelly looked through the window at the sandstone clifftop across Bluebird Bay: that distinctive crag above the marina, the place they looked at across the water from The Lodge every single fucking day. As if their eyes could wear down the sandstone and make it drop into the blowhole.

And that one dumb word in graffitists' paint:

BLUEBIRD

'Mum.'

Kelly leant into the mattress. Ben tolerated her hugging the breath out of him. She tried to get his arms around her. His effort to tolerate her felt worse than no effort. She felt the pain radiating off him like fire. Boys should need their mothers, she thought. Boys should need their mothers.

For the ages

BEN HAD SPECIFICALLY ASKED HIS FATHER NOT TO DRAG THE whole crew along to the cricket final. Gordon failed again as a parent. He felt a wild reckless pride in his son and didn't give a bloody-minded fuck who knew it, Ben included. So in the menacing early heat, dew glistening on the Father McInally Oval, as Daniel and the Cobcroft Boys' captain walked to the pitch to toss a coin with the solemnity of dignitaries at a state funeral, a talkative group of Gordon's guests was settling into the Father McCroorey Grandstand.

No other players had supporters present. Ben Grimes's family entourage comprised Gordon, Kelly, Lou, Ron and Norma. After the first surfing shift, up from the beach came Sam Eastaugh, Red Cap and Josie, Tonsure Man, Snake, Cnut, Chook, Macca and the three-time state champ. It was quite a mob. Japan Ned was watching cricket for the first time. He pronounced cricket neither good nor shit. The only crony missing was Dog, rumoured to be in hiding with a head the size of a pumpkin and two dozen fresh stitches.

Lou had cleaned out her gear from The Lodge and stowed it in her car for the drive south, where she was to start a job the following week.

'I'm happy you came,' Gordon said, a catch in his throat. 'You owe me nothing.'

'Well, now that I think of it, that's true,' Lou said and gave him a soft punch across the jaw. 'I have to pop back there later to get the machine out.'

The La Marzocco was the property of Lou and Afterpay. She was determined to finish owning it in her new life. 'If you take it, that's one less misdemeanour for the council to pin on us,' Gordon said.

'And I'm the only one who knows how to use it.'

'How will you get it up the stairs?'

'I've got a brilliant idea. But it involves the StairLift, if I can get it working.'

'Want me to help?'

'You stay here. If I've learnt one thing about The Lodge, I won't have to wait long for help.'

As the game started, with Ben's team losing the toss and having to bowl first, Gordon shuttled among the crew.

Red Cap had brought a card table and a jigsaw puzzle, and Ron Grimes turned out to be a surprisingly sharp-eyed asset. Perversity was Ron's last great joy: when the worst was expected of him, he would deliver his best. As they worked separate sections of the jigsaw, Gordon and his father exchanged reminiscences about family holidays, which were happier in memory than at the time. Maybe, Gordon thought, the only true moment is the present, and if I am content in our fictitious constructions, they overwrite the facts. Ron had come with his usual overnight bag, crammed, as if for a long stayover, with pyjamas, toiletries and the obligatory manila folders and file envelopes. Gordon didn't press. It was such an uncommon morning, uncontentious and companionable, he wanted to preserve it.

Ron was convivial, behaving politely towards Norma. Red Cap talked jigsaw tactics with Ron, Josie brought cups of tea from the pavilion, and Tonsure Man listened with interest as Norma prattled about a golf club friend's father who had been Tonsure Man's dentist in the 1970s and removed a young TM's impacted, infected molars.

Out in the middle, the gentlemen's game proceeded in a manner befitting this cultured audience. The Cobcroft Boys' wickets fell in an orderly sequence, Daniel bowling out the opposing captain and Ben staying out of harm's way. He only had to field two balls in the first hour, and when he threw from the outfield nobody was audibly laughing. Gordon counted this as a win.

The sun burnt off the dew after the drinks break, and the batsmen dug in. When Mr Stoyle, as umpire, gave a Cobcroft batsman run-out, the two coaches faced off in mirror teapot postures, but presently the game settled back into its cricketly rhythm. Gordon's friends, having made the big effort to turn up, lost enthusiasm as the length of the match hit home. They had come to support Ben—but would they have to wait all day to see him do something? Sam Eastaugh, remembering why he had given up cricket at age twelve, left the group and sat under a Moreton Bay fig tapping on his phone. Japan Ned's eyes glazed over and he looked around hopefully for a lift to the beach. It might be good out. But nobody could leave: they had made a vow to Gordon, and Bluebirders were nothing if not loyal to their vows.

Gordon walked a lap to soak up the day before it got too hot and to escape the creeping sense that he had played a successful trick upon his friends. Jude Oxenford was walking a lap in the opposite direction and they met in front of the Father McCann toilet block (affectionately known as the 'Father McCann cans'), near the poplars on the eastern side where Ben was fielding on the boundary, walking in and out with each ball as seriously as if he was playing a test match. He dropped his head when his father wandered into his eye line.

The Cobcroft lower-order batsmen were staging a fightback, and Jude commented that what had looked easy pickings for St Pat's was turning into a total that would require good batting to chase down. Daniel waved his arms like a traffic policeman as he changed the fielders and bowlers. In exasperation, he brought himself on to bowl, but the Cobcroft tail-enders connected with a few swishes and Daniel kicked the dirt. Coach Stoyle engaged him in a long conference.

'I'd have thought as umpire Mr Stoyle was meant to be impartial,' Gordon said.

'Neither partial nor impartial but somewhere in between,' Jude said. 'That's how he put it to me.'

'I'm sorry,' Gordon said.

'Sorry that I have to work with dills?'

'Sorry that Carl coming back to Bluebird has caused you so much grief. I'm assuming that had something to do with your decision to leave.'

Jude chewed this over. A Cobcroft batsman went for another swing, missed and was bowled.

'Only one to get and our boys will be chasing, what, a hundred and eighty?' Jude turned her full face to him. 'I've run schools for a while. Things like Carl happen every week. The other day I had to restrain a parent from physically attacking one of our teachers over a homework detention. I'm a crisis manager. It's what I do.'

'Carl hasn't made it easier.'

'We have to deal with the trade in ADHD drugs like our teachers used to have to deal with tuckshop lines. It's the way things are. You don't have to take responsibility for everything that happens in Bluebird.'

'I'm beginning to learn that.'

'Just beginning?'

'I'm glad Daniel's playing today.'

'Glad because it was the right thing, or because it made Ben happy?'

'I'm taking your advice. I don't care about the right thing anymore.'

'That's good,' she said. 'Because making the other boys happy was his only reason for doing it.'

'I'll miss you,' he said, feeling like he wanted to cry.

'Gordon.' Jude's face turned in upon itself. 'Not everything you've brought to Bluebird has been bad.' She had more to say. She took a breath and exhaled through pursed lips as if blowing out a candle. But her eye was caught by something behind Gordon and she said, in a freeze-drying tone, 'Anyway, nice seeing you.' She walked briskly away.

Gordon, puzzled, was about to continue his stroll when he saw Jude's reason for suddenly terminating their conversation. A carnelian red Prius Hybrid had pulled up. Half-running down the slope past the Father McCann cans was a man on an unkempt warpath.

'Frontal,' Gordon said.

Frontal was in no mood for light chat. His wispy ginger hair fluttered in the breeze and his beard was uncharacteristically ragged at the edges and fluffy around the jowls. A ruff of neck and back hair sprouted, bringing to mind a border collie. Instead of his usual slacks and business shirt, he was clad in dirty Billabong shorts and an Australian Crawl T-shirt.

'I warned you and you ignored me,' he said, waving his finger in Gordon's face.

'Nice to see you too. Daniel's taken two wickets. The tail's wagging though. Have you been sleeping rough?'

Frontal was red-eyed like he had been drinking, or crying, or both. Gordon was familiar with the look, having seen it in the mirror most mornings. But whereas Gordon employed his insomniac hours in self-pity, enumerating his sorrows, Frontal looked like he had been fomenting conspiracy theories.

'You don't appreciate the trouble you're in.'

'I have a full appreciation of the trouble I'm in.'

'You're the worst type of fool: an arrogant one.'

'Why don't you lower your voice to a scream.' It was a cricket match. Frontal's voice was carrying across the field, all the way to Gordon's artificially generated crowd on the far side. 'If it's about the retaining wall, I can't do anything about that until David Archer's buyer moves in.'

'Bugger the retaining wall! And his name is Archer David!'

Frontal's eyes were bulging. He really did look unwell. His dismissal of the importance of a retaining wall grabbed Gordon's attention.

'I sent you a *letter*! On council letter*head*!'

Gordon didn't know how to respond to this. He was tempted, like his mother, to pick up on the most trivial sidebar and express a polite sentiment, to say, 'I'm sure you will still have access to the letterhead, no need to hit the panic button just yet,' when he realised that Frontal had no doubt about getting his job back. Frontal was a winner. Daniel was a winner. Daniel would win today, Frontal would win tomorrow, they would toast themselves in their champions' lounge, and Frontal would be reunited with his letterhead.

'I lost it,' Gordon said.

'You lost it?' Frontal's face fell, expressing not outrage but a passing cloud of disappointment, as if this was all his long career in public service had come to: victory without satisfaction.

Gordon thought: I lost your letter, and my brother slipped and fell off the cliff while we were playing. Or . . .

'No. I burnt it,' he said.

That felt better.

Recovering, Frontal laughed, apparently with genuine humour. 'Well, you'll deserve all the costs that are about to hit you. Don't say I didn't warn you.'

A caw from the cricket pitch interrupted them. The last Cobcroft batsman was out, and Daniel, having spent the morning sulking and swearing, had ended up with three wickets and was being clapped off. He raised his hat in acknowledgement. Only now did his father notice the game.

'Good job, Danny boy!' Frontal clapped above his head. 'Go get 'em!'

Daniel ignored him. Ben trailed into the pavilion last, talking with Zane Dwyer, the cricket team's bits left over.

Frontal said, 'That boy is an out-and-out champion.'

'Hundred percent,' Gordon said, feeling as articulate as Japan Ned on the subject of cricket. 'I heard the investigation over the surfboat thing is going away?' The Capri rower had been discharged from hospital with minor injuries. Funny how justice works, Gordon thought: Daniel could have killed that boy, but it's the consequences, not the act, that determine the punishment.

'He's a fraud,' spluttered a voice from behind Gordon.

'Hello, Ronald,' Frontal said complacently. 'How are your plans to move into The Lodge?' He smirked at Gordon, as if their interests were aligned and Frontal, with his punitive wave of costly demands, had come to Gordon's rescue. 'If you end up out on the street, you won't have to worry about the old man moving in. Glass half full!'

Gordon felt his insides coil, uncoil, recoil. At that moment, he hated Frontal. Or maybe the daily effort not to hate Frontal became too much, and what he was feeling was not hate but the absence of restraint.

'You threatening my son?' Ron said. 'You of all people ought to know not to play that game.'

Gordon, watching Frontal, did not immediately understand the change that came over him. The smug pleasure dissolved, and was replaced by, if Gordon was not mistaken, bug-eyed terror.

'Oh, come on, I was joking,' Frontal croaked. Gordon turned to see that his father had produced, from the overnight bag at his feet, a manila folder which he held up teasingly.

'I knew I had this somewhere,' Ron said. 'Gordon, you have nothing to fear from this pinhead.'

'I don't understand,' Gordon said. Frontal and Ron most clearly did.

A dry rasp came from Frontal's throat as Ron slid a plastic-sheathed document from the folder.

'See?' Ron said with peak vindication, and handed Gordon the document.

'Dad, why have you got Daniel's birth certificate?'

'Does it matter why? Look: the date.'

Gordon read the date twice. He looked at Frontal, then read the date a third time.

'Doesn't that kid look like a nineteen-year-old to you?' Ron said. 'This is a copy of the original.'

Gordon shook his head, not in response to the question. In response to everything.

'Why bring this up now?' Frontal said desperately.

'Why have you got it in the first place?' Gordon asked. He read the certificate again. Daniel's parents, Michael and Soula Abottemey. Place of birth: Sparta. According to the date of birth, Daniel was twenty-six months older than Ben, two years older than all the other kids on the field. Daniel was eighteen. No, nineteen. What the fucking fuckery.

From his folder, Ron now produced a second birth certificate. Same details, except Daniel's date of birth nineteen months later.

'I know a falsified document when I see one,' Ron growled. 'You could say it's my special subject. I tell you what,' he said, levelling an accusing stare on Gordon, 'if this town had a decent newspaper, it would be the first place I would take this little scoop.'

'Why have you got it?' Gordon repeated. He was reaching an understanding of the scandal—and a scandal it was if Daniel's age had been falsified. Frontal's vicarious revenge, his scheme to get back at Bluebird for every last one of his humiliations, through the success of his golden child, his Greek god, was a fraud. Daniel's achievements exceeded those of everyone else in his age group because they were not *in* his age group. To finally be the big boy he had failed at being, Frontal had scammed the school, scammed the town, scammed his own flesh and blood. Of course. He had rigged the paperwork at source.

'I was proud of being a Justice of the Peace,' Ron said, puffing his chest. Now was his moment. He had been rehearsing this speech. 'But my office led me to shameful acts.'

Gordon's knees went weak as he heard his father's declaration. As a young engineer, Ron had had professional dealings with the Bluebird town clerk, Conal Abottemey, a man to be feared and respected, or at the very least complied with. Ron's engineering projects routinely passed over Conal's desk. The town clerk's power was absolute, and Ron had learnt, from his profession—its first law, the law of preservation of mass!—that such force could only be leveraged, never eliminated. 'In my day,' he said, 'we didn't call it corruption. We called it business.'

Conal Abottemey's favourite functionaries were distributed across the beaches. He had his accountant and his turf accountant; he had his solicitor and his barrister; he had his builders and his certifiers and his surveyors and his agents and his developers. He had his politicians. And Ron Grimes was Conal's Justice of the Peace. When documents needed to be altered, they required a JP to authenticate them. If you controlled the facts at their documentary source, you controlled outcomes.

'I needed to feed my family,' Ron said by way of mitigation, showing sufficient mercy, or discrimination, to fix his accusing eye on Frontal rather than Gordon.

Ron, discreet and trustworthy, had certified the altered documents the town clerk brought him. 'That's what was required of you, and that's what you did': the two dimensions to the little box, at the bottom of his mind, where he consigned these acts.

'You . . . you wouldn't dare bring this up now,' Frontal said, but his expression betrayed his shrinking hope. Why wouldn't Ron bring it up now? What did he have to lose?

'You learnt your filthy trade at your father's knee,' Ron said. 'You took over what was to all intents and purposes a hereditary position, and you continued its practices.' He turned to Gordon. 'The soul of rectitude, the picture of integrity. Along with his father's processes, he inherited his father's trusted functionaries. I kept on verifying documents for this one as I did for his father. When he came back from Greece, ready to take over the kingdom, he brought me that boy's birth certificate. And the deed was done,' Ron concluded, reverting at the last moment to the passive voice.

More than anger or surprise, Gordon felt acute embarrassment. To have this level of criminality—personal, family, inherited corruption—exposed, to see Frontal caught out, was secondary to the shock that his father had participated in it and the Grimes family had profited from it. You could never put your finger on it, but you saw the residue—the misanthropy, the anxiety, the fear, the intolerance, the nest egg. Gordon felt that he had finally solved the mystery of who his father was. And he wished he hadn't.

'Does Daniel know?' Gordon asked.

Ron gave Gordon a look of alarming directness. 'Some things, between fathers and sons, are best left unsaid.'

In the shocked silence, they watched the cricketers file back onto the field, the Cobcroft Boys' fielding team followed by the two St Pat's opening batsmen. Ben looked on from the pavilion. A space away, sitting in his pads and helmet, loosening up with twirls of his bat, was Daniel.

'But does he?' Gordon repeated to Frontal, who came to his senses as if recovering from a head knock.

'You won't do it,' Frontal said to Ron. 'Do this to Daniel and their team will be disqualified from the competition. You're killing your own grandson's dreams.'

Ron thrust his jaw. 'I want my conscience to be clear.'

Frontal put his index finger to Gordon's chest. 'You let him do this, and I will destroy everything you value.'

Gordon watched Frontal walk to his Prius. He had developed a slight limp, or it could have been that he was trying to keep his right shoe, which had lost its laces, connected to his foot. It was true what they said. The longer you knew a man, the deeper the mystery. Gordon sincerely wished he could understand this guy. He had made an enemy of the person who could do him most harm or the most good. Which was how the world went.

'Looks like you might have stuffed everything up for everyone,' Gordon said.

'I dare say he is overestimating his powers,' Ron murmured. He put the certificates back into the plastic, the sheath into the manila folder, and the folder into his overnight bag, which he handed to Gordon, like a porter, before commencing his long shuffle back to the stand where Norma, Kelly and the others were sitting, unaware of what had just occurred.

Catching up to his father, Gordon said, 'Are you really going to do it?'

'I'm not one for empty threats,' Ron said. 'I will be presenting this to the proper authorities before the day is out.'

'Why? After all these years? Don't you realise what it'll do to your own reputation?'

'Tell someone who cares. He has been threatening you, my boy, and when I saw him there today, I had to act in your defence. I told you I could help.'

'Come on, Dad,' Gordon said. 'There has to be something else.'

'Well, if you must know . . .' Ron stopped walking so he could gather the breath to speak. This was the beauty of his father, Gordon thought. He had no ordinary shame. As long as his comfort was not at stake, Ron lacked the human propensity to take offence. If you denied him his five-thirty drinkie, he would murder you. If you asked him to reveal why he was a lifelong fraudster, he would answer candidly.

'You were there,' Ron went on. 'At the prison.'

'What prison?' Then Gordon realised that his father so loathed the nursing home, he could not bring himself to utter its name. 'Oh, when he came to your room.'

'As he has done over the years, with documents.'

'I thought it was a coincidence he came across us.'

'For the unknowing, there are always coincidences,' Ron said. 'He didn't do it as often as his father, but these people can't help rigging the game. I asked myself the same question you have asked me. Why was I doing this? What did I need that he could give me? You know what I want. I have submitted my request again and again and again. What, you think I would give up just because you and Norma wouldn't get me out? I went to a higher power. I gave him his chance. I told him that if he did not get me released from my cell, I would disclose his secrets. The boy is a fool. I told you that. He thought I was a silly old goat. He thought I was bluffing.'

'So this is what, retribution? Blackmail?'

'I am not proud of what I have done. I have notarised building certificates, passport applications, approvals . . . Don't ask me what I have done for them or what the consequences are. I do not know. The burden of not knowing how much corruption I have enabled has weighed heavily on me. Do you understand? I am a crook. The great misjudgement that boy and his father made was to think that my respectability would protect us all. They were wrong. I am not good or respectable. Never have been.'

'Dad, I don't believe you're a crook.' Gordon swallowed. He wondered at the despair that must have overwhelmed his parents when Owen died. If Ben went off a cliff today, perish the thought, whatever the cause, Gordon's anger would be limitless. He could beat to a pulp the first person who stepped into his path. Kelly's voice came back to his mind—what had she told Ben? That 'your grandparents already think Owen jumped'? Was that what had turned Ron from an honest man into a cynic? Had Gordon's lie created a vacuum into which Ron's worst instincts had flooded? There was a connection that his father might, must, have made. 'It wasn't your fault.'

If Gordon was not mistaken, there was forgiveness in the watery-eyed look his father was levelling at him. Maybe even a glimmer of comprehension.

'I know it wasn't my fault.' Ron frowned. '*What* wasn't my fault?'

Gordon was about to explain. Surely his father must have blamed himself. Ron would never have believed the story about Owen slipping. He must have been solving the puzzle, on his own, left to his imagination. What theories about the true cause of Owen's death could he have cooked up, tested, discarded, rebirthed, and finally settled upon? Gordon understood that he had created his father's bitterness. By lying about Owen's death, he and Sam had wanted to save Bluebird. Instead, they had preserved Bluebird's worst, unleashed its fantastic powers of disappointment and blame.

'Dad, I need to tell you something.'

'Not interested.'

'It's really important to me. To us.'

'Look, they're serving lunch.'

In the grandstand, the spectators were supplementing the school-provided chicken and salad lunch with some purchases from the bottle shop. Leaving Gordon dumbfounded and silent, Ron beetled towards Red Cap, who knocked the cap off a stubby and offered it to the thirsty and grateful old man.

'Don't get me wrong, Gordo,' Red Cap said when Gordon came over, 'we're here to support Benny, but jeez, why didn't anyone tell us cricket takes a whole day?'

Gordon, given no choice, surrendered his father to the mob. Meanwhile, the St Pat's innings hiccupped. The openers were out and Daniel came to the crease, to defend against the new ball and set a platform to chase Cobcroft's score of 199.

'At least they've got plenty of time,' Gordon said, watching the back of his father's head.

'Yeah, time,' Tonsure Man said, looking stricken. 'Anyone know if that new swell's kicked in?'

Gordon focused on the game. Daniel was batting with a boy whose name was Joel Something, and the St Pat's innings began to settle. Daniel and Joel were talented, even Gordon could see that. Pity Ben couldn't. Or maybe Ben could, but didn't care? He still believed he would play for Australia. The poor kid had drunk the Kool Aid about 'desire' and 'will' and 'hard work' and 'belief'. It was almost an article of the national faith in sports that natural talent was less important than desire. You never heard a champion

431

attribute their success to the talent they were born with. It was only ever desire, will, hard work and belief. Ben believed. He did not realise that the mantra of desire, will, hard work and belief rested on a foundation of natural talent that was beyond not only Ben, but beyond the best boys Ben had ever played with, and the best boys *they* had played with. But Ben believed in belief, and you had to love him for that. What would it do to him to discover that Daniel was a fraud? Leave aside the disappointment of forfeiting today's final: what would it do to Ben's belief in *belief*?

Gordon glanced at Kelly. He had still not dared to speak with her today. He set off on another circuit of the ground.

There was a 'Howzat!' and the Cobcroft boys converged in the certainty that they had taken Daniel's wicket. They were surprised, not to say appalled, when Coach-Umpire Stoyle folded his arms and shook his head. A conference ensued between the opposition players and their coach, and then between their coach and Stoyle, but the umpire is always right—particularly, Gordon thought, when he is an arrogant little shit in cargo shorts. Daniel continued batting, and after this let-off the Cobcroft team attacked him verbally: the price he paid for his teacher's favouritism. As if admitting his guilt, Daniel began to bat carelessly, swishing hard at every delivery, trying to get his ordeal over with. Stoyle spoke to him. Daniel lowered his head in the teenage-boy stance of 'Say what you like, I'm not listening', and went on hitting balls in the air.

Gordon felt sorry for Daniel, who was playing this dashing innings, leading his team towards death-or-victory, without knowing about the bomb Ron was about to detonate. It didn't matter that Frontal was the perpetrator; Daniel would be seen as the criminal. The kid was a dickhead, but did he deserve a bonus two years added on to a childhood under his father's protection? Gordon pictured Daniel receiving the man-of-the-match award and, as per the formula, thanking his parent for supporting him, and Frontal wouldn't be there. The bomb would be ticking.

As if this image of Daniel's success produced a kind of hex, there was a cry of collective joy, mixed with quieter groans, as Daniel lost his middle stump. Some Cobcroft boys gave Ryan Stoyle the surreptitious finger. Their celebrations had a triumphal tone, and indeed, although Daniel had blasted a half-century, St Pat's still needed seventy more runs to win and were now at long odds. Gordon watched Daniel slouch off, dragging his bat. Every few steps he looked balefully over his shoulder at the yahooing opposition. When he got near the boundary, he flicked his bat at the fence and it let out a gunshot crack. Even petulance Daniel achieved with timing. His bat was intact, but the paling was shattered. He threw his gloves down and disappeared into the pavilion. His teammates affected the studied professional indifference of their heroes, fixating on the game. Only Ben was watching Daniel. He got up and followed him into the darkness.

Gordon continued circling the ground. His heart sank when he saw Lou standing by her car, apparently waiting for him. He wondered if he could keep walking past her. He dropped his head and quickened his step. If he couldn't say goodbye, he thought hopefully, then maybe she wouldn't leave.

'Don't avoid me, Gordon.'

He paused, then walked up the grass bank.

'Hey.' Lou opened her arms. 'Let's make this painless.'

Gordon put his face into her hair and tried not to make a fool of himself.

'We'll probably still be getting that coffee machine out when you come home later,' she said.

'Right. Let's not make this goodbye. Might see you later.'

'Right,' Lou repeated. 'Got a job to do.'

'Have you found someone to help?'

Gordon heard a tapping on the inside of Lou's windscreen. Jude Oxenford was in the car, flashing her Annie Lennox teeth. Gordon let Lou go to the driver's side and leant in the passenger window.

'Thanks for helping her.'

'Pleasure!'

'Has my father spoken to you?' he asked. 'About Daniel?'

The way Jude's eyes narrowed, Gordon could see that she knew.

'Not my problem, Gordo. My last official day at St Pat's was yesterday.'

'Well . . . okay.'

Lou started the engine.

'You've got to let us go.' Jude smiled. 'We've got a long night ahead of us.'

'I'm sure the coffee machine won't take that long . . . Ah. Oh.'

Lou threw the car into reverse, and the way she slung her arm around the passenger's headrest to see through the rear window stopped Gordon's voice in his throat.

'Always the last to know, right?' Jude called out to him as Lou reversed onto the street.

⌣

Gordon walked on, watching the play. In a day of surprising twists, now came another. Joel Something and his batting partner became mixed up running and both finished at the same end of the pitch. There was an argument about which batsman was out, Stoyle trying to convince the Cobcroft coach that the other boy, an inferior batsman, should be the one to go, but the Cobcroft coach (and his players) insisted on Joel. Resentfully, Joel left, and then the other boy tossed his wicket away. St Pat's, suddenly five wickets down with sixty to get, were in a tight spot.

When he got to the stand of Moreton Bay figs separating the cricket ground from the boundary of the Bluebird Country Club, Gordon detected a movement to the side of one of the sinuous trunks.

'Jesus, you lurk like a peeping Tom.'

'Persona non grata, forced to live on the margins.'

'Even at a kids' cricket game, you have to sound like fucking Yoda.'

In Carl's hand was his ever-present battered *Don Quixote*.

'Not finished yet?' Gordon said.

'Only three hundred and ninety pages to go. But I feel I've broken the back of it.'

'You want to join us? There's still some lunch.'

Carl shook his head. 'My oil has never mixed with Bluebird's water. And yeah, that one's mine.'

Gordon didn't know if he meant his epigram, or Daniel, who Carl was watching walk towards them with his cricket bag.

'Nice of you to come to support the boys, anyway,' Gordon said.

'I only came for one boy.'

Daniel was upon them. 'Ready to go?' he asked Carl.

'We have business,' Carl explained to Gordon.

'You're leaving before the end of the match?' Gordon asked Daniel.

Daniel looked to Carl, as if requesting permission to speak.

'He saw you and your father talking with Frontal,' Carl said to Gordon. 'Then he called me and asked for a lift.'

Daniel was turning impatiently towards Carl's Camry, flicking his chin to beckon Carl to hurry up.

'He doesn't want to be here when the *merde* hits the *ventilateur*,' Carl said. 'And he doesn't want his father turning up again. He doesn't want either of them to be here.'

'So . . . he already knew.'

Carl's noncommittal response passed for assent. He followed Daniel up the slope to his car, into which the boy had loaded his cricket bag. Seeing Gordon still watching them, Carl called, 'You all right?'

'What do you mean?'

'I mean . . . everything.'

Gordon pondered this. What was all right, in Carlian terms?

'I don't know.'

'Good.' Carl nodded, as if this was the answer he had been seeking.

Norma was sitting alone on a park bench under a stand of casuarinas beside the pavilion. Gordon dropped onto the seat beside her. She was distraught at the direction the match was taking. 'They're hopeless, those boys—absolutely hopeless!' she said hotly. Gordon didn't know if she was talking about St Pat's or Cobcroft. Maybe both.

'It's all set up for Ben to save the day,' Gordon said.

Norma rolled her eyes. 'You know I love him to bits, but the last thing we want is for the match to be in his hands.'

The good thing about cricket for a family like Gordon's was that it took the awkwardness out of long silences. Even Norma's need to talk eased off. Watching cricket granted her a peculiar freedom. As he sat beside her trying to summon the courage to ask what he had come to ask, Gordon also felt the comfort of not being expected to speak. They were watching cricket. Things happened very, very slowly.

'Mum,' he said, but the word stuck his tongue to the roof of his mouth. He tried again. 'Mum?'

'What is it?'

'I've been thinking about Owen.'

He saw a tremor in her dewlap, but she had the fortitude—or was it the preparedness?—or the presence of mind?—not to respond.

'Mum?'

Again she made him wait. Two overs passed.

'Spit it out, Gordon.'

'I was eight. And we've never talked about him. Never. Not once. Not you, not Dad. Don't you think that's a bit strange?'

'Well, maybe we are *a bit strange*.' She said it dismissively. But her mouth and cheeks were puckering. Her eyelids fluttered. He noticed her hands gripping each other. 'What's brought this on?' she asked.

'Maybe I'm at that time of life. I don't know. We don't have to, it's all right.'

'Do you remember the funeral? What a beautiful eulogy your father gave?'

Gordon barely remembered anything about the funeral beyond seeing the toughest adults he knew, the superheroes of Bluebird Beach, in tears.

'He rose above himself. He spoke with such love and admiration for our son. My heart was already broken. It broke again to hear your father speak like that. He talked about the boy Owen was, how graceful and intuitive and loving and kind, and how sensitive he was too. He said nothing about what Owen was *really* like, and he said nothing about—the end. We couldn't do that to you, of course. We did everything to avoid any further attention falling upon you. It was our wish that you didn't even go to the funeral. But we reconsidered, and I was glad that you could hear your father speak about your brother. Ronald was . . . I think Ronald was *in love* with your brother. That love came out so eloquently and movingly in his tribute. Simply beautiful. It was his finest hour. But something finished in your father that day. He became . . . empty. He lost his belief in the goodness of people. It was only the bad, the nothingness, that he could see. It killed something in him. He never rose to those heights, and he would never talk about Owen again. Even in the dead of night.'

Not for the first time, Gordon wondered at the boy he had been. How the fuck had he got through that? It was Sam, of course, then and now. In the instant of Owen's death, Sam had doubled in size. He had told Gordon what they would do, what they would say, and Gordon had obeyed. Gordon had accepted both fictions: the fiction of Owen and the fiction Sam had helped him create of himself. Who was that eight-year-old? He seemed a stranger and a myth to Gordon now, as spectral as his dead brother. He had grown up so fast, all in one afternoon, and from that point he had not grown up at all. His dedication to The Lodge, to the past, to preserving every trivial little detail of Old Bluebird, down to his destructive friendship with Dog and his submission to his parents, were all in some way deliberate failures, thrown up as sacrifices to gods who might return what he had sacrificed to them the afternoon Owen died. And yet he wasn't just protecting himself. Sam was right. His failures were also the fulfilment of his actions: what he had done, he had done for Bluebird. In saving himself, he had relinquished a phantom version of his fate. The scared little boy who had kicked Owen in the face was the man Gordon might have become. Owen had held on to that man and taken him over the edge.

He allowed the cricket match to swallow up moments, minutes, rolled-out lengths of silence. His mother's face conveyed that the silence of her marriage, in the dead of night, was not limited to Owen's death.

'What your father wouldn't talk about at the funeral,' Norma said, 'was how Owen adored you. Four years was an unusual gap between children but Owen always wanted you with him, tagging along, sharing in what he was doing. I think Ronald cherished the exclusivity of their father-son relationship, but Owen insisted that you be included. Owen would do anything for you, Gordon. Anything. And I suppose in the end, he did.'

He didn't take me surfing that day, Gordon thought.

'I remember him always treating me like I was a pest.'

'Not at all! But see, dear, you were very little, and it was a horrible time. I wouldn't place too much trust in your memory if I were you.'

'I don't remember Dad speaking at the funeral.'

'Well, there you are. You shouldn't think about it too much, you'll only start inventing things.'

Gordon's heart thumped against his throat. 'Is that why you and Dad never talk about it? You're afraid you'll start inventing things?'

Norma sniffed gently. She did not break down or begin keening, as she might usually have done. This was a new species of her emotionality. She seemed calm, relieved, almost happy to be having this conversation. He had expected more resistance, certainly more tears. Norma appeared to be undergoing some kind of blissful transcendence. Her eyes were fixed on the leaves of the Moreton Bay figs, hard and shiny as patent leather.

'I used to try to get him to talk about it, but he would get very worked up. It's years since I tried. Honestly, darling, I believe it would do him in.'

'Do him in?'

'Finish him off.' She smiled. 'Don't worry, I've considered it from time to time! But I really think it would.'

At her turn of humour, she patted Gordon's hand, briefly letting hers linger.

'I'm not blind, darling. I know what it's done to you. But you might want to think of our course of action in that light. We put Owen behind us. We thought the world of him, but he was gone. To keep talking about Owen would only make things worse for you, I thought, and I'm fairly sure this is what your father thought. To make too much of what we had lost would be putting too much expectation on you. We thought that by helping you—and ourselves—to forget him, we were doing you a kindness. I'm aware that you might not see it that way.'

Uncertainty cut Gordon through his centre, like a spike hammered through the crown of his head into the base of his spine. Had he invented his entire memory of his big brother hauling him up the cliff? Had he invented himself kicking Owen? Amid the horror and shame and panic, had he buried another story, the story that others might have believed, the story that Kelly herself and, for all he knew, his parents, had poured into the lie-shaped mould that he and Sam had left vacant? Had Owen fallen backwards on purpose? Had his last face been a smile of relief?

'Mum, do you know if Tony Eastaugh ever interfered with Owen?'

'Why on earth would you ask me that?'

'Did he?'

She shook her head. 'No.'

'No he didn't, or no you don't know?'

'That man—whatever we think of him, whatever we wondered, we just couldn't afford to think about things like that.'

'He perved on kids at the surf club.'

'That isn't the same as . . . other things,' Norma said. 'There were whispers, of course, but in those days you just steered clear of it and got on with your life. What was to be gained?' Norma chewed on her lip. 'Owen was a terrible accident, nothing to do with all that.'

Gordon knew, at this point, that he would not tell his mother what he had come to tell her. He would not reanimate the dead. Owen was gone. It was an accident. There were no witnesses to Gordon's state of mind, only one to his action, and it was all so deeply buried that it might as well be a fable. Telling her now what he still remembered, or thought he remembered, would be the worst kind of cruelty. As Ben had said, it would be a secret doubled.

Instead: a kindness for a kindness, a lie for a lie.

The consequence of that fiction—the promise Gordon and Sam made to each other—might have tied a knot that only tightened with each pulling year, but when Gordon observed the faraway smile on his mother's face, he could see that through keeping his secret, he had kept Owen alive for her. She had never managed to close off the past; the lie, the doubt, the story about the accident, had left open a space in which Norma and Owen still spoke to each other. Forty-two years had not been wasted.

'There is absolutely no doubt in my mind that it was an accident,' Norma repeated with finality.

By lying to himself, too, Gordon had kept Owen, or the chance of Owen, alive. Fucking let him go.

'All the same, I can only speak for myself,' Norma said. 'Your father might have his own ideas.'

Gordon's courage to speak failed him, again. Maybe all that failure of courage had been the victory of something else. Hard for him to call it love, but what else could it be?

Personal effects

HER HEART SET ON ST PAT'S WINNING, NORMA REFOCUSED ON the game. Gordon continued walking around the perimeter until he reached the fig tree under which Sam Eastaugh sat. Sam got to his feet and dusted the dirt off his bottom.

'Sorry, brother, I can't take it anymore.'

Gordon grimaced. 'You've stuck it out all day but can't stay for the most exciting bit?'

'The boredom's not the problem,' Sam said. 'It's the nerves.'

'Do you care that much?' Gordon scanned the field to see if he had missed anything. 'From what I can see it's still eleven pimply boys on eleven.'

'It's an affliction,' Sam confessed. 'I start watching and soon I'm caring too much.'

'I'm not sure about all this either,' Gordon said. 'You're nervous, I'm nervous.'

Sam gave him a wretched look. 'You're getting cold feet.'

Another jubilant cheer came from the field, where St Pat's were on the way to losing the game without Ron's assistance. Zane Dwyer was walking out to bat, wearing board shorts instead of cricket whites, nothing matching except his attitude. They needed thirty runs to win. Umpire Stoyle shoved his hands in his pockets and scratched the turf with his toe.

'I don't know if what we agreed on is the way to go,' Gordon said.

Sam let his eyes fall on the field, where Zane hit the ball in the air. The Cobcroft fielder dropped it, amid groans from one side and impolite laughter from the other.

'This is killing me,' Sam said. 'I knew if I waited too long it'd go pear-shaped.' He climbed up the grass mound like a capital offender who was ready for the gallows but wasn't sure if his resolve would last. Over his shoulder, he called, 'It'll work out, brother. You just gotta give it time.'

'Brother?' Gordon said, but his voice was too faint to carry.

The ninth wicket fell with St Pat's still needing twenty-three runs to win. Ben, who had been padded up with box, thigh pad and gloves since the fall of Daniel, did some knee bends and touched his toes to limber up. This was his test match. He was playing for Australia. He unzipped his kit bag, took out his magic bat and walked onto the field to join Zane.

Over the next half-hour, Ben's heroism was not that of St George or David. Ben's dragons and Goliaths were in his head. He was cast in a supporting role while Zane swatted and clobbered and for the most part missed the ball. But when Zane missed the ball, the ball missed the stumps. When he hit the ball, it stayed hit. He scored runs behind his back and between his legs and over the wicketkeeper's head, unorthodox no-man's-lands where no fielding positions could be set. When you had no natural talent, no desire, no will, no hard work, no belief and no parental support, what else was there but pure dumb luck? When you had no idea where you were hitting the ball, how could the opposition?

While Zane put on this outrageous show, Ben, who had only to face one or two balls at the end of each over, contrived either to miss them or snuff them at his feet. He walked to the side of the pitch to adjust his gloves and pads like a test match batsman. When Zane called him for a madcap run, Ben sent him back. Avoiding a humiliating run-out was Ben's chief contribution.

The only piece of gear he couldn't seem to keep tidy was his bat. The stickers were peeling off. He was trying to smooth them by hand and even lick them, but they would not stay, instead curling up like autumn leaves.

⌒

'I'm going to the coach,' Ron said, getting to his feet.

'Stoyle won't listen to you,' Gordon said.

'I don't mean him! The other coach! The one who'll do something about it!'

'Both coaches are on the field,' Gordon said.

'Then I will go onto the field.'

'Can't you just watch your grandson?'

They were in the Father McCroorey Grandstand. Amid the excitement of Ben's appearance in the middle, Ron's agitation was gathering its own curious crowd. He was surrounded by Josie,

Red Cap and Tonsure Man, even Snake and the two-time state champ, all telling him to be quiet. In response, he waved his manila folder and maintained, cryptically, 'I've known this for years!'

Kelly was standing to the side of the argument, arms folded, a non-smoker looking like she craved a cigarette.

'What's your father on about?' she asked Gordon, the first she had spoken to him since the previous night.

'He's about to lose St Pat's the final.'

Kelly looked at Gordon as if it could only be his fault. And it is, he thought. It is. Nothing made sense when it came to his family. They were a bit strange. Gordon was only now coming to terms with quite how strange.

He barrelled through the cluster and swept Ron up in his arms. It felt parental, what he would do with a misbehaving toddler.

'What are you doing?' Ron shouted. 'Put me down, you idiot!'

Gordon felt a rise of such anger he could have hurled his father off the steps like a bag of trash. Alas, too many witnesses. He felt exhilarated. Release! Fuck, that felt new.

'Gordon, put him down.'

This was Kelly. Life was queuing up at a coconut shy to have a go at him. The others had scored glancing blows, but here was Kelly, with the biggest coconut, standing so close she couldn't miss, and a load of power in her cocked arm.

Gordon gave her a nod and set Ron down on the bench. Out of the corner of his vision, he thought he saw a dark shape, wearing a broad-brimmed hat, silhouetted against the sky on the crest of the grass bank south of the Father McCarthy eucalyptus grove. Leonie had been avoiding him, he was now sure, for weeks. He had thought he was avoiding her. He realised, at this moment, that he could walk over to her and say whatever he wanted. She had no leverage over him. Did she realise that? In all the shuffling of property titles, tightening her grip on this Bluebird she hated with a vengeance that was like a duel to the death, she had made one critical lapse in judgement: she had taken him for granted. She had counted on his loyalty. But she had no hold on him anymore, for he was literally, materially, actually as opposed to morally, bankrupt. Owning nothing, he had nothing to fear. As far as he was concerned, she could fuck off. They all could. He was free.

He bent in front of his father.

'You won't be taking that document to the coach or anyone else. They're kids, Dad. Ben's out there. Let them have their day.'

Gordon would have liked to see his father regard him through newly opened eyes. He had never asserted himself like this. He would have given anything to win his father's respect, to overcome his resistance, on a point of doing the right thing. But instead, Ron gave an easygoing shrug and said, 'Fair enough. You always get more out of them with the threat than if you follow it through. Oh, look at that.'

Gordon glanced up to the grass bank. If Leonie had been there, she was gone now. Maybe he had only imagined her. Then he saw what his father was seeing.

⌐⌐

Ben was facing his one ball at the end of the over. As per the plan, his purpose was to block it out and hope Zane could hit the winning boundary next over. But, in the effort to keep the ball out of his stumps, Ben leant forward in a correct defensive pose with such a determined, definitive shift of his weight that his bat descended with unexpected sweetness and timing. The ball rocketed off the meaty centre of the blade with the peeling stickers, bounced hard on the pitch, top-spun between the bowler and the mid-off fieldsman, and rolled into the outfield. Ben began running but Zane held up his hand. Ben ran anyway. Evidently, Zane did not want to risk Ben taking the strike for the next over. Ben yelled, 'Two, two!' in hopes that he could get back to his end and be out of danger, while scoring his first two runs for the St Pat's First XI. But when Ben got closer to Zane, he realised his friend was not holding up his palm to stop him running. Zane's glove was clenched in a fist. Having been closer to the ball as it fizzed past him, Zane saw how fast it had travelled off Ben's bat. The chasing fielders were not going to get it before it reached the fence. Zane knew that Ben had hit the winning shot. St Pat's by one wicket! Ben Grimes, match winner!

'Uh-oh.'

Zane also saw the stickers falling off Ben's bat.

The St Pat's boys, minus the departed Daniel Abottemey, ran whooping onto the field. The Cobcroft boys slumped to the turf. The coaches coldly shook hands. The crowd went as crazy as only a bunch of middle-aged and elderly cricket-flummoxed men and women can after cleaning up two cases of Toohey's Old. Norma Grimes's hand was fluttering at her throat. Red Cap was hoisting Josie in the air. Japan Ned was sprinting onto the ground to join the boys, Tonsure Man stumbling behind him. Kelly was crying out Ben's name.

Ben was chaired off by Joel and Jai Something. Zane Dwyer, who had scored most of the runs, was happy to let Ben take the plaudits, but he was sticking close, an oddly worried look on his face.

The boys celebrated like the men they watched on television. The Bluebird crew were soon upon Ben, who was trying to capture it all, put it in a bottle and keep it, every last microsecond. He would remember looking over the top of all those cheering faces to the distant and strange sight of his grandfather brandishing a manila folder. He would remember the murmur that arose among his mates as Joel and Jai lowered him to the ground. Zane Dwyer was discreetly pestering him to put the magic stick in his kitbag. But not even a guilty conscience could save Ben when Joel, spotting the ghostly white Gray-Nicolls-shaped patches unveiled by the peeling Puma stickers, stopped Ben's heart in his mouth.

'Oi, that's me fucken Gray-Nic!'

Ben would remember it as something akin to a rear-end crash, the worst moment in his life zooming up behind the best. Zane was trying to bluff Ben's way out of it, telling Joel he was 'full of shit, let the kid take the glory, who cares whose bat it is, we won, didn't we?'

This was only briefly the worst moment in Ben's life before it became the second-worst. This was a real high-speed pile-up. The worst came next, when, finally back on his feet, looking for his dad, shaking his embarrassed face free of his grandmother's hugs and his mum's kisses and his dad's mates' hair-ruffling, his eyes travelled over the crowd to the eastern horizon, past the cricket pavilion towards Bluebird Beach, where the perfect blue sky on this most perfect day was smudged by a line that looked like the smear of a filthy finger.

'Wait, what?' Ben said, and, because he was the hero of the hour, everybody followed his gaze.

Sacrifice

YOU READ IT HERE LAST. KELLY PROMISED TO WHACK IT ON HIS gravestone. 'Even when you die,' she'd often rebuked him, 'you'll be the last to know.'

While Ben had run towards him across the cricket ground, mute with panic, his cricket bat pointing at the sky to the east, Gordon thought his boy must have had a premonition. Or perhaps he knew something. No, these thoughts came later. At the time, Gordon was drowning beneath one thought:

Lou.

The last to know, and the last to think things through.

Lou.

A blur of action. He was in the back seat of his car and Ben was speeding after Kelly and Norma from the cricket ground to Bluebird Beach. Ron was insisting, even in this altered universe, on giving Ben driving tips, telling him to accelerate into roundabouts. Ben, fresh off this stunning achievement on the cricket field, then accused of stealing the bat with which he achieved that success, was fixed on a pillar of smoke rising from the south headland of Bluebird, a pagan signal that might reconcile his confusing opposites.

Gordon was insentient.

Here is that runaway storm, and we are in its path.

Lou.

What they saw, when they turned into Cliff Street, did not immediately penetrate Gordon's consciousness. There were road blocks. Ben wove around a hastily marked detour to the top car park. Sirens tore the air. Gordon perceived this dimly. And even when Ben pulled into the overflowing car park, Ron directing him into an illegal space because 'Who's going to book you anyway?', Gordon felt detached, as if what was before his eyes was the dream and he was impatient to wake into the reality he had to deal with. When he heard Ron speaking, he thought about the permanent realignment of his father as a man. Was this why Ron and Norma were, despite Ron having worked mid-level jobs and Norma not at all, pretty damn loaded? Had Ron been on the take the whole time? Was he a career blackmailer as well as a career forger?

Academic questions he might get back to one day.

Once he found *Lou.*

Dusk was falling. Some in the crowd gathered on the grass slope at the top car park, while others on the beach used the torches on their mobile phones for illumination. Most stood in nature's darkness, lit only in gold and silver, taking a primal appearance, like cave dwellers at a sacrifice.

Fire was the paramount element, Kelly was thinking. Here was the cataclysm that their lives had been hurtling towards, the thing they most feared, and yet her honest feeling was elation. Her arms tingled as if the blood was returning to them after a long blockage. The knot of anxiety that had taken up residence at the base of her sacrum was dissipating through her chakras, shattering into a thousand stars. Her heart was filled with a formless hollow bliss. Her brain felt alive as if given a shot of painkillers, stimulants, euphorics, tranquillisers, a cocktail of love chemicals. Inside, she was dancing.

She was not allowed to dance in front of the hundreds who had come to Bluebird to see the fire so they could say they were there. Faces floated out of the dark and nodded their condolences. Disbelief; numb shock; anger and outrage; Kelly felt like a cyclone's motionless eye.

'Nobody was in there, right?' she asked a random policeman, who didn't have enough information to confirm.

Then she saw Gordon. His stricken face intensified her almost indecent joy.

'My poor darling,' she said. 'For some reason, I thought you might have had something to do with this.'

'Lou.'

'What?' For an instant she thought he had lost his mind and was misrecognising her.

'Lou,' he repeated. 'She and Jude came back to get the coffee machine.'

'Have you tried to phone her?'

'Phone?' He looked at her mutely. She took her own phone from her pocket.

'Fuck. I don't have her number. Gordon, where's your phone?'

'Phone?' he said again.

'Lou's number!'

Against all likelihood, Gordon's eyes half closed and he recited Lou's phone number.

'You can never remember mine,' Kelly said as she pushed the buttons, 'but you can remember your omigod-daughter's. Hello?'

'Hello?' said an unmistakable low voice.

Kelly said to Gordon, 'Why the fuck is Jude Oxenford answering Lou's phone?'

'I heard that,' Jude's voice said.

'Are you all right?' Kelly said into the phone, her eyes on Gordon.

'The traffic's pretty shit, but we're past the worst of it now.' Kelly handed the phone to Gordon.

'What's up?' Jude said.

'Nobody was in there,' he stated, his inflection falling.

❧

'Omigod, you're okay!' the former state champ cried when she saw Gordon, hugging him for the first time in the three decades they had known each other.

When more spectators heard Gordon was watching the fire from The Bench of Broken Dreams rather than perishing in the defence of his house, they came to kiss and hug him as if he deserved a hero's welcome for not being up there. The rumour that he had been caught in the fire had taken hold so swiftly that people now wanted to touch him, to make sure they were not imagining his survival. He would never have guessed that anyone cared. He barely cared enough himself.

His face was burning from the heat, even though the firemen had kept the spectators cordoned more than one hundred metres away. The air smelt of chemicals. People were pinching their noses in pain. Most of the fire-smothering activity was concentrated on the real estate surrounding The Lodge. More valuable houses, duplexes and boutique apartments were being sprayed with fire-retardant foam and water to make a barrier against the incendiary construction, the terrorist building, the threat to its innocent neighbours. Archer David's mini-excavator could not be saved.

The Lodge, that culprit house, was sucking in the onshore breeze, creating its own fire whirlwind and curling in upon itself. Unlike the brick and masonry and glass surrounding it, The Lodge was nine-tenths flammable. Up went the driftwood balcony, up went the bleached timber walls of the main floor, up the floorboards, up the weatherboard lining, up the staircases, the shingles of the roof, the mouse-eaten electrical wiring, the dried-out insulation. Up went the jigsaw puzzles, up went the packs of cards, up the board games and the melamine table, up the beds and the bedsheets, up the kitchen bench, up the linoleum. Up the saloon door. Up went all those mountains of opportunity-shop synthetic fibres. Up went the French jacquard tablecloth from Eastons, up went Ben's Atlas penholder, and up went all of Gordon's other high-end purchases. Up went the books, all those books, the cleansers as democratically flammable as Carl's editions of Baudelaire and Beckett and Cortázar. Up went the Shitfuckerpoobum. Up went the brown macramé kitchen curtain. Up went the shower curtain with the naked ladies. Up went the laundry chute. Up went the diagonal pine veneer feature wall. Up went a million other things nobody had noticed. Down went the sloped floor, giving in to gravity with a profound sigh. The blaze entered the sky like a flag in a gale, the most spectacular victory Gordon had seen.

In silence, the roof gave way. Embers erupted like a dragon's sneeze followed by tubes of smoke dispersing into the sky.

Up, up and away.

'What did you say?' Kelly asked, giving him a sidelong look in a marriage composed of sidelong looks. She leant into him, as if they were in the audience for a show.

'I didn't say anything.'

Kelly was doing all she could not to smile. The thing that had taken flight and left her had also let go of Gordon.

'You look ten years younger,' she said.

He was unafraid to let it show.

'In this light,' she added.

The Lodge is on fire. The Lodge is on fire! He tried to formulate the sentence in his mind, like an actor rehearsing. *The Lodge! It is on fire!*

The peak of the flame mountain was beginning to shrink against the night. The fire had had its fill of Gordon's home, Gordon's shit, Kelly's shit, Ben's shit. Sated, it was snuggling into itself like an animal digesting its meal. The basement floor, all that salt-wettened cement, would be blackened but intact. Cracks rang out as each new section collapsed, prompting cries from the crowd.

'Notice that we're the only ones here who aren't in tears?' he said out of the side of his mouth.

'Don't let anyone hear you say that,' she shot out of the side of hers.

Gordon would not have wished for anyone else at his side. He squeezed her hand.

The firemen remained busy around the perimeter of The Lodge, even as the flames died under the hoses and the basement issued exhausted wheezes of steam and smoke.

'Show's over,' Gordon said. He felt a weight against his side and arms around his chest. It was Ben, inconsolable. He was still wearing his cricket whites, his pads and his batting inners.

The crowd began to dissolve, abuzz from the show, to head to the Hilton, which would soon be heaving. Sirens were still wailing and the full complement of emergency services, police and ambulance and SES and men in hi-vis, as there always had to be men in hi-vis, were shepherding the spectators. Event Management, Gordon thought as he stood with his arm around his weeping boy.

'Show's over,' he said again.

Red Cap came by. He had to take Josie home, and could barely speak as he clasped Gordon's shoulder. Tonsure Man shook his head in mute sorrow. Japan Ned gave Gordon a ceremonial bow. Cnut came by and said, 'I left me boards in there, that's five grand's worth,' and Gordon said, 'Don't worry, there's insurance.' Cnut didn't press the point, but Gordon could see his disappointment. All this, and five grand's worth of high-performance boards too. And whatever was packed into their hollow cores.

'Have you seen your mother?' Kelly asked.

'Not since the cricket,' Gordon said, as if referring to an event a week or a month ago. He would have said Norma belonged to that other era when he still had problems, but here she was on cue, hobbling down the path from the car park.

'*Where is your father?*' Norma cried with such thought-ending anxiety that emergency services personnel stopped what they were doing, like kangaroos in a field.

'He came back with me and Ben,' Gordon said. 'He wasn't anywhere near . . . that.'

As if to remind everyone that it still had a beating heart, The Lodge's basement exploded, bringing down the last of the balcony. The remnant spectators cried, or cheered.

Gordon freed Ben to put an arm around his mother. 'You know Dad. He'll pop up somewhere.'

'He's a very sick eighty-year-old! We have to get the police!'

Kelly was nodding at Gordon: Not the time for a smart-arse remark. You really do need to find your father.

Gordon turned to Ben. 'I'm a bit blurry about when we arrived. Did you get him out of the car?'

Ben was frowning, mentally retracing his steps, drawing a blank. Welcome to adulthood, Gordon thought.

'He wouldn't have tried to get into The Lodge, would he?' Gordon asked.

'Don't say that!' his mother cried.

'Maybe go back to the car,' Kelly said to Ben. 'He can't have wandered far.'

'Oh, you people!' Norma cried again.

'Calm down,' Kelly said. 'We'll find him. Ben, do you want me to come?'

Ben had flung off his cricket gloves and was smacking his hips and his chest. For a moment, Gordon thought he was having a reversion to one of his childhood anxiety attacks, those Tourettish self-smacking tics which had faded since he was nine or ten; maybe the trauma and excitement was bringing them out from wherever he had buried them.

He wasn't having an attack. He was searching his pockets.

'The keys.' Ben looked at Kelly. Norma was mouthing, 'Oh no.'

Gordon's heart skipped a beat. 'The house keys?'

'The car keys!'

So it was that when the police were trying to locate the inhabitants of the burnt-down house on the cliff side, three of those residents, instead of absorbing the grief and import of what had happened before their eyes, instead of comforting each other, instead of caring and nurturing and beginning to accept the magnitude of this event, were running up the dune path to the top car park. In front of the Beach Cafe, Ben said to Kelly, 'This is where I think I parked.'

By the time Gordon—who had lagged behind, as he was assisting Norma—caught up, his memory came back.

'This is where we got out.'

'Your car has been stolen?' a policewoman was asking Ben. 'Shitty what people will do, even in a fire.' Kelly recognised her as the sidekick police officer who had come to their house to deliver Frontal's letter. To Gordon she said, 'You the owner?'

Gordon nodded.

The officer took out her notebook, still shaking her head in outrage.

'What kind of car is it?'

She stood with her pen poised for a long moment while waiting for Gordon.

'Sir?'

Gordon's head was shaking.

'He doesn't know,' Kelly said.

'He doesn't know his own car?'

'Give him a minute.' Kelly put a hand on the back of Gordon's neck. 'He'll get there.'

Perfect peace

A PITY NONE OF HIS FAMILY HAD THE KINDNESS TO GRANT A dying man his last wish. Well, not a pity, Ron thought as he sped down the dipper where the road dropped into the bushland. An opportunity.

The pity was that his travelling companion didn't seem to appreciate how lucky they were. Ron was extolling the engineering genius of Chester Dam—the beauty of the sluices, the water-carrying capacity, the life-giving boon for the people of the region—but his companion was silent, even morose. No gratitude. Ron put aside his irritability. He was in too fine a mood—driving! There's a life-giving boon for you!—so he decided to regale his companion with stories of camping at Chester and other locations, back in the day. Mostly these stories ended up in complaint about how his son was as useful as a priest on a honeymoon, and how when Norma wasn't nagging she was whingeing. Never mind though. Like two tidal waters rising over a sand spit, memory and expectation converged to drown out experience, which, old men knew, was only a brief and painful illusion.

Ron's commentary on the unreliability of memory brought a disapproving growl from his companion. Two hundred miles to go, and the man was offside already.

'But you remember the last trip to Chester, don't you?' Ron said. 'The trip after we lost our boy.'

As his companion shrivelled into the passenger seat, Ron pressed the accelerator to the floor. God, driving was good. He felt sorry for every human born before the automotive age. Speed! He tried to wind down his window and feel the breeze on his cheeks, but there was no winder. He eventually located the button, but that only lowered the window on the passenger side, and when that window slid down Ron's companion shrieked in alarm. So Ron found a way to close it and gave up trying to open his own. He would fix that at the petrol station. He checked the gauge. Quarter of a tank. At least he thought that was the petrol gauge.

'We'll fill up at the next service station. But no snacks, all right?'

His travelling companion murmured sulky nothings.

They were at the lights turning onto the highway when Ron started thinking that maybe he shouldn't have swung by the fire-house to collect his passenger; he should have taken this trip on his own. What's the use of a travelling companion who only snarls and slobbers and shows no appreciation? What is the bloody use? Those other trips, with Norma and the boys, came back to Ron. To be honest—and if he wasn't going to be honest now, when would he be?—he hadn't wanted them with him and they hadn't wanted to be with him. That was true in Ron's expectation of those trips, it was true in his memory, and it was most certainly true during the events themselves. Torture for him, cruel and unusual punishment for them.

Even for Owen, when they had him. That boy was the image of Ron, every bit his father's son.

A bit of an arsehole, to be honest.

'Why did we do it?' he asked. 'Why did we bloody well do it?'

'Because you're a fuckwit,' his travelling companion said.

'Oh! It speaks!' Ron said with a sarcastic yelp. He had never liked this fellow. Amazing how the speed of this car worked like a key that unlocked memory. Memory of family, memory of Chester Dam, memory of his travelling companion. Those bad men of Old Bluebird.

There had to be more to it. He had spent most of his life with the penny stuck on the lip of the slot, refusing to drop, the truth frozen forty-two years ago. Of course Owen hadn't slipped. You could see Gordon was lying the moment he opened his mouth. There had to be more to it. You just had to join the dots. Kids threw themselves off cliffs like it was going out of fashion now. Owen had started it. Pain. In pain.

'You really are a fuckwit,' his companion said again, to make sure he was heard.

A peeper, this one. That was all he'd been done for. Had he interfered with Owen? Those bad old men. Bad men kept in power by small men.

He'd have liked to tip the whole bucket on them with that birth certificate, but given how that might affect his own repu-tation, and spoil young Ben's day, probably Gordon was right to hold it in reserve, keep it as a threat. Gordon was right! First time for everything!

But this one, this peeper: Ron had a plan for him.

'Aren't you listening?' his companion gurgled.

So consumed was he with thinking up some fitting retort that, as he turned onto the highway, Ron only looked to the north, not the south, and not to the arrow light which, unlike the circular traffic light, was red, and so Ron's last thought when the Car With No Name was T-boned on its passenger side by an eighteen-wheel semitrailer was that when he got to that service station, he would trick his travelling companion into thinking he could go inside and buy snacks, and while he was inside, Ron would leave him there and head on to Chester Dam all alone, in perfect peace.

Past its best

TONY EASTAUGH'S FUNERAL WAS A SUITABLY MODEST AFFAIR. His generation was long gone, in honour, dishonour, or simply unaccounted for. Gordon recognised, in the faces in the smallest and cheapest of the available crematorium chapels, friends of Sam, not Tony. The past showed little interest in being preserved. Those men of the past were a figment of the imagination. One poke of a firestick and they went down in minutes, and once they were gone, like The Lodge, those who had kept them alive wondered what all the fuss had been about.

A secular celebrant laid out some shadowless facts of Tony's biography. She was the only person in the room who did not know him. Sam delivered a tribute, calling Tony 'a father who loved me the best he could' but stopping short of extolling the man in any light that might have risked a disbelieving guffaw from the pews. The mood was neither mournful nor glad. You could say the audience were still in shock over the fire at The Lodge, and the death of Tony Eastaugh the same night, but this was Bluebird; they were getting on with it. The past was worn out, not as solid as it was made out to be. Past its best. Red Cap and Tonsure Man came, some of Sam's old colleagues from the Bluebird Building Society and the voluntary firefighters' unit, all, like Gordon, out of duty to Sam. They were checking their watches during the montage of photographs.

There was no wake.

'How's your old man?' Red Cap asked Gordon as they filed out of the chapel.

'Disqualified for unlicensed driving. At least that settles the argument about whether his doctor's certificate was valid. There's a suggestion it was a forgery.'

'Ouch,' Red Cap said, 'that's gunna hurt him.'

More than killing a man, Gordon thought.

'The old man's out of hospital?'

'Back in the nursing home.'

Gordon's Car With No Name and Tony Eastaugh were totalled, but somehow Ron had emerged without a scratch. The first responders found him wandering away from the accident site with his sleeping bag and primus stove, trying to flag down vehicles travelling north. The first driver to stop had got out and run towards the smashed-up car and semitrailer. Ron cursed him for not taking him up the highway.

'He always said you can't kill him,' Tonsure Man said with an appreciative stroke of his unshaven chin.

'Lands like a cat,' Gordon said.

The accident had been reported in the metropolitan newspapers and television bulletins, which named the victim but not the perpetrator. The licence charge against Ron was a first step, Gordon had been told by the police liaison officer who had come to the hospital the night of the accident. Negligent driving would follow, perhaps other charges, but not manslaughter. The police questioned Gordon at length, suspicious over his vagueness in describing the make and model of his car, but eventually left satisfied.

There was no hanging around after the funeral. Gordon waited for a quiet word with Sam, who was shaking hands with the last guests. In a business suit and tie, Sam looked oddly comfortable. Gordon had almost forgotten that he had spent his career in a suit, a side of Sam that had been both essential to Gordon and a foreign country.

'You all right?' Gordon asked as they fell into step through the crematorium gardens.

'You got a lift home?'

'I came with TM,' Gordon said. 'Looks like he's pissed off back to the beach.'

'There were some waves forecast.' Sam gave a humourless cluck. 'Up to me to get you out of trouble again.'

In the car, Gordon said, 'You heard anything from Dog?'

Sam shook his head. Nobody had seen Dog since the day he was beaten up by Japan Ned.

'He would have been welcome, you know,' Sam said. 'I thought that fucker had the hide of a rhinoceros, but it seems that you hurt his feelings when you wouldn't let him into The Lodge.'

'You know he's been questioned by the cops.'

'Over the fire?'

'He's a person of interest.' Dog was one of a long list of locals whose whereabouts on the night of the fire were being ascertained. 'There were plenty of witnesses when we shut him out of The Lodge. He had a motive for revenge.'

'Ah well.' Sam seemed about to say something, but he found a space in the traffic to pull out of the crematorium grounds and join the stream heading back towards the coast.

'They talked to me for a long time. They were collecting alibis,' Gordon said. 'I told them who was at the cricket match and who wasn't.'

'They haven't called me.'

'I told them the truth, brother. You were at the cricket with me all afternoon. You left with the lot of us, when we all saw the fire. My dad backed me up.'

'You told your dad to say that?'

Gordon smiled. 'I can't tell my dad to say anything. It was his clear memory.'

'I must've made a real impression.'

'Anyway, they're very interested in Frontal. And Carl, of course, he's high on their list. He and Daniel left the cricket just before the fire started. They'd been lurking around together like they were up to no good. Once the cops get Carl in their sights, they won't want to let go.'

Sam was intent on the road. 'But they can't find him?' he said.

'He's Carl Chidgey. No fixed address.'

'Is Frontal's kid talking to them?'

'One word: lawyer,' Gordon said. 'Strong little fucker. Tougher than his father, who's spilling his guts. You know, Frontal had been warning me. He was saying he'd make me pay. I thought he was talking about my rates.'

'He's admitted that to the cops?'

'When it comes to having a motive to burn the joint down, nobody was more motivated than Frontal. And he did disappear

466

from the cricket game. People heard him say he would destroy everything I value.'

Sam wiped the back of his hand across his mouth. 'So it's down to Dog, Frontal and Carl?'

'They look at people's histories. Carl's a career firebug.'

'When we were kids.'

'And the odd one since. He did burn down the sign.'

Sam's eyes bugged. 'Sign?'

'The Visitors Welcome sign at the top of the path. Years ago. Carl burnt it down.'

Sam half laughed. 'Who said you can ever stop learning something new, no matter how long you've lived in a place?'

'They even tracked down Lou and Jude driving south. Lou's car cracked its axle when it hit a pothole. Apparently it was badly unbalanced.'

'The coffee machine?'

'The La Marzocco. They questioned her about why and when she'd left The Lodge that day. It takes them a while to figure out the causes of fires. But they seem very interested in the StairLift.'

'The electric chair.'

'Possibility of an electrical fault. She told me they were asking her all about her installation and if there was a chance the wooden staircase could have been set alight first, and then it spread to the house.'

'So it could have been an accident?'

'Everything can always be an accident.'

After a lengthy silence, Sam said, 'Shit of a week, eh.'

'I've seen The Lodge burn down and my father taken to hospital after causing the death of yours. We could call it quite a week.' Gordon felt guilty at the thought, but his gut told him that

Ron had engineered the car accident to rid himself of Tony. The most meaningful conversation anyone had heard them exchange consisted of two words. 'Ron.' 'Tony.' Those men.

'Do you reckon he meant it?' Sam asked, reading Gordon's thoughts.

'I don't think we'll ever know.'

'But what do you reckon?'

'What do *you* reckon?'

'I asked you first.'

'How old are we, twelve?'

'I'm twelve,' Sam said seriously, 'and you're eight.'

After a pause to take this in, Gordon said, 'Who else was left for him to blame? Me?'

Sam averted his eyes, as if he had seen in Gordon, buried—in a shallow grave—in his paternal DNA, a capacity for violence that he had never before suspected.

'So who were you protecting?' Gordon said. 'Me or your father?'

A tremor in Sam's neck told Gordon that he didn't need to explain.

'Bluebird. We were protecting Bluebird, so we could stay.'

'You talked me into telling a lie.'

'I was shitting myself, brother, I didn't know what I was doing. We just had to cover our arses. I didn't want you to have to live with being the kid who kicked his brother off a fucking cliff, and you can't tell me I was wrong.'

'And look where that got us. I don't even trust what I remember anymore.'

'We're no different from anyone else, brother. We made our bed and shitted our own shit in it.'

'Who do you think killed him?'

A sad whistle, like the signal for the end of a factory shift, came through Sam's nose. 'All of us. None of us. An accident. What's the diff?'

'Something *happened*, Sam. That's the diff.'

'Okay. Okay. It was you.'

'The way I remember it? Or the way *you* remember it?'

'You were a kid, you panicked, it wasn't your fault. And then we bullshitted our way out of it, and yeah, you're right, I was scared, we were scared, and we created a whole world of new shit. And yeah, I can't say I wasn't thinking about my old man, but I was just shit-scared he'd give us a flogging.'

'And?'

'And I saw Owen smile when he went. He was smiling at you, Gordo. He had one moment to tell you he forgave you. He wanted to tell you it wasn't your fault.'

Sam was nodding, a thick film of sweat on his meaty brow. Gordon knew they would never have this conversation again. Perhaps any conversation. They were done. Sam had told him what he wanted—what he needed—to hear. It felt good, but dirty. Like everything now.

'How long are you staying on Norma's couch?'

'Until I lose my shit,' Gordon said. 'She's saying it's lovely to have me, but I give it a week before we drive each other round the bend. I don't think she wants a house guest interrupting her routines.'

'You can't go to the Hilton?'

Ben and Kelly were staying in the Hilton, at Leonie's invitation. After the fire, Leonie had acted with unusual generosity toward Kelly. The shake-out of the legal proceedings over The Lodge would take months, but from what Kelly had told Gordon, the pair of them, plus Carl, would get something. The Lodge and its contents were virtually worthless other than a handful of valuables purchased from Eastons homewares, but the land was worth considerably more without the house. The land title came under an obscure piece of legislation—dating to the Depression, when it was enacted to protect squatters and fishermen—that awarded ownership, in case of *force majeure*, to its most recent continuous occupants. In this case, Kelly, Carl and Gordon were the continuous occupants of a block of land that could not be redeveloped, but must, should an act of God destroy the dwelling, be compulsorily acquired by the state at its most recent valuation. Records revealed that the valuation of the property lay with the last assessment made by the Bluebird Building Society. Gordon, whose habit was to fill out forms stating that he had 'No occupation', had been wrong. He had one occupation, which was occupation itself. It had just made him a millionaire. If the fire was an act of God, then this God had revealed an unexpected sense of humour. Leonie had outsmarted herself: in that window where she was not the titular owner of the property, where the names on the holding company documents were Gordon's, Carl's and Kelly's, Leonie was vulnerable. She had banked on nothing changing during that time. But one act of God had left her with nothing of The Lodge, and a now-perilous collateral situation for her development of the Hilton.

'Turns out that Leonie's legal advice wasn't as sharp as everyone thought,' Gordon said.

It would take time for the money to come through. Leonie had offered Kelly an interim deal, whereby if Leonie covered Kelly and Ben until the payout, Kelly would cut Leonie in on the settlement.

'Is Kel going to accept?' Sam asked.

'She told Leonie to go fuck herself. But Leonie's playing the long game.'

Sam smiled. 'And Benny? What does he want?'

'Same as ever. He reckons I'd be happy if I pissed off Up North.'

To this, Sam was Buddha-silent. They arrived at the nursing home. Norma's car was parked outside. Sam left his engine running.

'Brother?' Gordon said.

Sam was sitting with his hands on the steering wheel, ten past two, as if he was speeding up the highway.

'Thanks.'

'For what?'

'Being a good bloke.'

'All part of the service.'

'We made our bed and filled it with our shit. You're right.'

'And sometimes the only way forward is to blow it up.'

'Hey. I'm sorry about Tony,' Gordon said. 'They might be fuckwits, but they're still our fathers.'

'And I'm sorry about what had to happen.'

'What had to happen?'

'To The Lodge.'

'Yep. You're sorry.'

They hugged across the centre console. When Gordon drew away, he saw tears in Sam's eyes. The last of the Eastaughs. Sam waited until Gordon had stepped out of the car and was about to close the passenger door when he said, 'You know what makes me real sad?'

'What's that?'

Gordon bent down to the window. Sam had put on a pair of reading glasses and was peering significantly at Gordon over the rims. Tony's reading glasses. Gordon felt a bubble of laughter rising in his chest.

'If we still had a volunteer fire brigade,' Sam said, 'it could have saved the joint.'

Jada was at the reception desk of Banksia floor when Gordon arrived, feeling drained from the funeral and his heart-to-heart with Sam. Her luminous smile lifted him like an amusement park ride. Amazing that a show of human teeth could have this power.

'I'm sorry, your father has been moved from this floor.'

'Oh?'

'He's on Acacia.'

Jada escorted Gordon into the lift, and squeezed his elbow sympathetically as the doors opened at the Alzheimer's floor. An elderly woman in a dressing-gown sat in a chair in the lobby holding out a donations jar for the Salvation Army. A man in his pyjamas was laughing uproariously while being wrestled down the corridor by two burly staff. In the distance was a cacophony of shouting. Terror, only terror.

'It's very confronting,' Jada said.

'Does he have to be here?'

'It was a condition of the court hearing,' Jada said. 'There were phone calls this morning, and he was moved.'

Tim Phelan, the duty magistrate at the Capri courthouse, had spoken with Norma, the police and the nursing home management. Norma wanted Ron in the nursing home, but due to fears of escape, it was negotiated that he be accommodated on Acacia floor where, even though he did not suffer from the disease, the restraint facilities could be utilised.

In a corner of the lobby, Norma sat in an armchair, reading the *Weakly-Daily*. When she saw Gordon she smiled faintly. He noticed in her arms a photo album.

Gordon read the spine. '*FAMILY HOLIDAYS 1979–83*. You brought it in?'

'Your father had it in his room.' Norma looked uncertain for a minute, as if deciding on a course of action, and then opened it. Gordon used to pore over this album and he knew the photos off by heart. But now, all the photos, page after page, had been removed. In their place was a single photograph that Gordon had never seen. Norma propped up the album. Gordon looked at the photo: their families, the stone wall of a high lake, the impressive machinery. Him and Sam. Between them, with one hand on each boy's shoulder, stood a bald man in a collared shirt and a pair of shorts. The sun caught the crease ironed down the centre of his thighs.

'He even turned up on our holidays,' Norma said, gazing at the photograph. 'With documents for Ron to sign.'

Gordon met his mother's eye. If he wasn't mistaken, Norma looked at peace.

'I know why Ron did what he did. Why it mattered so much.' Norma nodded at the man in the ironed shorts. 'Those men.'

'Wow. No wonder I'm so fucked up.'

'Well, that's not exactly the way I would put it, but . . . Oh, darling. Life didn't really turn out the way we wanted.'

He waited for her to start crying, but she was dry-eyed. Something had changed in Norma. A sad smile crossed her face. 'I don't know whether to laugh or cry,' she said. 'But at least I feel like I have the choice.'

Her gaze stayed on the photograph.

'Since Owen, I don't think your father lived a day when he wasn't angry. Those men who did so well, he wanted them to pay. For getting away with it.'

'With what, Mum?'

Norma looked at her son as if just now realising how little he had always known and how he never had a hope of catching on. 'Darling, when you get to a certain age, it's not important what "it" is. We paid, they didn't. It really doesn't matter what they did, only that it was so damned unfair.' She rapped the photo album with her knuckles. 'One thing he had was stubbornness. His anger could lie in wait forever, until it found its chance.'

Gordon thought: How long could my father's anger have lain in wait if he knew that I killed Owen?

'I am glad you're out of The Lodge, darling. It's the best thing for everyone. But we do love you, you know.'

Gordon thought: Would my mother still love me if she knew?

'I guess so,' he said. 'Just . . . you have a strange way of showing it at times.'

'Well, yes. That's us, I suppose.'

Norma snapped the album shut, its claws closing on that photo Ron had taken with Tony's camera, of all of them with Conal Abottemey in his ironed shorts, the impressive machinery and the high lake.

Norma led Gordon to Ron's room and opened the door. Gordon's heart, which had been bending and twisting ever since the night of his fiftieth birthday, finally buckled. Ron was a bag of bones under his blanket, his eyes turned to the ceiling, his mouth opening and closing silently as if he still had to get the last word. Where had he all gone? He was the size of a cat. Gordon drew his breath into his chest and followed his mother in.

Up north

THE WAVE STANDS UP ENTICINGLY ON THE OUTER BANK, DARK-faced against the gauzy grey air. Gordon slides across the water to the take-off spot. He glances to the inside to check nobody is taking the wave. Madness—there *is* nobody—but a lifetime of being hemmed in by competition, overtaken by the younger, the fitter, the better, is a hard habit to break.

He pops up and trims across the wave, so silken underfoot it feels like a fourth element, a kind of plasma. He turns his eyes to the horizon and takes in the view from the black cobbles at the base of the headland along the line of forest that stretches to the north, the lagoon inlet a morning's walk away. Not just a beach; the idea of a beach. Everything in its right place. Beneath his feet, the crumbling wave casts a shadow onto the green-ribbed sand floor.

As the wave empties into the channel, he steps onto the tail of his board, flips it up, and falls softly prone onto his stomach, in the same motion swivelling into his paddle back to the take-off spot.

'You looked blissed out,' Ben says when Gordon joins him.

'You're enjoying it?'

'Wait, what?'

'The solitude.'

'The solitude? But you're here.'

'Nitpicker.' Gordon splashes water at Ben and pivots for the next wave. He is too far behind, and it leaves him.

'Nobody else in the water and you're still missing waves!' Ben quips, stroking into the next, a better one. Gordon watches him rip three frontside turns and disappear into the pit before emerging in the channel, tilting his board up so he can fall back onto it and paddle, effortlessly, back out. One of the sad things about having a teenaged son, he thinks, is that the boy doesn't realise that when he competes with you, you want him to win.

'Going in, Dad! I'm meeting someone!'

Gordon stays in the water. Even though he has this break to himself every day, he still can't believe his luck, so he surfs like a chipmunk, storing waves against some bleaker future.

His onsite van is a three-minute drive up the dirt road from the point. When he gets there, Kelly is waiting. It is her first visit since Gordon moved a few months earlier, after his father's funeral. Ben, who still needs to get his hours up for his licence, coaxed Kelly into acting as his instructor for the return trip from Ocean City.

The van sits on the border of Rachel and Jason's property. Gordon finds Kelly smoking a joint with her feet on the balcony rail. She seems pleased to see his fifth-hand ute. He's already told her, proudly, that it's an '03 Commodore. He hoses down his surfboard and rinses sand off his feet, drops his board shorts, dries himself and changes into a pair of Okanuis with a hibiscus pattern that Kelly gave him as a going-away present.

'Don't mind me,' she says.

'Just reminding you of what you're missing.'

'Where did Ben go?'

Gordon smiles. 'Guess.'

'Aw, he didn't want to come all the way up here for some Mum time?' She stubs her roach into an empty UDL can by her feet. The fact that Ben has reconnected with the boy prompts unspoken celebration between her and Gordon. Ben was knocked about by the events at the end of last year. He was in trouble for stealing the cricket bat, and devastated over The Lodge, but his deeper sadness lingered over Daniel's sudden departure from St Pat's. Daniel was never his true friend, he knew that, but all the same, to find out that he was a fraud, an adult, cut Ben deeply. He knew Daniel had his torments and his secrets; he'd thought they sprang from a different source.

'Glad you've improved your habits,' Gordon says, nodding at Kelly's litter can.

'Wouldn't want to cause a fire.'

Gordon pulls a face and leans into his bar fridge, grabs a can of beer for himself and another UDL for Kelly, before settling down to watch the forest turn blue in the setting sun. He can never stop loving this about Kelly: she was the first to laugh with him about the fire, and the first to cry with him about his father. Ron's death, coming so soon after the loss of The Lodge, hits him subcutaneously. He can be fine for ninety percent of the time and raving mad the rest. At Kelly's urging, he accepted an invitation from Rachel and Jason to come up here as the 'probationary editor' of their regional newspaper, to live on their farm, to recuperate, and maybe to contemplate a future. So far, it has been so good.

'You heard about Capri Council?' Kelly asks.

Gordon nods. 'Frontal's gone?'

'Fifty years of Abottemeys running Bluebird, just like that. Cheers.'

They clink cans.

'Daniel went to Greece to meet his mother's family.'

'Frontal too?'

'I don't know where Michael is going. There's nothing left for him in Bluebird.'

Gordon closes his eyes and tries to remember the last time he saw Frontal, at the cricket final, driven mad by paranoia. That unexpected development was only a foretaste of the bizarre business to come. Having left the cricket match threatening Gordon, and disappearing from view just before the fire broke out at The Lodge, Frontal was repeatedly questioned by police. When the police phoned Frontal to tell him they were forming a theory that Carl and Daniel had left the cricket match, gone to Bluebird and lit the fire, he presented himself at the Capri station and confessed to the arson attack.

Frontal's confession set the city talking: a council deputy general manager, a second-generation stalwart of local government, set fire to one of the historic homes of his area because—why? Because he harboured a lifelong hatred for the family who lived there? Because it was an unsafe building, violating zoning regulations? Because they hadn't paid their rates? It seemed bizarre, but people agreed that the Abottemeys had a vindictive side.

Sure enough, Frontal had fucked up again. When the police pieced together his movements on the afternoon of the fire, he could not evade his own alibi. He went from the cricket match to his council chambers, where he was caught on CCTV removing documents. Cameras on the streets of Capri showed him dumping a file in a skip outside the ferry wharf. There was no getting out of it. Cameras were everywhere. Frontal wasn't the arsonist.

By the time the police released him without charge—though he was now being investigated for public nuisance—Frontal had sabotaged his career. His erratic behaviour, his false confession and the publicity it attracted rendered his position untenable. His mental health leave period was extended to a course of assessment and treatment, where he admitted to making his false confession as a means of protecting Daniel, who, he was convinced, had lit the fire while under the malign influence of Carl Chidgey. Frontal believed Carl was 'hypnotising' Daniel with the use of 'mind-bending drugs' to commit crimes. He claimed he had warned Gordon Grimes about this, but Gordon had ignored him.

Conveniently for council, the long-touted mega-maxi-merger, amalgamating the entire beaches region under one authority, was announced soon after Frontal was cleared of arson. The old roles of general and deputy general manager were vacated. He had been restructured out of his job.

'I feel sorry for him,' Gordon says.

'He hated us and wanted to bring us down. He got what he deserved.'

'Harsh.'

'But fair.'

'He was only trying to protect his boy.'

'He made his own kid live a lie, all so that he could, what, be the big swinging dick in the cricket team and the surfboat crew? I can't believe you feel sorry for him.'

'Carl messed with his head.'

'Carl's a fucked-up acid casualty. He's too hopeless to pull off any grand schemes. Here, that reminds me . . .'

Kelly reaches into her bag by her feet and fishes out a small shoe polish tin, from which she takes a fresh joint. She offers it to Gordon, who shakes his head. She digs into her bag again and comes up with a document in a clear plastic slip.

'What's this?'

'Duh. You're a Justice of the Peace now, aren't you?'

Gordon sniffs. His father's renal failure had advanced swiftly after he was relocated to Acacia floor. His kidney specialist said Ron had defied the odds in staying active for as long as he had, and his sudden decline had nothing to do with the car accident or the move to the locked ward. Gordon and Norma could not help but link it with his escapade, though. With the smash-up of his getaway vehicle came the obliteration of his hope. He did not speak to a soul for three weeks after the abortive trip to Chester Dam. Gordon and Norma sat by his side every day. The staff tended him and gave him medication, but he had decided to die. Gordon consoled Norma through this final act. Dying: it fucks you up even worse than your mum and dad.

And then, in the final days, after Ron stopped eating and drinking, a glimmer of beauty. The old misanthrope, a skeleton of bad intent, whispered something to Norma.

'I can't hear you!' she shouted.

Norma wanted to put her ear to Ron's mouth, but she could not flex her hips. Gordon acted as go-between, getting onto his knees to hear what Ron was whispering.

'What's he saying?' Norma demanded.

Gordon heard the words rustle from Ron's lips. He stood up and held his mother.

'He said he's been lucky to have us.'

Ron was saying something else. Gordon got back down and bent his ear to Ron's mouth. His father's lips shaped a wordless breath. Gordon stayed there for long moments, but couldn't hear what Ron was saying.

'What?' Norma said. 'What!'

Gordon sat back on the carpet, on his bottom.

'He said he loves us, even if he has a strange way of showing it.'

Norma looked at Ron, and he bobbled his eyebrows. Whatever he had really said, Gordon thought, he approved of the translation. Norma subsided into a fit of crying so heart-rending that the staff shifted her off the floor, as she was causing several of the Alzheimer's residents to become upset, some of them bursting into contagious tears.

When he got back to Norma's that night, Gordon applied to become a Justice of the Peace. At one o'clock in the morning, while he was completing the online form, his phone rang. It was Jada from the nursing home, delivering the news that Ron had passed away. Gordon thanked Jada and went to Norma.

Since moving Up North, Gordon has certified a couple of drivers' licences. Now, with a cheeky smile, Kelly presents him with a passport application. Gordon's jaw drops.

'Carl doesn't have a passport?'

'Believe it or not, he's never travelled outside Australia.'

'I had the impression Paris was his second home. Where's he going?'

'Spain. He wants to walk in Cervantes's footsteps.'

'Fuck me. The things people will do when they come into money.'

Two weeks after the fire, Carl had emerged from a drug house in the inner western suburbs. To the police's disappointment, he too had an alibi. Carl had taken Daniel from the cricket match with mischief in mind, but not to The Lodge. They had gone to St Patrick's College and broken into the sports department, where Daniel defecated on the desk of Mr Ryan Stoyle and Carl photocopied his buttocks then pinned the image to Stoyle's door. They committed further acts of petty vandalism before heading to the residence of the chaplain, the outside wall of which they had painted with the words *Pedos die!* Initially, someone had thought it was classical Latin, a first hint that Carl Chidgey might be involved. It was in Northern Beaches English, but the substance of the paint had given away the identity of the authors. When analysed, the paint was found to contain traces of human urine, faeces and semen. Due to his criminal history, Carl's DNA was on file. Further evidence from a school caretaker confirmed that the vandalism had taken place between four and six o'clock of the afternoon in question. A wharf surveillance camera then showed them sharing a certain Fast Ferry season pass, registered in the name of Douglas Oscar Gilsenan, to travel across the harbour before the fire was lit. It was beyond doubt. Being vandals meant Carl and Daniel could not be arsonists. Daniel pleaded guilty and received a good behaviour bond. Carl contested the charges and received a suspended three-month jail term and a fine of fifteen hundred dollars, plus responsibility for damages amounting to five thousand dollars. Leonie paid his fines for him.

Leonie? She put the Hilton on the auction block and moved back to the Gold Coast to reunite with Tino, her son from her first marriage. Now in his mid-thirties, Tino is recovering from a rough stint in a Thai rehab facility. Leonie has delegated the handling of the Hilton sale to her new legal adviser.

Gordon signs Carl's passport application.

'Sure he's going to get it? He's got a lot of shit on his record.'

'There are still a few hoops for him to jump through, but he never did anything major.'

Kelly stubs out her second joint, breathes luxuriously and unfolds into her chair.

'So comfortable,' she purrs. 'You know I saw Sally again at the country club? I haven't seen Dog around, but she was giving me enough evils for two. He's fed her some bullshit, no doubt, like it's them against the whole world. I really dislike that woman; I can't help it. Too loyal to him. Loyal as a . . .'

'As a dog? No dogs.'

'Ha. We were up against each other in a match. I reckon she cheated.'

'Really. Who won?'

'Who do you reckon, Gordo?'

He shifts in his seat and unpicks his Okanuis from where they have become wedged between his balls.

'If anyone knows Dog, I do,' Kelly says. Gordon's heart sinks a notch. 'He can't have done it. I know every other main suspect has been ruled out. But I don't think he'd be up to doing something that decisive. And clever! There's nothing they can pin on him. But if he did it, you've got to hand it to him. Respect!'

Gordon gives a noncommittal shrug. It suits his interests to let Kelly and others speculate about Dog burning down The Lodge. It suits him if she spreads it around the whole of Bluebird and Capri and Ocean City. Dog deserves his reputation: only a lawyer could commit such a perfect crime.

The misinformation suits Gordon because he knows who did it. There was someone else who slipped away from the cricket match, unnoticed, that afternoon. Someone with expertise in fires. Someone who wanted to expose the scandal of Bluebird Beach having its volunteer fire station closed down. Someone who wanted, above all, to expiate his guilt. Someone with nothing to lose. Someone who cared enough for Gordon and his family to liberate them from The Lodge and its tyranny. Someone who had carried the guilt of what he had persuaded an eight-year-old boy to do, in that faraway time on that clifftop. Someone who wanted to stop seeing that ledge from the surf every single day. Someone who could think of no other way to say sorry. Someone who has made Gordon happy. Someone who set Gordon free.

Someone who burnt down The Lodge out of love.

Someone who honoured a deal.

'Any news of Sam?' Gordon says.

'You haven't heard?'

'Heard what?'

'The new local government administrator wanted to offer a sweetener to the people of Bluebird for losing their council. You didn't know this?'

'I'm a million miles away. I don't answer the phone.'

'Shit, Gordo. The firehouse development got canned. The old firehouse is being done up as a museum to the history of volunteering. I can't believe Sam didn't tell you.'

'I haven't spoken to him for a while.'

'Well, he's been busy. He quit the bank, no questions asked. He's been earmarked as the curator of the museum.'

'Wow.'

'I'm surprised you haven't spoken,' Kelly says. 'You two are so close.'

'We're good.'

'Hm.'

'A man's got to have some mystique about him.'

Kelly narrows her eyes and looks out at the bush. 'Do you miss it?'

'Miss what?'

'The Lodge.'

'Do you?'

She shakes her head. 'I feel like I've been carrying a burden all my life and suddenly someone's told me I don't need to anymore. Sure, I miss it. I got used to the pain.'

Gordon eases into his chair and passes Carl's application back to Kelly. She slides it into its plastic folder, which she puts into her bag. Gordon notices: an Italian designer job. A rich divorcee like her can take her pick of the field down Bluebird way.

So why. Why is her leg extended and her toe outstretched, tracing a circle on Gordon's calf. Why. He watches her toe like it's a zoo animal, and then he meets Kelly's eye.

A set of headlights appears at the end of the dirt road; the crunch of a manual car's gears. Kelly's new BMW kangaroo-hops up the hill.

'Little bugger,' she says. 'I told him he wasn't allowed to drive alone.'

Gordon nods towards the approaching car. 'He's not,' he says, and fixes a steady eye on his ex-wife's toe, which is still on his calf. 'He's not alone.'

Acknowledgements

I OWE A GREAT DEBT TO THESE HONORARY BLUEBIRDERS WHO read drafts of this novel and contributed to its development: Christos Tsiolkas, Michael Robotham, Jon Casimir, John Edwards, Lyn Tranter and Christa Munns; and especially to my two loyal partners in crime, Jane Palfreyman and Wenona Byrne. Thanks also to the whole team at Allen & Unwin. Appreciation to Stevie Harris, John Hopkins, Sarah Hopkins and Helen de Mestre for sharing their love of books for many years and for wondering why there isn't an Australian Richard Russo. Russo is a source of some of Carl Chidgey's mutterings, as are Cervantes, Beckett, Philip Larkin, Martin Amis, and the Dandy Warhols, among many other scraps from which that bower bird built his nest. And a special note of gratitude to Ali Lavau, who turned herself into a Bluebird local and knows what lies under every rock.